The King's Dogge

the story of Francis Lovell

The King's Dogge

the story of Francis Lovell

Nigel Green

Matador
9 Priory Business Park
Kibworth Beauchamp
Leicestershire LE8 0RX, UK
Tel: (+44) 116 279 2299
Fax: (+44) 116 279 2277
Email: books@troubador.co.uk
Web: www.troubador.co.uk/matador

ISBN 978-1783061-846

British Library Cataloguing in Publication Data.
A catalogue record for this book is available from the British Library.

Printed and bound in the UK by TJ International, Padstow, Cornwall
Typeset in Aldine401 BT Roman by Troubador Publishing Ltd, Leicester, UK

Matador is an imprint of Troubador Publishing Ltd

To Alex, Jake, Josiah and Charl

HISTORICAL NOTE

Strictly speaking, this is not a book about the Wars of the Roses, but because there are references to Yorkists and Lancastrians, I have included a brief note to give the historical background.

In essence, the Wars of the Roses were conflicts fought between the rival descendants of King Edward III and their respective supporters.

The conflict started in 1399 when Henry Bolingbroke, Duke of Lancaster overthrew King Richard II and went on to become King Henry IV. The Lancastrian dynasty (Henry IV, V and VI) ruled from 1399 to1461.

Due to a number of factors, not least Henry VI's ineptitude as king, the Wars of the Roses flared up during the 1450s. Eventually the House of York prevailed and, following his victory at Towton (1461), its leader, the Duke of York was proclaimed King Edward IV.

The Yorkist Kings – Edward IV and Richard III – ruled England from 1461 to 1485, although the Lancastrians staged a brief comeback to power in 1470-71. After 1471, as a party they were almost totally defeated and the last Lancastrian claimant to the throne, Henry Tudor, languished in exile.

Against this chronological background, *The King's Dogge* begins in 1470 and concludes in 1485. The second volume of Lovell's biography, *The Last Rebel*, takes up his story thereafter.

THE RELEVANT PART OF THE HOUSE OF YORK IN THE 1470s

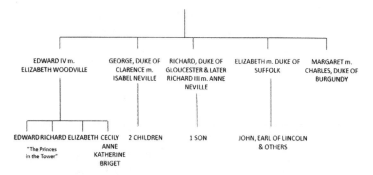

EDWARD IV m. ELIZABETH WOODVILLE	GEORGE, DUKE OF CLARENCE m. ISABEL NEVILLE	RICHARD, DUKE OF GLOUCESTER & LATER RICHARD III m. ANNE NEVILLE	ELIZABETH m. DUKE OF SUFFOLK	MARGARET m. CHARLES, DUKE OF BURGUNDY
EDWARD RICHARD ELIZABETH CECILY ANNE KATHERINE BRIGET "The Princes in the Tower"	2 CHILDREN	1 SON	JOHN, EARL OF LINCOLN & OTHERS	

THE RELEVANT PART OF THE NEVILLE FAMILY IN 1470 - 71

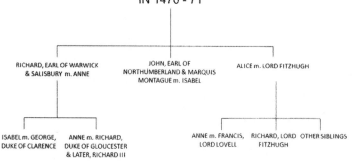

RICHARD, EARL OF WARWICK & SALISBURY m. ANNE	JOHN, EARL OF NORTHUMBERLAND & MARQUIS MONTAGUE m. ISABEL	ALICE m. LORD FITZHUGH
ISABEL m. GEORGE, DUKE OF CLARENCE ANNE m. RICHARD, DUKE OF GLOUCESTER & LATER, RICHARD III		ANNE m. FRANCIS, LORD LOVELL RICHARD, LORD FITZHUGH OTHER SIBLINGS

PART 1:
1470 – 1481

CHAPTER 1

I shuddered as another blast of icy wind howled through the trees. When Sergeant Jervis selected this particular spot he had worried that we might be seen by the enemy. I had been ordered to keep as still as possible. Jervis had chosen a position by the ridge as when we crouched down we had a panoramic view of the village below us, whereas to anyone looking up the hill we would be hidden from sight.

Ignoring Jervis's rhythmic snoring, I looked down on the sleeping village. Nothing had changed since the last time I inspected it. The twenty or so huts stood out clearly against the whiteness of the snow, and the large frozen pond glittered brilliantly in the moonlight. I inhaled the smell of the drifting wood smoke with envy as it rose up to me and rubbed my hands together to warm them.

Satisfied that all was well with the village, I looked towards the south. It was from that direction that the attack would come. I could make very little out in the darkness. I frowned as I tried to remember what I had seen of the landscape when I arrived here yesterday. As I recalled, the village was nestled between two immensely steep hills covered in trees. To the north and south the old riverbed meandered into the adjoining valleys, but because of the contours of the hills, it was impossible to see beyond the confines of our own valley. That had been another worry for Jervis. He had chewed uneasily at his lip and studied the steep slope behind us as he mulled over different tactics. If he placed us higher up the hillside, we would have greater advance notice of the Grey Wolves' attack, but the view of the village would not be so good. In time he arrived at the only possible decision.

'Since you are here to be tested, we should prioritise that over safety,' Jervis said firmly. 'But be sure to wake me when you get the first sight of the Grey Wolves.'

After Jervis left me, I continued to peer to the south looking for any sign of movement. The sound of a stone being dislodged made me spin round quickly. I froze as I heard more stones rattling down the escarpment and a rustling in the trees. A moment later first one, then another and then a third dark shape stepped out of the tree line and into the valley. I initially thought them to be horsemen, but then I heaved a large sigh of relief. The deer picked their way delicately across the snow. In the total silence of the night and in the absence of men, they felt completely safe and stopped to graze at islands amid the patchy snow.

But then they were off, bounding away as fast as they could. I scrutinised the landscape, wondering what had frightened the deer, and then gasped in fear at the shadowy figures now emerging. I waited until I was certain my eyes were not deceiving me and then prodded the snoring figure on the ground.

'The Grey Wolves have arrived!'

Jervis rose silently. Together we watched the stealthy advance of the Scottish raiders. They approached cautiously, taking advantage of the lie of the land, at times seeming to vanish but then reappearing once they were closer to the village. As the Wolves came, they split into two groups and dissolved into the woods close to the village.

Jervis bent down.

'One of those bastards will be just below us,' he whispered. 'So keep very, very quiet.'

I listened as his snores threatened to countermand his own instructions and speculated as to what the lord that I served was doing. Ever since the news of the devastating raid into Northumberland had reached him, my Lord Montague had remained shut up in his council chamber. Messengers had been sent out in all directions to gather men and supplies, and it was clear that England's foremost soldier was preparing to counterattack the

Scottish war party. If my lord was too busy in his preparations to see me, he must have thought of me because that night I was sent for by Jervis.

'My lord has learned that it is the Grey Wolves who are raiding,' Jervis told me.

I swallowed uneasily. The Grey Wolves were the most feared of all the Scottish raiders.

'And he would like you to take his little test,' Sergeant Jervis added, 'so I'll be taking you with me tomorrow to see just how obedient and loyal you are.'

Alone on the hillside, I swallowed hard. Whatever Montague's test involved, it would be starting soon.

★ ★ ★

The first flicker of dawn was visible as I shook Jervis awake. He groaned as he rose but immediately went to the ridge to inspect the valley. His eyes narrowed, and he pointed silently towards the distance. I followed the direction of his extended finger, but all I could see was a cloud of dust moving up the old riverbed.

Beneath us the village was coming to life. A man sauntered out of one of the huts. I heard the sound of voices and a baby crying. The dust cloud was growing ever nearer, and I could see glints of steel in it now. Two small children ran down to the frozen pond and laughed happily as they slipped and slid on the ice. At the sound of their play, other children ran down to join them, but the ice cracked ominously under the added weight. Still squealing with delight, the children slid back to the safety of the snow.

Their merriment evaporated into the cool air as they heard the noise of drumming hooves. They looked around in bewilderment as the noise of the horses drew closer and closer. All at once the Scottish horsemen erupted into the waking village. They swept through it, bellowing out curses of hatred as they hurled burning brands onto the thatched roofs of the huts.

Within a matter of minutes, the tranquil village descended into chaos. The children scattered, screaming loudly, as they desperately sought to avoid the terrifying grey-cloaked men on their wild horses. The Scots ignored the cries as they lobbed yet more flaming torches onto the straw roofs.

When the men of the village finally showed themselves, the Scots were ready for them. The horsemen wheeled and charged with outstretched spears. Their sharp lances beat aside feeble opposition and plunged through flimsy jerkins. The impaled villagers screamed in agony as they staggered and fell. Their wails were cut off abruptly as the Scots rode their horses over them.

Smoke was billowing from the roofs now and spread across the village. Horsemen darted in and out of the patches of smoke as they hunted their victims down. The wind caught the sparks from the burning houses and blew them on, creating yet more fires. Men and women stumbled out of the smoking interiors, waving their arms and choking. They too were met with the brutality of the Scottish horsemen.

There was movement now by the tree lines. The Grey Wolves had left their concealed positions and were steadily closing in on the stricken village. I turned to Jervis, but to my surprise he was not beside me.

'Look straight ahead, boy!' came his stern voice from behind me. 'Your test is just beginning!'

I did not understand, but I obeyed the order.

The huts were burning steadily now and, as the flames rose higher, screaming women clutching their crying children emerged from the huts. They ran wildly, colliding with one another, striking out desperately at anyone who barred their path. Seeing the frenzied crowds, the Grey Wolves closed in faster and swiftly encircled the village.

The Grey Wolves moved into the smoking village, and herded the frightened children in one direction and the women in another. The women struggled in the grasp of their captors, and the piteous cries of the separated families rose shrilly above the crackling of the fires. Their appeals were in vain, and I watched immobile as the children were roped together.

'They will look to sell them,' the harsh voice behind me said.

I looked away in disgust. Two immensely strong hands forced my head back into its former position.

'Keep watching, boy!' growled Jervis.

The Grey Wolves moved forward in groups of threes and fours and used their greater numbers to separate out the terrified women. They swiftly identified their prey and closed in on them. One raider blocked the path of a fleeing girl, making her swing away from him, only for her to find another in front of her. Outnumbered and pursued, the exhausted girl collapsed, sobbing in despair.

One girl managed to break through and sprinted towards the frozen pond where the children had played only that same morning. She began to run round the large pond, but the horsemen had already seen her. They cantered forward with their spears outstretched. The girl looked round desperately. The quickest route to the safety of the woods was to cross straight over the ice. The girl tested the ice tentatively with one foot then the other. With no time to spare, she stepped on and began to slide across. The Scots made no effort to follow her. They reined in at the edge of the pool and hurled their spears over the head of the fleeing girl. I watched nervously as the girl reached the middle of the ice sheet. Then she stopped.

'The bastards' spears have broken the ice,' grunted Sergeant Jervis.

The girl looked down at the strip of water that was now in front of her and then further on to the next thin sheet of ice so tantalisingly close. She began to sob in desperation and turned in miserable resignation to trudge back to the Grey Wolves on the shore.

They in turn shouted obscenities at her, and the jabbing movements of their spears told the girl what her fate was to be.

7

The girl stopped. For a moment she let her gaze rest on the smouldering village. She could hear the screams of the other women and the heartbreaking wails of the children. A raider dismounted and hurled a rope across the ice. The girl bent down to pick it up. Two of the Grey Wolves began to pull the girl towards them. The girl looked up at her ruined village once more. She flung the rope away suddenly. Raising her head, she spat in defiance and whirled around. Gathering her ragged robe up as high as she could, she sprinted towards the widening crack in the ice and leaped into the air. The energy of her bound made me think she would make it, but then I heard a loud splash. I breathed a sigh of relief as the girl's head and shoulders rose above the water's surface, and she tried to pull herself onto the ice sheet in front of her. The ice fractured in her grasp. Once more the girl seized the ice in front of her, but her motions were slower now and her splashing less frenzied. The ice audibly began to crack. Again the girl reached up for the ice, but this time only her head was visible above the water. I lowered my eyes as the sound of her splashing became fainter and fainter.

'The Grey Wolves will be rounding the survivors into the church soon', the stern voice behind me growled.

I blinked away my tears.

'You mean they can claim sanctuary?'

Jervis made no reply. His grip on my head became tighter.

I watched as the remaining villagers were forced towards the wooden church. They moved on without protest, their bowed heads and haggard faces testament to the cruelty of the Grey Wolves. Once the villagers were inside the church, the raiders rolled large stones against the door to seal it while others brought over timber from the ruined huts. I stirred uneasily; the grip on my head resolved into a vice. Still more Grey Wolves appeared carrying branches. They laid the timber and branches methodically around the church.

With strength I did not know I possessed, I snatched Jervis's hands from my head and turned away from the awful sight. He made no attempt to replace his grasp. He rose and looked down at me contemptuously.

'You were given an order, weren't you?' he snapped. 'You were told to watch everything.'

'But I can't watch that!'

There was a blurred movement as the back of his hand hit my cheek. I fell to the ground stunned. Sergeant Jervis stood over me.

'If you are truly loyal to my lord, you obey all his orders without exception,' he said stonily. 'Now am I to tell him that you are disloyal?'

I could not be disloyal to the man I served, but this was more than I was willing to bear. Sergeant Jervis hauled me up.

'I'm going to give you one last chance, Lovell.'

I looked down at the church. The Grey Wolves were putting kindling on top of the timber now.

'What do you wish to do?'

There are moments that shape our lives and this was mine. I realised I could not betray the trust that my Lord Montague had placed in me. So I watched.

I watched as the Grey Wolves shovelled burning embers on the kindling and it started to crackle. I watched the fire as it spread along the kindling and took hold of the wooden walls. And I watched as the flames rose up the walls and touched the thatched roof crowned with a cross. I listened to the screams of the dying prisoners and the laughter of the Grey Wolves. Even after Jervis had withdrawn his hands from my head, I watched.

★ ★ ★

Ratcliffe whistled as I finished my tale.

'I heard that my Lord Montague defeated the Grey Wolves a couple of days later,' he said, 'but it must have been horrific.'

I glanced at my friend.

'I had nightmares for a week afterwards.'

Ratcliffe nodded sympathetically, but made no reply, so I sat content to be with him. The two of us and Dick Middleton were the only three aspiring squires in my lord's household. Dick Middleton was a lively fourteen-year-old, small but with a love of horses and a wish to serve on the border. Richard Ratcliffe was older, a dark-haired boy with a brusque manner that concealed a keen mind and a burning ambition to succeed in life. He and I used to talk a lot, as friends do.

'Although in reality I should hate you!' he burst out one day as we spoke of the future.

I sensed what was coming and tried to deflect it.

'Look, we are not even squires yet and…'

He cut me off with a characteristic snort of impatience.

'You know what I'm talking about!' he snapped.

I did and felt guilty about it. The truth of the matter was that I had been handed all the good things in life, and Ratcliffe had not. I contrasted our situations unhappily. To begin with, there was the question of inheritance. My parents had died when I was very young; I had hardly known them. When I was older though, as if to compensate for my loss, I learned that as their only son and heir I would inherit their vast estates and would become a wealthy lord.

Richard Ratcliffe, in contrast, was the second son of a minor Cumbrian family; he would inherit nothing. Then there was the question of having access to influential people without whose help a man cannot rise in the world. Ratcliffe knew none of these. His training here was, he confessed, an act of charity on the part of Lord Montague. Again fortune had smiled on me though, as before they had died my parents had arranged two things which would prove immensely advantageous to me. When the wars between the Houses of Lancaster and York ended some years before, the victorious King Edward, aided by his chief supporter, the Earl of Warwick, had swept to power. My Lord of Warwick was the premier nobleman of England and, in wealth and power, he was second only to King Edward. Together with his brother the Marquis of Montague he ruled over the North of England. To have even a tenuous connection with such great men was potentially extremely useful, but thanks to my parents I had far more than that. Not only had they arranged for me to have my knightly training done at the Earl of Warwick's home at Middleham, but they had also persuaded my lord to allow me to marry his niece, Nan. As if all of this was not enough, I had a further claim on my Lord Warwick and his brother, for it had been to Lord Montague that I had been sent to complete my training.

I met Ratcliffe's gaze.

'I've been very lucky.'

He gave a hoot of laughter and punched me lightly on the arm. 'You're set for life!' He grinned, but then his face fell. 'If I'm to get anywhere in life, I need a good and generous lord to serve and a good marriage too.'

He looked down at the table.

'I know I can succeed if I get the right chance,' he said wistfully.

Considering his intellectual abilities, there was no doubt that Richard Ratcliffe would be an asset to anyone once he had completed his training.

'I'm sure you will,' I reassured him.

★ ★ ★

As our military studies continued our friendship deepened, but our interests diverged. While I remained fascinated by all aspects of soldiering, increasingly I sensed that Ratcliffe wanted more. Politics rather than warfare attracted him. Such was his interest that he pounced on every piece of news and gossip and dissected it meticulously. Then he passed the news on to me with his own analysis of what would happen next. As a friend I feigned interest in his speculations, but usually my mind strayed as he talked. For all that I will never forget what Ratcliffe told me the day I returned from the Scottish borders. He had sought me out directly.

'Have you heard the news?'

'Dick Middleton and I have spent the last two months with the light horse on the border,' I laughingly protested. 'Men up there are more concerned with the Scots than politics.'

Ratcliffe waved away my excuse. To him the danger from the Scots was irrelevant. What really mattered were the actions of the great men of the world.

'The world has been turned upside down.'

'Again?' Ratcliffe's political world was always being upended. His grey eyes met mine.

'This is serious Francis,' he corrected me sternly, 'because it affects both my Lords of Warwick and Montague.'

That got my attention instantly.

'Tell me your story,' I begged him.

* * *

According to Ratcliffe the current situation had been caused by problems in the past and so, to make better sense of it, he elected to start his tale during the times of the wars between the rival houses of York and Lancaster. I listened spellbound as first one side and then the other gained the ascendancy until the issue was decided once and for all at Towton.[1]

With the Lancastrians defeated and their King Henry VI ultimately imprisoned, the Yorkist leader had been crowned King Edward IV. England was at last peaceful. Discord lurked below the blanket of peace which shrouded the country though, as before too long King Edward and his greatest magnate, the Earl of Warwick, had fallen out. There had been talk of that when I was in the earl's household at Middleham, I recalled. Men said that King Edward did not pay heed to the earl's advice; others claimed that the king had not rewarded my Lord of Warwick sufficiently.

But if my lord's followers differed in their views on these points, on one issue they were unanimous; King Edward's new queen, Elizabeth Woodville, was wholly detrimental to the interests of my Lord of Warwick. For not only was the new queen wholly unappreciative of my lord of Warwick's substantial part in elevating Edward to kingship, she additionally brought to her marriage a great crowd of greedy relations, all of whom required rich marriages and lucrative posts. Swiftly the queen and her attendant Woodville family became a force in the land. Gradually my Lord of Warwick had found his influence with King Edward declining, Ratcliffe continued, and eventually he had risen in rebellion preferring to install King Edward's brother, the Duke of Clarence as king in Edward's place.

'Warwick married his eldest daughter to Clarence,' I recalled.

'She would have been queen,' agreed Ratcliffe, 'but in light of what has happened now, I don't suppose that matters now.'

'But what has happened?'

Ratcliffe leant forward confidentially.

'You remember that Warwick's first rebellion did not succeed?'

'Yes, no one else wanted Clarence as king. Warwick and Clarence fled to France.'

Ratcliffe grunted.

'But Warwick is not defeated – in fact far from it. He recognises that Clarence is seen as a poor substitute for King Edward, but he is still determined to overthrow King Edward and his Woodville wife.'

'Well, I can understand him hating Elizabeth Woodville and her family; after all, they cost him his power and influence.'

I defended my former lord and kinsman.

'Possibly, but listen to this Francis. Warwick is so determined to overthrow King Edward that he has transferred his allegiance from the House of York.'

'What?'

'And he is now planning to restore the previous Lancastrian King Henry VI to the throne.'

Amazing though the speculation was, it was speedily proved to be correct. My Lord of Warwick invaded England and with the help of his brother, the Marquis of Montague, chased King Edward out of England. The Lancastrian King Henry was reinstated, and Warwick and the Lancastrians were victorious.

★ ★ ★

With my Lord of Warwick's victory I assumed that the matter would end there, but a few months later Ratcliffe sidled up to me.

'I happened to be passing my lord's chamber the other day,' he murmured, 'and I overheard him say two things…'

'I bet you slowed your pace down to that of a snail.'

He flushed, but continued regardless.

'The news is that the Yorkist King Edward is planning to invade soon. He wants his crown back.'

I thought quickly. Presumably my Lord Montague and his brother Warwick with their Lancastrian allies would oppose Edward of York's attempt to regain his crown. The forthcoming battle would decide once and for all whether Lancaster or York would rule England.

Ratcliffe cocked his head and grinned at me.

'Do you want to hear the second thing this little snail overheard his lord say? Apparently the Marquis Montague intends to take you to war with him as his squire.'

CHAPTER 2

In warfare, the duties of a squire are both simple and numerous. In theory, you simply need to ensure that your lord has what he wants when he wants it. In practice, you have to second-guess his every need, whether for food, wine or weaponry. You have to take his messages when they are too important to be entrusted to others. You need to anticipate his need for a spare mount, and in battle you must protect your lord without getting in his way. If the duties are varied, there is one rule that can never be broken – you must not leave your lord, unless he commands you to.

Thus it was that I had been in constant attendance on Marquis Montague from the time our contingent had arrived in Coventry. Neatly avoiding the forces of the invading King Edward, my lord entered the town to be reunited with his brother, the Earl of Warwick. For a while, the two spoke privately, but later Montague summoned his captains.

'The situation is as follows,' he told them abruptly. 'Currently our numbers and those of the enemy are broadly equal. This is because King Edward's army has been reinforced by the force led by his brother, Clarence.'

There were groans at Clarence's treachery and duplicity. He had already proved a traitor to his brother, Edward, by allying with Warwick against him. Now he was betraying his father-in-law, Warwick to ally with his brother, King Edward.

'However,' continued my lord, 'the remainder of our army, namely the contingents led by our Lancastrian allies – the Earl of Oxford and the Duke of Exeter – will shortly join us. Once our forces have converged, we will easily outnumber the enemy. Aware of this, King Edward has moved south to London, desperately trying to win support there. We will follow him south once we are fully assembled.'

'And your plan, my lord?'

The Marquis smiled grimly.

'King Edward cannot remain in London indefinitely. He must emerge from his hole. When he does so, I will grind him underfoot, as you would a snake.'

★ ★ ★

A few days later we were encamped a few miles north of London close to a village called Barnet. I was working on the scroll for my lord, when I received his curt summons; I was to attend him at a meeting in his brother's tent. Rolling my scroll up carefully, I followed the page.

The Earl of Warwick's striped tent was not only larger but much better furnished than is customary on a campaign. Tapestries hung round its sides, while chairs encircled an unusual black-and-white patterned table in the centre.

A moment later, a short heavily perspiring noble pushed his way through the guards and, without acknowledging the others, sat down with a grunt and helped himself to one of the silver goblets of wine. Shortly after, a tall grey-haired man entered and bowed briefly to the other three. At a signal from the Earl of Warwick, the two guards inside the tent moved outside and the flap was closed.

The Earl of Warwick was the first to break the silence.

'Our scouts advise that King Edward's army is less than a day's march from here. Accordingly the purpose of this meeting is to discuss how we shall defeat it.'

He looked at his brother.

'I propose that the Marquis Montague takes overall charge of our forces. Do you agree?'

There were murmurs of assent; Montague was the best soldier

among them and they knew it. My lord raised his hand and, moving forward, I passed him the scroll that I had been clutching. In anticipation of being declared the army's general, my lord had already devised his battle plan and ordered me to commit it to parchment. Montague spread the scroll on the table. The other three eyed it curiously. He gestured to the drawing.

'I have, of course, inspected the likely battleground and will explain my plan in a moment. But first we need to verify that our own force outnumbers the king's army.'

'How many men do you command, John?' He looked at the short sweating noble, who must have been John de Vere, Earl of Oxford and dedicated Lancastrian. Oxford looked at his former enemy suspiciously. Circumstances might have made it necessary for him to ally with the Earl of Warwick and Marquis Montague, but it was obvious that he found it both unnatural and distasteful. The Marquis Montague held his gaze steadily and, a moment later, Oxford came to a decision.

'That's what I was doing before I was summoned here,' he said tightly. 'My captains assess our number to be about 2,500.' He must have sensed the air of disappointment at the paucity of his numbers. 'I am not as wealthy as some earls; I have brought all that I could to crush the House of York.'

Ever the diplomat, the Earl of Warwick was quick to smooth over trouble. He thanked Oxford and turned to the older noble.

'My lord duke?' he enquired politely.

Henry Howard, Duke of Exeter, another committed Lancastrian, looked at him impassively.

'3,000.'

Montague glanced round the table.

'That puts our force at 15,000 – we outnumber Edward of York.' He gestured to the parchment again. 'This is a simple diagram of my proposed order of battle. Our army will straddle the road that connects London and St Albans up which Edward has advanced. To our left, the ground falls away, making our flank more defensible.

On our right flank, and for much of the centre, a thick hedge provides some protection.'

The others nodded; in countryside devoid of natural defensive positions, the Marquis had probably chosen the best battle site.

'I would like you, my lord duke, to hold our left flank and you, my Lord of Oxford, to command our right,' continued the Marquis. 'I myself will take the centre and my brother will support us with the reserves.'

The Earl of Warwick spoke up.

'Edward's captains are not as experienced as you,' he said. 'We expect Edward of York to hold the centre.' He jabbed the diagram to illustrate the block of men facing those of the Marquis Montague. 'He is likely to put his younger brother, Richard of Gloucester, to face you, my lord duke.'

The Duke of Exeter glanced at the plan on the table.

'From what I hear, Gloucester has never fought a battle. I imagine I will be able to hold my position against an inexperienced youth fighting uphill.'

'On his left flank, Edward will probably put Lord Hastings to face you, John,' continued Warwick. 'Now let's hear my brother's plan.'

My lord put down his wine and gestured at the parchment.

'It's simple,' he said. 'We will use our numerical superiority to strengthen our right flank so that you, my Lord of Oxford, vastly outnumber Lord Hastings. You will defeat him quickly while the Duke of Exeter and I hold our positions. Once you have beaten him, you swing round to your left and attack King Edward's flank.'

He paused and looked at the others, while they stared at the diagram intently.

'At this point,' the Marquis continued, 'King Edward will have you, my Lord of Oxford, attacking him from the side, while I push forward from the centre. We will advance all our reserves and the Yorkists will be crushed.'

There was silence round the table as my Lords of Exeter and

Oxford absorbed the plan and glanced at each other. I could sense their unease – plainly the battle plan looked to be a good one, but could they really trust their former enemies not to double cross them?

The Duke of Exeter looked at my Lord of Warwick.

'Ten years ago you and I fought against each other at Towton, my lord,' he said softly. 'How do I know that I can trust you and your brother today?'

The Earl of Warwick flushed.

'I have sworn an oath to put King Henry back on his rightful throne.'

The duke nodded thoughtfully.

'Then God help you if you break it,' he said grimly. 'Now, my lords, despite our respective loyalties in the past, we find ourselves in a situation where not only do we have to trust each other, but additionally we must display that faith to our men. As such, I suggest that we and our captains should all fight on foot, leaving our horses in the camp. That will demonstrate to our men that we are all resolved to fight and die next to each other.'

Montague and Warwick stared back at him. It was common practice for knights to ride into battle and fight on foot, but their horses were usually kept close at hand to facilitate flight, if defeat seemed likely. While the duke's suggestion would undoubtedly make a positive impact on our troops, unless our side secured victory it would be unlikely that any of our leaders would be able to return to camp. It was an effective death sentence for them. My Lord Montague looked at his brother who nodded as if the matter was of no importance. The Marquis Montague's face hardened.

'We agree,' he said grimly.

★ ★ ★

By the next morning, I was profoundly frightened. The little sleep I had managed had been frequently interrupted by the sounds of

19

Warwick's cannons booming away. Tiredness added to my fears, and I fumbled badly as, by the light of flickering candles, I helped my lord on with his armour.

He must have realised how I felt, as he gave me countless tasks to keep my mind busy. I was dispatched to see whether the Duke of Exeter's men had moved into their appointed positions. Then I had to check that Oxford's force was placed behind the thick hedge. I blundered around in the darkness and mist getting helplessly lost but eventually returned to camp to find men milling about aimlessly. The confusion did not worry me; my lord had warned me about this when he had talked to me last night.

'King Edward's men are close at hand, Francis. Now, given that they will suspect that we outnumber them, what tactics do you think they will employ?'

I did not know. He shook his head in mock reproof and smiled at me.

'And after all my teaching too! What King Edward will do is to use the element of surprise; he'll attack before daybreak and try to catch us unaware. Accordingly, I have given instructions that all troops are to be up and in position long before the sun rises so Edward's plan won't work. But never forget to use the element of surprise, Francis.'

I shook my head in admiration at my lord's kindness as I re-entered the teeming camp. On the eve of a major battle, not only had he found time to add to my learning, but he had the forethought to explain what I would see. It was down to him that I understood that what seemed like confusion was, in reality, men mustering under their captains by the light of spluttering torches prior to advancing to their battle stations.

I found my lord and followed him and his men through the dark woods until we came to the place where he had ordered marker stakes to be placed in the ground. There were frequent cries of 'close up' and gradually the mass of soldiers were driven into some form of order. Around my lord and myself, I glimpsed the reassuringly large shapes of his personal bodyguards. They were armed with halberds – eight-foot spears with an axe blade on one side and a vicious spike on the other. Behind us a dozen lightly armoured horsemen, all bearing Montague's griffin emblem, waited to carry his instructions.

There was the sound of shouts ahead of us and I heard the answering roar of insults from our men. A moment later, some unseen force threw us back a few paces and, ahead of us, I heard the clashing of weapons. For a few moments, we were carried forward and back. One of the tall bodyguards caught my eye.

'Surprised us in the mist!' he shouted. 'Our archers would not have got many shots.'

I was about to question him, but my lord held out a metalled gauntlet, and I passed him the leather water flask. He grunted and glanced to the right to search for Oxford's troops.

The pushing and shoving continued, but it was impossible to make out what was happening. I could see little, nor could I work out whether we were advancing or retreating. I tried to fix our position by pinpointing a tall tree on my right, but when I looked again later somehow the tree had got behind me. Even more confusing was the fact that while we were constantly moving there was no sign of the enemy. Men passed us on either side but, apart from the clanging ahead, there was little sign of a battle.

The sudden whirr of an arrow made me slam my visor down and my sense of disorientation instantly worsened, my vision being restricted to the little I could see through its narrow slits. I stumbled on something large beneath me and would have fallen had a halberdier not grabbed me. Flinging my visor up, I swallowed uneasily. The ground beneath us was covered in bodies. My lord signalled to me and I moved over to where he stood, talking anxiously with one of his captains. Without being asked, I handed him the water flask. The captain ignored me.

'What's Exeter doing?' he demanded.

'Holding his own, but only with the help of all our reserves,' the Marquis Montague replied bitterly.

21

The captain looked startled.

'He shouldn't have needed them. We'll want them here presently.'

My lord made no reply, but looked out for Oxford's men. The captain followed his gaze.

'Lancastrians – untrustworthy bastards,' he muttered as he moved away.

My lord looked worried and, because I knew him, I could sense his thoughts. If the situation on the army's left wing was unexpectedly disappointing, what was happening on the right wing was a total mystery. Oxford's division appeared to have disappeared into thin air and none of the messengers, who Montague had sent, had returned.

There was a lull in the fighting and we stopped moving. I realised later that men in armour cannot fight indefinitely, and there are times when the battle almost stops while men regain their strength. It was now that my lord commanded me to take the last two mounted messengers to find Oxford.

'Tell him to break through Hastings immediately!' he ordered.

We rode behind the army to the hedge where Oxford's men had been stationed and found it completely flattened. There was no sign of Oxford or his men, only a number of bodies on the ground.

I rode forward anxiously, hardening my heart to the sound of the feeble moans of wounded men. There were large numbers of weapons strewn randomly; I guessed that they had been thrown away in flight.

'No further, master,' the older messenger called out. 'There may be enemy troops hiding.'

The mist had cleared completely now, but no matter how hard I looked I could not see Oxford's men.

'We'll go on!' I ordered.

The older man glanced at me scornfully.

'You'll never find them. They will be long gone.'

'What do you mean?'

He gave me a pitying look.

'Oxford's attacked and the Yorkists have fled. Oxford has chased after them.' He dismounted abruptly and started running his fingers through one of the dead soldier's clothing.

'Stop that!' I ordered.

He looked at me defiantly and moved on to another body. His colleague was doing the same. I drew my sword, but he picked up a mace and his comrade a fallen sword. For a few seconds, we all just stood there stiffly eyeing each other.

'It's the right of soldiers to loot,' the younger messenger said truculently. 'Always has been and always will be.'

'Course it is,' agreed his friend. 'You can't stop us, master; Oxford's men will be doing exactly the same thing.'

He hefted his mace.

'But if you do want to stop us master, you just try.' His companion came to stand next to him. He waved his hand back in the direction from which we had come. 'Or you can just ride back and forget about us.'

The two of them watched me closely. I cursed them and rode away. The important thing was to return to my lord and tell him that, while Oxford had completely routed the Yorkist left wing, he and his men had totally disobeyed instructions. There would be no flank attack on the Yorkist centre.

It had all gone horribly wrong, I reflected, as I made my way back. Evidently the prospect of plunder and revenge had proved too much for the Lancastrian Oxford and his men. There was little chance of him reforming his troops – most would just sneak away with what they had stolen and, even if they did return, given that most of them were foot soldiers, it would probably take too long. Worse still, by giving Oxford the extra men, Marquis Montague had obviated our side's numerical advantage and already our reserves were engaged in propping up Exeter's flank.

I skirted the rear of our army anxiously until I found my lord and told him the news. He cursed Oxford as an impetuous fool, but then a messenger arrived from Exeter; his men were suffering badly, and he needed reinforcements urgently. My lord gestured to a number of his immediate companions and his halberdier bodyguard to return with the messenger, and looked longingly to his right, doubtless hoping that Oxford's troops would return to save the day.

The noise from the front was louder now and I could actually make out the sun banners of the enemy. There was a sudden roar from ahead of us and we were jolted backwards. My lord frowned.

'I believe that King Edward has thrown in his reserves.'

'Hold hard!' he yelled and snapped his visor down, but we were all pushed back again. In front of us the clash of weapons grew louder and the ground beneath us more muddy and treacherous. Another squire seized my arm.

'Tell my lord that enemy horsemen threatened our right flank,' he gasped. 'They have been repelled by arrow fire, but they might attack again.'

I turned to my lord but his gaze was focused to our left flank. He summoned his captain again grimly.

'Exeter's force is crumbling,' he said briefly. 'Prepare to strengthen our left flank.'

The captain glanced at Exeter's position.

'Their line is buckling,' he confirmed, 'and already a few of his men are starting to slip away.' He looked at my lord. 'Gloucester will be upon us soon, my lord. We'll be squeezed between him and King Edward's reinforcements.'

I felt an icy chill. It was not so much what they said that panicked me, but the calm way in which it was said. Two experienced soldiers had evaluated the situation extremely quickly and had come to the same inevitable conclusion. In a short while we would be totally overwhelmed.

Others spotted the increasing desertions from Exeter's division and there were cries of 'treason' and a general edging backwards.

The Marquis stood tall so he could be seen by those around him and gestured to advance. Temporarily reassured, men moved forward. My lord beckoned to me.

'Francis!' he said urgently. 'Find my brother. Tell him the day is lost. Tell him to flee quickly. I will hold the ground here as long as I can.' He smiled at me briefly and then, snapping his visor down, turned back to the battle.

A squire may only leave his lord during battle at his express order. I pushed my way to the rear with eyes streaming. It was obvious that the Marquis Montague's instruction was not only designed to save the life of his brother but mine too. It was typical of the man that when he could have sent anyone with the message, his first thought had been to preserve the life of his own squire. Equally characteristic of the man was his decision to mount a rearguard action. For while he stood firm, Gloucester's victorious troops would not pursue Exeter's fleeing men, but would attack him. He was, I realised then, the bravest and most generous man I had ever known.

Behind the lines, it was pandemonium. Men raced frantically in all directions, jostling one another and striking out when another got in their way. I looked round wildly for the Earl of Warwick, but all I could see were Exeter's men running away. A knight on his armoured horse spurred his way into them frantically, using the flat of his sword to make them turn and face the enemy, but he was quickly pulled off his mount and the mob raced on.

Already I was being overtaken by a number of Montague's own archers. They dashed past me, flinging away bows and swords, their ragged breath and wild-eyed expressions evidence of their terror. Sensing this, my own fearfulness grew ever greater and I lumbered desperately after them.

Suddenly, I spotted the Earl of Warwick in the throng. He moved slowly accompanied by only two knights. I forced my way through the mass of fleeing solders to get to him. With him I would be safe.

'My lord, your brother sent me. The battle is lost and he bids you to flee.'

The earl's face was flushed and his breath came in quick gasps. He nodded at me and raised his voice to the knights.

'Bring the horses here!' he ordered.

They hurried away obediently.

I offered him my flask of wine and he snatched at it eagerly. Even as he gulped at the drink, the roar of battle grew ever louder and there was a sudden shout.

Gloucester must have launched his flank attack, I thought miserably. By now my lord would be under attack from two sides.

'Where are the horses?' the earl panted.

I looked round desperately, while the numbers of men hurrying past us was increasing, I could see no sign of Warwick's knights returning.

'They will be here presently, my lord.'

We waited anxiously as the noise behind us grew louder still, and more and more men slipped past us.

'Where are they?' demanded the earl furiously.

Despite all my fear, my heart went out to him. It was obvious by now that his knights had decided to save themselves and not their lord. The great Earl of Warwick, who had ruled the North as a king and who had nurtured thousands of his retainers, had been abandoned by them all. It was not right to leave my lord like that.

I gestured in the direction of the camp.

'We will find horses there, my lord.'

We started to move slowly towards the wood. The earl's panting was growing ever louder, and his face was turning increasingly red. He stumbled a couple of times, and his eyes met mine in mute entreaty. I offered him my shoulder to steady himself.

There was a great shout from behind us and I heard the cry 'Montague's down!' An instant later, the trickle of men racing past us became a torrent. We were jostled and my lord was flung to the ground. I shielded him as best I could until the crowd had passed, but it took all my strength to get him up.

He swayed unsteadily, his breathing ragged.

'The camp is only a little further,' I said encouragingly.

He glanced at me dully and the weight on my shoulder became heavier as we staggered on.

We came to a clearing and, just as I was daring to think we would make it to the camp, my lord fell heavily. I laid my poleaxe on the ground and bent over him. He lay with his eyes closed, his rasping breath coming very slowly.

The sudden crack of a snapping branch behind me made me spin round. A few yards away, six or seven men were advancing stealthily towards us. For a moment, I imagined that they were the earl's men come back to help him, but to my horror I saw them draw their swords and spread out in a crude semi-circle facing us.

They were Yorkists.

The rasping noise from behind me told me that the earl still lived, so I slowly bent down to pick up my poleaxe and then closed my visor. Stepping forward a pace, I swung at the nearest man and did not wait to watch him fall. I jabbed quickly at another, but I was too slow. The others must have rushed me, as there was now a terrible pain in my left leg and then something hit my head and everything went dark.

I must have drifted in and out of consciousness; at one point I believed that a group of men came and peered at us, but eventually my head began to clear, although I found it difficult to see properly. As my vision improved, so my concern for the earl increased and, ignoring the pain in my leg, I raised myself up on one elbow to attend to him. But then I retched uncontrollably. The Earl of Warwick's face had been sliced open and his blue eyes gazed sightlessly at me. Looking down, I saw that much of his armour had been ripped off and even his gauntlets had been taken. I peered at his hands and vomited. The thieves had hacked off his swollen fingers to steal his jewelled rings – his hands now ended in bloody stumps. I wiped my mouth and thought back bitterly to what the two messengers had said about looting. What an easy target the earl must have seemed to his murderers. I cursed them and brooded darkly on the evil that could cause men to do such a thing.

My thoughts were interrupted by the sounds of horses. I propped myself up to watch the knights dismount. Judging by their magnificent armour, I guessed that these were nobly born Yorkists. The approaching men must have noticed my movements, as two of them advanced on me with swords outstretched and stood threateningly over me.

'The earl, Your Grace.'

There were murmurs of consternation from the knights when they saw what the thieves had done.

'Anthony – care for him and Montague. Have them cleaned up. I want them displayed in St Paul's so all men know they are dead.'

'Yes, Your Grace.'

In response to some unseen gesture, the two guards removed their swords and the group clustered around me.

'Get up!' an immensely tall man commanded me.

'I can't.'

The giant gazed down at me.

'Who are you?'

'Lovell, squire to Lord Montague.'

A metalled foot booted me in the ribs.

'You say, Your Grace.'

'Leave him, Anthony,' the tall man said.

He glanced down at me curiously, lying next to the dead earl. Then he narrowed his eyes suspiciously.

'If you were Montague's squire, why did you leave him?'

So I told His Grace – for this must have been King Edward himself – of how my lord had sent me to warn his brother to escape and how Warwick's knights had run away. I explained how I had tried to help him. I gasped out the remainder of my sorry story quickly as the memory was so painful. The tall fair-haired

Duke of Clarence, who stood next to King Edward, eyed me incredulously.

'So you stayed with Warwick when the others deserted him?'

'Yes, my lord.'

He shrugged contemptuously.

'Then you were a fool to have done so.'

I looked up at the traitorous Clarence with loathing.

'Doubtless you would think so, my lord.'

The pain as his foot hit my wounded leg was indescribable and sweat, mingled with tears, ran down my face as I waited for the next blow. But someone must have pulled him away for another blow didn't come. The knights waited for the king to decide my fate.

'Have him tended, Anthony,' King Edward said.

He looked down at me coldly.

'In future, Lovell, show your allegiance to me, not to my inferiors.'

A man-at-arms remained with me as the group departed. He systematically searched the body of the Earl of Warwick. A series of muttered curses indicated that he had been unable to find anything of value. I ignored him and lay perfectly still. I guessed that presently men would come and I would be treated. Until they arrived, I dwelled on the murdered earl and his dead brother Montague. I grieved for them; the two men whom I had respected most in the world were no more.

CHAPTER 3

I sighed with pleasure as sunlight suddenly flooded the abbey garden. Its warmth would not only enhance the colours of the flowers but also bring out their scent. It was peaceful here now as the brothers were no longer weeding the cellarer's vegetable garden nor tending the physic plants. They had left a few moments ago, some to work in the neighbouring cherry orchard, others to weed the abbey's fish ponds.

I closed my eyes and sniffed the air to see which of the herbs I could identify. I had only got as far as thyme, meadowsweet and peppermint when a more pungent smell told me that my self-appointed guardian was once again checking that all was well with me.

Sure enough when I looked up I saw Esau's great shaggy head inches from my face with concern in his eyes. I stroked him to reassure him and, with a contented sigh, the enormous hound sank down again. As I looked at him, I wondered for the hundredth time about his ancestry. There was something of the mastiff about him and his sheer size hinted at wolfhound, but then neither wolfhounds nor mastiffs are covered in tangled brown hair, and both breeds have tails, which Esau did not. It seemed that he had simply appeared at the abbey a couple of years before and the kindly monks had felt pity for the half-starved dog with a length of cord tied round his neck. They had taken him in and cared for him. Within weeks, the newly named Esau had become a fully-fledged member of the community. Ostensibly he served as a watch dog, but in reality his role was to be an outlet for the affection of these loveless men.

My own arrival at the abbey must have caused Esau considerable anxiety for by now he was used to the routine of abbey life and familiar with the sounds around him. He had grown used to the tolling bells and subsequent chanting that came from the abbey church, and he knew to expect to hear the soft pad of sandals on worn flagstones when the monks left their services. And, above all things, Esau was used to long periods of monastic silence.

I was not quiet, though, which worried Esau. Unlike the others, I did not move serenely in a contemplative manner, clicking my paternoster beads but rather thudded my crutch into the ground and heaved myself forward panting loudly. And there was my whistling; no one else in the abbey whistled. I whistled, when occasionally I had the breath, to tell myself that my leg did not hurt when it touched the ground, and I whistled to try and ignore the pain from the chaffing under my armpit. Esau did not know this though. My movements were strange and my noises unfamiliar. With his wooden cross on its chain bouncing against his chest, he bounded towards me to investigate.

Quite what he made of my crippled figure leaning on the crutch, I do not know. But his growling stopped and his hackles went down. He sniffed me curiously and evidently decided that far from being a threat, I plainly needed his help. He licked the sweat and tears of frustration from my face and then moved protectively to my side.

Thereafter, in the two years that I spent at the abbey, he never left my side. He escorted me on my painfully slow journeys of exploration around the abbey. We fell into following the same familiar route, starting at the guest houses and stumbling towards the granary. At the brew house Esau would stop to allow me to catch my breath, and then he would nudge me on towards the almonry. I fell frequently, but on each occasion Esau was always there. He would stand over me protectively while I scrabbled for my crutch and then moved over so that I could use his bulk to haul myself up again. And it was the constant presence of Esau that gave me the confidence to venture further and further each day.

But the confines of the abbey were stifling and I welcomed my wife's letters since they exposed me to events in the world outside. It was from Nan that I learned that having defeated her Uncles Warwick and Montague at Barnet, King Edward had gone on to defeat a second Lancastrian army at Tewkesbury. There was a rumour, it appeared, that the former King Henry had been put to death by the victorious Yorkists and that, with his death, the wars were finally over. I had received the news indifferently since the wars had ended for me with the deaths of my Lords of Warwick and Montague. On re-reading Nan's letter though, I could not but note how formally it had been written. Why, it could have been sent to a stranger. Then I supposed that we were in effect strangers to one another. We might have been married for several years, but we had only met on three occasions and knew next to nothing of each other. With Esau panting at my side, I resolved to write to Nan to tell her of my life under her Uncles Warwick and Montague and ask her about her own family.

A few months later, after the exchange of a few letters, I was more familiar with their lives in Yorkshire and described my routine in the abbey in return. Clearly my letters amused Nan, which I had hoped for. She was glad I had a companion in Esau, but urged me to ensure that he got at least some meat to supplement his fish diet.

As our correspondence increased, so did our confidence. We talked of where we would eventually live in the North when I inherited my estates and of my desire to serve on the Scottish borders before settling down. It had been Nan's Uncle Montague who had trained me in that particular branch of warfare, and I owed it to his memory to put his teachings to good use.

Gradually news of the outside world infused Nan's letters. She wrote indignantly of King Edward's lack of sensitivity in appointing his younger brother, Richard, Duke of Gloucester, to rule the North. Nan understood that someone had to fill the political vacuum left by her Uncles Warwick and Montague's deaths, but obviously no loyal man would accept Gloucester as their successor.

I shared her opinion. No one could replace Warwick and Montague in the North and no one would swear loyalty to Gloucester. I realised that this refusal, in my own case, would rule out any chances of serving on the Scottish borders, but that did nothing to shake my own resolve.

As the months passed, Nan's comments about Gloucester became less hostile and at times almost placatory. She wrote fair-mindedly of what she had heard about him.

'…from all that I have heard men account him to be a good soldier who fought well at Barnet and Tewksbury and people here are impressed by that because we need good soldiers to keep the Scots at bay.

And then people say that Gloucester will be no absentee landlord but rather he will look to make his home among us in the North. My brother Richard told me that he has heard that Gloucester is exchanging his holdings in other parts of England for estates in the North and Richard believes that this sounds promising for us here.

But on top of all that Francis, everyone can see that King Edward is backing his brother Gloucester. He is positively showering him with honours and it is said that the king wants to make his brother even greater than Uncle Warwick and Uncle Montague.

Of course, dearest Francis, this will never be the case but while I am embarrassed to admit it, I do wonder whether I might not have been a trifle hasty in my initial reaction to Gloucester's appointment…'

Almost before I had time to consider this, yet more news arrived from Yorkshire. Gloucester had consolidated his position in the North still further by marrying Anne Neville, the younger daughter of the late Earl of Warwick. Nan was, of course, delighted with the news. She and her cousin, Anne Neville, had always been close and she was pleased that through the marriage Anne would regain her father's old home at Middleham and her rightful place in the North. Of course, Nan admitted, the marriage was probably not a love match, but it was undeniably very advantageous to both Richard and Anne Neville. Clearly Nan was coming round to the idea of Richard of Gloucester ruling the North, but I was not. I had no antipathy to the man for I knew little of him. What I did know is that he could not replace my dead Lords Montague and Warwick.

★ ★ ★

'One hundred!'

I flung myself onto the bench in exhaustion and, ignoring the ache in my leg, looked triumphantly round the sunlit cloisters. Yesterday I had only managed fifty paces.

The sounds of clapping came from the shadows on the far side of the rectangle. I glanced up curiously. A richly dressed man in a fur-lined cloak stepped out of the shadows. He looked strangely familiar. Richard Ratcliffe grinned at my amazement.

★ ★ ★

'You have done well for yourself!' I told Ratcliffe a while later. 'As we've known each other since we were boys, I am not going to call you Sir Richard.'[2]

I noticed that he was taller now with prematurely grey hair, but was still as boisterous as ever. He had demonstrated considerable acumen by attaching himself to Richard of Gloucester as soon as he had arrived in the North. He had been entrusted with a number of missions by the duke and the combination of his brains and energy had served him well.

'The Duke of Gloucester has been good to me, Francis,' he confessed. 'He arranged my marriage to Lord Scrope's daughter and presently I am to be made Constable of Barnard's Castle.'

'Well you once said that you needed a good lord and a better marriage,' I laughed, 'and you seem to have acquired both.'

Against his tale of success, I had little to tell, but as shrewd as ever, Ratcliffe probed and prodded until he was totally familiar with my situation.

'So you want to serve on the borders, but you won't swear loyalty to Richard of Gloucester?' he summarised. 'A pity that; we could have used you in the West March.'[3]

His mouth hardened.

'We need to do something though; matters are going badly there.'

I was intrigued.

'Why's that?'

'The West March has been neglected and yet the threat of the Scots is still great there. Carlisle, our main bastion close to the border, has been allowed to decay and successive defeats have eroded morale. Most of the important people there were followers of the Earl of Warwick and have no time for Gloucester.'

What an opportunity, I thought wistfully.

'Richard of Gloucester is eager to have men forget their former loyalties,' Ratcliffe continued casually. 'The way we see it now is that the North will be much more secure and prosperous if people forget about Warwick and Montague and swear loyalty to Gloucester.'

He gave me a sidelong glance.

'So tell me old friend, how do you feel about that?'

'I won't swear loyalty to him.'

Ratcliffe smacked the table impatiently.

'Stop being so sanctimonious, Francis! Warwick and Montague are dead, whereas Gloucester – who incidentally was trained by Warwick – is very much alive in their place.'

He rose to go.

'Gloucester will send for you. You know that, don't you?'

'Why will he send for me?'

Ratcliffe snorted impatiently.

'I thought there was one thing you had not thought of.'

'What's that?'

'Well, everyone knows the story of how you tried to save Warwick's life when all his other followers had deserted him. Richard of

Gloucester will believe that if you, of all people, transfer to his service and swear loyalty to him, then others will follow your example.'

Ratcliffe flung back his cloak.

'Make sure you give him the right answer when he calls you,' he advised, 'that is if you ever want to have a military career.'

★ ★ ★

Ratcliffe's prediction proved to be correct. Indeed, I had only been back in Yorkshire for a few months when Gloucester's summons arrived.

'I'm not entirely sure that you should refer to it as a summons,' Nan said thoughtfully as we walked beside the river that evening.

I bent down to lift her trailing blue dress. The path ahead looked slightly muddy.

'Thank you, my love. But Francis, I would have said that the message from my cousin was more of an invitation. Anne Neville bids us to visit her and her husband Gloucester at Middleham. She writes that she and I have not seen each other for a long time and that she wishes to meet the man who tried to save her father.'

Nan looked at me proudly.

'Who also happens to be my husband.'

I smiled down at her sweet, upturned face and thanked God for the love that we were beginning to share. I gently steered her back towards the ivy-walled castle of Ravensworth.

★ ★ ★

'Come, Lovell.'

Richard was small, so I moved slowly. He waved his attendants away and headed over the drawbridge at Middleham. It was not until we were on the moors that he spoke again.

'You would be amazed at the number of the Earl of Warwick's supporters without whose defection and assistance the king and I would not have won either Barnet or Tewkesbury.'

This did little to endear me to him, and perhaps he sensed it for he stopped and looked up at me. He had a strong face with a heavy chin. He regarded me steadily. His clothes were, I noticed, rich but without ostentation and his voice quiet and firm.

'Warwick's supporters have flooded to me,' he said.

It was a statement of fact, not a boast.

'All of them pledge loyalty and commitment to me and ask me to be a good lord to them.' He smiled, almost boyishly. 'This means that they want offices or annuities, yet apart from your friend Ratcliffe, I don't know which of them to trust.'

It seemed hardly tactful to point out that if the duke and his brother, the king, had not killed Warwick they would not be facing this situation, so I maintained my silence and we walked on slowly.

'Warwick was like a father to me,' he said eventually, 'as I hear that he and Montague were to you. He taught me much of men and their ways and how they should be governed. He took me into his family; he planned for me to marry his daughter.'

Richard glanced up at me.

'He treated me even better than he and Montague treated you, Francis.'

'And, like you,' Richard continued, 'I never knew my own father; I was young when he was killed, and my brother Edward was always too busy with other matters to bother much about me. He made me a royal duke, and yet I had few lands and less influence. Warwick, on the other hand, promised me estates amounting to ultimately half his own lands were I to marry his daughter.

'I think that, to be honest, I was frightened of Edward,' continued the duke. 'He is truly awe-inspiring when he is angry. Clarence, my other brother, could stand up to him for a while, but in the end he always backed down. When the final split between Warwick and Edward became apparent, my initial impulse was to side with Warwick and defy the king. I, like Clarence, would have worked with him to overthrow the king.'

'What stopped you?' I asked fascinated.

He smiled at me.

'All of us have a duty to our lord, who in turn has obligations to support us and reward us for that loyalty. Without that loyalty, Christian society ceases to exist and men become mere brutes.'

His chain of thought echoed mine, but I made no response.

'The question I faced,' Richard continued in that quiet voice of his, 'was whether I should give my loyalty to the man who treated me as a son and who had promised me a great inheritance, or a distant brother who had largely ignored me and offered me little but who was the king.'

He shrugged.

'In the end, the choice was obvious. With Edward, the anointed king on the throne, there would be a far greater chance of peace and stability in England than with Warwick and his faction ruling the country.

'So I gave my loyalty to Edward and walked away from Warwick, whom I had loved as a father, with infinite sadness, but it was with the certainty that I had made the right choice. I tried to persuade Clarence to follow me, but he would have none of it. I think that Edward recognised my loyalty. He has given me much of the North to rule. I have offices and estates here and will create a greater power here than Warwick and Montague ever had.' He looked at me calmly. 'The difference, however, will be that I shall hold this land loyally for the king, not against him.'

He smiled ruefully.

'But there is much to do. The Earl of Northumberland has to accept the subordinate position. Lawrence Booth in Durham had to learn his proper station. We need to strengthen ourselves against the Scots and trade needs to be developed. The fleet needs to be built up and Scarborough made a more secure harbour. Oh, the list is endless, but I believe we can achieve all of this and more given time and effort.'

He paused for a minute.

'And, of course, loyal men to help, Francis. Would you be such a one?'

I hesitated.

He laughed.

'I saw you with Warwick at Barnet. In fact, it was I who pulled Clarence away from you. Warwick had to die, Francis, but it would have been better if he had died in battle, not as he did. But what was shameful was that at the end he had but one attendant – you.'

I kept silent.

'You were loyal to Montague and Warwick and I respect that, but they are dead now.' He looked round at the rolling countryside, resplendent in its variety of colours. 'I love this place, Francis. I was brought up here, and when I die I will be buried in York. Before I die I have a dream, which I wish to fulfil; I want to build the North up into a rich, prosperous land where men can live safely, move about without fear of harm and their families dwell in peace and security. A land where men can freely obtain justice and where there are great monasteries to care for the sick and well-run churches to prepare men to meet their maker.'

He gestured for me to sit. After a while he looked at me.

'To do all of this, Francis, I need men. If I asked for your loyalty, would you give it to me?'

I stared back at him. From all that I had heard of Gloucester and what he had told me, I had no doubt that he would be an excellent ruler in the North. Despite my instinctive reluctance, I found myself liking him for his openness and directness. Additionally, he was correct – Warwick and Montague were dead and I had no other loyalties. To pledge loyalty to him would undoubtedly lead to an offer of a military role. In time, I came to a decision.

'No, my lord.'

His head snapped up.

'No!' he said in a surprised voice. 'And why, may I ask, is that?'

I hoped my ineloquence would not make me seem blunter that I wished to appear.

'Because I do not know you, my lord,' I said. 'I was with the Earl of Warwick and Marquis Montague for four years and in that time their kindness and care made me want to give them my loyalty. It did not happen immediately but grew over time, and it was, I believe, reciprocal. At Barnet, Montague made sure that my life was spared.'

Conscious of the fact that I was damning my future I blundered on.

'If I agreed to give you my loyalty today, my lord, it would only be because I wished you to send me to fight on the borders, and that would not be the honest way to agree to give you loyalty.'

He looked at me silently for a while and I knew that I had probably offended him very deeply. I sighed. I had quickly come to respect Gloucester and felt the potential of growing to like him immensely.

Then he smiled; his small, even teeth gleaming white in that strong face.

'I did not say, Francis, but I probably admire honesty more than loyalty as a quality. I wish I had more such as you; it would make my task here easier.'

He rose to his feet and we walked back slowly towards the squat castle of Middleham in the distance.

'If you refuse me loyalty,' he said after a while, 'would you give me something else?'

'Of course, my lord,' I said.

'Without even asking what it is?'

His eyebrows rose. I stared down at him.

'No, tell me what you want and I will give it.'

'You won't give me your loyalty, and yet you will give me something else. It could be the lands you stand to inherit or your wealth or something else you would not want to give up. Why is that then?' he teased.

I paused.

'I suppose I respect you, my lord. I admired the way you fought at Barnet and, from what I hear, at Tewkesbury. I respect the loyalty you showed to your brother, and I admire your vision of how you will make the North peaceful and prosperous.'

I paused, a little embarrassed.

'I like the way you have spoken today,' I added. 'You had no cause to be so honest.'

It was a pity that it had all been in vain, but I would give him what he wanted and depart.

'So what is it that you want from me, my lord?'

He smiled.

'Your friendship, Francis?'

It was the last thing I expected.

'Why?' I said without thinking.

Gloucester laughed at my astonishment.

'I have hundreds of followers and, until today, no one has ever said no to me. Men protest their loyalty and some may mean it but most do not. By saying what you have today, I know that I can trust you.'

I nodded in confusion. The day was turning out to be rather different than I had anticipated.

'I have a job for you,' continued Gloucester. 'I want you to go to the West March and restore order in that region. Recruit men, drive the Scots out and make it peaceful. I will keep Sir William, as deputy, in nominal control, but he'll stay here with me. You will be in charge there by my express wish.'

'You're putting me in charge!'

He nodded.

'Ratcliffe told me that Montague anticipated you would be an excellent soldier one day and, frankly, the place needs a lot of attention and someone with skill. We can talk tomorrow about what resources I can help you with, although these are few.'

'I do not know how to thank you, Your Grace.'

'Perhaps,' he suggested gently, 'you could call me Richard, and do not thank me yet for it will be a hard job, but you will always have my support and friendship.'

I walked on happily; the future looked suddenly very exciting.

'Tell me about Montague's plan at Barnet,' Richard said. 'What was he aiming to do?' He grinned. 'Edward thought that we would have great difficulty in winning the day.'

I hesitated. I still felt immense loyalty to my old masters Warwick and Montague, and it seemed to be wrong to betray them by revealing their battle plans. On the other hand, Richard of Gloucester plainly trusted me and had requested my friendship.

Richard gave me an amused glance. I guessed he could read my thoughts. With reluctance, I told him of the plan and he whistled softly when he learned of how Oxford should have turned Edward's flank.

'That would have crushed us,' he said soberly.

'How did you overcome Exeter on our left flank?' I asked with growing confidence. 'He had a good defensive position and the support of Warwick's reserve.'

'By luck mainly,' said Richard. 'In the fog, we overshot his line and came up on his flank.' He narrowed his eyes. 'To be truthful, Francis, I am not sure how committed to Warwick he or his men were. They did not put up the resistance they should have done.' He smiled. 'I expect one day Exeter will pay the price for that.'[4]

I made no reply. The talk of Barnet had brought back memories which saddened me and, for a fleeting moment, I felt a sudden surge of resentment towards the small man who walked alongside me.

He stumbled suddenly; instinctively I grabbed him to prevent him from falling. He straightened himself and glanced down curiously at the uneven ground before smiling up at me.

'I trust you will support me this well in the West March,' said Richard of Gloucester.

CHAPTER 4

I t was with considerable misgivings that I led the small party of servants, guards and three wagons to Carlisle, the capital of the West March. Richard's ducal council had, I learned, been less than enthusiastic about my appointment and I feared a similar reception in Westmorland and Cumberland. I was, after all, only nineteen and a squire with limited military experience who knew nothing of the region. I had talked of my fears to Richard Ratcliffe after my final briefing at Middleham.

'As I see and understand it Richard, the duke sees the situation there as being a mess. Carlisle was successfully defended against the Scots in 1461, but since then the city and the castle have been allowed to decay. Most of the people in the region have little time for the duke – he admitted as much, saying that they were all Warwick's people and feel no desire to pledge an oath of allegiance to him. To top it all off, this is the one place on the border where the Scots are particularly belligerent.'

He nodded soberly.

'It's worse than that, Francis,' he replied. 'Certainly many of the people there were Warwick's men, but with his death there is a void. The duke cannot afford to spend time there and all the old families – the Musgraves, the Salkeds, the Armstrongs and so on – do not know him.'

He snorted.

'They have little time for the king either. He has never been there, and all he wants from them are their taxes. They argue that, instead of paying, they should receive financial help against the Scots, but they receive nothing. Since Warwick's death – and he *did* help them – they have become more independent. They will defend their lands and homes but ask them to fight outside their own region or in Scotland; they will laugh at you outright.'

'So what is Richard of Gloucester expecting me to achieve? A miracle?' I said in exasperation. 'How am I supposed to motivate these people when neither the king nor his brother are prepared to help and the one person they did respect is dead?'

Ratcliffe shrugged.

'In reality I don't suppose anyone is expecting you to achieve a great deal. Just do the best you can.'

The only comforting factor I could think of was that I had the backing of the Duke of Gloucester and, apparently, his friendship. He had acted decisively in sending messengers to announce my appointment. I had been given wide-ranging powers at a young age to assess the situation and take what actions I deemed suitable to repel the Scots and improve security. Having done this, I was free to harry the Scots.[5] In a year's time, I should report back to the duke, although Ratcliffe would come over from time to time to see how I was managing.

Built on a defensive ridge to control the crossing from Scotland on the River Eden, Carlisle had been established by the Romans and had remained the main fortress in the western part of the borders since those days. It should have been a thriving city with its cathedral and markets full of bustling pilgrims on the way to St Ninian's or St Kintigern's in Glasgow. I found it quiet and depressing.

'The number of citizens has declined with the decrease in trade,' explained Sir Christopher Moresby, the keeper of the royal castle in Carlisle. 'There is a prohibition against trading with the Scots and merchants fear to bring their goods up so close to the borders for fear of raiding parties.'

'There is no port nearby?' I asked.

'Maryport is the nearest and then there is Ravenglass further to the south, but we cannot safeguard the track between here and Maryport,' replied Sir Christopher. He looked grim. 'We cannot protect the merchants or the pilgrims and, given their condition, I am not sure we can defend the city walls or even the castle for very long.'

We left the cathedral and walked up to the castle. I noticed the masonry at the main gatehouse was badly decayed, although the drawbridge seemed sound.

Inside, the castle's condition was much the same with the defences weakened. In theory, once an enemy broke through the gates he would find himself in the outer bailey under fire from all sides. In reality, parts of the walls were actually crumbling so only limited firepower could be used. I felt downcast at the signs of neglect evident everywhere. I asked after the garrison's strength.

'The castle should have 300 men,' Sir Christopher replied. 'With that I could maintain an effective defence and keep the paths in the immediate vicinity secure. Currently I have sixty-two.'

'Why so few?'

'Lack of wages,' came the prompt reply. 'Soldiers tend to desert when they do not get paid.'

'Your own wages?' I asked suspiciously.

It would not be the first time a garrison commander had pocketed his men's wages. He looked at me steadily.

'I am owed two years' pay,' he said firmly, 'since the little we actually receive I give to the men.' He paused and frowned. 'The whole place has been allowed to decay, Gloucester ignores us, and so before you run back to him, Lovell, I'll tell you what I believe, so that there are no misunderstandings.'

He paused in thought for a moment, a small earnest man with grizzled hair and a determined expression.

'There are three Marches. The Earl of Northumberland has the East, and he has the money, the resources and the castles to make that secure. The Middle March is also safe. But here? Gloucester is our warden, but he does not come. He has sent no money, no soldiers and,' he waved his hand about, 'you can see the result.'

He looked at me defiantly.

'In Warwick's time, the place was prosperous. The Scots kept their distance so there was security and trade. Since then, as you have seen, the city is quiet and will soon be almost empty. The Scots are rampant and people are frightened.'

I looked at him curiously.

'Then why do you stay?' I asked.

The defiance faded from his face; he spoke calmly and with total conviction.

'I was appointed as constable here and I will remain as constable for as long as I am able to. I won't just run away.' But then his expression hardened. 'I have always done my duty. Given help, I could make this castle strong and maintain order in the surrounding area. Given encouragement, I could persuade others to assist against the Scots, and with money I could pay my men and recruit more. But we have had none of these things,' he said sadly. 'Our appeals are ignored.' He eyed me up and down. 'And now Richard of Gloucester sends us a young squire without lands and influence, and we are expected to obey him.'

He gave a little laugh.

'You asked why I have remained as constable, Lovell? I don't suppose I'll be in the position much longer when you run back to your absentee duke to tell him what I have just said. Frankly, I don't much care. It might actually make him do something useful in the region he is supposed to command.'

He looked at me contemptuously.

'So, will you leave tonight or wait until tomorrow?'

For a moment I was tempted to leave there and then. The situation was much worse than I'd imagined, and already my authority was being questioned. Evidently I was seen as a stranger and a servant of an unpopular lord. I looked down at him squarely.

'Neither, Sir Christopher.'

He blinked rapidly.

'What do you mean?'

'What I just said,' I replied. 'I am not going back to the duke. I have been appointed to do a job and I will do it. If you wish to remain as constable here, I would be pleased. If not, then go.'

He looked confused.

'But we need help!'

'And you will get it,' I said.

He looked doubtful.

'In the meantime, prepare quarters for me and my people in the castle.'

He nodded and turned away.

I sat quietly rubbing my chin. Despite my brave words, I had not the slightest idea of what to do first.

★ ★ ★

'With the extra men, we will need to make further changes to accommodate them all in the castle,' Sir Christopher observed cheerfully at dinner.

It had taken six months to win over this prickly little man, but now that all the arrears of pay had been settled and recruitment for another two hundred men had begun, he had begun to lose his distrust of Richard of Gloucester. By the time the masons had been summoned to provide estimates to replace the worst of the stonework and the carpenters had rebuilt the stables, he had become positively enthusiastic. So much so, in fact, that he was begging me to approach the duke for money to recreate the defensive ditch in the courtyard.

'Extra arms too, my lord,' continued Sir Christopher.

My title was now in common usage in the castle, since it was assumed that I had some extraordinary ability to coax money out of the ducal council.

'We still have not resolved the bigger issue,' observed Sir Thomas Broughton, 'of how we are actually going to stop the Scots from raiding.' His eyes twinkled. 'Unless you can ask the duke to send us some Saracen horsemen – I hear they are the best in the world.'

I laughed heartily; I liked Sir Thomas. He was a landowner from southern Cumberland with black, straggly hair and a wild beard. It was curious that he and Sir Christopher were friendly, I thought. They seemed to have so little in common. Sir Christopher was devoted to his position in the castle, while Sir Thomas was a natural wanderer. He had spent many years travelling in Europe, although he was vague about what he had actually been doing in this time. I suspected he had been a soldier of fortune, until he had finally returned to England with a French wife half his age.

His position in the castle hierarchy was ambiguous. He had arrived a few weeks previously to see his old friend and had stayed on to help. Like Sir Christopher, he had little time for the country's recent wars; what mattered to him was overcoming the danger of the Scots. I found him humourous, his common sense invaluable and his military knowledge extensive.

'Strengthening castles alone won't stop the Scots,' continued Thomas. 'I accept that they have to be maintained but the Scots are manoeuvrable and we're not.'

I had heard it all before. The Scots on their short, shaggy ponies were capable of covering an amazing sixty miles in a day and a night. They were a fearsome foe with their eight-foot spears, swords and knives. For protection, they had sleeveless jacks, helmets and small shields; most worrying of all was their ability to move with the minimum of supplies and raid freely in Westmorland and Cumberland.

Such troops as could be mustered on the West March were primarily infantry used to defend fortifications that the Scots largely avoided. Attempts to use our archers, supported by men-at-arms as infantry patrols, proved useless. The supply chains required for such a force slowed our men down and the Scots raced around burning villages and farms carrying off livestock, and attacking solitary farms and travellers.

To my mind, the solution was obvious. I determined to build

up our own force of light horse, which could not only counter the Scottish raids but, in due course, raid into Scotland. The problem was that I had neither the men, nor money, horses or anyone to train our force. Additionally, with the Duke of Gloucester abroad with the English Army in France, I could neither ask for his authorisation or support. But I knew it was the right policy and Ratcliffe agreed. Hesitantly, I took the problem to Thomas Broughton.

He stroked his wild beard.

'You are serious about this, aren't you, Francis?'

'It is the only way to stop the Scots.'

He pondered for a while but then grinned at me.

'We will have to start to bluff,' he said. 'If it goes wrong, you will be in so much trouble you would have done better if you had died at Barnet.' He winked. 'Mind you, if it works out then you will have bound both counties firmly behind Richard of Gloucester, which is probably what he wants.'

He paused.

'You'll have to tell lies and make promises you can't guarantee to keep, but, with Moresby and myself to back you, you'll win a lot of support. Then, all you have to do is to get the duke to agree to what you have already done.'

His unkempt hair fell over his forehead; impatiently, he pushed it back.

'Mind you, that should not be hard with all that he currently owes you.'

I looked up sharply.

'What do you mean?'

He grinned.

'Sir Christopher might believe that the costs of repairs and funding of the wages for the garrison all came from the duke, but I don't,' he said. 'You've spent your own money and are now probably heavily in debt because you believed it was the right thing to do. Am I right?'

I nodded bashfully.

'Well it needed someone to do something,' he said, 'so that's why I'll help you in Cumberland and get Moresby to do the same in Westmorland. You are probably completely mad – but we will help.'

Leaving Moresby in Carlisle, we journeyed south to Broughton Hall. I was surprised to see that this far south it had a piel tower, but Thomas advised that it was a necessary defence against the Scots. Having sent out messages, we began to tour the county to visit the homes of those men who had previously supported the Earl of Warwick. The message we put over to them was simple: Warwick was dead. I had been with him when he died – I received surprised looks at this point. Gloucester was not only the warden of the West March but also Sheriff of Cumberland and the Earl of Carlisle. More importantly, he had married Warwick's daughter. Their son would be Warwick's grandson. Furthermore, Gloucester – despite all his other duties – had shown an interest in the West March. As testament to his efforts, Carlisle Castle had been strengthened and partially rebuilt. I argued with them that to remain permanently on the defensive was not a sensible military option. We needed to create a mobile force better than that of the Scots to stop the raids and harry them over the border. Gloucester had promised to supply horses and men to train the troops but, in the meantime, he needed their support in men and loans to raise a force of 1,000, and perhaps even more than that.

It was solely due to the influence of Thomas Broughton and, later, Christopher Moresby that we got the support of the landowners, and when eventually I realised that we had 1,000 men pledged for two years' service, I judged it advisable to go to meet Richard of Gloucester.

I found him at Sheriff Hutton. I reported the situation I had found as concisely as I could to him, beginning with the decayed situation in Carlisle and the antipathy of the gentry to anyone who was not the Earl of Warwick. I briefly described the improvements we had already made to Carlisle and the plan to establish a mobile force to wage war on both sides of the border.

★ ★ ★

'So Richard of Gloucester heard you out in silence and told you that he would give you his decision in the morning,' Ratcliffe clarified.

I shifted uncomfortably.

'Yes, I assume that he will want to take advice before he agrees or disagrees with what I have done.'

'What we have done,' Ratcliffe quickly corrected me. 'Don't forget I authorised your plan to commit Gloucester to pay for your horsemen.'

'I had not realised that I would drag you down with me, if things go against me,' I apologised.

Ratcliffe fell silent and I guessed that he was assessing how great the threat to us was. In truth, I was not optimistic of the outcome since Gloucester would obviously turn to his ducal councillors for advice. The problem was that I had heard that many of them were already prejudiced against me. It seemed that a number of them felt that a more experienced man should have been appointed to the West March. Doubtless they would listen carefully when Richard presented them with an account of my actions, but then would happily recommend my dismissal on the grounds of impetuousness and irresponsibility. I passed on my opinion to Ratcliffe gloomily. He glanced round the little chamber that had been allocated to him and absent-mindedly rolled two of the scrolls on the table from side to side.

'Gloucester might not ask his councillors,' he said slowly. 'If I'm right – and it is a very big "if" indeed – I think he will ask Anne Neville about what you have done.'

I stared at Ratcliffe in amazement.

'But why would he ask his wife?'

He drummed his fingers on the table irritably.

'Francis, I'm not certain that he will. Perhaps I'm totally wrong, but I think that Richard relies very heavily on Anne.'

'Why do you say that?'

Ratcliffe drummed his fingers on the table in frustration.

'As I said, perhaps I'm wholly incorrect. But you can make your own mind up when I tell you my story. But first of all, what did you make of Anne?'

I thought back to our meeting. Anne Neville had been sitting in a high-backed chair, but as we approached she had passed her embroidery to one of her ladies and had risen to greet us. Pleasantries were exchanged, and Nan and her cousin spoke of childhood memories. Then it was my turn, and it was not until I actually came face-to-face with her that I realised just how like her father she was. It was not just that she shared his love of expensive apparel and gleaming jewelled rings nor was it simply in their same pale blue eyes and warm smiles. I spotted these similarities of course, but when Anne Neville used the same mannerisms as her father Warwick, I felt time move backwards. He'd had a number of course, but you could always tell when he was trying to assess the truth of what someone was telling him. He used to cock his head slightly to one side and tap his forefinger slowly. I saw his daughter do the same when, at her request, I told her my story of the battle where her father had died. For obvious reasons I sought to improve it, but even as I did so, with her head slightly cocked, her long finger began to tap the side of her chair.

The tapping stopped shortly after I had finished speaking.

'I do not believe that poor father's death was quite as heroic as you claimed it to be,' she said softly. 'But thank you for what you did.'

I reported this to Ratcliffe. I added that I thought Anne Neville was very shrewd and my wife's comment that her cousin had always been extremely clever.

Ratcliffe narrowed his eyes and began his account.

★ ★ ★

When he first started in Richard of Gloucester's service, Ratcliffe was determined to make a success of his role. It was a unique career opportunity for a man such as himself. To make himself as useful as possible to Gloucester, Ratcliffe decided to study the man and to identify areas of potential weakness. Once he discovered these he reasoned that he could look to excel in places where Gloucester was weak and thus make himself indispensible.

As time went by, Ratcliffe's analyses became more comprehensive, but his conclusion was not a happy one. In his view, Richard, Duke of Gloucester, was not a natural leader of men. Instead of inspiring trust, he seemed cold and secretive in his manner.

'But that is nonsense,' I interrupted Ratcliffe. 'I can distinctly remember my first meeting with Richard. He was none of those things.'

Ratcliffe nodded sagely.

'He had been transformed by the time you arrived back here, but just listen to this.'

In the face of such a chilly personality, it was unsurprising that few of Warwick's former supporters rushed to serve Gloucester, Ratcliffe continued. The contrast between their former charismatic leader and his unattractive successor was too great. Accordingly it proved increasingly difficult for Ratcliffe to fulfil his role in converting the dead earl's supporters. At this juncture Anne Neville had intervened directly. She had visited a number of the major families whose loyalty had been to her father and had used her own influence to win them over to her husband. Anne's efforts swiftly bore fruit and, as they did, Ratcliffe began to notice a subtle change come over Gloucester. Whereas previously he had been awkward, even abrupt, with people, he now seemed more at ease as – with Anne at his side – he welcomed Warwick's former supporters fulsomely.

At first Ratcliffe assumed that the change was due to Gloucester's enjoyment of his newly found popularity, but then it occurred to him that certain other disagreeable traits in Richard's character were gradually being eroded. Where was that fatal impulsiveness of his that had caused so many problems? These days he seldom rushed at things and his speech was measured and controlled. Likewise his natural suspicion of things he did not understand appeared to have been replaced by an open-minded curiosity. Ratcliffe credited Anne's influence in the transformation of her husband and welcomed it. It was perhaps a surprising development, but one that made his job easier. But if Gloucester's revolution was unexpected, what truly astonished Ratcliffe was the day that Gloucester had sent for him. With a smile, the duke had presented him with a list of ideas all designed to enhance Gloucester's prestige in the city of York.

'But why was that so unusual?' I asked.

'Because that was what I was supposed to be working on!' Ratcliffe exploded. 'As soon as Warwick's supporters started to come over to us, I thought it was time to go on the offensive. So I drew up a plan to build up Richard's reputation in the North.'

'But if he knew what you were working on, it's not totally unexpected if he had a few ideas of his own!' I objected.

Ratcliffe shook his head.

'Normally I would agree with you. But we are talking of Gloucester here. In all the time I had been with him, I had seldom heard him venture a single original idea. He's not stupid of course, but he does not have the imagination to resolve matters innovatively.'

I must have looked doubtful. Ratcliffe jabbed his finger at me.

'Think of your own situation in the West March then. Has Gloucester ever suggested any specific ways in which you could improve the situation there?'

I thought back.

'No.'

Ratcliffe slammed his hand down.

'Exactly! So up to this point I admit that I had thought

Gloucester pretty unimaginative, but when he called me that day his suggestions flew at me faster than archers' arrows. Did I not realise that the city of York was getting poorer? Why had I not thought of drafting a letter to his brother, the king, with the aim of getting York's taxes reduced? Why had I not suggested that one or two of York's more prominent citizens were drafted onto the ducal council, which would be very popular in the city?'

'Miles Metcalfe from York is on the ducal council,' I remembered ruefully.

'Of course he is now!' Ratcliffe barked. 'But tell me, Francis, how could someone as uninspired as Gloucester have suddenly come up with the brilliant idea of putting him there? It was totally out of character.'

'An isolated incident?'

'It could have been,' Ratcliffe admitted, 'but when you hear the rest of the story I'm not sure you will think so.'

A few days later Ratcliffe had been summoned back again, he continued. On this occasion he had been reproved by Richard for not devising a plan to demonstrate Gloucester's undeniable piety. Why, Richard had demanded, had Ratcliffe not thought of this? A list of abbeys and churches to be endowed was produced and Ratcliffe was told to get on with it. Ratcliffe protested in vain that he had considered the duke's military reputation as the key message to be put across to the people of the North. He was corrected instantly. A more holistic approach had to be adopted immediately and, while they were on that subject, why had Ratcliffe not seen fit to instigate a plan which demonstrated the duke and duchess's concern for their poor and needy people? Ratcliffe had admitted to himself afterwards that these ideas were much better than his own, but, as he did so, he began to feel distinctly uneasy. Obviously, Gloucester was not coming up with all these schemes, so someone else was clearly doing the work that Ratcliffe was supposed to be doing. What worried Ratcliffe was that the other person was doing it a great deal better.

Ratcliffe sensed that he would be dismissed imminently. To his immense surprise, he found himself being promoted twice in rapid succession.

'It made no sense!' Ratcliffe burst out. 'On each occasion I was thanked and given greater responsibilities. But why? All I ever did was to execute my unknown rival's schemes. So why was I being promoted and not him?

'But then I had a thought,' my friend went on. 'Suppose I was merely being moved up the ladder because I was proving useful in implementing my rival's ideas? Was it just possible that my rival did not see me as a threat, but as a helper?

'That threw me,' confessed Ratcliffe, 'because it is against the natural order of things. Everyone knows you don't promote your rivals; you knife them in the back at the first opportunity. After a while though, it occurred to me that my rival knew that I could never be a threat to them, no matter how high I rose in Gloucester's service.'

'And from that you deduced that it was Anne Neville who was feeding all these ideas to Richard of Gloucester?' I asked Ratcliffe.

'I don't know,' moaned Ratcliffe. 'I cannot prove it and yet it is the only way that it all makes sense. Anne Neville is determined to make her husband as great as her father was, so she brings her husband her father's supporters. Then she builds him up to make him a more charismatic figure. Finally, she helps him to rule by providing him with ideas – and good ones too.'

He turned to me.

'What do you think?'

It was hard to fault Ratcliffe's reasoning and I told him so but added that if his theory was correct I was pleased.

'Why do you say that?' asked an astonished Ratcliffe.

I made no answer because I was still thinking it through. Hitherto I had seen Richard of Gloucester as an unwelcome interloper, intruding in the realms governed by my dead lords. Although to be fair, I was grateful to him for my appointment in the West March and had liked him when I had met him. The news that Anne Neville was helping her husband to rule put things in a different perspective. After all, if Warwick's own daughter had the desire to help Richard, should I not do so too? Then I had another thought. If Anne Neville was effectively ruling alongside Richard, was it not possible to view the pair of them as the natural heirs of Warwick and Montague? I put this idea to Ratcliffe excitedly. He nodded soberly.

'I think we all have a duty to help Gloucester,' he agreed. 'The North is not an easy region to run, and, whatever our various motives, we all need Richard and Anne Neville to be successful.'

He chewed his lip nervously.

'We'll find out tomorrow if I'm right about Anne Neville.'

'How have you worked that out?'

He gave a mirthless smile.

'Well the ducal council hate you, so if Richard of Gloucester goes to them, both of us will be out of a job. But,' and he crossed his fingers now, 'if he asks Anne Neville, she will probably endorse your actions since, by doing what you did in the West March, you probably brought a good number of Warwick's followers over to Gloucester.'

★ ★ ★

The next day Richard publicly announced his approval of what I had done in the West March. He dispensed with his attendants and invited me to describe my future strategy.

'What is your plan?' asked Richard.

'I'll put Thomas Broughton in charge of all the men-at-arms and archers we recruit and I will get Dick Middleton to train up the light horse – that will probably take about two years. We need to co-ordinate the use of all of them offensively and we need someone to organise the money and supplies.'

'Do you have someone in mind? I might be able to help you there,' he said.

I thanked him.

'We will start by clearing the area round Carlisle and reopen the track to Maryport. We will get patrols out on the major routes to encourage traders and merchants. After we have done that, we will start probing the borders and then I will clear out the Debateable Land.'

'The Debateable Land?'

'It's a piece of land about twelve miles long by four miles wide, but no one is really sure. It's between England and Scotland and bounded by three rivers: the Sark, the Lyne, and the Liddel. It's of little value, but it is the home of every thief and robber, English or Scots.'

'Why is that?' asked Richard.

'Because it belongs to no one. Some years ago when the borders were reset, no one could agree whether it should be English or Scottish. In the end, it was agreed that it belonged to neither and, as such, there is no law enforced there,' I replied. 'There are reports of an unofficial leader there, an Englishman called Skiam, who directs raids on both the Scots and English with the utmost ferocity.'

I finished my wine.

'After we have done all that, I will carry out raids into Scotland itself. Perhaps you will bring men, and we can capture and burn Dumfries.'[6]

Richard eyed me curiously.

'Despite the difficulties you will face, Francis, I sense that you are relishing the task ahead of you. Am I right?'

I frowned. It was something I had not thought about, but now that he had voiced it, I realised that he was correct. He grinned at my bemused expression.

'You can forget the conventional response that – as a soldier – you are naturally delighted to serve me to the best of your abilities…'

'I was not going to say anything nearly so ridiculous!' I protested.

I realised then he was teasing me and smiled ruefully.

'Well, why do you enjoy your work so much then?' he demanded.

I drew a deep breath.

'I suppose that I like trying to solve all the challenges in the West March. I like working with men who I respect – people like Moresby and Broughton. I'm proud that others in the region are beginning to support us because it means that they believe in us.'

I looked at him squarely.

'I'm also proud of the fact that today you backed me. It shows that you have confidence in us and what we are going on to achieve.'

Richard of Gloucester nodded thoughtfully.

'We do, Francis. Believe me, we do.'

CHAPTER 5

I glanced round the table.

'So that is my plan. What are your own views?'

There was silence in the council chamber of Carlisle Castle as my colleagues digested my strategy. I glanced round the room as I waited. As befitted a frontier garrison, it was uncompromisingly masculine. No colourful tapestries covered the grey-stoned walls, and there were no scented rushes under foot. Instead we furnished it to reflect the life we lived, so that massive antlers and spears lined the walls. On an old wolf skin in front of the fire, Broughton's dog slumbered noisily.

I suspected that the wiry cavalryman opposite me would speak first, and I knew that his words would carry great weight with the others. Dick Middleton was respected by everyone for his sheer professionalism. I recalled his look of horror when I had first shown him the volunteers who comprised the Carlisle horse.

'You lured me over from the East March to command this rabble,' my boyhood friend had moaned. He glanced at me reproachfully. 'You're deluding yourself! There's no chance of turning them into proper light horse.'

Despite his gloomy forecast, he had set to with a will; under his firm guidance the Carlisle horse was gradually transformed from a collection of enthusiastic amateurs into a disciplined body of horsemen. Next to Dick, Thomas Broughton and Moresby's gaze lingered on the final member of our group. For a moment I wondered why they were staring so hard at the tall, fair-haired figure, but then I understood. The issue of supply was central to my plan; Broughton and Moresby were trying to speculate whether

Edward Franke could deliver what we would need. For my part, I had no doubt that he would. Ever since Gloucester had seconded Edward to the West March, he had proved invaluable. Within weeks of him arriving he had gained my total trust, and, accordingly, I had delegated to him all matters relating to pay and supply. Contrary to my expectation, it was Broughton who broke the silence.

'To summarise your thinking, Francis, you believe that it is essential to destroy Skiam and his thieves in the Debateable Land before attacking the Scots. This, we have agreed in the past. But now,' and his voice shook with these words, 'as a result of the Anderson atrocity you want to obliterate the Debateable Land completely. To achieve this, you are proposing to attack it in winter. Am I correct?'

It was not a strategy I relished, but it was my duty to our people in the West March to ensure that there could never be a repeat of the atrocity.

'Yes.'

Broughton pulled at his straggly beard.

'After what Skiam did to Anderson's men no one in this room is going to disagree with you. So it is only a question of how we do it.'

'Those thieves and felons in the Debateable Land are worse than the Scots,' agreed Dick Middleton in disgust. 'We will make your plan work, Francis.'

I turned to Edward.

'Well?'

His blue eyes met mine.

'Skiam's raids are the most savage,' he said simply, 'so I agree. But as for Anderson...' His voice trailed off.

I thanked them; when they left, I let my thoughts drift back to Anderson's patrol.

★ ★ ★

Anderson's men had been late in returning, I recalled. In itself this was a concern, but not a major one. We had followed routine practice and a day later another patrol was sent out to look for them, but they found no trace of them and our worry steadily increased as subsequent searches failed to find any survivors. As we grieved them and cursed the Scots, an emaciated figure stumbled up to Carlisle's main gates. He was ragged and exhausted, indeed so unrecognisable was the man that the guards initially refused to believe that the man was whom he claimed to be. I understood their confusion as the Anderson who was brought to me was so terribly different from the man who had ridden out just a few weeks before.

★ ★ ★

His story came out incrementally. He had led his patrol out to the Bruntshields and then decided to do a sweep to the west. On the fourth day, they spotted a small number of Scots and Anderson pursued them.

They chased the Scots hard for a full half day until they came to a thick wooded area. The Scots disappeared into it, and Anderson and his men followed, but the increasing thickness of the wood, and the absence of paths, made it hard for them to keep together. After only a few moments, he had only half his force with him and had lost sight of the Scots completely. It was then that he heard shouts to his right and turned to investigate. They reached a clearing where suddenly his troop was hit by a volley of arrows coming from all directions. Almost all of the horses were hit and at least two of his men. He and the remaining eight huddled together in a crude circle, as there was no enemy in sight – only total silence.

There was another volley of arrows and Anderson saw three more of his men go down. In desperation he threw his lance and sword on to the ground. His surviving five men followed suit. The silence continued as the six of them looked nervously at the undergrowth. Slowly from all sides men in half-armour emerged with spears and swords pointing at them.

The Scots bound the six of them together and took their surrendered weapons. The Scots made sure that the men in his patrol who had been hit by arrows were definitely dead, and the survivors were marched a few hundred paces to another clearing, where they found more Scots. A burly man in a fur cloak, who seemed to be the leader, indicated with his double-sided axe the fate of the missing men of Anderson's troop. They all lay lifeless on the ground before him; some had been killed by arrows but a number had simply had their throats cut. The six remaining men were marched onward in deathly silence.

Once out of the wood, they were taken westward. Anderson estimated that they covered three or four miles in the dark. One of his men, who was wounded, found it difficult to continue, but being bound they were unable to assist him. The Scots noticed this and halted the group. The man was untied and was killed with a spear thrust to the throat. In horrified silence, the five survivors were marched on until, at length, they came to a crude settlement.

There were four or five huts; in the centre a huge fire burned. Seeing his badge of office, Anderson was separated from his four men and tied to a post by the fire. He watched, in disgust, as a group of ragged men, women and children emerged and started to strip his men of their armour and clothes. As they stripped the men, so the clamour rose and the villagers began to quarrel then fight each other for the best plunder. He watched helplessly as his men were injured in the ensuing scuffle. The Scots were like animals, as they fought one another by the light of the great fire. He was tormented by the screams from his men and he struggled ineffectually against the ropes that bound him.

There was a sudden shout and a small man came out from one of the huts, followed by the hulking figure still holding his double-sided axe. As they moved to the shivering, naked prisoners, the crowd of villagers collected the armour and clothing and scurried away. The small man looked at the remainder of Brian Anderson's troops and then came over to him. The man had cropped hair and only half of one ear. He wore a stolen English breastplate and carried a small axe. In anticipation of death, Brian braced himself and observed his executioner with contempt.

'Your name?'

The eyes never left Anderson's face. He told him and the other man nodded.

'I have a message for Middleton and Lovell,' he said, his eyes fixing him with a cruel stare.

'Francis, I asked him what the message was,' muttered Brian, 'because I was confused. The Scots would surely not be sending you messages. Then I realised that these weren't Scots, as the small man with the axe spoke in English. These were the thieves from the Debateable Land.'

'What was the message?'

Brian Anderson buried his face in his hands and then slowly looked up.

'He stood there for a minute just looking at me, Francis, tapping that axe of his against his legs.

'"I think my message to Lovell will carry more impact if you watch something first," he said to me slowly.'

There was a long silence and I feared that Anderson must have fallen back into a trance, but he suddenly leant forward and seized my arm.

'Francis, he and the large man with the double-handed axe attacked the other prisoners,' he gasped. 'They just kept chopping at them. They were bound; they didn't stand a chance. Their screams grew louder and louder and then the villagers joined in…'

Brian dissolved into tears.

I put my arm around his shoulders, but he shook me off roughly.

'You know the worst thing I saw,' he said wildly. 'It wasn't the dead men; it was the two who were still alive.' He buried his head in his hands and said brokenly, 'and it was not the screams that were the most harrowing, it was the laughter.'

I sat in silence imagining the horrific scene that Anderson had witnessed.

'At last it finished and the little man with the axe came over to me and looked up at me. He was covered in blood and his axe had pieces of hair and gore on it. He never took his eyes off me, but he ran his hand over the axe to wipe it and then wiped my cheeks with his hand.'

Anderson fell silent again.

'Then what?' I prompted.

'The villagers and his men crowded round him and I thought I would be hacked to death like my men. I didn't care, after what I had seen, but he waved his followers away with the axe. He rubbed more blood off his axe and said to me: "Tomorrow you'll be released and taken to the border; all you have to do is remember what you have seen tonight. This will help you." Then he wiped more of the gore on my face. "Now to the message," he carried on. "Tell Middleton and Lovell that I rule in these parts, not them or the Scots and they would do well not to stand in my way, now or in the future."'

Brian Anderson looked at me.

'Then, Francis, he said to tell you that this is the only warning you will receive from Skiam.'

★ ★ ★

During the next month, the rest of us worked with grim determination. While previously I had planned to clear the Debateable Land, I now intended to destroy it forever. Fodder for the campaign proved to be the biggest problem. By November it was proving hard to find oats and hay. I sent messengers to the duke to beg his assistance and to my surprise, three weeks later a small number of wagons arrived, accompanied by Richard Ratcliffe.

'Why are you planning a winter campaign?' he demanded once we were in my quarters.

I poured him wine.

'Firstly, Skiam and his followers will not be expecting us, so we have the element of surprise. Secondly, the ground should freeze over, so there will be no retreating to secret hiding places in marshes and bogs. Finally, once his horses and supplies have been destroyed, he will have no way of replenishing them.'

Ratcliffe nodded and rose. I watched him prowl round the room carefully avoiding the scattered pieces of armour and discarded weapons. He bent to pick up a mace but dropped it when he felt the weight.

'How soon can you go on the offensive once you've destroyed the Debateable Land?' he asked casually.

His tone was too nonchalant to be convincing, so I grinned at him.

'What's the problem?'

Ratcliffe gave a rueful smile.

'You know me too well, Francis. The fact is that we need a success.'

I reached for the wine.

'Tell me what has happened.'

Ratcliffe's story was narrated hesitantly. He apologised for this at the outset; clearly it was not that he did not trust me or wished to withhold sensitive material, rather, that he was dealing in overall impressions and not facts.

Nothing could be proved, Ratcliffe explained, but he believed that people were stirring up trouble for Richard of Gloucester and Anne Neville. A recent spate of rumours had apparently been spread in the South of England, all of which hinted that the North was not being as well managed as it should.

'There was talk it seemed about the recent Scottish raids,' Ratcliffe told me. 'Men say that the raids could have been halted sooner. The damage need not have been so great.'

'But that's absurd!' I interrupted him. 'Anyway who's behind these rumours?'

Ratcliffe could not say for certain.

'Up until now Gloucester has been well respected in the

country. He was seen as a loyal brother to King Edward, serving him well in war and peace.'

'So who is trying to cause trouble for him?' I demanded.

Ratcliffe glanced round quickly and lowered his voice.

'I believe that the Queen, Elizabeth Woodville, and her family are.'

'But what has Richard done to harm them?'

'On the face of it nothing,' Ratcliffe admitted. 'But Francis, the Woodvilles are constantly looking to increase their own political power. Maybe they are trying to weaken Gloucester's hold on the North so that they can encroach here as they are elsewhere.'[7]

Ratcliffe shrugged.

'And then of course there is Anne Neville herself.'

'How does she come into it?' I asked.

'Her father, Warwick, rose up in rebellion against King Edward and the Woodvilles,' snorted Ratcliffe. 'In fact, come to think of it, he killed two of them.'

He paused reflectively.

'Possibly, had he lived longer he would have got rid of them all. Anyway that is one major grudge that the Woodvilles could have against Anne Neville.'

'How does she view them?'

'With contempt!' came the uncompromising retort. 'To Lady Anne, the queen is wholly undeserving of her title. Her numerous relatives are to her greedy and selfish and their ambition far beyond their abilities.'

He glanced at me.

'Well, she is Warwick's daughter, Francis. Anyway the last thing anyone wants is the Woodvilles intruding in the North. We need a success to stop these rumours. Can you help us?'

I thought quickly.

'There would need to be a period of rest and recuperation following the campaign in the Debateable Land, but I could keep this to a minimum and so advance the timing of the raid into Scotland.'

Ratcliffe's face lit up when he heard this.

'That will stop the damaging talk against Gloucester,' he said happily, 'and it will prevent the Woodvilles from meddling where they are not required.'

He rubbed his hands together.

'Yes, this will turn the tables of that family. You'll find Gloucester and his wife grateful to you, Francis.'

I shook my head.

'I'm not doing this for reward.'

Ratcliffe gave me a look of pure amazement but then nodded.

'I suppose you are rich enough not to be motivated by money,' he agreed. 'But as a matter of interest, why are you helping?'

The simple answer was that I by now knew I was of use to Richard. Over the past two years I had come to know him better and increasingly liked what I saw. Moreover, when Nan and I had visited him and Anne Neville, we were treated not only like friends but as confidants. As far as I could see they held nothing back. They spoke freely of the challenges that faced them in the North and, as they did, I began to gain an idea of the sheer scale of what needed to be done if their region was to be made prosperous and secure. At times, when he and I were alone, Richard would speak of his own unfitness for the role that he was called on to play. At first I was suspicious of this, fearing that such humility was feigned, but after a while I knew it to be genuine. I sympathised with him too as leadership, whether it was for the West March or all of the North, is a lonely position and what man does not at times feel wholly inadequate for the task ahead? I believed that it helped Richard sometimes to have someone to confide in apart from his wife, and in turn this began to bring out in me the desire to help and protect him and Anne Neville. This was not a concept that Ratcliffe would comprehend.

'I believe it is my duty to help,' I told him.

Ratcliffe snorted approvingly.

'Well, try not to fail him in the Debateable Land or in Scotland afterwards, because we are all relying on you.'

★ ★ ★

The results exceeded all my expectations. Operating from secure bases, our fresh troops and well-fed horses erupted furiously over the south and east of the Debateable Land, cutting a swathe of destruction and leaving nothing in their wake.

Initially, our men operated cautiously, using guides and outriders, but as the trail of destruction grew, so did their confidence. They began to leave the fortresses while it was still dark to maximise their range. Fortunately, they were blessed with bright days of snow on the ground, rather than in the air.

The method of destruction we devised was simple. Scouts would identify potential targets, and our troops force would surround the hamlet, forming a circle around it. The outer buildings would be set fire to first and then the troops unleashed. Resistance was light, except from Skiam's followers who, while invariably heavily outnumbered, fought in the desperate knowledge that death awaited them, even if they surrendered. Any male villagers who attempted to fight were to be killed, but the remainder, as well as women and children, were spared. Anyone trying to escape from the village was ridden down – an easy target for mounted men with long spears.

A few survivors made it to the borders and were found half dead from cold and hunger at Solway Moss, but with our ruthless system of destruction, the majority of the population perished. Despite the necessity of this course of action, it was not a campaign of which I was proud, but it proved successful beyond all our hopes. Within three weeks, the whole of the east and the south had been cleared completely and Dick sent a messenger on to us. He wished to mount a final series of raids, culminating in an all-out assault in the north-west of the region. He guessed, at this stage of the campaign, that this was where Skiam and his remaining followers would have fled. He asked me if I would bring up the remaining 200 Carlisle horse and supply additional fodder for a two-week campaign.

I rode north a few days later at the head of a number of creaking wagons, escorted by the Carlisle horse, who were eager to join in the assault. Presently I rendezvoused with Dick and Thomas Broughton.

'How many men do you think Skiam has left?' I asked them.

Broughton shrugged.

'There can't be many and they must be more or less exhausted by now. They will be no match for us.'

Dick Middleton proposed to divide our 800 men into two groups operating on alternate days, a tactic that had worked well so far. We would further subdivide the two groups so that one could approach from the east and one from the south.

'To be honest though, Francis, in Skiam's place I would try to flee north into Scotland. But let's finish the job.'

I rode with Middleton and his men a day later. We passed through burnt-out hamlets and destroyed farmhouses, but otherwise the country was white and empty. Far to our left, twin spirals of smoke indicated that our fellow patrol had found something worth destroying but of Skiam and his followers there was no sign.

We patrolled for much of the day and returned to camp, following this same routine for a week. Nevertheless we were thorough in our search. Still we found no trace of our enemy either in the bleak salt marshes or in the oozing peat bogs and deserted beaches. We were making the last patrol of the campaign when Dick finally signalled a halt and rode over to me. He exhaled clouds of breath when he removed the wool wrap that he and his men wore across their lower faces.

'I think that we are probably in Scotland now, Francis. We'll go three or four miles to the east and then return to Carlisle. There's nothing and no one here.'

He gave instructions for the men to water their horses and returned to me.

'I would say that this is the end of the Debateable Land. We'll rest here for a while and then we'll be back in half a day.'

Half frozen, I nodded back; it was the end of the campaign. We had not found Skiam, but I was not overly concerned. No one could live in the Debateable Land for a long time, let alone use it to attack from. It was victory, but I was too cold to enjoy it.

A little later we crossed the Kirtle Water on our way back to camp. The winter campaign was over. It was now time to launch the first major raid into Scotland.

CHAPTER 6

'Horsemen!'

Edward Franke pointed up the valley.

The archers had seen them too. At the sound of sharply issued command, they dismounted. Their horses were led to the rear of the column to join the packhorses, guarded by a small number of men-at-arms. I sighed as the captain signalled for his men to notch their bows. This was the second time in two days that the Scots had threatened our advance but were too cautious to attack, which was a pity as we would have destroyed them with ease. The Scots would not be reckless enough to attack bowmen head on, but they would try to manoeuvre round to strike at our flanks or to our rear. Of course, they would have been unaware that the Carlisle horse was out somewhere to our right and left, poised to take the Scots on their flank as they attacked.

The Scots had not obliged us last time though. On this occasion, I suspected they would hold their position for a short time and then withdraw. Our advance up the valley would continue and I was hopeful that we could break into the heart of Scotland.

'They're leaving!' someone shouted.

Sure enough, the small band of Scots ahead of us retreated further north up the valley. I looked to the hills on the right and saw that a small number of Middleton's horse were now in sight. There were probably some to our left, but I couldn't see them. I gestured to John Fennell to remount his archers.

'That's the trouble,' said Broughton. 'They won't stand and fight.'

He looked wistfully after the departing Scots.

'Why did you bring him?' he gestured at John Fennell, the giant captain of archers. 'You could have picked anyone.'

'He doesn't have the keenest mind, I know, but his men trust him, and when he heard about the raid he came to me and begged for the opportunity to join us. He pleaded with me – I couldn't refuse him.'

Broughton nodded.

'It was good of you to give him the chance when there are other more experienced leaders. Now Francis, we must move on; the days are long up here and we should be able to cover a good few miles before nightfall. Then perhaps tomorrow we could move out of the valley and continue our trail of destruction into the heart of Scotland.'

He moved back to his position at the rear of our small column, and I turned to Edward Franke.

'Tell me, Edward, what have we achieved so far?' I asked as we resumed our march.

He rummaged in his saddle bag and produced a rumpled piece of parchment.

'Eight villages, twelve large farms and sixteen small ones destroyed.' He turned to me. 'Mind you, Francis, we won't be able to keep going much longer.'

'Why not?'

He consulted his parchment.

'Allowing for the fact that we have been advancing from side to side for the past ten days, I believe we are now fifty miles from the border. At the moment, it takes the packhorses two to three days to bring us supplies. From today, we will be moving due north; each day we advance adds another day to the supply chain and we require thirty packhorses worth of supplies a day. You are extending your line of supply too far.'

I bit my lip irritably; any hope of a quick campaign, organised with minimal supplies, was proving futile. It had been impossible to live off the countryside, as I had hoped we might.

It would be infuriating to have to return now. Once we were

through this valley, I was certain we would find ourselves in the heart of Scotland. Our raid had been highly successful so far. We had faced no opposition and, despite the lack of ale and wine, morale was high among the officers and men.

'There are more supplies coming up tonight,' I said. 'We can go on a bit further, Edward. After all, when we return the supply chain will become shorter.'

He looked sceptical.

'I suppose so, although we are low on most things and the supplies are late – they should have reached us yesterday.'

I felt he was being too cautious, but by the end of the next day, when the packhorses had still not arrived, I began to grow similarly concerned. I asked Thomas Broughton to take men to bring in the errant supplies.

'I'll do a sweep of the South, Francis, and watch out for any Scots. Mind you, I don't suppose I'll see any. All they seem to do is run away.'

I spent the day with Dick Middleton examining the horses while the men rested. My own presence in the inspection was pretty superfluous; his knowledge of horses exceeded that of any other man. He found little fault in the small, shaggy horses that comprised the Carlisle horse, but he was scathing about the condition of the palfreys that carried the archers and men-at-arms. Being large men, the archers required bigger mounts than those used by the Carlisle horse. He took the matter up with the giant captain of archers, John Fennell.

'Your men care nothing for their mounts. They don't look after them – look how many are missing shoes and those over there are lame. Do you know how many of these poor beasts have sores on their backs? No, of course you don't.'

Captain Fennell was unmoved by this outburst. Like all archers, he viewed horses as a convenient way to move his men into battle and his priorities lay elsewhere with the numbers and types of arrows, dry strings and the direction of the wind, but he was sensitive to Dick's passion and promised to look at the worst cases. If Master Middleton could advise on treatments, he would be grateful.

'That lumbering ox of a man,' Dick snapped, as we walked away. 'He doesn't care for his animals at all – I tell you Francis, it's shameful how they are treated.'

'You've always loved horses, Dick, haven't you?'

'I'm sorry Francis, I get excited, but yes I do love horses.' He looked round at the grazing beasts. 'Sometimes, I believe they are like friends.'

I pointed down the valley.

'There's Broughton. Let's see what he's found out.'

★ ★ ★

Thomas was grim-faced as the three of us sat down on the bank of a small stream that trickled down the valley.

'It's bad news, Francis. We're in trouble.'

He had found the pack train – well, a number of dead horses that were members of it – midway between our current position and the old road. The escorts were dead.

'All fifteen of them?' asked Dick, surprised.

'Mostly from arrow wounds,' grunted Thomas. 'But some were hacked with axes.'

We looked at each other in confusion. The Scots carried spears, short swords, daggers and occasionally short crossbows, but not axes.

'Skiam must have joined the Scots.'

'Or else he has recruited another band of followers,' brooded Thomas. 'But there's worse – we have the Scots behind us now. I saw one large group coming up from the south-west, and there's a large cloud of dust in the east.'

'Numbers?'

'I would say more than us.'

We sat in silence for a while.

'The Scots are in too great numbers to be mere random patrols,' Middleton said slowly.

Broughton narrowed his eyes.

'My instincts tell me that this is not a coincidence,' he growled.

He was right.

'I think I've completely underestimated the Scots,' I said bitterly. 'Our initial raid must have caught them by surprise, but while we were destroying their farms and villages, they were systematically assembling their own forces behind us.'

'They have fooled us altogether!' Thomas burst out. 'As we advanced, they gradually joined their forces together and just tempted us further and further into Scotland.' He gave a mirthless chuckle. 'That's why they sent those horsemen in front of us – to lure us deeper into Scotland.'

'With a larger force between us and the border, we're cut off,' Middleton said grimly. 'God knows if Skiam and his band are working with the Scots, but either way it looks as if both our lines of supply and retreat are cut off. We're trapped!'

I got up slowly, avoiding their gaze, and walked along by the stream, feeling the ever-increasing weight of failure. This was all my fault; I had been too reckless. It was I who had led this impetuous advance into enemy territory that had resulted in us being snared.

I paused to pick up a handful of pebbles. It was also my responsibility to get us out of this mess, I quietly reflected.

There was little hope of sending messengers back to Moresby to request reinforcements, as the Scots would intercept them. Even if, by some miracle, a messenger actually got through, if I were in Moresby's position, I was not sure I would send reinforcements. Having taken effectively half the strength of the West March on this raid, the remainder was required to guard Carlisle and our English forts.

The second alternative I considered was to fight our way back to the border, which was only two or three days away. The problem with this lay in the mixed composition of the force I led, which would severely restrict the speed of our march. The issue, of course, was that to use their bows the archers had to dismount. Given the Scots would be attacking us tirelessly, most of the journey back to the border would have to be done on foot. With fresh supplies and sufficient arrows this might be feasible, but we had little food and only a finite number of arrows. On top of this, Dick Middleton's horsemen were outnumbered by the Scots and would be destroyed over time.

I threw a series of stones in the stream. If somehow we could overcome the Scots, we would weaken their Western March considerably, since they must have assembled much of their available manpower. Although, it rather looked like it would be our own West March that would be weakened, due to my disastrous handling of this raid.

I flinched and felt my cheek; it was bleeding. A stone that I had thrown had not fallen into the stream, but had hit a rock and broken in two. A shard of the stone had bounced back and struck me. I knelt down to wash the trickle of blood in the stream and suddenly had an epiphany. It was an extremely risky idea but it might just work. Even if it didn't, at least half our force might survive. I walked back to where Broughton, Fennell and Middleton were sitting to seek their counsel.

★ ★ ★

I looked at the three of them.

'So what do you think of the plan?' I asked briskly.

Thomas rubbed his head.

'It's risky, Francis. Conventional military wisdom advises against dividing up your force when facing an enemy who outnumber you.' He paused. 'On the other hand, if it does work we could inflict a severe defeat on the Scots. I have no better plan.'

Dick shook his head.

'Let's be totally clear, Francis. You are saying that Broughton and

I break out tonight with the Carlisle horse. In the darkness, we will try to elude the Scots, before they are fully joined up, and then get to the border. That's possible if we move quickly and the Scots have not already joined all their forces together. Now, if we make it to the border, you want Sir Thomas to tell Sir Christopher Moresby to strip Carlisle of all its troops and send them to guard our fortresses.'

'Which I will then take charge of,' added Broughton, 'while he garrisons Carlisle Castle with his friends and servants. That way the border is safe.'

'Meanwhile, I bring up the whole of the Carlisle horse – there will be 700 or 800 of us – and attack the Scots, who will be attacking you and the archers in your fortified position,' continued Middleton.

'Yes. The way I see it, Dick, is that they expect us to split our force and try and save the Carlisle horse, but,' – I felt my cheek gingerly – 'what they will not expect is for you to bounce back with a large force, let alone so quickly.'

His face lit up.

'They will get the surprise of their lives and, with any luck, we will outnumber them. I suspect, Francis, that if we can break out, they will chase us all the way to the border. It should take us two days to reach there, two days to muster the men and another two days to return. If we can get through, you will need to hold out for six days.'

'No, Dick. If they follow you to the border it will take them two days and another two to return. We will only be under attack for two days. We can manage that easily enough.'

'I'll take the archers' palfreys with me. We can use them as remounts; I'll not leave them for the Scots. They deserve better than that.'

Dick and Broughton looked at each other.

'It might work,' said Thomas, 'but only if we can break through the Scots tonight. We'll leave you whatever rations there are. If we make it to the border, we can eat there. If we don't, well it won't matter. Francis, are you certain you will not come with us?'

I shook my head meditatively. It was my fault we were in this situation and it would encourage the archers if I remained. I suddenly had a thought; Broughton and Middleton had agreed to the plan, but courtesy demanded I seek the advice of the giant, albeit slow-witted, captain of archers, John Fennell.

I was not certain if he had been listening, as he seemed engrossed in cutting notches into a stick with a knife that seemed too small for his huge paw of a hand. I relayed my plan to him. When I was finished, he put his knife on the ground and looked at the hills around us.

'So I will find a good defensive spot for us, my lord,' he said slowly, 'and then we'll hold that ground until you and Master Middleton return to ambush the Scots.'

'No, I will remain with you.'

A simple smile spread over his face.

'That's good, my lord. It will do everyone good to know that you're here.' He rose to his feet. 'Let me go and look for a good place for us to defend.'

He started to move away, but I stopped him and gave him his little dagger.

'Thank you, my lord. I would not have wanted to lose that. It's my brother's.'

'Is he an archer too?'

'No my lord, he was a soldier; killed last year.'

He paused as if he was going to add something, but changed his mind and began to move away. He stopped and turned back to look at Broughton and Middleton.

'It's a cunning plan that my lord has devised.'

We watched his huge frame amble off and Dick Middleton's face creased in amusement.

'Do you know, Thomas, he's totally right and I'm completely wrong. I didn't realise that my lord's plan was a cunning, strategic device. I thought it was a plan born out of desperation to get us out of a rather nasty trap.'

Broughton smiled slowly.

'Ah, but you are unaware of my lord's strategic genius. Not many great generals would have carefully marched their forces deep into enemy territory to act as a decoy for the ambushing of their enemy. I doubt Julius Caesar would have thought of such a ruse.'

I bit my lip trying not to laugh as my two friends teased me mercilessly, but when Broughton referred to me as the Hannibal of the West March, and Dick swore that men in the future would talk of Alexander the Great and Lovell in the same breath, I burst out laughing and raised my hand to stop them.

'You two will move out of here late in the afternoon. I agree, Dick; you should take all the horses, as we will not need them. If you leave us the rest of the rations, we can probably make them last four or five days.'

'If we break through tonight,' said Dick, 'I will be back in six days at an outside guess. I think I know how we might get through without losing a man, but it's a gamble. If we do get through, the Scots will pursue us to the border. After all, they can always come back for you afterwards.'

★ ★ ★

With Captain Fennell at my side, I talked through the plan, and the role and tasks of the archers and men-at-arms before the Carlisle horse left us. Otherwise, they would have been worried when they saw their comrades depart. There were no questions, which surprised me, as archers are generally very quick to express their views.

I asked Fennell about this afterwards. He frowned and played with his little knife.

'There's not much to ask, my lord. The fact that you've stayed here proves that you believe Master Middleton will come back to defeat the Scots.'

'What you said was reassuring to them anyway,' Edward Franke added. 'It's true that Scottish horsemen are ideal for fighting other horsemen or attacking marching troops, but against archers in a defensive position, they would be shot to pieces before they reached our lines.'

Captain Fennell shook his head.

'The men trust you; that's why there were no questions. Now, my brother, he was a great one for asking questions. Not that it helped him in the end, him leaving a widow and four children behind.'

'If I can help them in anyway?' I began. 'I would…'

He looked down and smiled at me.

'No, my lord, no more is necessary.' Obviously, he was supporting the family himself. 'But it is kind of you.'

He looked around the valley.

'I need to find a hilltop for us, my lord; so if you don't mind, I'll start looking now.'

I watched him amble away. He appeared very helpful, as far as he was able, but I was still feeling very uneasy. Everyone remaining here seemed to have total confidence that Middleton would break through the Scots to the south of us and return in six days. Dick was a good leader, but the Scots outnumbered him and knew the ground intimately. They would know where to water their horses and lay ambushes and, of course, if he could not break through them, our group was going to be stranded here with dwindling rations. I began to feel sick as it hit me that, due to my impetuosity, I had probably condemned Middleton's force to annihilation at the hands of the Scots and the rest of my force to a lingering death on a lonely hilltop.

'Five days, I estimate,' Edward Franke interrupted my thoughts.

I looked at him blankly.

'We have sufficient rations for five days, Francis, but when Dick Middleton returns, he might bring some with him. I suppose we could just go hungry until he gets us back to the Debateable Land, though. Mind you Francis, on the next raid I think we should try to

81

establish a series of supply points as we advance. What we could do is…'

I clenched my hands and bit my tongue. There was not going to be a next raid; the chances were that Dick was not going to make it through the Scots, but I was going to have to keep the truth to myself.

'Yes, of course.'

I interrupted his ideal plan for supplying a raiding force.

'But Edward, this valley is not suitable as a defensive position; we need to be on top of one of the surrounding hills. Additionally, we need timber for palisades and wood for fires. The timber, wood and supplies have to be manhandled up the hills. We need to do all of this as quickly as possible; can you form the men into groups?'

'I know what to do,' he smiled at me. 'Mind you, in two days Dick will be back at the border and the Scots will want to rest before they return here, so the earliest they will be back is in five days' time, with Dick only a day behind them. Is it worth doing all this, Francis?'

I looked into his trusting blue eyes.

'Yes. It will give the men something to do and stop them worrying.'

'But no one is worried,' he hastened to reassure me. 'Captain Fennell has told the men about the defensive position we need to establish and has told them that we can slaughter the Scots while we sit there safely. Then when Middleton returns there won't be so many for him to defeat.'

'And they believed him?'

He furrowed his brow.

'Oh yes, of course. I know that he isn't at all clever, but to the archers he's a natural leader. He can outshoot any of them and he's a man of long sight, which is highly valuable. Apparently he can see things in the distance that any other man could not. And he's not a man to argue with – somebody tried to quarrel with him last year and Fennell knocked him unconscious with one blow. The men believe in him, Francis… and in you.'

I crossed to the east side of the hill and peered into the valley where yesterday afternoon Dick Middleton had led his force south to the cheers of the archers. They made a fine sight, spears aloft, the afternoon sunlight glinting on their breastplates and the silver embroidery of their saddlecloths. Dick argued when I suggested such a spectacle, thinking it would make his men too conspicuous, but had backed down when his troops had taken to their ostentatious saddle wear with enthusiasm.

I wondered where he was now. If he had broken through, he must be halfway to the border with the Scots in hot pursuit. If he had not, the Scots would be back here in a day or so.

★ ★ ★

Unlike the exhausted archers who sprawled everywhere on the hilltop, I was unable to sleep. I had forbidden the making of fires, so as not to reveal our position, but the moon was almost full and gave sufficient light as I walked round the small camp. To my surprise, I found Fennell on the southern side, his burly frame hunched as he peered down to the entrance of the valley.

He pointed into the darkness.

'Can you see it, my lord?'

I looked out uneasily.

'No, what is it?'

He rubbed his eyes.

'It's a long way off, my lord, but I think it's a fire or fires.'

I went cold. If Middleton had broken through, he should be near to the border now and the Scots would be with him. There should be no one close to our camp now. Either the Scots had abandoned the pursuit or they had defeated Middleton, but there was no reason why the Scots would have called off the chase – they outnumbered the Carlisle horse, knew the country and the quickest routes, and it was clear Dick and his men were fleeing for their lives.

'How far away would you say that fire is?' I asked.

'Difficult to say my lord – could be half a day's march, maybe more?' Fennell squinted through the darkness.

I thought hard. Men generally believe what they want to believe and hoped Fennell's men were no different.

'Middleton left yesterday so he must have been able to break through and the Scots decided to abandon the chase,' I said confidently.

Fennell was silent for a long while as he absorbed this.

'Could the Scots have defeated Master Middleton?' he asked slowly.

I swallowed; this was the difficult part.

'No. If they had, they would be busily pursuing all the survivors. Think about it; Middleton's men fight in groups. They're not just one single body of horsemen. There would be a series of battles between the Scots and the groups of Carlisle horse, but even if the Scots had won some of these they would have wanted to wipe out the whole force. They would not have come back here; they would have chased the survivors, hoping to kill them before they got to the border.'

'So the Scots would have chased the survivors to the borders,' Fennell asked hesitantly, 'if there had been a battle?'

'Yes, the fact that there are Scots half a day's march away suggests that Middleton eluded them completely.'

'I'll tell the men what you've said, my lord.' He straightened up slowly. 'They will be glad to hear that Master Middleton has broken through.' He paused for a moment and then added. 'I am glad you're here, my lord. I would not have thought of what you have just told me.'

With that he lumbered off, while I thanked God for his lack of wit, as clearly all of Middleton's horsemen had been annihilated speedily. There were no survivors, which was why the Scots were returning. I sat silently grieving Thomas and Dick Middleton, as well as their men. It was my fault they had died, along with the 300 men of the Carlisle horse. Soon all the archers and men-at-arms here would be dead as well. Even if Middleton or Broughton had escaped, or there were any survivors, the defeat of the Carlisle horse settled the fate of the men on the hilltop. Sir Christopher Moresby would retain what was left of the forces of the West March to protect it. The last thing he would do was weaken the numbers in the West March still further by sending more troops to reinforce failure. Besides which, he would not know where to send them.

I thought of my two friends and their men. I had known Dick since we were boys, but was closer to Thomas Broughton – our thoughts and speech were attuned to one another, but now he was dead as a result of my actions.

Another idea struck me – with the defeat in Scotland, our West March was badly weakened, which would add fuel to those harmful rumours of Gloucester's poor handling of the North. By destroying half the available soldiers in the West March and its military leadership, I had probably destroyed its chances of survival. Dear God, instead of helping Gloucester, I had probably ruined him and Anne Neville.

'Captain Fennell said you were here, Francis.' Edward Franke broke into my thoughts. 'I brought you some wine; there's a little left.'

I grunted out my thanks.

'And Dick Middleton has broken through, Captain Fennell told the sentries. The fact that the Scots are about half a day away is good news. If they had found Middleton, they would have chased him to the border. We will need to hurry up with our defences, Fennell's told them – but Middleton should be back in four days.'

He peered out into the night.

'I can't see anything though, but then Fennell can see farther than most. Do you think the Scots will attack tomorrow?'

It hardly mattered when they attacked now; our force was doomed. I had destroyed it, as I had destroyed the Carlisle horse.

'I doubt it, Edward. In their place I would come at us slowly and carefully inspect our position. Then I would probably try to offset our advantage of archers by attacking at night. Edward, we will be busy tomorrow, get some rest now.'

I sat alone on the south side of this hill for the remainder of the night, thinking of my friends and the men I had sent to their death and how I had failed Richard and Anne.

★ ★ ★

There were happy smiles in the camp the next day. While I slept, Captain Fennell had spread the news that Middleton had broken through and the men worked eagerly on our makeshift defences. I left them to their work and eyed the approaching Scots as they moved up the valley towards our defensive position. It was a slow advance. They were in no hurry, as they knew that they had us trapped.

They came at us cautiously. I watched them ride through the valley and up and down the defiles on either side, entering the little woods further up the valley to check that we had not concealed men there. It was only when the Scots were satisfied that there was no chance of an ambush that the main party rode up and started to water their horses.

Their next moves were fairly predictable. They identified our position and sent patrols round the hill to find the easiest slopes from which to attack upwards. They quickly discovered that the western side would be the simplest route, given the steepness of the other three sides. Then they had a fairly obvious choice whether to attack us or starve us out.

To attack uphill against a large number of archers capable of firing ten arrows or more a minute would be suicidal. Even if they attacked at night, I would back the archers to win, since the contours of the hill made it impossible to come from more than one direction. In the Scots' place, I would only attack if I needed to finish the job quickly. But as the Scots had defeated Middleton, they had no need to hurry at all. They could simply starve us out. Eventually the lack of food would force us to leave our defensive position and try to break out towards the border. Once on open ground, they would ride us down.

'I've counted about 700 in the valley and there are those thirty or so on the hill opposite us, my lord.'

Fennell had obviously been watching them closely. I had been so pre-occupied that I had not noticed him approach. He gestured down to the horses by the stream.

'It looks like the Scots have captured some of our palfreys.'

My heart sank as I saw our larger horses drinking next to the small Scottish horses.

'There must be about 200 of them,' he added. 'They must be ours, as the Scots don't use them. How do you reckon they got hold of them?'

I turned away so he could not see the tears in my eyes. The answer was obvious; Dick's fondness for horses was such that he would not have surrendered a single one – let alone 200 – while he still lived. The presence of the palfreys confirmed finally that he had been heavily defeated.

I thought quickly. Apart from Edward Franke and myself, there was probably no one else in the camp that knew of Dick's love of horses and I could deal with Edward later. Casually, I turned back to Fennell who was staring across the valley at the thirty or so men on the opposite hill. Inexplicably, he was smiling happily, but then he was a simple-minded fellow.

'Middleton has used those palfreys as a decoy,' I said firmly. 'He would have let them go in order to draw off the Scots and let the main body escape.'

Please let him believe me, I prayed silently. With reluctance he tore his eyes away from the far hillside and looked down at me.

'That's clever of him,' he said with admiration. 'It's a good job you know him so well, my lord. I would have never of thought of that.'

I tried to work out if there was a hint of sarcasm in his voice but found none. Thank God he was so gullible.

'I'll tell the men in case any of them start wondering about those palfreys.'

'You see that explains how Middleton broke through?'

A relieved smile came to his face.

'Of course it does, my lord. It's sort of proof that Master Middleton escaped. I'm glad you are here, my lord. I'll go now, if I may?'

I nodded and went to find Edward Franke. With a little luck I should be able to persuade him that while we both knew of Dick's obsession with horses, Dick and I were boyhood friends. Naturally, Dick would have put friendship and comradeship before his devotion to horses. He had surrendered the palfreys to act as a decoy so they could escape. My explanation would have to be particularly convincing; it would be difficult as I didn't believe a word of it.

CHAPTER 7

'There aren't enough Scots for us, my lord!' called out one of the archers to roars of laughter from his colleagues.

I delayed inspecting the barricade and smiled back at the ring of confident faces.

'Why won't the Scots attack?' shouted another.

'They're scared of you!' I answered with a smile.

This was the story I had put to Fennell when, after two days and two nights, the Scots had still not attacked. It was obvious that with Middleton's troops defeated, the Scots, wisely, preferred to starve us out rather than risk an all-out assault on a fairly narrow front. I had pointed out to Captain Fennell the difficulties the Scots would face if they tried to attack and how, in their defensive position, the archers would have the natural advantage.

'So they're afraid?' he growled.

He seemed disappointed there was to be no attack.

'It's the only reason I can think of.' I was lying barefacedly. 'You'll destroy them before they get to the barricade and they know it.'

His face clouded over. Clearly he had been hoping to slaughter the Scots.

'You're right, my lord, of course. Mind you, they'll have to do something soon. How many supplies do you think they have?'

It was an unexpected point. I had assumed the Scots would be able to starve us out, but while they travelled light and consumed little, after two weeks in the saddle they must be nearing the end of their own supplies. As such, it was probable they would try to complete their defeat of the English forces soon. I decided to inspect the barricade with a new conviction that tonight would be the night they launched their assault.

'Master Middleton's men will be back in three days!' another archer shouted out.

There was a round of cheering. Morale was high; everyone believed what their Captain had told them.

'Well it might be four days if he's bringing supplies up with him.' I sought to calm them with a strained smile.

'Three days, four days,' the man called back. 'Why won't the Scots attack?'

'They're terrified!' his friends chorused loudly and there were roars of derisive laughter.

I looked at the barricade; it seemed smaller every time I stared at it.

'What happens if they get round the flanks?' I wanted to know.

A number of them patted the long swords they wore and one produced a heavy bullock knife.

'Can't say, as they won't, my lord, but if they do, they'll be sorry.'

There were murmurs of agreement and I moved away, feigning an air of confidence, to the eastern side of the camp. It had been agreed that Fennell would command his men on the exposed western side and I would cover the remaining perimeter with the thirty men-at-arms. We had agreed that it would be unlikely there would be an attack other than from the west, but it would be foolish to leave the remaining ground unguarded. If necessary, my men could reinforce Fennell.

I found Edward Franke peering at the small group on the hill opposite us.

'Who do you think they are, Francis?'

They seemed the least of our problems.

'Probably Scottish scouts watching to see that we don't try to escape when the Scots attack from the west.'

'I suppose so, but Captain Fennell told me that they don't have spears like the other Scots. Perhaps, they are just looking after the captured palfreys.'

'Edward, how are the supplies?'

'We can last two more days, but then Dick Middleton will be back the day after that.'

I bit my lip. I had to give Edward something to do before I lost my composure and told him the truth.

'Edward, I think that the Scots will attack tonight. I want you to be the messenger between Captain Fennell and myself. Base yourself on the western side, stay away from the barricade, and bring me word when he needs reinforcements.'

'Yes, my lord.'

In the valley, the Scots were on the move. I saw them mounting and forming small groups. They rode south and, presently, began to loop to the right. It certainly looked as if they would attack tonight. I settled down to keep watch.

★ ★ ★

Edward Franke nudged me.

'Captain Fennell sent me,' he whispered. 'There are noises on the western approach.'

I got up and looked down the sloping camp to where the three great fires burned by the marker stands. The night being cloudy, they provided the only light. With them as a background, I could make out the shapes of archers rousing themselves and slowly making their way to the barricade.

Edward helped me into my harness; I picked up my gauntlets and gave him my helmet, as I reached for my war hammer. It had been a gift from Sergeant Jervis when I trained under him. He had narrowed down the choice of weapon that most suited me to two – the war hammer and the poleaxe. After watching me in combat training for about ten days, he decided on the hammer.[8]

'The poleaxe has a longer reach and it has an axe as well as a hammer,' he had said in the end. 'But you need to be quicker than you are. If you manage this weapon correctly, you'll only need to use it once against any opponent. With your size and strength, I doubt there are many who could stop you. Now let's take it slowly…'

I spotted Fennell in the centre of his men. He towered over them and shouted for them to form two crude lines. They all shuffled into position and bent down. I assumed they were placing arrows in the ground in front of them.

I left my helmet off; once it is placed on the head most sound and vision is impeded and, while it would be impossible for the Scots to ride up the other three slopes, I needed to watch and listen for enemy foot soldiers.

There was a great shout from the other end of the camp, and I heard the thunder of a hundred horses' hooves. In a moment, the ground in front of the fires was full of horsemen galloping frantically towards the barricade with spears outstretched, screaming as they came. I could neither see nor hear the arrows that were being poured into them as they charged.

It would be carnage for the Scots. They were advancing on a single front and, silhouetted against the blazing fires, the front rows would be quickly destroyed by concentrated arrow fire. The bodies would then block the charge of those following them and bunched together they would be easy, if unseen, targets for the archers. Judging by the babble at the west side of the camp, I was right. The Scottish whoops were turning to screams and the frantic neighing of their horses was gradually being silenced. Simultaneously, the triumphant roars of our bowmen grew louder and more confident.

I saw our archers gradually relax their stance; I guessed they could hear a distant drumming of hooves signalling the retreat of the Scots. I imagined none of them had got close to the camp and, since there were no mounted figures on our territory, any attempt to outflank the barricade must have failed.

'Fennell reckons he's used about half his arrows,' Edward Franke panted. 'He's not going to try to recover any arrows until it's light.'

'Any losses?'

'He didn't say, but I don't think the Scots came close enough. I don't know how many of the Scots died, but we'll find out in the morning.'

His white teeth gleamed in the gloom.

'Dick Middleton will be angry when he returns and finds that there are no Scots left for him. He should be back…'

'Edward,' I said quickly, 'tell Captain Fennell that nothing has occurred at this end of the camp, but we will continue to keep watch. Go now in case he's worried.'

'Oh he's not worried. In fact, I think…'

'Just go!' I yelled at him.

There would be no further attacks that night, I guessed. The Scots had been badly hurt. I looked out into the darkness and tried to anticipate their next move. In their position, what would I do? There were probably sufficient numbers of them left to mount another attack tomorrow night, and by that time the three great fires would have burned themselves out. They could attack with the advantage of total darkness, but suppose that attack failed too? The obvious thing to do would be to bring up reinforcements and get further supplies. They would know that with Middleton dead; we were stranded with no food and few arrows left. They could either starve us out or mount a third attack, which would probably succeed.

At dawn, I went down to the western side. Despite the hour, the place was a hive of activity with archers recovering whatever arrows they could find and looting the Scottish dead.

'158, my lord.'

I recognised the archer who had joked about the Scots the previous day.

'What about their wounded?' I asked.

He looked at me in surprise.

'There aren't any now,' he said patiently. 'But you'll find that figure of their dead to be correct; Captain Fennell went to look at the bodies himself.'

That puzzled me, but I did not ask him about it when later I congratulated him on his men's shooting.

'Easy pickings, my lord. We couldn't miss at that range. I don't know how many of their wounded managed to ride away,' he added thoughtfully.

'How many arrows have your men got left?'

'Probably thirty or so a man. We'll see off the next attack and then Middleton will be back.'

He roared with laughter and put his great paw of a hand on my shoulder.

'Did you hear what Edward Franke said, my lord?' His shoulders heaved. 'He said that Master Middleton will be angry to find we have destroyed half the Scots when he gets back.'

A few men smiled openly at the sight of their giant captain laughing happily with Lord Lovell safe in the knowledge that their clever plan was working out as they had hoped. Soon Middleton would return and they had already killed a large number of Scots without losing a single man. I bit my tongue and suggested that we use the Scottish spears to line the bottom of the trench – Edward Franke could take care of that. With any luck it would take him all day.

'Another good idea, my lord,' John Fennell chuckled. 'Mind you, we'll have to pray for moonlight tonight; we won't be able to build more fires. You'll find that those Scots will lurk around here just out of arrow shot. Maybe we won't even see them, but they'll be there. If you sent a man out of camp today to rebuild those fires, he would be ridden down and spitted before he knew what had happened.'

I had guessed this would be the case, but it was interesting, and curious, that Fennell had come up with the same thought.

'Then tonight we are reliant on the moon and the stars, so there's a greater chance that the Scots will throw everything they have at us,' I said to him. 'Even that little band of thirty or so have moved off the hill opposite us.'

For some reason his head jerked up. For a moment his eyes blazed excitedly.

'In the darkness, I think they might be able to outflank you, so I'll give you some of the men-at-arms to strengthen you and, if it's desperate, I'll bring the rest down to join you.'

He nodded, but I sensed his mind was elsewhere; he toyed with his little dagger in his hand. I moved away from the happy chatter of the archers. Morale in camp was undoubtedly high, and the men clearly relished the prospect of taking on the Scots again, but what would happen when Middleton failed to return? I could stall it for a day or so. If he were bringing supplies, Middleton would have come slower, but how long could I keep up the pretence? Morale would plummet, the Scots would gather more provisions, and with reinforcements, they would attack for the final time. The sharp swords of the archers would be no match for the longer spears of the Scots.

There was no way out. I had thought of trying to get the men down the hill to the captured horses, but we would have been ridden down shortly after we left camp. Even if we got to the palfreys, we would be outridden by the Scots and outreached by their spears. On balance, it was better to die on this hill. At least some of the men would die without knowing that Middleton was never going to come back for them. With any luck, most of them would die without knowing that it was I who had caused their deaths.

★ ★ ★

One of the men-at-arms shook me awake. I looked up blearily. The Scots must be massing at the western end. As I made the final adjustments to my half armour[9], I peered down the camp. The full moon and stars provided some light, but clouds obscured large areas of the ground.

In the distance, I could hear the rumble of the Scottish horsemen massing beyond the burnt-out fires, but the barricade and archers were a black shadow. Then the hubbub turned into a rhythmical thudding sound and I heard the whooping of the Scots as they launched their charge. The cloud moved over and I could see no more.

The yelling of the Scots was much closer now, so I put my helmet on but kept the visor up and signalled to the men-at-arms to close up on me. I guessed that the Scots must have made it over the trench and were probably now at the barricade. Some Scots seemed to be crawling over the barricade, or were they but shadows? What was certain, and far more worrying, was that some of their horsemen had definitely outflanked the barrier and were riding into camp behind the archers. The men-at-arms vigorously contested their passage.

I glanced at my fifteen or so men; they were needed there, not here. There was no point in waiting, so I raised my hand. The screams were audible behind me despite my helmet. I turned horrified; the Scots were flooding over the eastern side of the camp. They were all on foot – clearly they had climbed the steep slope in the darkness – and were running towards us. I cursed and slammed my visor down. All was suddenly quiet. Forget the western side, I thought. Forget that you have been surprised; defend Fennell's back. I waved the men forward and lumbered ahead clutching my hammer. All I could hear were the nasal tones of Sergeant Jervis.

'Left foot forward, left hand to the base, right hand higher and swing, right foot forward and recover. Now, left foot forward, left hand to the base... Ignore anyone that is not in front of you... Left foot forward, left hand to the base... Tired? You're not tired! You're only just starting! ... Left foot forward, left hand to the base, right hand further up and swing... Don't stop you fool, a stationary man is an easy target! ... Left foot forward...'

He was a hard man, Jervis, but a good teacher, as he made you forget the sweat, tiredness and the immense jolts that ran down your arms. You learnt to ignore the blows that struck you. He taught you just to keep moving inexorably forward, until the pressure opposing you began to slacken, as it was doing now.

I risked a quick sidelong glance. Some of the men were still with me, but the Scots were shrinking back. I raised my visor to look out properly, gasping for breath, and saw that the Scots were fleeing back over the brow of the hill.

The cloud cover had moved away completely now and it was easy to see the bodies on the ground. I estimated that I had lost perhaps half my men, but there seemed to be a lot of dead Scots. The remaining men-at-arms were using the ends of their poleaxes to finish off the wounded enemy. Clearly, despite being outnumbered, our men's armour and weapons had proved far superior to the short Scottish swords and their thin jacks. Indeed, there had only been one opponent I faced who had proved a problem, as he had used a large double-bladed axe.

The surviving Scots had fled now – but no, over there were three more. The one in the centre appeared wounded and was holding the shoulder of the man on his right. The one on his left had been wounded in the leg and was staggering. I signalled my men to spread out and we moved slowly towards the trio. We would finish this, I thought; then we would go down to the western side to help there. Then I gazed in amazement for two of the three men suddenly collapsed with arrows sticking into them. Unable to support himself, the little man in the centre slowly slid to the ground. I removed my helmet; if there were archers here, the western side must be secure.

'You've been busy here, my lord,' Captain Fennell greeted me and strode over to examine the little man.

'And you?'

'Probably lost thirty men, but they were badly hit, the Scots. The ones who got inside the camp will have been dispatched by now.'

'You mean, you left your men fighting to come up here?' I said horrified. 'Why did you leave the major battle to come and help in a skirmish?'

His actions were unbelievable.

'It's all quiet there now and this was the major battle for me anyway. I came as soon as I heard Edward Franke say we were being attacked at the rear. As a matter of fact, I've been hoping we would be.'

His speech was quick and confident now and I noticed a new

authority about John Fennell, as he ordered the men-at-arms and archers back to the western side of the camp.

'They won't attack again, my lord, and they won't come up here anyway.'

He moved a few feet away from the sprawled form on the ground.

'Fair devil you are with that war hammer, my lord. I watched you batter your way through them, as easy as anything.'

'You watched? You could have…'

'Do the men good to see you in battle,' he said admiringly. 'Mind you, I'm glad you didn't kill him,' he gestured at the ground. 'We had to stop the man who wounded him.'

This made no sense at all.

'Why?'

He smiled genially at me.

'Men think that I am simple-minded, my lord, but of late I think I've been rather clever. Shall I tell you why?'

'Go on.'

'I've had you fooled, my lord, haven't I? There's me applauding your clever plan, when all the time I knew the situation was a total disaster. There I was telling everyone that Master Middleton had broken through the Scots, when a child could have worked out that he'd been defeated quickly. And there was me telling everyone that nonsensical story about the decoy Master Middleton made, when he surrendered his palfreys.' His shoulders shook gently. 'You were there, my lord, when he told me off – proper angry he was. You could tell that he loved horses; my brother told me that before. He would not have surrendered those horses to the Scots – the Scots captured them when they defeated him. I expect you're wondering why I went along with all of that nonsense?'

He paused and then went over to prod the wounded man on the ground. There was a rattling groan. Fennell came back and grinned at me.

'Still alive – that's good. Now, my lord, can you recall the names of the widows you provided for after the news of Anderson's patrol became known?'

I shook my head.

'It doesn't matter. It was kind of you to think of them anyway, but among them was one Alice Fennell. She was married to my brother Christopher and you gave her more support because you took time to find out that she had four very young children.'

'Your brother was with Anderson?' I asked stupidly.

Clouds had covered the moon and I could not see his face.

'He was my twin. Mind you, no one would have guessed; he was much smaller than me, but we were close, very close.' He fell silent for a moment. 'You know how it is with twins, my lord; you're closer than brothers, sometimes even closer than with wives. We'd been together all our lives as boys, then as men.'

He drew out the little dagger and played with it, a sudden shaft of moonlight illuminating the blade.

'He was one of the five men who were taken with Anderson,' he said softly. 'When I heard how he died, at first I wished I was dead. Then I realised that I had to help Alice and her children, but you'd provided for them so generously that there was no need.'

The clouds had broken up completely now and I saw that he was gently stroking his brother's dagger.

'So I only had one thing to do, my lord. I swore that I'd find my brother's murderer and that he would die a slow, painful death.'

He glanced down at the collapsed form.

'You know who that is now, don't you?'

'Skiam?'

'The very same. After you and Master Middleton devastated the Debateable Land, everyone thought that he'd have to go to Scotland. I was wondering if I could try to find him myself, but I couldn't by myself in Scotland. Then I heard you were planning a raid and I thought the only way that Skiam could win himself a bit of trust with the Scots was if he attacked you. That's why I pleaded for you to take me with you, my lord. I hoped that there might be a chance.

Then, when I heard about how the supply packhorses were attacked, I thought he might be close. Finally, I thought hard. The only way I could come close to him was if he and his men joined in the Scottish attack. That's why I went along with you, my lord, after Middleton was defeated. We had to keep the morale strong enough to ensure that the men did not desert or try to surrender to the Scots, which they would have done if they had known that no one was going to come back for them. We had to be strong enough to resist the Scots and Skiam.'

'But how did you know that he was here?'

'I saw them on the hill opposite us when you were explaining to me how Middleton used the palfreys as decoys,' he smiled at me. 'I was wondering about that little group. They didn't have spears like the Scots and then I remembered Anderson's description of how he was captured by a big man with a double-bladed axe and I saw such a man in that group. I was frightened that we might have killed him with those other Scots last night. That's why I went to look at the bodies, but he wasn't among their dead. Then when I heard Edward Franke shouting that you were being attacked on the east side, I knew that it had to be Skiam and his men trying to take us in the back. The Scots were almost beaten by them, so I brought up a few men and then I saw him. It was obvious he was their leader as he was urging them on with his little axe. That's why I went to look at him afterwards. I just had to see if his face fitted Anderson's description. It was just as I had heard, down to the piece missing from his ear.'

There was an air of total satisfaction in his manner. He had done what he had set out to do and fooled me completely in the process. At least, it would be easier now that I knew he was aware of the fate of Middleton and the others. I got up slowly.

'We'll need to think about what we should do tomorrow and then the next day when Middleton doesn't return.'

He nodded vaguely. Clearly the threat of the Scots being reinforced and returning to crush us completely was of no consequence to him.

'We'll talk in the morning, my lord. You'll think of something clever and I'll tell the men. But you'll be tired now, so why don't you leave me and this one to have a little talk together?' He rose and put his great paw on my shoulder. 'Thank you, my lord.'

'For what?'

He gestured to the figure on the ground.

'For helping me to keep my promise.'

★ ★ ★

I woke to find the camp cleared of the Scots and our own dead. I walked to the barricade and looked over at the piles of Scots stacked in front of it. The stench was unbearable; all the same the archers and men-at-arms were busy working their way through the clothing of the dead.

Edward Franke joined me.

'They lost over 300 men last night,' he said in a shocked voice. 'They cannot have more than 200 or 300 left by now.'

'Do you know how many arrows we have left?'

'Not many, but Middleton will be here soon and even I don't believe the Scots will attack again tonight.'

I crossed to the east side of the camp to look into the valley. Fennell was already there. He pointed to the Scots milling about in the valley. We watched them as they formed little groups and rose away to the south. In a short while, they were out of sight.

'Going to get reinforcements, I suppose?' he said after a while. 'What do you want me to tell the men?'

I looked at him hopelessly. The events of the past few days had exhausted my powers of inventiveness. I shrugged my shoulders.

'I think I'll tell the men that you believe the Scottish scouts have reported a sighting of Middleton coming up from the south, and they are scared of being caught between him and us here.'

'And when the Scots return?' I said wearily.

'It won't matter by then, my lord. We'll all be too busy fighting to worry about where Middleton disappeared to,' he said cheerfully.

He was right, of course. Why bother telling the truth? Morale was sky-high as Middleton was expected any day now – better that the men lived their last day in hope rather than in despair. To maintain the fiction, I told Edward to distribute the remainder of the rations that night.

★ ★ ★

It was early the next day that the Scots returned. I did not see them, as all our men were on the southern side of the camp waiting for the first sighting of Middleton, while I was on the west with Fennell.

'When the Scots return,' he said quietly, 'we'll say that Middleton cannot be far behind.'

'I think we need to move into a central defensive position,' I interrupted him. 'The Scots will have learned their lesson by now and will attack from all sides.'

Edward Franke ran to us.

'There's a small cloud of dust in the south,' he panted.

We walked together to the south side, pushing our way through the archers. I could see nothing, but Fennell muttered 'horsemen'. A few moments later I could see a few specks on the horizon.

'Probably about 500. They've got their reinforcements,' Fennell added.

I knew they were Scots, but in my tired state I pretended for a moment that they were Middleton's men. My shoulders sank; there was no chance it could be them. Even the numbers were wrong. I remembered him saying, 'I'll bring up the Carlisle horse. They'll be 700 or 800 of us.' I pinched myself irritably; of course they were Scots. Middleton was dead anyway.

My daydream was dispersed by Fennell bellowing to his men to return to their posts; smiling broadly, the archers obeyed. With good humour, they followed him to the western barricade, and I waved my men-at-arms to the east. Edward Franke stayed with me.

It began to rain heavily, for which I was glad as it restricted visibility. With any luck the men would not know that they had been deluded for a good few hours, and we would all just fight this last battle. I pulled my cloak around me and sent Edward to the east side.

After a while he returned, his cloak steaming in the bright sunlight that had just replaced the rain.

'Horsemen are coming up the valley, Francis.'

There was an outbreak of cheers and shouts from the men on the east side of the hill. Turning round. I saw that the men from the north side had joined them.

I swallowed; Edward would be safer with Fennell's men when the attack started.

'Edward, will you go to Captain Fennell and tell him to prepare?'

The cheers swelled to a deafening crescendo. With an apologetic smile, Edward ran to the east. I watched him and the others shouting and waving their arms about. Some were even jumping up and down.

Dear God, I thought. I had better go and calm those fools down. I stepped forward wearily and looked down into the valley where the first horsemen moved towards our position. I sank to my knees in disbelief. While they had the same little ponies and spears that the Scots used, these troops were undoubtedly English – the sunlight behind me picked out the silver threads on their ostentatious saddle coverings.

Ignoring their captain, the archers begun to stream across the camp to see the Carlisle horse who waved back at them. I saw a party of horsemen ride up the valley to probe for Scots.

Edward Franke tugged my sleeve.

'Francis, what did you want me to do?'

'I'm sorry?'

'You said "Go to Fennell and tell him to prepare..."' he prompted me.

'Um... well yes.' My powers of inventiveness suddenly returned. 'Yes, Edward, go to Fennell and tell him to prepare to leave.'

There were tears in my eyes.

★ ★ ★

'You picked a good spot to defend,' Dick commented as we walked past the Scottish dead. I waved my hands about me; the flies were intolerable. 'Fennell tells me that you killed over 400 of them, and I intercepted another 300 or so on my way up here.'

It had been a running fight, but with many of their number wounded and badly outnumbered, the Scots had soon broken and fled. Dick had detached a number of his men to pursue them and then had moved up here with the rest.

He smiled happily at me.

'We've hurt them badly, Francis. They must have lost over 700 men and horses; they'll find it difficult to replace both.'

He chattered on while I looked at him uncertainly; there was a strange air of unreality about our meeting. I felt that I wanted to keep touching him to reassure myself that he was actually walking beside me.

'Mind you, that does not include their wounded.'

'Or Skiam's followers,' added Captain Fennell happily. 'How did you manage to break through Master Middleton, when you left us?'

Dick grinned.

'I had scouts ahead to the left and right. The Scots had not quite joined together, so I split the men into groups of twenties and thirties and we slipped through the gap in the darkness. I had all the palfreys released and then we went as quickly as we could...'

'You released the palfreys?'

He gave me a curious look.

'They are valuable animals to the Scots and by the time they had rounded them up, we were too far away to be pursued. It was a pity to lose them, but I thought the Scots would take them and leave us.'

'You mean you let the horses go deliberately?' I stammered.

He stared at me.

'Well, of course. In the darkness they provided an excellent decoy and what mattered most was to get to the border. Your lives were in danger here and, after all, they were only horses.' He frowned. 'You can't believe that I would value horses as more important than your lives surely?'

I avoided looking at Fennell.

'Of course not, Dick,' I said indignantly. 'As you said, they were only horses.'

Edward Franke joined us at the bottom of the slope.

'I've had all the men fed, so we can leave whenever you wish, Francis. I'm glad to see you Dick, although everyone knew that you would come back for us.'

'I'm glad everyone had so much confidence in me. Thomas Broughton was worried about you, Francis. He believed that by releasing the palfreys it would cause the Scots to return to you sooner than you thought they would and you might have believed that we had been defeated.'

Edward Franke shook his head.

'Oh no,' he said simply. 'Francis and Captain Fennell told everyone exactly what was happening and were so confident of the time of your return that last night Francis told me to hand out the remainder of the rations.'

Dick nodded in a relieved way.

'Well, Francis, thank you for your faith.'

Dick was an old friend and I swallowed hard. I felt bound to tell him the truth, but as I stepped forward I felt the giant paw of Captain Fennell on my shoulder.

'Edward Franke exaggerates my part in this Master Middleton. For it was my lord here who was clever enough to work out what was happening. I just told the men what he told me.'

Dick smiled at him and turned to me.

'I hear that Skiam is dead, Francis. How did he die exactly?'

Captain Fennell took his hand from my shoulder and cleared his throat but I thought it best to speak for him.

'He was wounded in the second attack and died later from his wounds,' I said casually.

Dick nodded.

'I doubt that there will be many who will mourn his passing,' he commented dryly. 'Now, when you're ready, we will return to Carlisle.'

CHAPTER 8

I n the two years that followed, we continued to build up the fighting strength of the West March. In one sense it was easier than before as, with the destruction of the Debateable Land and a decisive, albeit lucky, victory over the Scots, men were keen to serve.

What surprised us though were the numbers of volunteers. Even after weeding out the more unpromising ones, we still found ourselves with a large number of men all of whom required feeding, equipping and training, and above all organising. It was a task that stretched all of us to the limit, but it was a process that forced Broughton, Middleton, Edward Franke and me to function as a proper team. We began to think and act as one and, as we did so, we came to recognise each other's strengths and to rely upon them. It was both a frustrating and exhilarating time, but it was due to our teamwork that our force grew not just in strength of numbers but in skill and confidence.

Reports of this found their way back to Richard of Gloucester, and when Nan and I visited them, I sensed that our progress pleased both him and Anne Neville, as Ratcliffe's visits to Carlisle became increasingly infrequent. When he did eventually come, his inspection was done in a perfunctory manner, and he found little to fault. Instead he used his time to tell me how Richard and Anne were continuing to build up their position in the North. Indeed, he said, that they had been so successful that even the Woodvilles had given up trying to destabilise them and had probably turned their attention to easier areas of encroachment and growth. I had heaved a sigh of relief at that and, after Ratcliffe had gone, put the

Woodvilles from my mind and threw myself into our work. But the Woodvilles had deceived us all. It all started a few weeks later when I received a direct summons from Richard of Gloucester. I was to report to him and Anne Neville immediately. He regretted that on this occasion I should not bring Nan; indeed it was essential that I came alone and quickly.

★ ★ ★

The sun was just beginning to slip behind the distant hills as I slowly retraced my steps to Middleham. I stopped to gaze at the familiar outline of the castle; even allowing for its particularly squat appearance, it looked to be miles away.

I shook my head ruefully. Evidently I had been thinking so hard that I had not noticed how far I had walked. For the first time too, I noticed that I was not alone. All around me great flocks of sheep grazed peacefully on the heather-covered moorland, while startled rabbits scattered in front of me. Overhead swifts darted and swooped, while beyond them a solitary hawk circled tirelessly. I put the moors from my mind as I considered again what I had heard from Anne Neville. It had been she who had done most of the briefing. I pictured her for a moment sitting in her high-backed chair as she had shrewdly analysed the problems that confronted her and Gloucester.

As I watched the two of them, my admiration for them grew. Anne might have done most of the talking and Richard most of the listening, but you could see that theirs was the complete partnership and that Richard trusted his wife's judgement implicitly. For that I respected him. Any major decision would ultimately be his, but he was content with being guided by Anne Neville. Any man married to a woman such as Anne would have been. A man would have been a fool to have rejected such a powerful intellect and a complete idiot not to have spotted the passionate integrity with which it was being used. All of her thoughts and words were motivated by her heartfelt desire to assist Richard in every possible way. Without Nan, I arrived at the meeting feeling awkward. I felt like an interloper in their marriage. Anne Neville swiftly swept away my inhibitions. Within minutes their problems became our collective issues; they both relied upon me, she admittedly openly, and hoped that I would not fail them.

★ ★ ★

The first problem I recalled was a fairly simple one, but in an indirect way it impacted on the second and more major one. In itself the issue was a minor one. It seemed that Clarence, brother to both King Edward and Richard of Gloucester, had once again been plotting. For this he had been imprisoned and subsequently killed. Anne Neville handled the subject fairly. She freely admitted that to her mind Clarence always had been a traitor and that he was indirectly responsible for the deaths of her father and her Uncle Montague at Barnet. But, that said, in this instance she believed that Clarence might just have been the victim of a conspiracy. Her instinct led her to believe that it had been Edward's queen, Elizabeth Woodville, and her lowly born greedy family who had seen Clarence as a threat to their own power and ambitions and had consequently poisoned King Edward's mind against his own brother. I felt anger at the scheming of the Woodvilles, but on the other hand Clarence had always been a traitor. Surprisingly, Richard shared my view about Clarence. He admitted that he could have gone to plead with the king for their brother's life, but duty had to prevail over sentiment and the future of England was more secure with one less traitor. I respected his views and thanked him for his honest opinion.

'You are totally correct,' Anne interposed, 'but do you know, Francis, that unkind people are putting it about that my dear husband is cold and unnatural in not going to beg for Clarence's life?'

Her jewelled finger began to tap the side of her carved chair.

'There are grounds for believing that the Woodvilles are behind these rumours,' she opined, 'and are using them to try to damage my husband.'

She cocked her head to one side and the tapping became more staccato. Richard and I waited patiently until the drumming stopped.

'One day I do believe there will be a reckoning with the Woodvilles,' Anne Neville promised, 'and we can finish poor father's work for him.'

At this juncture, Richard took over to relay to me the second problem, which was of a military nature. Anne deferentially let him take the stage.

★ ★ ★

The former Duke of Burgundy[10] had married King Edward and Richard's sister, Margaret, eleven years before. Unfortunately, Duke Charles was an overambitious man and desired to enlarge his territories at the expense of the Swiss and the French. His attempts, Richard continued, had been a complete failure and he had been defeated in three battles, being killed at the last one. He left a daughter from his first marriage as heiress. As a result, the situation in Burgundy was critical. The duchy, wedged between the Holy Roman Empire and France, with a defeated army and Duke Charles's young daughter as its ruler, seemed to be doomed to extinction. To save Burgundy, Mary had married Maximilian, whose father was the Holy Roman Emperor.

'Effectively the only way that Burgundy could survive against France was to ally itself with the Empire,' Richard concluded.

I stared at his strong face.

'So what is the issue then? I heard that your sister – the widow of the last Duke of Burgundy – likes her stepdaughter Mary and that, additionally, she works well with her and her husband Maximilian. So with the strength of the Empire behind Burgundy, your sister is safe and Burgundy is secure. What then is the problem?'

Anne Neville rushed instantly to the aid of her husband.

'The problem, Francis, is this. The French claim that, since the late Duke Charles left no male heir, the duchy should revert to being French territory. Indeed, immediately after Duke Charles was killed, the French took over part of the duchy. Now the Holy Roman Emperor has not provided any assistance and most of the duchy's wealth and manpower was wasted by Duke Charles's defeats at Granson, Morthen and Nancy. The duchy is virtually defenceless.'

She paused and looked at me.

'If the French swallow up Burgundy, Francis, then not only does my husband lose his sister, but England loses its major market for wool and cloth.'

I had not thought of that, but when Anne made the point I began to grow cold. So much of the country's wealth came from exporting vast amounts of wool and cloth that the loss of a major market such as Burgundy would be a complete disaster. There would be great hardship and possibly starvation among so many of our people here in the North and elsewhere.[11]

An obvious question sprung to mind, but I hesitated.

'Speak freely, Francis!' Richard commanded.

'Well, given the threat to his sister in Burgundy and the dangers to trade if Burgundy is destroyed, why does the king not ally England to Burgundy?'

Richard and Anne Neville glanced at each other. I imagined that I had asked an awkward question.

'He cannot, Francis,' Anne Neville murmured confidentially. 'For some years now King Edward has been secretly in receipt of a pension from France. It is a very generous pension indeed and is largely squandered by the queen and her Woodville relations. But the pension comes with one condition: England must never ally with the enemies of France.'

Her pale blue eyes met mine.

'So Edward prefers to have the pension and will not help Burgundy. For the sake of the Woodvilles, he is prepared to sacrifice his sister and much of England's trade.'

★ ★ ★

I could make out the battlements at Middleham now, but if I was closer to the castle I was no nearer to finding a solution to the problems which confronted us. Yet I had to come up with something – Richard and Anne had implored me to do so. How was I, though, supposed to solve a problem that the pair of them could not?

I reviewed the facts moodily. As matters stood King Edward had decreed that England would not help Burgundy, so the duchy would be overrun by the French and trade would suffer badly. There would be hardship and ruin in the North as a result, and Richard and Anne Neville would be blamed for doing nothing to prevent this. All this because King Edward and his wife, Elizabeth Woodville, wanted to continue to receive their French pension.

How incredibly greedy and selfish of them, but oh-so-typical.

I frowned as I recalled the countless tales of the Woodvilles' cupidity. Why, according to Anne Neville, they had specialised in using marriage as a way of increasing their wealth and influence.

'But many men have married for money', I had protested when she told me of this.

'True, Francis, but at least their wives knew that they were getting husbands who were well born,' she retorted. 'The Woodvilles, notwithstanding their pretensions, originate from the gutter and have not risen from it.'

'But you said that no less than seven of them have married into the nobility, my lady. How can that have come to pass? No one can be forced to marry a Woodville.'

'Not physically of course', Anne Neville said darkly. 'But it would have been immensely hard for anyone to reject one of that family knowing that such a denial would incur not only the wrath of the king but the everlasting vindictiveness of the Woodvilles.'

I saw her point.

'But it was not just adult brides or grooms that those self-seeking schemers targeted,' she continued bitterly. 'They went after young and old alike…'

'…provided they were well born or rich.' I finished off the sentence for her.

'Precisely, Francis. Did you know that the Duke of Buckingham was but a child when he had a Woodville bride foisted upon him?'

He would not have been in a position to object, I reflected sadly.

'But then look at the other end of the scale', Anne Neville cried. 'My own father's aunt was selected to be the bride for the queen's brother solely because she was extremely rich. It did not matter to them that father's aunt was nearly fifty years older than her husband nor did they care about her frequent bouts of eccentricity. No, to the Woodvilles she was rich and that was sufficient for them.'

'Your father must have been horrified, my lady.'

'Of course he was, Francis, and at the first suitable opportunity he had the young John Woodville executed to wipe out the stain on our family's honour. But does not my story show you just how low the Woodvilles will stoop to win wealth and influence?'

She had convinced me of that, I reflected. But while the tragic story had emphasised the venality of the Woodvilles, it in no way reduced the current threat they posed to Richard and Anne. For in this instance Richard would be vilified for doing nothing to help his own sister, and doubtless the malicious Woodvilles would try and use that against him, particularly since he had behaved patriotically and had not begged for Clarence's life. On top of all this, there was a strong possibility that the grasping Woodvilles would look to exploit Gloucester's resultant unpopularity and seek to encroach into the North. The greed and the selfishness of the Woodvilles angered me. As a family not only were they corrupting King

Edward, but worse still they were influencing him to make policies that were manifestly bad for England.

How to outwit them and to protect Richard and Anne? For a long time I turned the problem in my mind, as I watched a solitary hawk that circled high above me. As I gazed at it, I suddenly had a thought. It was highly unlikely that I had been asked to join the two of them to merely give advice. Leaving aside Anne's unparalleled intellect, Richard has a whole host of councillors who were older and wiser than me. Was it just possible that both of them already knew the answer to their problem and in some manner expected me to execute it for them? Why could they both not tell me what Anne Neville's plan was? Why did I need to work it out for myself?

I flung myself down onto the springy turf in frustration and watched the lonely hawk on its ceaseless vigil. Surely the obvious thing to do was for Richard to send a force to Burgundy to help his sister's people. But then I halted. Not even the king's brother and royal duke had the power to act contrary to the wishes of King Edward. I jerked up as the solution hit me. King Edward had the authority to prohibit England from helping the Burgundians, but he was powerless to prevent volunteers from going out to fight for what they believed in. I rubbed my hands together in satisfaction. Everyone knew that I was close to Richard and canny folk would quickly guess that it had been his idea to get me to volunteer.

The more I thought about Anne Neville's plan the more I liked it. Once news of my volunteers spread, far from being damaged by the problems with Burgundy and Clarence, Richard was actually going to come out of them looking very good. All those who dealt in cloth and wool would see that Richard, at least, was making an effort to protect their livelihoods. It would be good for Richard that people saw him making an effort to help his sister, Margaret, particularly after that business with Clarence. I saved the best bit until last, as I suspected that this was the part that Anne Neville would have relished most. Not only was Richard going to come out of all this smelling sweet, but, in contrast, the Woodvilles' reputation with their total selfishness and lack of chivalry, would be irredeemably tarnished.

With a harsh cry the hawk suddenly left off its circling and flew south towards Burgundy.

★ ★ ★

Thomas Broughton and I had originally intended to spend a few days resting the men in Bruges, but within hours of arriving we received news that made these plans change quickly. Maximilian had laid siege to Therouanne,[12] a border town about nine days' march away, but was in trouble. Not only were the French supplying it from sea, but also they were sending reinforcements there. Within a day we heard news that a French Army was approaching the Burgundians from the south-west and, if the two French forces combined, they would outnumber Maximilian.

To make matters worse, it seemed there were no reinforcements to send to Maximilian and his was in fact the only army in Burgundy. If Maximilian was defeated the French could advance swiftly into the centre of the duchy completely unopposed. Clearly the sooner we marched the better.

I conferred with Thomas David, the captain of archers who Richard had assigned to me. In a town full of unemployed mercenary troops, he was finding it a simple matter to recruit men and estimated that our force of 500 could leave in two days.

In the heat of midsummer, we marched without stopping. Whereas in England archers will progress to war – where possible – on horses, here there seemed only a small number and the ones we could obtain were required for scouting and foraging. After a week, the men were exhausted and I ordered a period of rest while we awaited the return of Broughton and the scouts.

In fact, they arrived the next afternoon accompanied by two German officers from Maximilian's army, which lay only two days' march away. The idea, it was explained, was for them to brief us on the situation before we all arrived at Maximilian's camp.

I looked at them curiously. Both were clearly old soldiers, tough and determined ones at that. The face of the older one, Strolheim, was covered with scars; he spoke no English, but some French, and as we ate he talked at length with Thomas Broughton. When he finished, Broughton turned to Thomas David and me.

'I will not repeat what he has told me word for word, but I'll give you a summary and then you can ask whatever questions you want me to put to him.'

Thomas Broughton was concise. Maximilian's army comprised solely Flemish peasants and numbered around 10,000 men. It was made up of pikemen – 'I will explain about that in a moment' – and was situated thirty miles south of our current position. The siege of Therouanne had been abandoned due to the threat of the French Army approaching from the south. Equally, it was believed that the French troops in Therouanne had left the town and were trying to join with the advancing French. If they succeeded in doing this, the French would number 14,000 men.

Military intelligence indicated that the French Army was made up of men-at-arms, a few archers, a large number of crossbowmen and horse: both knights and light horse. They had cannons and were well supplied. The Burgundian Army comprised only pikemen with a few Burgundian nobles and their retinues. They had a small number of cannons, since most had been left at Therouanne. Supplies were low.

He paused and asked Strolheim a question, who nodded and yelled at his servant, who returned a moment later carrying something which he laid on the ground. We all rose to inspect it.

'A pike,' translated Broughton. 'Eighteen feet long, it can outrange any other weapon on the battlefield – except bows, of course. Now imagine you are a plain man-at-arms with your sword or poleaxe and you face a row of 100 of these. Behind them is another row of 100 – they fight in columns or squares – and the second row points their pike over the shoulders of the man in the first row.'

'You would not stand a chance,' observed Thomas David.

'Yes,' Broughton continued, 'you would be dead before you could even get close and if, by a miracle, you did manage to kill your man, they have tens of such rows behind them. Once a column such as this starts to move, the sheer weight and force of it allows it to just push through any opposition.'

I stared at the pike; this was a totally new form of warfare, but there was an obvious weakness to it.

'Hold on, Thomas; concentred archery fire could massacre such a column before it came up to the enemy position?'

'The pikemen have helmets, breastplates, sometimes even additional body armour – that would neutralise arrows to a degree. Crossbows, of course, could stop them, but you can only fire off one crossbow bolt a minute and be accurate at seventy or so paces.' He shook his head. 'So that would not be too much of a problem for the pikemen.'

Strolheim interrupted him; Broughton listened and turned back to us.

'He says he understands a little of what we are saying and tells me that the Swiss columns use their own crossbowmen to drive away enemy archers and this, perhaps, is a role we can perform?'

Strolheim continued to talk while I moved away to give instructions to begin the march down to Maximilian's camp. The sooner we arrived, the better.

Broughton resumed when I returned.

'Swiss pikemen defeated the Burgundian Armies of Duke Charles at three battles. Duke Charles tried everything to stop the columns – cannons, archers, crossbowmen, flank attacks – and each time he failed.' He pointed to Strolheim. 'He was at Nancy and said that to face a column of pikes advancing at you was the most terrifying experience he has ever had.'

We prepared to move, as Strolheim continued to talk.

'It seems that Maximilian is determined not to repeat the mistakes of his predecessor,' Broughton translated. 'He sent for the Count of Romount, whose estates are in Bern in Switzerland, and asked him to create a pike force. Maximilian sent his own officers to help him. For the Flemish peasants, the pike is an easy weapon. They are a stolid people and strong. The pike needs no special skill and the formation is excellent for inexperienced troops. You are closely surrounded by your comrades and feel safe, since your weapon easily outreaches the enemy. Also, unless you are at the front, you cannot even see the enemy, so you don't feel frightened.'

We marched on as Broughton continued his translation. The Flemings had apparently been training hard and were basing their formation on the Swiss pattern of having two separate columns; the one under the Count of Romount numbered 6,000 men and the other, under Engelbert, Court of Nassau, had 4,000. By creating two separate columns, not only did the army possess greater manoeuvrability but, additionally, each column was only vulnerable on one flank. The basic idea was that the larger column would smash into the French line first, the smaller one a moment later, to take advantage of the devastation that had already been caused.

Strolheim said something and Thomas looked at us both.

'He says do you have any questions?'

'Will the flanks of the advancing columns be vulnerable to cavalry?' Thomas David asked.

Strolheim said not. Unless a fully-fledged cavalry chase looked likely, the columns kept moving. If, however, a charge materialised, then the first two ranks of men on the exposed side extended their pikes and impaled the charging horses.

'Would broken ground, a river or a wood stop a column?' I wanted to know. 'Surely once a column is stopped it could be shot at continuously from a distance and, once it is sufficiently destroyed, you could send in men-at-arms.' I paused to think. 'At close quarters on a one-to-one basis, the pikeman with his long weapon would be at a great disadvantage to a soldier with a sword, surely?'

Strolheim agreed. The only way to stop the column was by using natural geographical advantages, but fortunately this part of the country was flat and, additionally, the total absence of rain for many weeks had dried out the rivers. There were no such obstacles. In turn, Strolheim wanted to know what protection our archers could give against enemy crossbowmen and it was Thomas David who explained the advantage we could add to the Burgundian Army. For one, our archers could shoot initially ten times faster than the crossbowmen and had a greater range. Also, as we had 500 archers, not only could we protect the flanks as we advanced, but we would be able to fire on the French line as the column   advanced – right up to the moment the column smashed through. Strolheim smiled as this was relayed back to him.

I walked round our little camp that night with Thomas Broughton. He was hoarse but excited.

'It will be a massacre, Francis,' he said while taking swigs from his wine flask. 'The French must be more stupid than Duke Charles – the combination of pikemen with English archers will annihilate them.'

We spoke of how to best deploy the archers in the forthcoming battle, although that was fairly simple. As we parted, though, I felt uneasy; everything seemed too straightforward. And the more I thought about it, the more disquieted I became. Until today, I had little or no knowledge of the potential of mass pike formations and had not realised that Duke Charles owed his three defeats to pikemen, but undoubtedly the French would have done. Equally, they would have known that Duke Charles had cannon, crossbowmen, archers and cavalry and had still been beaten, and they would know that Maximilian's army was made up of pikemen. Yet despite this, they were not only preparing to fight the Burgundian pikemen on terrain that offered them no significant advantage, but were preparing to do so with the same types of troops that Duke Charles had taken with him when he lost on three separate occasions. To make it even more puzzling, they were advancing towards the Burgundians fairly swiftly, with no doubt a degree of confidence.

I couldn't conclude that the French were ignorant of military affairs, since only a few years ago they had driven the English almost completely out of France. The only logical explanation for their action was that somehow they had a plan to defeat the pikemen. Defying recent military precedents, they must know of a way of achieving what Duke Charles had failed to do – namely, beating an army of pikemen while using conventional forces.

Sleep eluded me completely. I could not see what the strategy of the French could be. Cannon fire would cause casualties – but a cannon can take up to an hour to load and fire. Our archers would outshoot their crossbowmen. Their horsemen would be unlikely to attack an unbroken pike column and, according to Strolheim, there were no natural geographical barriers to stop the columns. Logically, there was no way that the French could beat the pikemen, let alone pikemen whose advance would be protected by English archers. So why were the French advancing so confidently?

★ ★ ★

It was hot in Maximilian's tent, but it afforded a degree of privacy in the camp that was required for the meeting. We were amazed at how sparsely the camp was furnished. The lack of water had caused many of the draught oxen and horses to be slaughtered and, as such, it had been impossible to move much from the camp outside Therouanne to the present location.

The issue of supply was critical. Occasionally lumbering wagons would arrive, but the lack of rain had severely reduced the water supply. Food was only slightly less of a problem; all the surrounding area had been ruthlessly looted to try and satisfy the needs of 10,000 hungry men. No one at the meeting seemed to have any idea how to resolve these problems. The Burgundian nobles, threadbare but proud, stood silently, more concerned with the future of their duchy than the needs of their army.

Maximilian's German officers pointed out that since the French were only two days' march away, battle would commence soon; the best thing to do was to reduce rations still further and slaughter what remained of the draught oxen, retaining only those necessary to move the three cannons.

Maximilian, richly dressed, young but with a remarkably strong jaw-line, sat silently as all this was relayed back to him. He said something and Haldi, the aide that had been assigned to us on our arrival, translated.

'He says that he requires the most up-to-date information on the French positions and the composition of their army.'

One of the Germans stepped forward and the small, fair-haired Haldi began talking quietly.

'The French are two days' march away. They number between 12,000 and 14,000; 3,000 of these are crossbowmen. There are a small number of archers. There are 8,000 men-at-arms and a large number of horse. The French have made camp and are receiving many wagons bearing pavises.'

Haldi stumbled on the word and looked to me for clarification.

'Pavises are big wooden shields that archers use for protection.'

There were chuckles at this news. Clearly both the Burgundian nobles and German officers found it amusing to think of the cowardly French crossbowmen cowering behind their shields, as they harassed the flanks of advancing Burgundian columns. No matter how many of these pavises they bought, such craven-heartedness would not help them avoid defeat.

Maximilian's voice cut through the mocking laughter and Haldi quickly translated.

'He says we have practised the order of the battle. The Count of Romount,' he indicated a small dark-haired man, 'will lead the right flank column and the Count of Nassau,' a tall silent aristocrat, 'the left. As has already been agreed, the others nobles and he will take up pikes and personally lead the columns. The three remaining cannons, and the few horsemen we have, will guard the flank of the

Count of Nassau, and the English will guard the right flank and advance in front of it.'

Haldi paused to listen.

'He says that he is disappointed that the cities of the duchy have not seen fit to send him reinforcements, but he will force them to submit to his will after he has defeated the French.'

The Burgundian nobles all seemed to be behind this plan. Maximilian rubbed his brow and spoke again.

'He proposes to break camp tomorrow and force battle on the French. He says that he is totally confident of victory and invites any questions before the army marches.'

Haldi finished, out of breath.

Maximilian looked at me quizzically.

'Any questions, Lord Lovell?' he said in English. I found out later he spoke six or seven languages.

'He says…' said Haldi and then blushed realising his mistake.

I looked at Broughton and Thomas David who both shook their heads, and so I took a deep breath and looked at Maximilian.

'Your Highness, I don't know how it is being done, but I think the French are creating a trap for your army.'

He looked at me sharply with an arrogant expression.

'Why do you say that?' he snapped.

Hesitantly, I explained my misgivings. Would the French be stupid enough to attack pikemen using only conventional weapons? Particularly – I added tactlessly – after what had happened to the Burgundian Armies recently. Why had they not trained pikemen of their own order to take advantage of this new development in warfare? Surely, the only possible conclusion was that they had devised a method of beating columns of pikemen? In light of all this, I feared a trap.

There was a loud murmur of dissent from the Burgundians and the Germans. Broughton stepped forward loyally to stand by my shoulder, but Thomas David looked uncomfortable. Maximilan sat silently for a moment.

'I very much doubt that you are correct,' he commented dryly, 'and I am certain that none of my officers share your opinion.'

Ignoring the angry mutterings and hostile stares, I held Maximilian's gaze.

'I am convinced that we are walking into a trap,' I repeated.

Maximilian narrowed his eyes.

'Very well. I do not agree, but it behoves me to accept the opinion of an ally.'

He turned to Strolheim and spoke to him as Haldi rapidly translated.

'He says that the army will remain here for two days and, at the end of that time, you will present yourself to the assembled leaders of the army and demonstrate the nature of the trap and your plan to counter it.'

With a swift chopping movement of his hand, Maximilian signalled the end of the meeting and his officers and nobles began to drift out of the tent, ignoring me completely. I shrugged my shoulders, indifferent to their discourtesy. That I was correct, I was certain. The problem I faced was that I had no idea why this was the case or what to do about it.

CHAPTER 9

'It's funny how everyone hates us so much,' Broughton mused. 'You would have thought that the rest of the army would be grateful to us for trying to save their lives. Instead they just seem to regard us as the reason that they are getting less food.'

I shifted uncomfortably on the prickly stubble. By allowing us two days to find a solution, Maximilian had placed an even greater strain on the Burgundian Army's rapidly diminishing food stocks. Rations, already low, had been halved, and men spat on my shadow as I passed them in camp.

'We are going to be even less popular tomorrow evening when we tell Maximilian that we have not got the slightest idea what the French plan is,' I said irritably.

'Let alone how to counter it.' Broughton agreed unhappily.

He subsided into silence, as we brooded on tomorrow's meeting. At best, we were going to be made to look extremely foolish.

'Lord Lovell?' Surprised, I glanced up and saw Haldi together with an unfamiliar young man. Haldi gestured to him. 'This one is in the service of Maximilian.'

I swallowed uneasily.

'What does he want?'

'He wishes to know whether you have discovered the French tactics.'

I glanced up in surprise at the young man, who had crouched down next to us. He looked too frail to be a soldier. His high forehead and slender hands gave him the appearance of a scholar or a priest.

Broughton looked at the youth suspiciously.

'We report directly to Maximilian,' he grunted. 'What's his interest in us?'

A slight smile lit up the young man's features as this was put to him.

'He says that he can help you, provided you assist him,' Haldi replied. 'He has calculated how the French will defeat the Burgundian Army.'

Broughton snorted contemptuously and turned to me.

'Francis, we are in enough trouble already without wasting time listening to the theories of a beardless youth. Don't waste your time on him; he has probably not even fought a battle in his life.'

Broughton was right, so I turned to Haldi.

'Ask the young man why he has not advised his superior officers of the French plan. In any army, you have a duty to talk to those who command you before approaching strangers.'

The young man's face became flushed.

'He tried, but they did not believe him,' Haldi explained.

The young man said something. Haldi listened carefully before turning back to Thomas and me.

'He says his superiors are boneheaded idiots. They are afraid to be shown up for the fools that they are. Strolheim is the worst; he told this one here to come back and talk to him about warfare when he was not drinking his mother's milk any longer.'

Tactfully, I ignored Broughton's poorly suppressed snigger.

'Tell him that he is too inexperienced to help us,' I said shortly. 'Knowledge of warfare comes from practice and experience.'

I expected the stranger to depart, but, to my astonishment, he spoke long and earnestly to Haldi. Haldi appeared to try to argue with him, but the young man protested passionately. At last reluctantly, Haldi turned back to us.

'He says that through study he probably knows more about warfare than you will ever know, Lord Lovell,' he began apologetically. 'He has pointed out that neither of you have guessed the French plan, which he has. Therefore, he proposes a bargain. He will explain the plan to you. If both of you believe it, you will publicly endorse him when he explains it to the others in Maximilian's tent tomorrow.'

The young man spoke again.

'He says that you would all benefit from the arrangement because, while he knows the French plan, he does not believe there is a way to counter it. By working together, you could come up with a solution. He asks whether you agree to his proposal.'

Instinctively, I glanced at Broughton, who nodded slowly.

'We have nothing to lose, Francis.'

'All right we agree,' I told Haldi. 'But I will only endorse him if I think he is right.'

Haldi conveyed this message to the stranger who was already sketching some form of diagram in the dust.

'He understands, my lord.'

'Good. Now ask him his name.'

There was a rapid exchange between the two of them.

'His name is Swartz, my lord – Martin Swartz. He asks you both to concentrate as the key to the French strategy is the manner in which they use their large wooden shields or pavises, as they are called.

'He says it is obvious how the French will use the pavises. He would now like to explain to you the French plan to stop our columns and annihilate the Burgundian Army.'

We all squatted and looked at Swartz's dust drawings.

'Normally, when faced by attacking columns of pikemen, you would spread your crossbowmen out over your whole front. But then the enemy's archers or crossbowmen shoot at your own, so there is no significant gain for either side. Equally, you would, under normal circumstances, use your archers with cavalry to harry the flanks of the advancing column. These, however, are not the tactics that the French will use.'

Swartz gave a small smile and continued to talk to Haldi.

'He says what he would do – if he was the French – is try and separate out our two columns. He would do everything he could to slow down the smaller column of the Count of Nassau, but he would allow our own column to advance completely unopposed.'

Haldi gestured to the dust drawings.

'He says he would concentrate all of his crossbowmen behind the pavises, which he would lay out in a long line to face the bigger column of the Count of Romout. He would place the majority of crossbowmen behind the pavises and the others would go at either end.'

His finger traced the line of pavises in the dust.

'Now, while a crossbow is accurate at seventy paces, it has a range of 300 paces. He wonders how accurate you need to be to hit a target of 6,000 men all bunched together. He also points out that crossbow bolts can penetrate armour.'

Broughton and I stared at the dust. It was beginning to sound plausible.

'He would fire off the first volley of bolts – probably 1,000 – at a distance of 200 or 300 paces. The next 1,000 crossbowmen fire immediately afterwards. While they reload, the next 1,000 men fire. He estimates that at least two out of three bolts would find a target. In the confusion, there would be time to fire off at least two more volleys.'

Swartz smiled sadly and demonstrated the length of the line of pavises with a gesture; Haldi listened and turned to us.

'He notes that the cleverness of the French plan is that their line of crossbowmen is much longer than the width of the advancing column. Consequently, they are able to hit the front and sides of the column simultaneously. Additionally, their men are safe from the archers, since they are behind the pavises. It would require three volleys to reduce the column to a complete ruin. But they will probably use five or six before they send in the cavalry and men-at-arms to finish off what is left of it. Having destroyed the larger column, the crossbowmen would wheel to their right and fire at the flank of the Count of Nassau's column, which, of course, has been slowed down. Again, 3,000 bolts firing into tightly packed troops would cause havoc. The second and third volleys would destroy them completely.'

It sounded devastating but convincing.

'How can we use our archers to counter these pavises?' I asked Thomas David, who I had sent for. He looked despondent.

'Arrows will not penetrate the pavises, except at point-blank range. We could try firing over the top of them, but we would lose accuracy and most likely the French would have helmets and some form of upper-body armour.'

I turned to Haldi.

'Ask Martin Swartz whether he believes we could use the archers to make a flank attack. It would be hard for the crossbowmen to concentrate on what was in front of them if they were being shot at from the side.'

He considered the question for a few moments.

'It is a possibility, but with the French being superior in numbers, it is likely they will put a very strong guard on either end of their line: archers, crossbowmen, men-at-arms, possibly cavalry. He fears that your flank attack would not stop the columns being defeated.'

Broughton, who had been studying the dust drawings, rose up stiffly.

'There is no doubt he's right, Francis. It makes perfect sense to separate out the two columns, destroy the bigger one and then turn on the second, smaller one.'

Thomas Davis looked at him gloomily.

'And there is not much that we archers can do to prevent it.'

Without doubt, Swartz's analysis of the French battle tactics was totally correct. Safely protected behind their row of pavises, the French crossbowmen could wait for the huge column to come into range and then pulverise it with volley after volley of armour-piercing crossbow bolts. Packed tightly together in pike formation, it would be hard to miss and the moment the column began to disintegrate the French cavalry would complete the slaughter.

I stood up and gestured to Haldi.

'Tell Swartz that we believe he is totally accurate in his thinking.

'So now all we have to do is to think of a way of defeating the French.'

Broughton plucked at his beard, a sure sign that he was thinking, Swartz began to draw more lines in the dust, talking to Haldi as he did so.

I too began to think, but after a while I turned to Broughton.

'Well?'

'I can't honestly say that anything springs to mind instantly,' he admitted. 'It seems to me that not only do the French outnumber us, but they have useful things like cannon and cavalry that we don't.'

'Well, we have three cannon and then there are our archers.'

'Which will be rendered useless by the French pavises,' he pointed out.

We fell silent, but then Broughton gestured to Swartz who was still imparting information to Haldi.

'Judging by the way he's ticking the points off by using his fingers, I reckon that he has thought of something.'

We waited expectantly; Swartz's plan was obviously not a simple one. He was now on to the fingers of his other hand. Broughton cocked his head for a few moments and then turned to me excitedly.

'I understand maybe one word in a hundred, but I think Swartz is talking about a night attack,' he whispered.

I let Swartz talk for a few more minutes and then I poked Haldi.

'Can you give me a synopsis of his plan?'

'His plan?'

'Yes, for the night attack on the French.'

Haldi looked puzzled, but then his face cleared.

'You are mistaken, my lord,' he said cheerfully. 'Martin Swartz knows of no way to defeat the French. He was, however, explaining why a night attack could not work.'

I put my head in my hands and groaned – dear God, what a mess!

'Would you like to hear his detailed reasoning as to why it would not work?' enquired Haldi helpfully.

'No, I don't! Just ask him if he knows of anything that could work. Neither Broughton nor I can think of anything.'

A moment later Haldi turned back apologetically.

'He regrets that there is no logical way to defeat the French. The only way that the Burgundian columns could get anywhere near the French Army was if they were invisible.'

I don't know what reaction Haldi expected from me. Possibly he thought I would be angry at such facetiousness or just look disappointed, but my lack of response evidently worried him as, after a moment, he touched my shoulder and asked if I felt all right. With an effort, I focused on him.

'I'm fine, thank you.' Then I pointed to Swartz. 'Tell him that I know how to make men invisible.'

★ ★ ★

For a small man with a frail manner, Martin Swartz should have been an unremarkable orator, but as he spoke that evening in Maximilian's tent he had his audience's undivided attention and not just because he had my public backing.

Quietly, but with complete conviction, he took the Burgundian nobles, his fellow officers and Maximilian through the French's probable battle tactics. Watching the assembled crowd's faces change from scepticism to interest, it was clear they all believed him. But when Swartz described, with mathematical precision, how the French could annihilate both columns successively, their interest turned to despair.

After he had finished delivering his account, there were a number of questions, but Swartz answered these in a tone of calm efficiency and gradually, as his explanation of the French battle plan unfolded, the spaces between the questions became longer and longer. It was as if the men inside the tent came to realise the hopelessness of their situation and the inevitability of defeat.

Maximilian looked at Swartz heavily and asked a question. Swartz gestured at me and, prodding Haldi, I stepped forward.

'There is a solution, Your Highness. It is an unusual one, but it will work.' I paused, conscious that everyone was staring at me. 'The only way to counter the threat of those crossbowmen is to conceal your advancing column from them so that you can be on top of them before they realise you are there.'

A shouted question from Strolheim interrupted me. Haldi translated.

I winked at Broughton.

'I have it on particularly good authority that a night attack would not work,' I replied. 'It is difficult to advance pikemen in such conditions and the French would know we were coming. There would be sufficient light to fire at us and the result would be as Martin Swartz has already advised.'

It did not seem tactful to point out that as soon as it was explained to the Flemings that they had to attack at night because they faced 3,000 crossbowmen firing from a defended position, most would promptly desert. I tried to be diplomatic.

'Your idea is cleverly thought out though...'

There was another bellow from Strolheim. Haldi swallowed.

'He asks what your solution is.'

'To shoot fire-arrows.'

There was silence and then a murmuring in the tent, which I duly ignored.

'We will not use normal arrows, but will shoot fire-arrows in front of the French line. The stubble will burn easily in the ground, since it is so dry. There is no water to extinguish the fires and, after a few volleys, we should have created a fire sufficiently big to make enough smoke for the Count of Romount's column to approach unseen.'

There was total silence for a moment and then an excited babble of German and French chatter erupted. Haldi did not bother to translate, but I could see from the excited expressions and smiles that the idea had caught their imagination. A few moments ago, they had been facing the prospect of total defeat. Now they were imagining the vast column advancing through billowing fire and smoke to burst unexpectedly on the unprepared French. Instead of being destroyed before they had even reached the French line, they could now picture slaughtering the French without even so much as a shot being fired. I watched the happy expressions and heard jovial laughter.

Swartz and I exchanged smiles and I raised my hand.

'And now I would like my captain of archers to explain how we will operate the fire-arrows.

Prudently, Thomas David kept his speech short. Only a few of the archers would carry fire-arrows. The remainder would protect them and shoot at any French who attempted to leave their lines to try to extinguish the fires. Someone asked a question, which Haldi translated. Thomas David looked at me and I stepped forward to answer.

'There will be no protection to the flank of the column because there will be no attack on it. Remember that the French plan has one key objective – the separation of our two columns. It follows that if they are to slow down and harry our smaller column, then they want our larger column to advance as quickly as possible, so they may destroy it before firing on the smaller column. Now the way we will counter their plan is by starting the fires before the column makes its final advance. The range of the fire-arrow is shorter than that of a normal arrow, so it will be necessary to have all those archers advance in front of the column within range of the French crossbowmen, while their colleagues shoot at the enemy line and guard their flanks against horsemen. As such, the column should pause 500 paces or so from the French lines until the archers had done their job and advance when they see fit.'

There were sounds of approval and another question. I looked at Thomas David.

'We can fire three fire-arrows a minute,' he said, 'and at least ten normal ones. We are hoping that the French will not be tempted to fire at us, but will retain their shots for the column. When the fires start they will probably shoot, but by then it will be too late for them. Now, coming to what we will require; I need linen, ropes, fire-pots...'

Maximilian interrupted me, and Haldi gestured to the German officers.

'He says they will ensure that he has all you require immediately. He says that he will donate his tent for linen and ropes. He asks if anyone disagrees with either the analysis of the French tactics or the proposed battle plan.' I was relieved to see that no one did. 'Then it is the duty of everyone to assist and add improvements to the plan that has been outlined. The army will march tomorrow. The battle will be fought in three days' time and he is totally confident of victory.' There was the beginning of applause, but Maximilian held up his hand to prepare to make a final point. 'He says he is grateful to Martin Swartz and the English.'

The gathering broke up happily and Thomas Broughton nudged me.

'We seem popular, don't we?' he muttered. 'Shall we see if Maximilian's servants will let us have some of his wine?'

★ ★ ★

Later, Haldi found us and led us outside. He took us to Strolheim, who was surrounded by a group of six or seven olive-skinned, dark-haired men, some of whom wore aprons. They were shouting at him excitedly; one was waving an arrow, I noticed. Strolheim hushed the chattering crowd and spoke to Haldi who turned to me.

'He says that they are men from Milan. They care for Maximilian's cannons. They have watched your men shooting the fire-arrows and have a suggestion to help you, but we cannot understand them.'

Communication must always have been a problem for the mercenary forces of Duke Charles, I reflected, and now it looked as if Maximilian had the same problem. But surely there must be someone in the army who could speak to the Italians, or how else could they be instructed what to do or where to go? Unfortunately, he was not here now.

Broughton stepped forward.

'Shall I try?'

He turned and slowly began to talk. There was an eruption of noise from the cannon-master's assistants. Strolheim bellowed at them and indicated for the oldest of them – a small wiry-haired man – to come forward. Clutching the arrow, he began to talk slowly, with Broughton frequently stopping him, requiring clarification on a particular word or two. The discussion was lengthy, not least because, despite Strolheim's shouting and occasional kicks, the others kept interrupting in order to assist in the explanation.

Finally, Broughton turned to Haldi.

'I think I understand about one word in ten; they seem to be saying that they can make the fires much bigger.' He grinned and, mimicking the enthusiasm of the men from Milan, threw out his arms. 'Much, much bigger!'

'How?' Thomas David joined us with more of the German officers.

'I'm not sure I understand fully,' said Broughton. 'But I think they want to mix some of the powders they put in the cannon with linen. They wrap the linen round an arrow and aim it to wherever there is already a fire.'

We all frowned at each other.

'The powder would just blow off,' said Thomas David shortly. He looked at Broughton. 'Will you try again, Sir Thomas?'

Seeing our confusion, the Italians clustered round Broughton. Out of sheer frustration, one began to add miming gestures while the others spoke, not that it seemed to help. Then one of the German officers grabbed Haldi and said something quickly. Haldi nodded slowly.

'He says that the powder is stuck to the linen. He says it has something to do with the inside of animals.'

'The only animals here are the oxen for the cannon,' I said.

Using a stick, the German sketched out a crude picture of a cow in the dust. The men from Milan nodded and continued with a garrulous explanation. The older man took the stick and pointed to the cow and indicated that they needed two. Then, holding up the arrows, he looked at Thomas David and indicated that he should be given more.

The arrows were not a problem; we had sufficient supply. But with two oxen removed, the chances were that the third cannon could no longer be moved. I looked at Strolheim, who chewed his lip and then nodded to the cannon master.

'Give him the arrows he needs,' I said to Thomas David.

★ ★ ★

In the largely flat countryside, the French positioned themselves in the only place that offered them a small natural advantage. Not that the river had any water in it – the scouts hastened to assure us – but as it was dried out it provided a natural ditch. It was not deep though and would not be a serious obstacle when we eventually arrived at the site.

We advanced slowly towards the French position, as to march quickly with pikes is impossible. They are too long and heavy to be carried for anything but a short distance. Normally on the march, carts transport them, but the only carts available were required for the armour of the nobles and such food as remained. Accordingly, the march towards the French position took longer than expected, and it was a hungry and thirsty army that had staggered into camp that night.

Despite hunger, thirst and weariness, there were few desertions.

Haldi reported that the Flemish conscripts were pleased to be moving against the French, reasoning that the sooner they fought, the sooner they could return home, preferably laden with French booty. Haldi emphasised that after the battle they were going home to try to salvage what remained of their harvests. Clearly, the siege of Therouanne would not be continuing.

'It doesn't make too much difference to us,' Thomas Broughton remarked as we strolled round the battle camp. 'If all goes well tomorrow, there is no chance that the French will try and invade again before the end of the campaigning season and Maximilian will have bought himself enough time to raise a proper army.'

He looked towards the lights of the French campfires.

'They will have enough of fire by the end of tomorrow. Did you test out the ones the Italians gave us?'

I shook my head. The archers had arrived into camp exhausted from helping to carry the pikes and had simply collapsed on the ground. It was better, I felt, to let them rest rather than spending time practising. Accordingly, I had given the Italian arrows to Thomas David with instructions to select fifty or so men to be ready to shoot these as soon as the fire-archers, led by Broughton and myself, had started the fires.

He felt the weight of one of the arrows dubiously.

'It will be short range with these. Still, once you've got the fires going, we can just shoot a few and that will be it.' He paused, 'Maybe we will not need them.'

I tended to agree; the ground was so dry that anything would catch fire. But if we had the opportunity we could try them. I left Thomas and lay on the ground with the exhausted soldiers; it was odd that there were no stars tonight.

★ ★ ★

The storm that night raged fiercely for two hours or more. Lightning shot across the sky and the rumble of thunder grew increasingly louder as it moved towards us. An enormous crash overhead signalled the start of a very heavy downpour, which continued for some time. Without tents or any form of shelter, our men suffered miserably, huddling together on ground that got progressively wetter and muddier.

In due course the sound of thunder grew quieter, and the lightning moved further away; gradually men started to dry themselves as best they could in the mud. The noise of cursing filled the camp as men contested with each other for the dryer parts on the ground, but towards dawn the camp was perfectly still.

I watched the beautiful beginning of the dawn. Clearly it would be another fine day, but it would be a day in which the Burgundian Army would be defeated. So great had been the rain from last night that the ground around me was still soaked; the fire-arrows would just splutter out. Unprotected in their advance by fire and smoke, the Burgundians would be decimated by the crossbowmen and the Duchy of Burgundy lost.

I had been in Burgundy for several weeks now and there had been very little rain, yet now the only thing that could have wrecked our plan had happened just half a day before the battle. And we had no alternative battle plan.

★ ★ ★

'He's stopped again,' moaned Broughton.

I glanced to my left. Sure enough the column commanded by Engelbert, Count of Nassau, had halted for a third time. Despite the fact it was over 2,000 paces from the French line, large numbers of horsemen were threatening the Count of Nassau's column. Each time they came too close, the column halted and extended their pikes. This, however, acted as a signal for the French archers ahead of their column to fire volleys of arrows into it; then they retired and the horsemen withdrew.

Three times already this had happened because the Burgundian left flank was completely exposed. The few Burgundian knights had been chased off and the two cannon were captured. So now, facing the twin threat of horse and archers, the Count of Nassau's column moved forward in fits and starts. Their progress was slow in the extreme.

It had been decided at the meeting before the battle that there was not too much that could be expected from the fire-arrows. The only chance we had as an army was to try and get both columns to the French line at more or less the same time, in order to deny the French the chance to obliterate the columns one by one.

The Count of Romount had agreed to this up to the point when he was in the range of the French crossbows. He thought that to remain static while French crossbowmen pulverised his column was lunacy. Strolheim agreed to this but instructed that until that point our column was to advance at the same speed as the Count of Nassau's.

Thomas David was asked about the likelihood of the fire-arrows working. He was ambivalent. Clearly the longer the attack could be delayed the better, but Strolheim overruled him; they could wait to noon, he declared, but to expect the semi-trained levies to sit about all day without food and little water, knowing they would be fighting a battle later, would completely destroy morale. Ideally, the attack should be made immediately, but he reluctantly agreed to wait until noon.

The columns advanced again, but I groaned as I saw on the far left the French horse beginning to threaten again. Doubtless in a moment both columns would come to a juddering halt. I think it was at this point that the Count of Romount's patience ran out, and he decided that the only way he could assist the other column was to advance without it.

He might have hoped that by crashing into the French line he could relieve the pressure that the Count of Nassau was under and that all this stopping and starting was depleting his men's morale. He may have thought that the sooner he faced the crossbows the better. For whatever reason, though, our column moved forward to the measured cadence of drums and pipes.

Ahead of us, the French line seemed to fill the horizon. The huge number of painted pavises dominated their front, but it was possible to discern flashes of silver armour and see their gaily coloured flags. Their murmuring grew louder as we approached. Soon enough, it was possible to hear individual shouts.

The sound from our column was different; the tall Flemings in breastplates and helmets moved forward steadily, their rhythmical tramp almost drowning out the beat of the drums and squealing of the pipes. There was no talk, more due to exhaustion than fear, I believed, as to advance over a mile in this heat while holding a heavy pike upright calls for great stamina.

There had been no attempt to slow our column, and, at 500 paces from the French, we halted for the last time. I signalled to Broughton and Thomas David and we advanced the archers.

The noise from the French was deafening; moving against them was terrifying. About 300 paces from their line, we halted, and Thomas David led his men to the right to guard the flank. Broughton and I moved our men forward with the fire pots. There seemed to be a large number of horsemen massing on our far right. I trusted Thomas David to deal with those, while we quickly spread our men out.

The drill for shooting with the fire-arrows had been practised in camp – two men shared one pot. One arrow was inserted in the pot while the other fired. While this had worked well in practice, the situation here was so intimidating that I suspected a number of arrows were fired before they were properly lit.

I watched the first few volleys sink into the ground and then shouted to the archers to shoot faster. There were already crossbow bolts thudding into the ground around us. The noise from the French line grew louder and louder, and I saw that two of our archers were hit, then another handful went down.

'The horses are moving!' shouted Broughton.

'Keep firing!' I shouted, and after a moment signalled the recall. Our archers obeyed with alacrity – only a few of them actually remembered to kick their fire pots over – and we moved back to the rest of Thomas David's men, who stood to our right.

I looked back towards the French position. A few little fires took light in the stubble and small patches of smoke drifted across, but it was too little to conceal one man – let alone a column. I panted with exhaustion and felt sick with disappointment. The French yells of contempt at our pathetic efforts carried clearly across the distance.

'The column's moving!' shouted Thomas David.

Obviously the Count of Romount and his officers had drawn the same conclusion as I had and wisely decided that the failure of the arrows made it pointless to delay the inevitable any longer. I saw the front two rows of pikemen extend their weapons, and, with a lurch, the whole block of 6,000 men moved forward.

Thomas David kept a watchful eye on the French horsemen, signalling to his men to move further to the right, as we were in the path of the column that was, I remembered for some reason, 100-people wide. Then I remembered something else.

'Fire those Italian arrows!' I shouted to Thomas David.

'There's no time!' he yelled.

Frantically, he chivvied men out of the path of the oncoming column.

Broughton pushed me aside, drew his knife and seized Thomas David by the shoulder.

'Fire them!' he shouted.

Thomas David looked to start to say something and thought better of it. He gestured to the men with the yellow-circled arrows.

'Fire the shots, then run!'

He moved off swiftly with the rest of the archers. Broughton and I drew our swords and stayed with the fifty or so archers.

The noise from the French rose to a crescendo. Despite the clamour, I could hear the fearful tramping as the column advanced behind me and the sound grew louder and louder. The archers heard it too; one turned round with a look of horror and saw my sword pointing at him. He quickly blazed off the rest of his arrows.

It was over in a moment; we all moved as quickly as we could to join Thomas David's force on the right flank.

I heard, rather than saw, the column begin to march past us. The French horsemen advanced to surround us on three sides. They kept out of range, but any retreating movement on our part would provoke them to ride us down. Equally, no armoured knight was stupid enough to attack over 400 archers. For an uncomfortable few minutes we faced each other. A moment later, at the sound of a shouted order, they withdrew. Doubtless they were required for the final destruction of the column.

'Look!'

The man next to me grabbed my arm, and I swung around in the direction he was pointing. As more men took in the spectacle, we began to laugh and cheer. While only the men from Milan could have any idea of the effect of whatever they had put onto the arrows, the results were truly inspiring.

The little fires we had started were now burning fiercely and the gentle breeze was blowing the fire and smoke back towards the French line. Already the French line was showing signs of confusion, as men emerged to try and beat back the flames but were driven back by the smoke and the vision of the column that was now only 300 paces away from them.

A sudden series of explosions told me that the fast-spreading fires had now reached some of the Italian arrows that had carried further than the others. As they caught fire, so did the vegetation in the old riverbed and, being sheltered, the smoke and fire began to spread along the bottom of the ditch itself. But as the fire encountered moisture from the previous night's rains, the smoke rose and billowed along the length of the riverbed.

As the smoke was at its thickest, the Count of Romount's column crashed into the French line and, in turn, was lost in sight.

★ ★ ★

'Nice wine this,' Broughton said appreciatively.

He had found the large flask of wine; you could always rely on him where matters of food and drink were concerned. We sat on the ground in the French camp watching the Flemings and our own archers systematically looting everything and gorging themselves on all the food that they could find. Doubtless the remainder were busy going through the bodies of the enemy's dead.

Victory had come swiftly. Overwhelmed by smoke, most of the French crossbowmen had simply fled and the Count of Romount's column had easily smashed through the men-at-arms. They had then wheeled left towards the centre of the French line and had used their sheer momentum to roll through completely and slaughter the archers who had been delaying the Count of Nassau.

The enemy cavalry, seeing what had happened, promptly fled. Unhindered, the Count of Nassau advanced vengefully towards the enemy's right wing. Having punched his way straight through it, French resistance was put to an end.

'Mind you, I suppose Maximilian will be angry that he has no cavalry to pursue the French,' I said.

'I don't know.' Broughton handed over the flask and settled himself down more comfortably. 'He's probably killed half their army and built up his reputation in Burgundy. What are you going to do about Thomas David?'

I shrugged.

'If he has the courage to come and see me, nothing. If not, I'll tell the Duke of Gloucester that the man is a coward.'

He grunted and we sat and drank throughout the rest of the day as the French camp around of us was thoroughly pillaged.

★ ★ ★

The next day we prepared to return to Calais. I had already sent word to Nan that I was safe, but it occurred to me that a further message, to the Duke of Gloucester, might also be advisable. I was sending for a clerk to come to my tent when Thomas David entered.

He was pale and his hands were shaking. Quietly, but in a steady voice, he admitted that he had panicked. 'I don't know how it happened,' he muttered. 'Perhaps it was those fire-arrows that were new to me or maybe it was… well it doesn't matter now, does it?'

He looked at me.

'I'm finished now. It's taken me a good number of years to build up my reputation but when word gets out, everyone will despise me.'

'Why will it get out?'

'I imagine you'll tell the Duke of Gloucester,' he said bitterly.

He gave a half smile and turned to go.

'One error doesn't make you a bad soldier,' I said firmly.

He turned around.

'You made a mistake, but for the rest of the time you were a good leader. You ask me what I'll tell the Duke of Gloucester – it's simple. I'll tell him, and anyone else, that you brought your men safely here, recruited others and helped to teach them to fight in a new way.'

'Nothing else?'

'No, nothing else.'

'How can I thank you?'

He brushed past Swartz and Haldi on his way out.

'Maximilian is grateful to you and your men. The French are totally defeated and Martin Swartz,' Haldi told us with a smile, 'has been knighted by Maximilian and is to be given an important post.'

'He deserves it.'

Martin Swartz shrugged modestly and Haldi spoke again.

'He says Maximilian wished to reward you, but does not know how it should be done.'

They both looked at me expectantly; I declined their offer. The German officers had allocated more than sufficient rations for the two- or three-day march to Calais. The men had apparently done well for themselves after the battle and we had no wounded from the men we had brought from England.

'I did not come here for reward. I came because it would help a friend of mine and his wife.'

Swartz smiled and then said something slowly. Haldi turned to me.

'He says he's not sure if you are a very good soldier or a very lucky one, but he has enjoyed fighting with you and wishes you well.'

We clasped hands; it was time to prepare to depart for Calais and then on to England. It would be good to see Nan and be able to hold a conversation with someone without every other sentence starting with the words, 'he says'.

CHAPTER 10

I returned to the West March and slipped back happily into my former role. Working closely with Broughton and Dick Middleton, I gradually increased the strength of the Carlisle horse until we had sufficient numbers to mount two simultaneous raids into Scotland.

I briefed Ratcliffe on this when, after a lengthy absence, he came to Carlisle. I was surprised to find that he listened attentively and asked a number of perceptive questions. Not wishing to overdo the news of our success, I tried to steer the talk to other matters, but uncharacteristically Ratcliffe did not want to discuss politics. Instead he brought the conversation back to the attacks on Scotland that I was planning.

'Richard of Gloucester will wish to lead the next raids,' he said after a while.

'Of course and I will be there to assist him,' I reassured him.

He gave me a sharp look, but made no comment. Instead, he jumped up and started to pace round the room, carefully avoiding the chests and various items of armour that cluttered it. Watching his narrowed eyes and frowning face, I guessed that he was deliberating with himself about something.

I poured more wine and waited until he was ready. Eventually he seemed to come to a decision, as his head jerked up and he looked me straight in the eye.

'Richard of Gloucester, whom we both serve, is of course not yet well known in the West March,' he began. 'Admittedly, it is through your efforts that men here acknowledge him as their overlord, but he is not yet seen as their leader. You will have to do far more if we are to get people to accept Richard as their leader in all parts of the North.'

He shot me a keen glance.

'Particularly in the West March.'

I returned his glance blankly. All my subordinates here already knew that I was accountable to Richard of Gloucester and reported to him. What on earth was Ratcliffe talking about?

'Well, yes?'

Ratcliffe shifted his stance uneasily.

'So what do we – and you especially – need to do to ensure that he is viewed as the leader in the West March?'

Still I did not understand.

'But that's your job!' I protested. 'You spend all your time thinking about things like that. Why do you need my views when you probably already know the answer?'

Ratcliffe picked up his gauntlets and looked down at me pityingly.

'I have worked it out,' he said sadly. 'But the problem I have on this occasion is that it cannot be me who provides that answer; it has to be you. Now, I will leave you for a while and when I come back I want you to give me the answer.'

His words made no sense and I told him so.

'They will in a while, Francis,' he said gently, 'and believe me, I am truly sorry.'

And then he was gone.

★ ★ ★

It took time for the tears to dry. Indeed, it was curious just how long after Ratcliffe had departed that water still swam in my eyes. At least by now, I was over the worst of the shock.

When eventually I divined what Ratcliffe was talking about, I had found it impossible to accept. The proposal that I should stand down and leave the West March was both incredible and totally unfair. I raged against the ridiculousness of the notion. Dear God, I had built up this rundown backwater of a march, hadn't I? Was it not I who had financed much of its defences and paid for its troops? Who had then destroyed the Debateable Land and taken the war into Scotland? And, in return for this, I was supposed to step down so that Richard of Gloucester would be perceived as the only leader when he arrived. I was being sacrificed for his ambition! It was wrong for the region and blatantly unjust to me. Surely there must be a way in which both Richard and I could be accommodated here. I seized a pen and, summoning up every ounce of imagination and ingenuity I possessed, covered sheet after sheet with different structures and hierarchies, until at last I threw down the pen and faced up to the inevitable. While I remained in the West March, there was absolutely no chance of men here viewing Richard as their leader. Were I to stay, he would be seen as their ducal overlord and titular head, but no more than that.

For a split second I wondered whether I might be exaggerating my own importance, but with brutal honesty I put the thought aside. Richard was not known here and I had been in the West March a long time. If I were to stay, the entire officer cadre here would instinctively look to me, not him, for direction. With the mutual bonds of friendship and shared experiences that bound us all so closely together, it would be hard for them to do otherwise.

Ratcliffe had been right on another point too, I realised. I had to instigate my own departure. After all, there were no obvious grounds to remove me from my post. Indeed, such a move would be counterproductive as there was the strong possibility that such an action would provoke antipathy here towards my successor. While grudgingly I could see the logic of leaving, what truly angered me was the manner in which it was being done. It was bad enough to be ruthlessly cast aside to further Richard of Gloucester's ambitions, but to hear about it second-hand was intolerable.

I seethed as I brooded on it. Richard had not even had the

courage to tell me himself! My so-called friend had sent Ratcliffe to do his dirty work for him.

There was a tap at the door and Gloucester's executioner stepped in.

'Well?' Ratcliffe asked.

'I'm not resigning!' I said defiantly. 'After everything I have done for Gloucester, what he is proposing is blatantly unfair!'

I glowered at him.

'And in view of our friendship, frankly I would have expected you to have refused to be his errand boy on this occasion.'

'You believe this to be Gloucester's idea?' Ratcliffe asked incredulously.

'No. It would have to have come from Anne Neville!'

'But Francis...'

'And there's another thing too!' I exploded. 'They didn't even have the guts to tell me to my face!'

Ratcliffe's mouth tightened and he gestured to me to sit down. He poured wine and slid the glass over the table towards me. I waved it away.

'Drink it!' he barked and there was a steely edge to his voice.

I obeyed him as he watched me through narrowed eyes.

'In your position, I might have reacted in the same way,' he said tersely. 'So to make you see sense, I am going to tell you something that you will never repeat. Is that clear?'

I shrugged indifferently.

He smacked the table forcefully with his hand.

'I said, is that clear?'

'Yes.'

'Good. Now Lovell, understand first that neither Richard of Gloucester nor his wife know anything about my mission here.'

I hooted in derision.

'I don't believe you!'

His grey eyes met mine.

'Do you want to come to the cathedral with me and listen while

I swear an oath to that effect in front of the high altar?' he demanded. 'Anyway, surely you know me well enough to know I would never lie to you.'

Ratcliffe had always spoken the truth, I reflected.

'So whose idea was it then?'

'Mine.'

I reeled in shock.

'Yours?'

He smiled thinly at my surprise.

'Yes mine, old friend. Tell me, what do you know about my job?'

Ratcliffe spent his time building up Richard of Gloucester's reputation and I told him so. He nodded.

'That's reasonably well known. But there's another part to it which no one knows about, and it's a bit more complicated. You see, Francis, the way I see it, it is not enough to help Richard by building him up; I need to smooth his path for him.'

Despite myself, I was fascinated.

'How do you do that?'

He looked at me evenly.

'I anticipate that there will be obstacles in his way, and they need to be removed before they obstruct him. My methods vary according to the circumstances, of course. Sometimes it's fairly simple, at other times it can be more complex.'

He spread his hands as he spoke and I had no doubt that he was telling the truth. For an instant, I had a glimpse of the murky world in which he operated, for his ambition was such that, in the service of Richard of Gloucester, Ratcliffe would be completely ruthless.

'I've been watching you for some time now, Francis,' he murmured. 'If you had been less successful, I would not have needed to have this conversation with you. But, against the odds, you have done well, and when you started raiding in Scotland – well, I knew it was time to step in.'

He smiled sadly.

'You have become too big in these parts, Francis. If Gloucester came here now, you would eclipse him and you know it. So given that both of us want him to succeed here and elsewhere, by my reckoning, it is time for you to step down.'

'And if I refuse?'

He looked at me in surprise.

'With anyone else I would take drastic action, but I would do nothing to harm you.'

He stood up and put his hands on his hips.

'But what I would say, were you to refuse, is that you would be behaving very badly towards the man who entrusted you with the West March in the first place and you would be putting your own interests in front of his. Is that how you choose to serve him?' He stared at me. 'Are you really that selfish, Francis?'

His tone was reasonable and there was no hint of menace in his voice. As I looked at him, I realised that the talk must have been as uncomfortable for him as it had been for me. In all honesty too, everything he said was correct. The best way I could serve Richard was by not serving him here.

'So what reason do I give Richard for resigning?' I enquired slowly.

'You tell him that you have been in his service for a number of years and that you wish to spend some time with your wife on your estates,' Ratcliffe replied. 'Naturally Gloucester will be surprised and probably a bit upset, but given that you will be helping him, that doesn't really matter, does it?'

★ ★ ★

Richard's arrival in the West March was highly successful; he was precisely what the people there wanted. He came not as a high and mighty duke and brother to the king, but as a plain and honest soldier. He did not charm with idle flattery, but rather he sought advice and counsel. He gave few commands, seemingly content to listen. Above all for a region plagued by Skiam and the Scots, he arrived as a general.

Quietly and methodically he won people over. During our tour of the Debateable Land, he sent his own escort back to Yorkshire, saying that the Carlisle horse was all the protection he would need. Dick Middleton was elevated to the ducal council to advise them of the best ways of using light horsemen.

Sir Christopher Moresby was delighted to hear that not only were the remaining repairs to the castle to be carried out immediately, but the duke was proposing to oversee the work programme himself.

Broughton and I took Richard to visit some of the larger landowners; others were entertained in Carlisle and they all took to him quickly. Indeed, Edward Franke advised me that so great an impression was made by Richard that most of them not only wrote off his debts to them but offered yet more financial aid.

At last the time arrived when I knew that I could do no more to assist Richard and told him that I would depart in two days' time. His face immediately fell.

'But I have been comforted by your presence!' he complained. 'I wish you would reconsider your decision.'

I smiled down at him.

'I have been apart from my wife for too long,' I said with complete honesty. 'But when you have need of me again, send for me, and you know that I will come.'

My words seemed to cheer him.

'I know you will and I thank you – but Francis, delay your departure for one week more. There is something I wish to arrange.'

★ ★ ★

Broughton gestured towards the dark bulk of Carlisle's main gatehouse lay.

'It will be completely dark soon,' he said. 'Are you ready?'

I swallowed nervously.

'Not yet.'

He grinned at me and in the gloom his teeth glowed whitely.

'That's all right, Francis. And remember – I'm right behind you at all times.'

I smiled back gratefully. In truth, Broughton had proved an invaluable source of comfort over the past twenty-four hours. What exactly I faced, I did not know, except that at some point I would be formally made a knight. Normally the ritual can be carried out fairly quickly, but Richard delighted in chivalry and, accordingly, I had been instructed to participate in the entire ritual: the nightly vigil in the cathedral, the ceremonial bathing and the priest hearing my confession. These things I had all duly carried out, but now, as I stood outside the walls of Carlisle in my symbolic white tunic and red robe, I wondered nervously what was to come next.

Three torches suddenly illuminated the battlements, and I heard a creaking sound as the massive gates swung open. Broughton nudged me in the right direction.

'Come on,' he said, 'and remember to just keep moving forward towards the castle.'

I stepped out into the city and was momentarily dazzled by a mass of torches. I stopped and looked down the length of English Street. On either side of the road, dismounted troops stood with lances lowered, blocking my passage.

'Move!' hissed Broughton.

Trusting him, I advanced through the lances in front of me, which were raised to the upright position, their silver points glinting as they rippled upwards. I glanced at the soldiers as I moved between them; there were no smiles, nor did any man call out. In stern silence, the men of the Carlisle horse made their farewells with this final spear salute. Followed by Broughton, I passed slowly between them and was nearing the cathedral when the drum started. In the silence, its noise was magnified and its sound, though commonplace, added to the unreality of the occasion. The measured beat seemed to urge me on to where Moresby stood with his picked band of archers ready to escort me into the castle.

The courtyard was a sea of light, the fiery brands illuminating the burnished armour of the soldiers. Propelled on by the relentless booming of the drum, I walked slowly through the massed ranks of infantry towards a raised platform where I guessed Richard would be. There was total silence as I reached the dais and solemnly climbed up the steps. Then, without realising, I found myself on my knees in front of him. A moment later, I felt the top of his sword touch first one shoulder then the other.

'Arise, Sir Francis,' Richard of Gloucester ordered, 'and receive the tokens of your knighthood.'

He gestured to Broughton and Moresby, who now mounted the dais to proffer me my spurs, but he raised his hand when Dick Middleton reached to where my sword lay.

'I will attend to that,' he said quietly.

Removing his gauntlets, he girded my sword on. I turned to thank him, but at that moment, the trumpeters who Moresby had placed on the battlements all blew together and their clangour drowned out my words.

I waited for them to finish, but even as the last note died away, the cheering in the courtyard started. I believed that it would soon die away and stared at the ground in embarrassment, but instead the noise seemed to swell, and I realised in horror that the troops who had been on duty on the streets outside had now entered the courtyard.

Richard of Gloucester gently pushed me forward to face the men.

'You should acknowledge your men's acclaim,' he said quietly.

'It's not fitting with you present…'

'Do it, Francis!' he commanded firmly.

Even as I made the final salute to my – no, his – men, my heart went out to the little man who stood deferentially behind me. He had planned the whole ceremony. He would have known that the focus of the whole evening would have been on me, but he was prepared to walk in my shadow, so that I could have this moment of glory.

153

I turned to him.

'How can I thank you for all this?'

He grinned up at me.

'Promise me that you will return when I call for you.'

'But I would have done that anyway, without all this!' I protested.

His eyes twinkled.

'I know that, and I am grateful for your loyalty. But I owe you this evening not only for past services, but also for a more recent one.'

'It's just guesswork on my wife's part,' Richard continued, 'but if you have sacrificed something for me, should I not sacrifice something for you?'

He clapped me on the shoulder with a laugh.

'No, don't answer me; just come back when I need you.'

I gazed blankly across the teeming mass of cheering soldiers in the courtyard for a while. I was to go away from Richard, yet I had never felt so close to him than at this very moment.

PART 2:

1482 – 1485

"Ratcliffe, Lovell and Catesby the Devil
Ruleth all England under Anne Neville"

CHAPTER 11

A cross the river the Scottish patrol threaded their horses through the snow-covered trees. They moved slowly with spears aloft until they reached the shore. But even as the riders dismounted to water their beasts, their leader spurred his horse into the shallows and arrogantly inspected our camp.

I ignored his gaze and let my own eyes climb the steep slope behind the horsemen. High above them sentinels manned the high walls of Berwick[13] and even as I watched, a strong force of men-at-arms began to descend the hillside. I guessed that the Scots would be adopting forward positions so as to give additional notice of a surprise attack by our men.

Sourly I wondered why the Scots believed that they had to be so vigilant. After all, by now their spies in our camp would have reported that morale in the English camp was so low that our force was not even the slightest threat to their great fortress.

Angrily I clenched my fists. Morale was so bad by now that we had been obliged to place additional sentries round the camp. Officially it was explained that this was a precautionary measure against a surprise counterattack. In reality all our men knew that the sentries were there to stop them deserting.

In my heart of hearts I could not blame our would-be deserters, for our campaign at Berwick was proving disastrous for them. It was not just the lack of rations that was reducing our men to skeletons, nor was it the extreme cold which caused so many of them to lose fingers and toes[14], rather it was the defeats.

For twice now the Scots had beaten us and badly. Both of our frontal assaults had been bloodily repulsed and with such loss of life that no one in the army had the slightest confidence that a third attack would fare any better. Nor indeed that we could ever capture Berwick.

But we had to, I thought grimly. If we could not capture Berwick, then Richard of Gloucester would be exposed to complete and devastating humiliation. He would be ridiculed by his enemies the Woodvilles and reviled by the men of the North.

And that had worried Ratcliffe the most.

He had found Nan and I at Minster Lovell, my boyhood home, and from the moment that he politely asked to see round it I knew his business to be serious.

For Ratcliffe was only polite when he needed something desperately.

But for all his impatience, he had made an effort as I proudly showed him where generations of Lovells had lived and loved. He admired the siting of the old house by the river and liked my idea to build a tower in the south-west of the quadrant.

But when we came to the circular dovecot and he heard the cooing, he dropped his feigned interest.

'Doves are symbols of peace,' he had snarled. 'We need war.'

I had given up at that point and led him back through the crowded courtyard into the solar. Once the door had closed behind us I had asked what he wanted.

Swiftly Ratcliffe had summarised all that had happened while I had been abroad. Insofar as the North was concerned, it appeared that Richard and Anne Neville had used the time well to further strengthen their position as undisputed rulers of that region.

Wishing to minimise the constant threat from the Scots, Richard and Anne had actively promoted war with Scotland. They had argued that a successful campaign now would vastly reduce the Scottish military capability in the future.

King Edward had fully accepted his brother Richard's argument and had raised a special tax to pay for the war.

'It was originally envisaged that the king himself would lead the army,' Ratcliffe had added, 'but he was not well enough, so

Gloucester took command. Of course, that made perfect sense. Everyone knew that he was the man behind the war.'

'And the woman behind him, Anne Neville,' I had chuckled. 'After all a successful way led by her husband would greatly enhance his prestige, not just in the North but throughout England.'

Ratcliffe had winced at that, so I had guessed that we would presently come to the problem. I listened attentively as he had continued.

The strategy had been carefully planned. The invasion would naturally be launched from the English East March, since Northumberland was the English county nearest to the Scottish capital. It was quickly accepted that the key objective in the decisive first phase of the campaign would be to capture the Scottish citadel of Berwick. This clearly had to be secured, since to advance in strength into Scotland with Berwick still in Scottish hands, was too great a threat to the English Army's lines of supply and communication.

As preparations progressed excitement rose in the North, Ratcliffe had reported. So great was the antipathy of all northerners to the Scots that the prospect of defeating them in battle and having a peaceful border seemed a God-given gift.

Men began to see glory and gain for themselves in the campaign too and the numbers of those volunteering their services increased daily.

But even as Richard and Anne Neville rode ever-growing waves of popularity, it all went horribly wrong.

Richard made a terrible mistake.

Reverting to his fatal habit of impetuosity, he had tried to capture Berwick prematurely and had failed. Alerted to the threat to Berwick and their country, the Scots had poured reinforcements into that redoubtable border fortress. By doing so they made it impregnable.

Desperately the English had tried to maintain the siege or at least to contain the Scots in Berwick. Lord Stanley had taken his levies from Cheshire and Lancashire to try to do this, but Ratcliffe had not been optimistic. In his view, success was unlikely. After all, if Richard of Gloucester had failed in the campaigning season, how was Lord Stanley supposed to capture a reinforced Berwick in the middle of the coldest winter that there had ever been?

'But the invasion cannot proceed without Berwick being secured,' I had clarified.

'Exactly,' Ratcliffe had snapped. 'But since we cannot capture it, the campaign will have to be called off and Gloucester will be humiliated.'

I had not been able to disagree with his conclusion. Gloucester had instigated the war and had worked up everyone to fever pitch about it. But now not only was he going to have to dampen expectations, but also he would have to admit that it was his own impetuosity that had led to the cancellation of the war.

I shuddered as I thought about it. The Woodvilles would crucify him for that, and at their instigation even his supporters in the North would vilify him. How quickly they would forget all the good things that Richard and Anne Neville had done for them and how savagely they would turn on their benefactors.

As I listened to Ratcliffe, I felt my anger grow steadily. Of course Richard had acted both impulsively and foolishly in trying to capture Berwick prematurely. But what was one mistake when put aside all that he and Anne had achieved in the North.

Not that the Woodvilles would care about that, I thought miserably. They would see Richard's mistake as a golden opportunity to pounce on him and Anne, and would look to exploit the vulnerability of their position by poisoning men's minds against them.

And because human nature is weak and men susceptible, the malicious rumours and damaging innuendos would quickly take hold.

The more I brooded on the vindictiveness of the Woodvilles, the more I felt my hackles rise. Their cowardly campaign would doubtless be secretly devised and subtly orchestrated, but it would be devastatingly successful.

And, as a result, Richard and Anne's supporters would abandon them, as they had left my Lords of Warwick and Montague, I recalled. Well, I was not going to allow it to happen to their heirs in the North.

I met Ratcliffe's anxious gaze. I knew what I had to do even if I had no idea of how to do it.

'I will ensure that Berwick is captured,' I promised.

★ ★ ★

A few weeks later, I reported to Lord Stanley and placed myself and my men under his command, since he was older and doubtless more experienced.

But three weeks later, fearing that the tactics that he and his captains were using would never succeed, I put my own plan forward.

He had listened carefully with the twin lines of worry growing ever deeper between his eyes while he slowly stroked his pointed beard. He had asked a number of extremely perceptive questions and begged me time to consider. I'm not sure how many choices he had left to him though; he had already tried two other options.

The first, a seaborne attack on the eastern side of Berwick had been unsuccessful. His second attempt was two weeks after I arrived at Berwick. The idea of an assault on the north-west of the town had initially looked promising, since the ground there is more favourable than elsewhere, but the assault was a disaster. I grimly recalled it.

★ ★ ★

We had started confidently. The long columns of metalled men had easily waded across the river at low tide and, brushing aside the feeble Scottish defences on the far side, had skirted round the castle which dominated the south-west of Berwick. Moving inexorably northwards, they established a supply point out of enemy range.

Archers were moved forward to provide covering fire for the assault, while the men-at-arms prepared to advance towards the city walls.

The first attack was beaten off fairly easily by the Scottish archers on the city's battlements, but the second attempt was a much closer-run affair and, for a short while, the three great storming ladders rested against Berwick's walls, before we were driven back. As our troops withdrew from the attack, Lord Stanley and I conferred with his three captains.

'What do we need to do to succeed next time?' Lord Stanley panted.

The elder captain, a former mercenary, rubbed his chin thoughtfully, while his two colleagues remained silent. Clearly they were content to be guided by the older man's experience. He glanced at Berwick's castle on our right and then at Lord Stanley.

'The tide turns in two hours, my lord,' he began. 'So it's obvious that we only have time for one more attempt. We can't risk being stuck on this side of the river and not be able to cross back into England.'

Lord Stanley nodded. To be in hostile territory without any means of retreating was clearly folly.

'So it follows that we need to throw everything we've got into this last assault,' the captain continued. 'We need to lay down a heavier barrage prior to the assault so that the Scots will be keeping their heads down as the infantry approach the walls.'

'How do you do that?'

The captain gestured to our archers who were protecting our right flank from an assault from the Scots in Berwick Castle.

'Use those men to supplement the main assault, my lord. With their extra firepower, we can get our men's ladders up against the walls and Berwick will be yours.'

'But that would leave our flank totally exposed!' I protested.

'Against what?' he jeered. 'If there are any Scots in the castle, which I am beginning to doubt, why haven't they fired a single arrow against us so far? My guess is that they have mustered all their archers at the point we are attacking.'

He turned to Lord Stanley.

'My lord, it does not make sense to keep half our archers standing idle and watching for an imaginary danger when, with their assistance, the main attack can succeed.'

I began to object, but Lord Stanley courteously stilled me as the deep lines of worry furrowed ever deeper between his eyes.

'It's the quickest way to end the siege, my lord', one of the other captains started, but he was silenced with an irate gesture.

We waited for a few moments. Lord Stanley glared at Berwick Castle to our right and tried to assess the danger that lurked within. At last, conscious of the fact that shortly the tide would be turning, he reluctantly came to a decision.

'All the archers will join the main assault!' he commanded.

★ ★ ★

The three great ladders served as standards for the troops. The trio of assault groups grimly moved towards the walls of Berwick. Above them, massed volleys of arrows darkened the sky as our archers expended their stock to provide cover for the advancing infantry.

I am not sure how lethal those volleys were, but the absence of returned fire indicated that our archers' fire was serving its primary objective of keeping the Scots quiet.

Presently, the three great ladders were propped up against the walls and men clustered round them. A moment later, the first wave began their ascent. Seeing this, our archers ceased firing and, laying their bows aside, drew their swords in anticipation of joining in the assault.

A scaling ladder is not a place to linger, but Lord Stanley's men were faster than any I had ever seen and presently there was a great cheer as the first of them was seen waving his arms at the top of the battlements. And then another joined him and then a third. Sensing victory, the troops at the bottom of the ladders jostled each other in their eagerness to ascend. As they clustered together beneath the great ladders, the concealed archers in the castle suddenly opened fire.

It was devastating. From their greater height, the Scots had full view of the whole English force and, firing ten arrows a minute into tightly packed troops, they made it a killing field. Overwhelmed not only by the unexpectedness of the assault but by its sheer ferocity, men stood momentarily frozen while volley after volley pounded into them.

Within minutes the assault on Berwick degenerated into complete confusion. Men ran in all directions trying to avoid the deadly hail of death that was engulfing them, while others simply dropped or staggered out of the maelstrom, feebly pulling at protruding arrows.

Recovering from a daze, I moved quickly to where Lord Stanley stood.

'Sound the recall!'

He looked confused and gave the order reluctantly. Even as the trumpets sounded their doleful notes, I looked up at the city walls in horror. I realised now how cleverly the Scots had planned this.

Scottish men-at-arms flooded onto the city walls and began to swamp those troops who had ascended the ladders. Vastly outnumbered and attacked from two sides, Lord Stanley's men stood little chance. Presently, I could see that dark shapes were being hurled from the battlements.

Worse was to follow. Having secured the city, the Scots now turned their attention to the long ladders while the archers in the castle continued to flay the infantry below them. Ignoring the hysterical screams of the troops marooned on the ladders, the Scots used forked poles to push the ladders away. Two fell away completely, hurling the screaming troops to their deaths, but the third ladder swung out and then, for some inexplicable reason, bounced back against the walls. The violent jolt was sufficient to dislodge the majority of the men, but a handful doggedly hung on, unable either to ascend or to climb down.

They remained there for some moments, faces raised in supplication to the Scots on the walls. It seemed that they would be saved as no move against them was forthcoming. My hopes proved ill-founded; men approached the top of the ladder, two of them carrying what looked like a tub. The liquid poured from the tub seared through the upturned faces of the men on the ladder. They raised their hands instinctively to try to assuage the indescribable agony of the quicklime upon their skin. As they fell below, the Scottish archers on the battlements lined up; working in conjunction with the Scots in the castle, they shot arrow after arrow at the fleeing troops.

★ ★ ★

'We were routed.' Lord Stanley spoke firmly, but with fierce intensity.

I sat silently with him in his tent. The disastrous assault at Berwick had been bad enough, but the flight that followed had been a disgrace. In their panic to escape, our men had simply run, discarding weapons and bows. No attempt had been made to recover the stores or to assist the wounded.

I clenched my fists in anger. There had been many wounded who could have been saved as the Scots had made no attempt to pursue us. Many of these could have been treated, but neither Lord Stanley's captains nor his men had bothered with them in their haste to escape. Indeed, as far as I could recall, Lord Stanley's captains had appeared to be leading the rush to cross back over the river before the tide rose too high.

'We'll have to try an alternative plan,' Lord Stanley began. But then he froze in shock and looked at me wildly. 'What's that noise?'

I listened but could hear nothing. Excusing myself, I went outside and listened to the sounds that drifted across from the Scottish side of the river. At last, satisfied that I was correct, I returned inside.

'It's the Scots,' I told Lord Stanley grimly. 'They're torturing the men we abandoned.'

He bit his fist in horror.

'What a way to celebrate their victory! I pray they will be tired of it by tomorrow.'

He was wrong. In order to convince Lord Stanley's men of the inadvisability of making further attacks on Berwick, the Scots devised a cruel deterrent.

At the base of the long curtain wall that straggles down the hillside from Berwick Castle, there was a small stone fortification. Positioned on the very edge of the river, the fortress was designed to provide additional protection to the castle itself.

At low tide, the little fort could fulfil this role quite well, but when the tide rose the fortress' usefulness was compromised as it became submerged by the waters. Unperturbed by this defensive weakness, the Scots made good use of the fortress. Every day a fresh batch of prisoners was imprisoned in it at low tide.

For ten long evenings Lord Stanley's men watched petrified as the tide rose. They tried to block out the frantic screams of the comrades they had abandoned, as they slowly drowned in the dark.

★ ★ ★

Brutal though the Scots' tactics were, they succeeded. Even Lord Stanley lost his enthusiasm for all-out assaults.

A day later he agreed to my plan.

'So Gloucester will send ships in order that we can blockade Berwick by sea,' he summarised, 'while I and my men try to contain the Scots here.'

'That's right' I agreed. 'Now while you do that I'll take my horsemen and archers behind the enemy lines and stop all reinforcements and supplies reaching Berwick. With no supplies, the Scots will weaken and then we can capture it.'

Lord Stanley thoughtfully stroked his beard. 'It could work,' he admitted, 'but if you are defeated then I have not got enough men to capture Berwick. I would have to abandon the siege and the invasion could not proceed.'

And Richard of Gloucester would be shamed and ridiculed.

'I won't be defeated', I told Lord Stanley resolutely.

★ ★ ★

A few weeks later my confidence waned. The first Scottish convoy moving down the coast road to Berwick had been poorly defended and, not expecting attack, our archers made short work of the few Scottish troops. We had taken the wagons and draught animals to camp and buried the Scottish dead. It was as though the convoy had never existed. However, with the second convoy, we lost the element of surprise. While we captured the supplies, a number of Scottish horsemen managed to escape in the driving rain. Fennell's archers had been unable to shoot properly and, while our horsemen had killed a number of fleeing Scots, some got away.

'So what will the Scots do now?' Dick Middleton asked as we rode back to the camp in the great forest.

'I suspect what the Scots will do is to gather all their supplies for Berwick and send them down with the reinforcements. This would serve two purposes. Firstly, they would prove a strong escort on the journey south to Berwick. Secondly, if they could get their supplies to Berwick, they know we would have to retreat.'

He frowned. 'Why's that?'

'Because once they have all their men and supplies at Berwick the English invasion cannot go ahead,' I said irritably. 'They would be too strong a force for Richard of Gloucester's army to leave behind.'

Dick Middleton agreed hesitantly.

'Mm… well I suppose we'll just have to wait until they move their men and supplies down to Berwick. We might just be able to deal with them, providing they are not too strong.'

This was the issue that had caused me to worry. At the outset I had assumed the Scots would reinforce and re-supply Berwick bit by bit. They were, after all, moving supplies in their own territory and had no reason to fear attack. But with the knowledge that a hostile force was based in their country, their tactics would alter radically. They would merely muster the strongest force they could and send it down to Berwick along with the supplies. Nor did they have any need to look for us; the Scots knew that we would have to attack their force. If we failed to defeat it and the Scots reached Berwick, then the English plans for invasion would be ruined.

Back in camp, Sergeant Haxx greeted me.

'Have you learnt anything from the Scottish prisoners we captured after the first attack?' I asked him.

He shook his head as we walked together on the soft moss.

'Nossir! Scotch bastards refuse to give anything but their names, sir!'

'What nothing at all?'

Haxx halted reluctantly. 'One of those Scottish thieves has the same name as you have, sir – Lovell; he's called, Henry Lovell. Mind you, I wouldn't trust that little bastard.'

'Why not?'

He gave me a pitying look. 'Got clean hands sir. How many soldiers do you know that have got clean hands. It's not natural sir!'

'I'd like to meet Henry Lovell.'

'I'll have him sent to you.'

It was dusk when the mysterious Henry Lovell was brought to my tent. We inspected each other silently. He seemed shorter and slighter than me. He was probably a bit older too, I mused; there was grey in that sandy hair of his.

'I will tell you nothing that will assist the invasion,' he told me curtly.

I grinned at him.

'I wasn't going to ask you why a well-born man was going to Berwick, while it was under siege.'

'I would not tell you.'

'Nor why he sought to pass himself off as a common soldier.'

'It's none of your business.'

'Tell me about yourself.'

He looked amused.

'Do you think you'll succeed where your man Haxx failed?'

'No, but I won't try.'

To put him at his ease I told him a little of myself first. He listened attentively and, when I had finished, he got up and stretched.

'You're honest, Francis; I like that in a man.'

I choked on my wine.

'How do you know that?'

'What you've told me bears out everything that we already know about you,' he replied coolly.

★ ★ ★

But despite our mutual suspicion, Henry Lovell and I drifted closer to one another. If there were certain topics we would never discuss, there were a great many others which we could. We found we had common interests and drank together. One evening he told me of himself.

His own life had been an interesting one. He had done his military training in France and then moved to Burgundy to become a hired soldier for Duke Charles.

'I'm surprised you survived that experience.'

'So was I,' he admitted with a grin. 'After Grandson, I swore that next time I would be the one holding the pike, not facing it.'[15]

Lacking confidence in Duke Charles's ability to win a battle, he had returned to Scotland and married, but, sadly, his wife had died in childbirth leaving him a son. After a spell fighting in the East March, he had entered the service of the Earl of Argyll, the Scottish Chancellor.

'So what are your duties?'

He raised an eyebrow.

'What do you do for Richard of Gloucester?'

'Mm… All right, I see. So where's your home?'

'Ballumbie.' He grinned at my blank expression. 'You mean to tell me that you've not heard of it? It's near Dundee.'

I believed that Dundee was on the east coast near Edinburgh.

'Have your family always lived there?'

'Originally we settled in Hawick.'

'Oh yes, Hawick.'

I doubt I convinced him, but he continued regardless anyway.

'That's where the Scottish Lovells started,' he explained. 'Three or four generations after the Norman Conquest, one Ralph Lovell became quite a favourite of your king, Henry II. He gave him a wealthy heiress, Margaret of Hawick, to be his wife.'

I had never heard of any of this before.

'So the Scottish Lovells and the English branch descended side by side thereafter. Are there any more of us anywhere?'

'Well I suppose there must be the French line.' Henry smiled at my enthusiasm. 'Our mutual ancestor came over at the time of William the Conqueror and was given lands in England but the rest of the family stayed in France. They must have done well for themselves. My father told me that one of them rose to become Chief Butler of Normandy.'

'What does a chief butler do?'

'I've no idea,' Henry responded frankly. 'It can't be that important though or else we would have one in Scotland.'

We laughed. Soon the time for me to make a final circuit of the camp before nightfall was upon us.

'We'll talk again,' I promised Henry, 'and, since we are kinsmen, I will ransom you and you can go home again.'

But such an interlude was a rare moment of relief from my worry. Over the next few weeks we found no trace of supplies moving to Berwick. Obviously the Scots were gambling on supplying their garrison there with one large convoy escorted by all their reinforcements.

Two days later our scouts spotted it.

'Mother of Christ,' Middleton muttered again. 'Will you look at that?'

I ignored him. I gestured for him to be silent and concentrated on the enormous column below us.

I had to give the Scots credit. The long chain of wagons moved steadily along the track with the sea behind them and a protective screen of horsemen flanking the carts. Groups of men-at-arms marched alongside the wagons and a strong force of archers brought up the rear.

'They've got outriders and scouts ahead,' Middleton pointed to distant figures on horseback. 'There will be no way of surprising them.'

I continued to count.

'Mind you, it's not as if we could attack them,' he continued. 'There are thousands of them.'

The Scottish column was pushing hard. Wagons with broken wheels or axles were manhandled to one side and abandoned. Lamed horses were led away and replaced immediately. The loud and consistent cracking of whips indicated the pressure that the Scots were putting on their beasts to maintain the column's momentum. From our vantage point on the hilltop, we watched as the enormous column snaked below us generating clouds of dust. As far as I could see there were no Scottish cavalry shadowing the chain of wagons.

As the Scots passed our position and continued their march to Berwick, I rose from my prone position. Middleton leapt up and Captain Fennell groaned as he rubbed his cramped arm. I looked at each of them in turn.

'200 wagons or so. Several smaller carts. Sufficient replacement draught animals…' I began.

'Probably about 700-800 men-at-arms.' This was the estimation of our farsighted captain of archers. 'Maybe another 100 or so archers.'

'They could have more in the wagons. How many horse?' I asked Middleton.

By splitting out the counting we would arrive at a more accurate appraisal of the enemy's strength.

'Including scouts and outriders, I would say 400.'

So the Scots numbered around 1300 men. We had 600. They were prepared to defend themselves and the only area in which we held a slight advantage was that we had more horsemen. But the Scots could be reinforced, and we had not got the element of surprise on our side. To attack such a force would be to commit our small force to oblivion.

'We'll return to camp,' I said heavily.

I found no surprise in the faces of either Fennell or Middleton.

★ ★ ★

We led the horses as we would need them fresh for the return to Berwick, but as I trudged along my feelings of disquiet began to grow.

On the face of it, the decision not to attack the Scots was sensible. They vastly outnumbered us and could be reinforced. To withdraw kept my small force intact. But then I stopped abruptly – intact for what? As soon as the Berwick garrison was reinforced and re-supplied, there was no way that the town could be taken. Slowly, I led the horse forward as I faced up to the sobering truth – if Berwick could not be taken, the English invasion could not take place, and Richard of Gloucester would be humiliated.

I raised my hand to halt the column. Anne Neville and her husband were relying on me. Somehow I had to defeat the Scots and wipe out their entire convoy. None of it could be allowed to get through to Berwick. I needed time to think of a plan, so I called a halt to allow the horses to be watered. Then I summoned Middleton.

'Will you take a number of your men and check that there are no other Scottish forces within the vicinity?'

He looked up surprised.

'Even if there are, they'll hardly attack us while we're mounted and moving away from the Scottish convoy. Is it really necessary?'

He saw my glare.

'We'll be back in two hours.'

★ ★ ★

After Middleton's scouts had ridden out, I wandered away from the stream to think. I squatted down and drew endless diagrams in the dusty earth, discarding them one after the other until I came to see how the business could be managed.

A hand touched my shoulder.

'There's no indication of any reinforcements in the immediate vicinity,' Middleton smiled down at me. 'Shall we resume the return to camp?'

I stood up slowly. We would have to attack the Scottish column before it could be reinforced.

'Captain Fennell!' I shouted.

He raised his arm in acknowledgement and ambled over. I looked at the pair of them.

'We are not going to retreat. We will attack the Scottish column and destroy it.'

Middleton gaped at me.

'But that's madness!'

'Captain Fennell, take your men to the end of the moor. Cross the river past that abbey, and keep your men in concealment until I come to you.'

'You're going to attack the Scots without archers?' he stuttered.

'Correct. I want you to be a surprise for the second phase of the battle. Now Dick, get your men ready.'

They hesitated.

'That's an order!' I barked. 'Now move, both of you.'

* * *

Ahead of us the rising dust denoted the steady progress of the Scottish column. Presently, they would spot Middleton's approach. He had been helpful, I reflected. Once he had got over his initial shock, he had been quick to make improvements to the plan. It had been his idea to make his force's appearance as obvious to the Scots as possible.

'You want the Scots to see us coming a long way off. That gives them more time to move their cavalry and bowmen against my horsemen. But you'll have to work hard to ensure that your own angle of approach is concealed. Use every scrap of cover you can find.'

'They might be expecting a diversionary attack,' I agreed. In fact, they would probably have more men-at-arms at the end of the column to compensate for having moved their archers up to the head of the column to protect the Scottish cavalry. All right then, we'll try and stay concealed so that they think you're their only threat.'

Hopefully, Middleton's approach across the open moor would have been spotted by now and we could bring our men out of the old riverbed. I estimated that the rear of the Scots forces was not more than a mile away, but the further the Scots moved away, the greater the chances of our being detected as we moved up on it. Next to me, Sergeant Haxx glanced up at the sun.

'Master Middleton should be in position now, sir.'

To attack prematurely would be a disaster, but all the time the Scottish column was moving away from us. We would be best to move in a moment.

'You remember the order of battle?'

His eyes were steady on mine.

'We attack their rear, sir. You takes the right. I takes their left. If that doesn't work we makes a further attack to provoke that Scottish cavalry to come at us.'

'Very good. Now the Horse Dance.'

'To be done when you orders it, sir.'

There was no expression in his eyes.

'You've got volunteers?'

'With the bonus you've offered them, I've got volunteers, my lord.'

'They know the risk they're taking? Not many will survive.'

'Those bastards will do anything for money, my lord.'

'Then get the men mounted.'

And then it was back to a familiar routine. We eased into a trot, which turned into a canter, as we met the dust billowing from the Scottish column. We were galloping as we reached the end of the Scottish wagons and crashed into the men-at-arms guarding them.

CHAPTER 12

The surge was devastating. Razor sharp lances tore into the flanks of their bellowing oxen and frenzied draught horses. There was no time to cut the beasts free and allow them to escape. There were simply too many animals.

In front of me, a driver leapt from his high seat to flee. Instinctively my horse swerved to the left as I drove my spear through the man's chest. I glanced around quickly; panic was spreading fast as men desperately sought to avoid the tide of death and destruction that was engulfing them.

Maddened by the smell of blood, the horses pulling the wagons tried to flee. Their ears pulled back and, flanks heaving, they strained at the traces which bound them. Many wagons were without drivers and guidance now – they careered into one another. I saw two carts overturned and heard the frantic neighing of trapped horses.

Around me, our men chased the few men-at-arms that showed themselves. Some tried to fight, but a sword is poor protection against men on horses armed with long lances. As they fled, they found themselves colliding with each other or caught between wildly moving wagons. I saw a man-at-arms knocked down by a maddened draught horse and another was trampled by stampeding oxen.

Frantically, I urged our men forward. We had to force the Scottish horse to turn on us; this was the whole essence of the plan. My divisionary attack force was the bait. Once the Scots were tempted to turn on us, then Middleton could attack them without fearing the Scottish archers. Our spears tore into the backs of screaming men-at-arms as they sought to evade us. Panic was spreading up the column now, but where was the Scottish horse?

The plucky Scots fought back though. They must have had

archers concealed in their wagons for I could hear the whirring of arrows. Protected by overturned carts, their bowmen began to find their targets.

I guessed that in a moment we would lose the impetus of our attack. The horses were beginning to tire and we could not afford too many casualties. It was time to attack further up the column. I had the trumpet blown three times and as the men reformed I led them through the shattered convoy to Haxx's force.

'Casualties?'

'About a quarter, my lord. And you?'

'The same. We'll try again further up.'

We launched the second assault midway up the column. I guessed that we were out of range of the main force of Scottish archers and I believe that the bowmen who had been stationed at the rear of the column were not certain where we were. Despite the absence of archers, we were beaten back. Initially, our charge engendered chaos as it had before, but our horses were tiring now and the Scots sent spearmen against us. Most of our men had lost their lances by now. They were unable to counter the groups of Scots who stood out of range and jabbed at their mounts and then hacked at their riders as they slid to the ground. We were losing too many men. Soon the Scottish horse would have no need to move against us. We were becoming too few to pose a threat to our enemy. With the Scottish horse still protected by their archers too, Dick Middleton could not charge. We had to force the Scottish horse to move against us. I signalled to Haxx.

'Now', he snapped.

I could think of no other way.

'It's now or never,' he said curtly.

I let my shoulders droop. God forgive me, but this was the only way I knew.

'Do the Horse Dance.'

He signalled to the remaining volunteers who were close by. I left him immediately and pushed my mount through the bellowing oxen and crazed horses. We had to get our men out and quickly.

'Retire!' I yelled at a couple of troopers who were thrusting at a large man in a black breastplate.

'Retreat!'

Hurriedly, I seized the reins of a soldier's horse. Where was that fool with the trumpet? I used the flat of my sword to beat two of our men back towards the rear of the column. Dear God, why didn't these fools hurry? As soon as they saw even the beginning of the Horse Dance, the whole Scottish Army would go berserk.

'Move!' I yelled.

By now Haxx's volunteers must have targeted a couple of the fleeing Scottish men-at-arms.

I used the point of my sword to prick the rump of the horse in front of me.

'Faster, you fools!'

But our horses were slowing. Any moment now the Scottish cavalry would ignore their orders and charge us. The provocation of the Horse Dance would simply be too great. Their shock and revulsion would make them want to tear us to pieces. Originally the dance had been invented in the West March to punish soldiers who were found guilty of stealing from their comrades. In that harsh military environment, the barbarity of the dance proved a highly effective deterrent. Until today, it had never been used against the Scots. Dear God, but our men were moving slowly. I had to use the flat of my sword to speed our flight. By now, Haxx's volunteers would have caught up with the fleeing Scots and used their horses to separate a pair from the others.

'Move you fools!'

Approaching the Scottish cavalry, they would have used their horses to knock the pair to the ground. The screams of the two men-at-arms would have been plainly audible to the Scottish horsemen. Such collisions are commonplace in battle and result in injury, although they are not necessarily fatal, but the remainder of the Horse Dance is. At first the Scottish cavalry would not have appreciated that, like all dances, there is both a pattern and a rhythm to its movements. No weapons are used and the horses themselves are the dancers. After felling the two men, the horsemen make small bows to them and retire gracefully away from the prone men. Horses will not usually stand on men or seek to injure them deliberately. It can happen in the course of battle, but it usually occurs by chance and not by design; the Horse Dance, however, moves to a different beat. As the first men retire from the fallen figures, three more riders approach and bow to the men on the ground. Then, one after another, they steer their horses towards them. Their horses are familiar with the steps of the dance and know to trample the men beneath them. They move gently this way and then the other. Finally, in obedience to their rider's soft guidance, they courteously move away to allow the next three riders to take their places, already bowing to the men on the ground as they approach. And so the dance swirls on to the beat of the horses' hooves until the cries of the bloody forms on the ground subside and they remain completely still.

★ ★ ★

I felt, rather than heard, the Scots charge. The pressure behind me increased and I was jostled as men sought to flee past me. Their horses' flanks were streaming now as their riders desperately tried to outrun the Scots behind them.

Dead God though, we were slow. Already the Scots had sent men ahead of us on both our flanks. In a moment, once we were clear of the Scottish wagons, they would use their outriders to come at us from left and right. Striking at us simultaneously, they would force us back onto the spears of their cavalry behind us. In the open, we would be an easy target.

Frantically, I shouldered my horse forward and turned the direction of our flight back towards the wrecked Scottish wagons at the rear of the column. At least there we would have some protection since the overturned wagons and panicking animals would split the Scots and give Dick Middleton a chance to save us. But we were too late. The Scottish outriders caught us in the left flank as we were still turning. The momentum of their charge pushed the survivors towards the wagons. Without lances, we were outranged by their horsemen. Our small force fragmented into groups of dismounted men madly hacking at the Scottish horsemen. But their horses were fresh and they were quick. As soon as we beat off an attack from one direction, they rode at us from another. Their fury showed in the savage handling of their beasts and their cruel cries of triumph as their barbed spears drove into our horses. Men were falling quickly now as we sought cover desperately.

The air was thick with sweat and the smell of blood as they herded us back to where the dying draught oxen still bellowed mournfully in their traces. A group of four or five Scots rode out quickly from their ambush point behind the overturned wagon.

We turned quickly. Then we were running, leaping over fallen men and dodging the flailing hooves of wounded horses. But the Scots were playing with us. As we emerged from the debris of the column, directly ahead a large body of their horsemen sat waiting. There was a sudden shout and their cavalry began to move into a rough crescent formation.

I sighed as I wearily hefted my sword aloft. The Scots had smoked us out of the potential safety of the column and were set to complete their task. There were only half a dozen of us remaining, but it would be better if the older men stood with me. The younger ones might possibly survive and finish as captives. Before I could arrange this, I felt the drumming of hooves on the turf and, bracing myself, wheeled round.

Middleton's charge swept through the Scots like an immense wave. Attacking from their rear, his troops swept though the Scottish horsemen scattering them in all directions. Some turned to flee, but Dick must have launched a second attack as the scene ahead of me turned into a bloody brawl. Men were flung from their horses.

Riderless animals galloped wildly in all directions. As quickly as it had started, it was all over and the horsemen swirled away. The ground in front of us was clear of troops, except for the dead and wounded. We stood with chests heaving and hands shaking. I was covered in perspiration and desperately thirsty. I guessed the others were in the same state.

'We survived!' the man next to me wheezed incredulously.

The realisation that we would live seemed to come to us all simultaneously and we smiled in disbelief. I cheerfully clapped the shoulder of the youngest trooper and heard the sound of hysterical laughter. But then, only moments after, the whirr of a Scottish arrow.

I grabbed the nearest man.

'Let's get out of here.'

I led them away hurriedly from the Scottish column.

★ ★ ★

'Fall in behind the Scottish wagons!' I told Dick Middleton. 'Keep pushing them south, but don't attack them!'

He peered down the hill. Slowly the Scottish column had reorganised itself. All the injured beasts had been dispatched and immobilised wagons abandoned. The dead lay unburied.

'It's moving now,' Dick grunted.

Sure enough, with archers and men-at-arms flanking it, the Scottish supply train was heading south to Berwick.

'We'll attack again when they come to the end of the moor at the river crossing.'

'But they still outnumber us. We took casualties,' he reminded me hesitantly.

Ignoring him, I gestured at the abandoned wagons.

'Burn those and leave nothing for the Scots to take to Berwick. Now I'll join Fennell and you keep herding the Scots towards us.'

He would propel them to the place where I would seek to destroy them completely.

★ ★ ★

It was Captain Fennell who identified the likely crossing point the Scots would use.

'They'll bring their wagons over here.'

He pointed to that part of the riverbank which was flatter than the rest.

'There's probably a natural ford here. Now, how do you want to fight them, my lord?'

It was a good question. With the destruction of their cavalry, we had wounded the Scottish force, but it was not necessarily a fatal blow. Marching over the moors the Scots had sufficient archers and men-at-arms to repel Middleton's men. Had he attacked, their bowmen would have decimated his charge before he could close in and their infantry would have easily finished off any survivors.

Provided the Scottish convoy kept moving across open moorland and remained bunched together, there would be little that Dick could do except skulk after them. He could threaten them but that was about it, particularly since the Scottish archers would not worry about wasting arrows. The wagons would carry numerous arrows for the garrison at Berwick.

But coming to the river the Scots had a problem. Their archers had to counter Middleton's horsemen at all times. If Middleton crossed the river, the Scots had to send their own archers over. Conversely, if Middleton remained on the far side, the Scots would need to send their wagons over with some of their men-at-arms and only move their archers over when everyone else was safely across.

'Send a messenger to Middleton!' I told Fennell irritably. 'Under no circumstances is he to cross the river. He should threaten the Scots from the far side of the river and only attack when the enemy is totally confused.'

'Totally confused?'

'He'll know what it means,' I said impatiently. 'Now let's get your archers out of sight.'

'Where do you want them?'

I pointed to the pine forest south of the crossing.

'Keep them concealed in there. No one advances until I say.'

He wrinkled his brow.

'Their scouts will spot us.'

John Fennell's stupidity was making me angry now. Dear God, we still had the majority of the Scottish force to deal with and all he could do was make half-witted observations.

'What scouts?' I snapped.

He thought for a moment and then smiled broadly.

'That's true, my lord.' He paused. 'It's lucky that you destroyed their cavalry first, isn't it?'

I stamped my foot in frustration. His frowning face indicated that further profound pearls of wisdom were to be shared with me shortly.

'So you want Master Middleton to keep those bowmen busy on the other side of the river and we let some of the men-at-arms cross the river?'

'They'll send over half their men-at-arms and establish a protective screen.'

'Of course they won't be expecting us. It's lucky that you didn't use us in the first attack, my lord. They won't know about us at all – real good fortune, I'd say.'

'It was all planned!' I yelled at him, clenching my fists.

He looked dubious.

'No one could be that cunning. Men say you're good, my lord, but that would be really clever.' He shook his head and put his great paw on my shoulder. 'I'd say that you were just lucky, my lord.'

I burst out laughing as I looked at him. He was smiling now that he had got me to relax. He was a clever man, Fennell. He must have seen how strained and tense I had been when I'd arrived and set himself the task of altering my temper.

'That's better, my lord,' he said gently. 'Now what do you want to do with those fire pots?'

'Have them filled with pine wood but don't use them until I tell you. Now, will you get your men into concealment?'

I watched him chivvy his men into the forest. Then I looked towards the river and started to calculate the angles for arrow fire.

★ ★ ★

'Message from Master Middleton.' Fennell interrupted me as I placed the white marker sticks in the ground. 'The Scots have quickened their orders of march. They'll be here in another two hours.'

'We'll be ready for them,' I promised.

'What happens if the Scots don't adopt a defensive position when they've crossed the river,' Fennell wanted to know. 'What happens if they just keep going?'

I shook my head.

'They wouldn't dare. Some of Middleton's horsemen would cross the river and decimate them. The Scottish archers can't be in two places at the same time.'

He thought about that one, then he grinned.

'Suppose they divide their archers up, my lord?'

'They wouldn't have enough to deal with the bulk of Middleton's horsemen on the far side.'

He checked my angles of fire and adjusted two of them. Presently, he peered steadily through the trees.

'Can you see anything?'

'Dust, my lord. We'll move back in a while.'

★ ★ ★

'Do you want me to advance the men?'

Fennell's low tones would normally have been audible miles

away, but the noise of the creaking carts and lowing oxen drowned out most sound.

'Not yet.'

I signalled to him to remain where he was and quietly made my way to the edge of the forest.

About a third of the Scottish men-at-arms had crossed the river and were sprawled in a broad arc about 600 paces from the river. Two wagons had already crossed the river and had been moved away from the bank to make room for the remainder. Anticipating a lengthy wait, the drivers had unyoked the horses, which now grazed peacefully.

On the far side of the river, the remaining carts and wagons were preparing to cross. Behind them I caught a glimpse of Dick's horsemen who lurked out of range of the wary Scottish archers. Quietly I made my way back.

'Light the fire pots!' I told Fennell. 'Leave men to tend them with pine wood, but advance the rest of the archers.'

He leapt to his feet preparing to bellow out the order to the archers, but stopped when he saw my glare. Quietly, he moved round the supine men and formed them into small groups. We advanced silently through the trees. Twenty paces from the start of the clearing, Fennell signalled his men to spread out and I heard the sound of bows being notched.

'Seems they've decided to speed up the crossing,' muttered Fennell.

He was right. Whether it was the fear of Middleton's horsemen behind them, or whether the Scots wished to ensure that they reached Berwick by nightfall, I did not know. For some reason though, they had abandoned their previous policy of sending the wagons over one at a time. Instead they seemed to have a number in the river and on our side of the bank; the Scottish infantry was manhandling the heavy wagons up the steep banks.

Fennell looked at me expectantly. I shook my head. We would fire the first few volleys from the shelter of the trees. Obediently, he stuck his arrows in the ground in front of him and the others followed suit. Then, aiming carefully, he fired the first shot. Seeing this, his men did the same. The second volley was already in flight before the first shots hit the Scots.

Some arrows were perhaps deflected by trees and others missed their targets but most did not. The sound of screams and frantic neighing of horses filled the air as the third and fourth volleys slammed into the Scots on the field by the river. I advanced the archers to the marker beyond the treeline to take up the second position.

Ahead of us was a scene of complete pandemonium. Dead and injured Scots lay in groups on the rough turf. Terrified horses galloped wildly, following each other to who knows where. By the river, two wagons had overturned, crushing the men who had been working them.

'Keep shooting!'

Fennell's bull-like roar rose above the cacophony of shrieks, groans and neighing.

How necessary the next few volleys were, I did now know. The surviving Scots made no attempt to rush our position; instead they fled downstream or simply cowered behind the wagons. Gradually, the hubbub subsided.

'Out clubs?' the scar-faced archer next to me asked.

I shook my head. Some of the wounded Scots might recover and get away.

'Ask Captain Fennell to bring up the fire pots,' I told him.

We would advance to the riverbank now to complete the destruction of the Berwick relief force.

We moved forward ignoring the wagons and wounded beasts. On the far side of the river, there must have been well over a hundred wagons. The Scottish archers were still there of course and I guessed their numbers would have been supplemented by men-at-arms who had fled back across the ford. Captain Fennell raised an enquiring eyebrow. The wind was coming in from the coast.

'Fire at the ones on the right-hand side,' I commanded him.

At fifty paces his men could hardly miss the wagons clustered together by the ford. Presently I smelled smoke and saw clouds drift up lazily from some of the carts.

To my surprise, few arrows were fired from the Scottish side. I guessed that Dick was manoeuvring threateningly and the bulk of their archers were still guarding the northern side of the Scottish position.

A few of the braver Scots attempted to draw water from the river to extinguish the small fires but at short range they were easy targets and toppled lifeless into the water. Behind them the Scottish wagons began to bump into one another as the horses smelled the smoke and moved uneasily.

'Cease firing.'

I jumped as Fennell's bull-like roar resounded. I had not realised that he had come up behind me. I wheeled round.

'Why stop now?'

He pointed across the river.

'They'll try to rush us now. It's the only chance they've got.'

He was right of course. Boxed in by Dick on one side and us on the other, the Scots would be forced to use their greater numbers to rush one of us before the fire in the Scottish wagons spread uncontrollably.

'Spread out!' Fennell boomed.

They were brave the Scots, but even a ford can slow men down at a time when they need to move quickly. Only a few of them even reached the abandoned wagons in midstream; the rest were washed away in that maelstrom of arrows, their screams silenced abruptly as the water took them.

Some managed to make it back to the far bank but the ground was muddied badly now with the progress of so many wagons and horses. They found it hard to climb back out and in their panic scrambled over each other as our arrows sought out their unprotected backs. They began to fight each other in their desperation to escape the river and their shrill cries and curses could be heard above the jubilant shouts of our archers.

The river was now becoming clogged with Scottish corpses, and I glanced at the far bank. Soon the Scottish position would be totally untenable. They were descending into a state of total confusion.

A number of wagons were now burning fiercely and the flames, fanned by the wind, were moving on to other wagons. Up to now the Scottish drovers had been able to control their plunging beasts, but as the smoke and flames increased, the horses began to panic completely. The animals crashed their loads into other wagons causing the fire to spread more rapidly.

Men jumped from the moving carts but were trampled by flailing hooves or crushed beneath the wheels of moving carriages, their shrill screams cutting through the smoke and panic. Two of the wagons managed to disentangle themselves and, with their horses tossing their heads and whinnying in sheer terror, careered driverless along the riverbank.

'Cease firing!' I bellowed above the din.

'The enemy is not fully destroyed!'

The scarfaced archer leant forward to pull another arrow from the ground in front of him and made to notch it. Impatiently I struck it to the ground and gestured to where the wind had blown the smoke away for a moment. There were horsemen with lances among the Scots now – horsemen who rode down the Scots milling on the riverbank, horsemen who hunted the fleeing Scots and plunged spears into their backs, horsemen who plunged their mounts into the river to spit the desperate Scots as they tried to wade away.

I turned away from the sight. Presently we would fire the remaining wagons and dispatch the wounded beasts. There was no chance of Berwick being relieved now, and soon the city would either surrender or be captured. The invasion could proceed, and Richard's reputation would remain intact.

Yet as I looked at the dead and wounded, I felt little elation, just an immense weariness.[16]

★ ★ ★

'One, two…hup!'

'One, two…hup!'

The archers' voices were hoarser now I noticed and despite the cold wind they were sweating profusely.

'One, two…hup!'

Their perspiration was not caused by unnecessary movement as by now the powerfully built bowmen had perfected their routine to make it as efficient as possible.

They worked in pairs. One would pull the arrows from the body, while his partner ran his hands through the dead man's clothing. Sometimes the arrows snapped as they were jerked out but, if they were extracted intact, the pair would share them along with everything else.

Then one archer would take the Scot's arms while the other took his feet and together they would drag the corpse to the edge of the burial pit.

'One, two…hup!'

The problem for the men now, I observed, was the distance that they needed to drag the dead weights. When they had started this had not been an issue since naturally they had started with the bodies closest to the freshly dug pit. But, as the morning advanced, they found themselves roaming further afield which was why they were sweating now.

I glanced round. At the current rate of progress it was going to take at least another half day before all the Scots were heaved into the pits, so still thinking deeply I crossed over the ford.

On the far side two bloated bodies, with spears still impaled in them, bobbed and nudged against the muddy bank. For a moment I wondered why they had not drifted downstream with the others, but then it occurred to me that they must be entangled with roots or branches below the water.

189

I came to the place where the Scots had made their last stand. Being so close to the river I imagined that until yesterday it must have been a verdant, pleasant pasture with colourful wild flowers contrasting against the green reeds on the bank.

But now it was blackened and ruined.

All around me the charred remains of men, oxen and wagons still smouldered, while patchy grey ash covered the muddy soil.

I was still thinking hard when I heard a sound. It was high pitched, wild and desolate; a solitary wailing that cut through the chant of the archers on the far bank. Presently other voices joined in until the shrill keening sound rose to a crescendo of grief before brokenly falling away.

The Scottish women were mourning their men.

And it was their grief that made me answer the question I had been brooding over.

Why had I acted so ruthlessly in the service of Richard of Gloucester?

And it had been ruthlessness on my part because when I had planned the two phases of the Battle of Berwick, I had not just devised a battle plan. No, what I had prepared was a strategy to annihilate the entire Scottish host.

Nor could I pretend that I had no knowledge of how the battle might develop. On the contrary, from the moment I had unleashed the Horse Dance on the Scots I had known what their reaction would be and thereafter events had come to pass as I had anticipated.

In truth, I had not planned a battle. I had organised a massacre.

But in military terms, I had no other choice. If even part of the Scottish reinforcements and supplies had got through to Berwick, there could have been no invasion and Richard of Gloucester would have been ruined.

So, how far was I prepared to go to serve Richard, I wondered.

To answer the question I cast my mind back. I thought of Lord Montague testing me with the Grey Wolves and I thought of how proud I had been to have been able to demonstrate my loyalty to him and, at Barnet, to his brother Warwick.

Then my mind turned to their heirs in the North. I reflected how I had come to know Richard of Gloucester and Anne Neville and how they had trusted me and how, in time, I had come to serve them and want to help and protect them.

And how they relied upon me.

And it was the realisation of their reliance that pulled me up abruptly. For with lightening clarity it came to me that there was nothing that would cause me to fail them. Which was surely the answer to my question.

So now I would seal my commitment and make my oath of loyalty.

For a brief moment I reflected on the seriousness of this, as in making such an oath I was promising to serve Richard in war and peace. Moreover such an oath cannot be lightly made; it binds a man as tightly as his marriage vows tie him to his wife and is just as sacred.

For a moment I questioned my ability to make this pledge. But a final glance round told me that I was certain of it.

★ ★ ★

Next to me, Nan sighed gently.

'I suppose, dear heart, that Lord Stanley thought by capturing Berwick he would make a name for himself.'

'"The man who captured Berwick" is how Stanley would like to be described.'

I propped myself up on one elbow and smiled down at her. Nan gently touched my cheek.

'But it was you who came out of Berwick covered in glory,' she cooed lovingly. 'Why do you think that everyone is talking about you?'

'I'm sure they're not.'

'Of course they are, my foolish Francis. Everyone knows what you did in the West March and Burgundy. And now everyone knows that without you Stanley would have failed at Berwick.'

'It will be forgotten in a day or so.'

'Why do you think you're going to be admitted into the Order of the Garter?' Nan asked impatiently. 'I was so proud of you when my cousin told me.'

I jerked upright suddenly – what an incredible honour![17]

'And you are to be made a viscount too after Christmas,' Nan continued. 'Richard of Gloucester and my cousin feel that it is high time you were rewarded for everything you have done for them.'

She nestled up against me.

'But did Richard not tell you any of this when he returned to Berwick?'

'No.'

'He would have been too busy,' Nan mused. 'As you told me earlier, none of the original objectives of the war had been achieved but, provided the story was presented in the right way, it could be made to sound very successful.[18] Richard would be a hero and could demand the extra lands and offices he wanted, but both he and my cousin had to move quickly and cleverly.' [19]

'I suppose Ratcliffe would have helped him with that,' I mused aloud. 'But everyone will happily accept that Richard invaded Scotland and forced the Scots to make peace. Berwick is not a bad prize to win.'

'It will build up his reputation. It is an excellent thing for the North that Richard is seen as so successful. All the old nobles and even Queen Elizabeth Woodville's relatives served under him. Richard of Gloucester is now perceived to be the second most powerful man in the whole of England. What did he talk to you about, beloved?'

Despite not defeating the Scots in battle, Richard had returned to Berwick in high spirits and greeted me warmly. We talked of our respective campaigns and I was interested to hear that Henry Lovell had been particularly helpful in brokering the peace treaty.

'I didn't know that you had Scottish relations?' Richard smiled.

'And French ones,' I told him. 'One of the French ones went on to become Chief Butler of Normandy. Do you know what a chief butler actually does?'

He stopped to think.

'No I don't,' he replied, 'but I'll find out for you. Now, Francis, we'll meet in London in a few months and when we're done with the business at court and parliament, we'll return here in the spring.'

It seemed a pity to have to travel south.

'I think that you'll find it's worth the effort,' he said quietly. 'But when we return, I wondered whether you would care to go to the West March to start the conquest of the Scottish lands.'

He took my arm and we resumed our walk along the city ramparts. Below us, Berwick was slowly being restored; to my left, workmen were already starting to rebuild the outer wall.

'But would not you yourself lead?'

We were reaching the eastern walls now and Richard stopped again and put his hands on the parapet, breathing in the clean sea air. He smiled in pleasure and looked up at me.

'No, Francis, I have other matters which interest me, but I trust you and know that you will help me as you have always done.'

'Of course.'

He fell silent as we watched the glittering sea. When he spoke again, it was with calmness and certainty.

'We can make the North strong now, Francis. With the Scots forced to sue for peace, we are safe. We can use money and influence to build up our region. Our people will prosper and we can look after them in body and soul.'

'You've done well, Richard.'

His hands were still firmly resting on the parapet. It was almost as if he wanted to reassure himself that Berwick was physically in our possession but he turned to me and smiled again.

'Only because I had good men who served me faithfully,' he said quietly. 'And we are building on the foundations laid down by our former master, the Earl of Warwick.'

He turned back to the sea as seabirds squalled above us. I glanced at his small form with affection. Everything that he had said was true. Under him, the North would grow stronger and its people properly cared for. He would still need our help, of course.

'I will make my oath of loyalty now if you wish, Richard.'

He looked pleased but shook his head.

'I have your friendship; I value that more.'

Next to me Nan stirred as I relayed my conversation on the Berwick ramparts to her.

'So now you've committed yourself to Richard completely?'

'For as long as he needs me,' I said contentedly.

She reached for my hand and squeezed it.

'I would make that a very long time, if I was him,' she whispered.

CHAPTER 13

Even in defeat my king still wore his normal serene expression. Nor did he express any emotion at all as hurriedly I pushed him to what I thought would be a safe place behind his knights.

But I had selected the wrong position for him. There was a swift movement and a moment later my king was toppled over.

'Checkmate again, I fear,' said Anne Neville.

I threw up my hands in despair for this was the third game I had lost to her within an hour.

'My lady is too good for me,' I told her ladies.

I spoke the truth as while I thought myself a reasonable player, Anne Neville had proved herself infinitely superior. Time after time she had guessed my intentions, but at no time did I spot her own strategy until it was too late. It had been a humbling experience.

As the door closed behind her ladies I duly turned to face her but she did not acknowledge me. Instead she gazed intently at the pieces on the black and white board.

I waited patiently so as not to interrupt her thought process but after a few moments I saw her remove both kings from the board and place them carefully on an adjacent table.

'Can you play chess without a king, Francis?'

'Of course you can, my lady. All that we would do is to make one of our other pieces substitutes for our kings.'

Anne Neville's fingers began to drum on the side of her chair.

'So if you lost your king all that you would do is to get one of the other pieces to deputise for him until you had a new king carved?' she said thoughtfully.

'Exactly, my lady. Then when you get your new king you just return the substitute chess piece to its former position.'

The finger drumming stopped in mid beat.

'And that is the part I struggle with most' my lady said quietly.

Her words made no sense, but I made no reply as Anne Neville appeared deep in thought.

Presently she roused herself and smiled apologetically at me.

'There are times perhaps when I go too fast and think too far ahead, so forgive me, Francis. Now let us come to the heart of the matter. At this time, more than on any occasion in the past, my husband needs your help if he is to prevent England from degenerating into civil war…'

'…civil war?'

'…and I will explain how you can help him save England.'

★ ★ ★

The threat of civil war had arisen, Anne Neville explained, as a result of King Edward's serious illness just before Christmas and the fear that he might die soon. Having defeated her father and Uncle Montague, the king had ruled England peacefully. For the past twelve years people in England had accordingly got used to the end of war and no one had thought of what might happen if the king suddenly died.

'But he has two young sons, doesn't he?' I interrupted.

'The eldest, Prince Edward, is twelve. He can't become king until he's at least sixteen. Even that, Francis, is awfully young. The problem would be that he would be influenced and controlled by his mother's family. The queen and the rest of the Woodvilles would be ruling England effectively.'

I saw her point at once. Whilst our efforts over the past years had prevented the Woodvilles encroaching into the North of England, elsewhere things were different. Ever since King Edward had married the Lancastrian widow, Elizabeth Woodville, almost twenty years ago, her family had risen greatly in both power and influence.

'Even now,' Anne Neville complained, 'the Woodvilles are looking to acquire more power. The Marquis of Dorset – he's her eldest son, Francis, from her first marriage – is one of the king's favourites. Then King Edward appointed his wife's brother, Earl Rivers, to be his eldest son's governor. Rivers has the boy in Wales, where – incidentally – the Woodvilles are trying to build up a power base too.' Anne Neville frowned. 'Do you know that there are Woodvilles on the king's council itself? I tell you Francis, that family is getting everywhere.'

'Do they have much support?'

'Quite a bit in the South, I think, but we older nobility hate them for their lowly origins and grasping tendencies. We see the Woodvilles as arrogant and greedy parvenus. Not one of us would accept them ruling England through the young king if – God forbid – King Edward died shortly.'

'So that's why you fear civil war? But surely the king's council would forget their differences – if they have any – and work together for the sake of the country until the young prince is old enough to think for himself?'

Anne Neville nodded glumly.

'In theory, at least, were King Edward to die shortly, a number of different political scenarios could emerge. Obviously the most straightforward one is that the king's council would rule in the young prince's name until he is old enough to rule himself. It would only be for a few years, after all.'

'Is that likely to happen?'

She shook her head emphatically.

'The council's already split into two factions. On the one side you've got the Woodvilles with the queen's eldest son Dorset leading them, and on the other side you have some of the nobles who oppose them.'

'Who is leading the nobles?'

'Lord Hastings together with his ally Lord Stanley – Hastings' is an old friend of the king and his chamberlain, but he and Dorset are rivals, and it is only the king that keeps that rivalry in check. Without King Edward, there would be no chance of the council co-operating together. Both parties would try to get rid of the other.'

It began to sound as if the quarrels between these two factions would indeed precipitate a slide towards civil war. Bearing in mind Anne Neville's antipathy towards the Woodvilles, I wondered whether she and Gloucester would ally with Hastings and his faction. Before I had the chance to voice this thought, she spoke again.

'No one of course wants a return to the civil wars that were so ruinous for England,' she said quietly. 'Notwithstanding the ambitions of the Woodvilles, we all desire peace when King Edward dies. The moderates in the country are therefore talking of Richard of Gloucester becoming protector. A protector, Francis, acts more or less as a king until the young prince is old enough to inherit the throne. A lot of nobles seem to view it as a way of avoiding civil war.'

She smiled a little sadly.

'It is of course an ideal solution, although I'm not sure that Hastings would readily accept losing his power. And probably the Woodvilles would prefer it if they acted as the interim government.'

'Protector!'

'Well, why not? Richard has always been completely loyal to this brother, King Edward. Gloucester's seen as a good administrator and now he has an excellent reputation as a soldier. His rank and estates are second only to the king's and he's not allied to any faction. If you think about it, he's the obvious choice and already men are saying that it is our – that is, his – duty to step in and prevent a conflict between the nobles and the Woodvilles.'

Even to me this sounded a bit biased.

'But he's famous after his success in the Scottish wars!' Anne Neville protested. 'Don't forget another thing too. On that occasion everyone was very happy for him to lead the army in place of King

Edward and both the Woodvilles and all the old nobility accepted Gloucester as their leader. Well, if everyone followed him in time of war, why wouldn't they in peace?'

It was hard to refute her argument and I was full of admiration for the way in which both Richard and Anne Neville put their country's interests ahead of their own, particularly as this would be an immensely difficult role for Richard. Because I knew him so well, I brooded on this unhappily. While able, Richard was not, I judged, a natural leader outside of his own familiar environment, but if called on to serve he would have to go south to take control leaving behind him familiar friends and faithful servants and that, I knew, would worry him. On top of that he would find himself working with men who he would neither know nor trust. As if all that was not sufficient at a time of crisis, everybody would be looking to him for leadership and he would doubt his own capacity to supply it. I feared that the protectorship might be too great a burden for Richard and expressed my concerns to Anne Neville.

She nodded sympathetically.

'But in a while I will be there to help him, and, in the meantime, he will have good and faithful friends such as you to guide him.'

'What would happen if he declined the protectorship and stayed here in the North?'

Anne Neville cocked her head as she thought.

'Assuming that there was no civil war and the Woodvilles came to power, then that would be an even bigger worry for Richard and me. How long would the Woodvilles tolerate such a mighty magnate ruling the North? They would see us as a threat to them so they would take action against us. Gloucester would be excluded from power, gradually his offices would be taken away, and we would lose all that we have gained.'

I thought about that. Ever since she had married Richard, Anne Neville had toiled with total single-mindedness to build Richard up in the North so that she and her husband might be seen as the worthy heirs of her father and Montague. Clearly under no circumstances would she permit her work to be undone or to be ruled by the lowly Woodvilles. And why should she or Richard? The thought was totally unreasonable.

'So to protect himself, Richard of Gloucester, needs to be protector if King Edward dies, and by doing so he will prevent civil war between the nobles and the Woodvilles.'

Anne Neville's blue eyes met mine.

'That is correct, Francis. But are you prepared to accompany him if he is called on to serve as protector?'

I did not hesitate.

'Of course, my lady.'

★ ★ ★

'Of course Gloucester needs us,' Ratcliffe agreed. 'The pressure on him is mounting, despite the fact that King Edward is still alive. Do you know that when he was in London earlier this year, people were sounding Richard out about his intentions?'

'No, I didn't.'

'It was all done pretty discreetly; in fact, I didn't find out until later. It seems that men will support him to become protector but they all want something in return. It's not just the ones in government but the ones outside as well. Take the Duke of Buckingham, for instance.'

'I don't know anything about him.'

'That's hardly surprising. He's been kept out of power by King Edward since Buckingham's got royal blood too. Now admittedly, it's not the strongest of claims, but King Edward doesn't want any rivals. Consequently, Buckingham's been excluded from more or less any form of government, despite his rank and his extensive wealth. It's hardly surprising that Buckingham would support Gloucester to be protector, is it? It's the only way he'll fulfil his ambitions.'

''How do you know what his ambitions are?'

'His man, Persiwell, acts as the intermediary between Buckingham and Gloucester. Buckingham wants to control Wales, but, Francis, he's not the only one sending messengers. The Earl of Northumberland believes that Gloucester would make an excellent protector.'

'So that he would have a free rein in the North, while Gloucester was in the South,' I said sourly.

Given that King Edward was still alive, all this scheming sounded faintly treacherous. My tone surprised Ratcliffe.

'Francis, be reasonable. Men will always have ambitions and it's only been the strong hand and natural ability of King Edward that has kept order in England these past few years. But once that strong grip looks to falter, everyone will look out for themselves.'

He grinned at me.

'Myself included. After all, if Richard of Gloucester became protector, my own prospects would look distinctly rosy.'

I laughed at his honesty and was about to reply when a messenger appeared and handed a scroll to Ratcliffe. Ratcliffe's face became unusually solemn as he studied the contents.

'Now it has begun,' he announced gravely. 'A report has reached York that the king is dead.'

★ ★ ★

In fact the report of King Edward's death was premature, but we had no way of knowing it at the time. Indeed, it was not until the official notification of the monarch's death reached us nine days later that we realised what an incredible piece of luck we had been handed.

Of course, we failed to appreciate it at the time, but it meant we had extra time to prepare both ourselves and Richard of Gloucester were there to be a call for him to serve as protector.

Messengers arrived from London with considerable frequency. Some were sent by well-wishers who wanted to ingratiate themselves; others were from more reliable sources. Initially the reports were encouraging as the king's council was functioning normally and it seemed that trouble would be averted, but then a note of disquiet crept in. The council was operating but Hastings and his party were outnumbered by the Woodvilles. Indeed, Dorset and the Woodvilles were giving orders in council and Hastings was violently objecting, claiming that they were too lowly born to do so. There was a plan to bring young Prince Edward to London, where the prince would be crowned immediately. The queen would act as Regent until he reached sixteen, meaning there was no need for a protector. The young Prince would be escorted to London by an army. Hastings seemed at the point of declaring civil war.

★ ★ ★

'So Lord Hastings has sent a message to Gloucester saying that the late king left everything to his brother?' I asked Ratcliffe.

'So it appears. Apparently King Edward bequeathed everything to Richard of Gloucester's protection: the realm, its goods and its heir. Hastings advises Richard to secure the prince and bring him to London.'

I frowned.

'But if King Edward's will says that Richard should be protector, why didn't the late king tell everyone while he was still alive? If he'd made his wishes known then – not least to Gloucester – all this quarrelling and these threats of civil war could have been avoided.'

Ratcliffe grinned at me.

'Francis, from you that's good, very good. But it doesn't really matter now; events have moved on. Now whether or not Hastings' note is truthful, it tells us one important thing.'

I was confused.

'What's that?'

'Both Hastings and Lord Stanley know that they are losing ground to the Woodvilles. Both of them are shrewd enough and have sufficient political experience to know that they face political annihilation at the hands of the victorious Woodvilles.'

'If not worse.'

'True. But equally they both know that they lose a great deal of power if Richard is protector. What Hastings' message really means is that they will now support Gloucester if he wishes to be protector. They probably see him as the lesser of two evils.'

'Mm… so what happens now? Do we move to secure the prince as Hastings suggests?'

'Not quite yet. She's instructed me to write to the council in Gloucester's name, before he rushes into anything. I am to state that Richard was always loyal to the late king and only desires that the new government is established according to law and to point out that his brother's will names him as protector.'

Ratcliffe glanced at me quickly.

'She's clever, Francis. If we do it this way, we justify our actions.'

I had no need to ask who 'she' was.

★ ★ ★

Anne Neville's plan to secure the Protectorate of England for her husband was probably one of the best pieces of planning I have ever witnessed. I doubted whether even her father could have done better.

'Clearly the prime objective in all of this is to separate the young prince from his Woodville escort and to secure his person,' she began. 'Once you have possession of the prince, it will be impossible for the Woodvilles to crown him quickly and deny you, my lord, your rightful protectorate.'

'But how do I do that?' her husband asked.

Anne Neville narrowed her eyes as she considered the question, but then her mouth twitched as if in secret merriment. She raised her hands to obscure her face.

'Tell me, my lord, am I frowning or smiling?' she asked.

Richard looked puzzled.

'Well, how can I tell? Your face is hidden.'

Anne Neville put her hands down on her lap.

'And that, my lord, is precisely how you will secure possession of the young prince; but before I explain further, allow me to tell Francis his role, as he must depart immediately.'

★ ★ ★

The twin furrows on the face of Lord Stanley grew even deeper as he listened to my message. When I had finished, he turned sombrely to his ally Lord Hastings.

'Not for a moment can I see Gloucester actually pulling it off,' he said slowly.

The great leonine head of the late king's chamberlain and best friend nodded sagely.

'I have to agree with you – Gloucester will never be able to extract the young prince from a heavily armed escort of 1,000 men. Lovell says that Gloucester is only taking a small force, mostly unarmoured, so as not to arouse suspicion, but what use is that? He'll just be brushed aside. The Woodvilles will bring the prince to London and crown him.'

He glanced at Lord Stanley.

'You and I are finished now; Gloucester was our last chance.'

To my surprise, Lord Stanley glanced back to me.

'Just remind me, Francis,' he murmured. 'If – against all odds – Richard of Gloucester did manage to secure the young prince, what is it that he wants us to do?'

I repeated Anne Neville's instructions.

'He wishes for Lord Hastings to use his considerable influence among Londoners here to ensure that the city affords Richard a favourable reception. This is essential; as soon as word gets out that Richard has gained control of the heir to the throne, fears and rumours are bound to spread. Men will question his motives and ask what his true intentions are.'

Lord Stanley looked up sharply.

'Of course they would, but we can deal with that. Lord Hastings can reassure the mayor.'

'If I thought that Gloucester stood a chance of getting hold of the prince, I'd personally ensure that the Mayor of London and all his aldermen were outside the city walls to greet him,' snorted Lord Hastings. 'Sweet Christ, I would have 500 of the most prominent citizens all clad in violet standing with them to honour our future king and his protector.'

His colleague nodded.

'If Gloucester can manage this, he need have no fear of his welcome in London. We will use all of our influence to ensure everyone understands that all he wants to do is to protect his young nephew.'

But then the twin lines of worry deepened.

'But, for the life of me, I can't see how he's going to manage it. The Woodvilles have over 1,000 men and he has far fewer, you say?'

'Yes. Most of them are not in armour, I believe.'

Lord Hastings groaned deeply.

'Then Gloucester's a fool. The Woodvilles will trample over him and deal with him as they intend to deal with Lord Stanley and myself.'

His tawny eyes bored into mine.

'The Woodvilles have won,' he muttered dejectedly.

★ ★ ★

They were laying leafy branches and scattering blossom on the hawthorn in the hall of Crosby Place. I smiled at the sight, since the copious foliage totally transformed the mood of the austere room. It was pleasing to see the younger servants bustling around happy, not only with the novelty of their task, but in keen anticipation of their May Day holiday.

I reached into my purse for some pennies and groats for the steward to distribute to them.

'My lord?'

I spun round. The messenger's face was scratched by brambles, his face and clothes filthy with mud. Clearly he had ridden both long and hard.

I held out my hand for the proffered scroll and unrolled it apprehensively. Shortly after I felt an immense surge of happiness as I read Ratcliffe's enigmatic scrawl.

'Woodvilles deceived. Prince retrieved.'

So Richard had managed it! In his evident haste, Ratcliffe had omitted any details of where, when or how Richard had done this, but it scarcely mattered for the moment.

I smiled broadly, so great was my joy. Seeing this, one or two of the servants regarded me curiously, but I paid them no heed for now Richard could become protector and we would be saved from civil war. I glanced around for someone to share my happiness, but then I had an idea. Crosby Place was the house Richard used sometimes when he came to London. These were his servants.

On impulse, I dug deep into my purse and flung a handful of coins into the air. There was an excited rush towards them even before the cascade of copper and silver hit the floor and rolled in all directions, the servants scampering after them.

I left to find Lord Hastings. His own joy this May Day would probably exceed that of Richard's servants.

★ ★ ★

The entry of Prince Edward into London, together with his Uncle Gloucester and the Duke of Buckingham, was managed magnificently. But while the young prince was cheered by the crowds, it was Richard who was the man of the hour.

Word had spread quickly; the crowds had learned that he had prevented the unpopular Woodvilles from seizing power for themselves and they were grateful to him. I watched how they cheered him as he deferentially presented King Edward's son to them. He had chosen to wear subtle dark clothing to lend greater emphasis to the prince's purple velvet and he bowed repeatedly to show the people that he was merely their servant.

Lord Stanley chuckled next to me.

'They love him, don't they? Hastings thinks the same. Mind you, he's positively bursting with joy now that the Woodvilles have been neutralised.'

It was curious just how quickly the Woodvilles had collapsed, I reflected. With the head of the family, Earl Rivers, and the queen's son Grey already arrested, they had been at a disadvantage. Of course, once the news of Richard's action became known in London, they had tried to fight back. The queen's eldest son, Dorset, had tried to raise an army but to no avail. As a result, he had joined his mother and the remainder of her children in sanctuary at Westminster.

'I would like to know how Gloucester actually managed it,' Lord Stanley murmured.

I tore my eyes away from the cheering crowds and smiled at him.

'I imagine we'll have to wait a few days.'

I pointed at the tumultuous scenes around us.

'This is going to keep Richard busy for a while.'

★ ★ ★

But I was wrong; the following night a page summoned me from my chamber. The Duke of Gloucester had arrived at Crosby Place and, despite the lateness of the hour, was desirous of speech with me.

I hurried down and greeted him delightedly, but he waved away my congratulations claiming that I should be praised for arranging the successful reception in London.

Looking at his flushed cheeks and glittering eyes, I suspected that the heady events of the last few days were catching up with him and called for wine.

'So how did you manage it?' I asked after he had dismissed the servants.

'It all went according to plan,' he said smugly.

He then gulped down his wine and held his glass out to be refilled, which was completely out of character for him.

'Of course, I hadn't realised just how good her planning could be. You see, we knew that Earl Rivers was bringing Prince Edward up to London from Ludlow, so we simply sent word to him that we would join him en route and would journey on together.'

'But surely he would have been on his guard? He would have suspected your intentions.'

Richard winked at me conspiratorially.

'Why should he? His force, he knew, easily exceeded mine and he probably viewed my offer as a natural surrender to the power of the Woodvilles.'

'And Buckingham, who was with you, is married to a Woodville,' I said thoughtfully.

Richard clapped my shoulder and used his other hand to push his empty glass towards me again.

'Rivers is a clever man, but he suspected nothing,' he chuckled. 'Do you know that when Buckingham and I got to Northampton, he even came trotting back to meet us?'

'So what did you do?' I asked as I handed his glass back.

'We charmed him.' Richard grinned. 'We asked him to dine with us and told him that he could sleep in the inn next door. Then Buckingham praised that book of his, while Ratcliffe plied him with wine.'

I shared in his amusement.

'Did you have to carry him to bed?'

'Almost, but the next day he felt bad.'

'On account of the wine?'

Richard roared with laughter and slid his glass back towards me.

'No, he felt bad because we imprisoned him in his inn and set up sentries and road blocks to stop anyone getting to him. Then we galloped about fourteen miles south – ah, thank you, Francis – and presented ourselves to my nephew and his escort.'

'So how did you separate him from them?'

Richard's shoulders shook in merriment.

'We told him that we had urgent news fit only for his own ears, so it would be best if he and his half-brother, Grey, accompanied us to a private place.'

'What was the news?'

'There wasn't any!' Richard bellowed with laugher. 'The whole thing was just a ruse. Anyway, as soon as we had separated them out we told him plainly that Rivers and Dorset were plotting against us and insisted that he dismiss his attendants and come with us. Of course we arrested a few of his key people; left leaderless, the rest of his servants and troops dispersed peacefully.' He grinned at me. 'A neat piece of work, I think you'll agree?'

'A bloodless coup that saved England,' I said honestly. 'But weren't you a bit worried? I mean, suppose something had gone wrong?'

He pushed his glass towards me. His face was now very red and his eyes animated as he relived his moment of triumph.

'No, I wasn't worried, Francis,' he said slowly. 'My wife's plans usually work out extremely well, although this one was probably one of her best.'

I nodded. As a model of deception it could not have been bettered.

'I'll tell you something though, Francis.'

'What?'

'It was when I rode into London and everyone was cheering me that I thought to myself how easy this has all been.'

'Well, the people love you, Richard, and admire what you have done.'

He smiled at me.

'But it's interesting that it's actually a lot easier to gain power than you imagine.'

I was proud of his success, so I paid no real attention to the ambition concealed in his words.

* * *

Richard quickly consolidated his position. All lords were required to swear an oath of loyalty to the young king, and the coronation was arranged for the end of June. The young prince was lodged, at Buckingham's suggestion, in the Tower. A committee was set up to work out how to persuade Elizabeth Woodville to come out from sanctuary, and the king's council was strengthened by the addition of the Duke of Buckingham and a chubby lawyer called Catesby, whom Hastings recommended.

I had little time for Buckingham. He had a naturally haughty manner and an overdeveloped sense of his own importance. He was quick-witted and spoke well, but instinctively I mistrusted him.

Catesby loathed him too; he had worked for Buckingham previously and spoke badly of him as he took me around London. He knew the city well and we must have dined together half a dozen times. Gradually I came to appreciate the depth of his intellect and his shrewdness, but I was unprepared when he asked if he might be permitted to serve the Duke of Gloucester.

He plucked at his red and white doublet as he spoke. It was curious for a man of his age how colourful and youthful his clothes were, and I found his habit of sniffing his scented handkerchief oddly effeminate.

I forced my mind back to the subject.

'But you are Lord Hastings' man. You're on his baronial council.'

'Which would, I imagine, make me extremely valuable to the Duke of Gloucester,' chuckled Catesby. 'How useful it would be for him to know what was going on in the minds of Lord Stanley and Lord Hastings.'

'You'll consider the matter, my lord?' Catesby enquired.

'I'll mention it to Richard Ratcliffe.'

'The busiest man in London,' sighed Catesby. 'What an honour it would be to serve under him!'

★ ★ ★

Catesby's description of Ratcliffe was highly accurate. Ratcliffe was to be found everywhere in London these days, using all opportunities to sing the praises of Richard of Gloucester.

He was singularly successful in his propaganda, but then people were open to hearing reassuring words. Slurs and rumours were flying around and many people knew nothing of the Duke of Gloucester. They wanted to know that he was an honest brother and uncle. It pleased them to know that he cared equally for both great and lowly people, and he was desirous only of working with all men harmoniously in good Christian fellowship.

Ratcliffe was also sufficiently experienced to know that one of the easiest ways to build someone up is to denigrate their opponents. Consequently, his arrival in London coincided with a spate of derogatory rumours about the Woodvilles. At times he went too far. His attempt to persuade the citizens of the city that four wagonloads of rusty armour left over from the Scottish wars was conclusive proof that the Woodvilles had been planning a coup, had been received with polite scepticism. But with so much gossip in the air though, this was speedily forgotten. To my surprise he was greatly excited at the prospect of acquiring a spy in Lord Hastings' camp.

'He could be very useful indeed.'

'I can't see why; Hastings is an ally. Richard's only going to be protector for the next three years then Prince Edward will become king.'

Ratcliffe shook his head impatiently.

'In theory if no one thought about their own advancement we could use the three or four years to give Prince Edward an excellent start. But it's not working out like that.'

'Why not?'

'Because, after Richard himself, Buckingham is now the most important person in government and Hastings doesn't like that. He's jealous of him, as is Lord Stanley. They don't like the fact that Buckingham has been given most of Wales. They take issue with Northumberland who is likely to be given extra powers in the North and they certainly don't like the new men, like you and me, influencing Richard. Hastings and his allies want to regain their old power.'

'But unless Richard rewards his supporters, few of them are going to follow him,' I protested.

'But there's not enough to satisfy everyone,' Ratcliffe snapped. 'There's another problem too. What happens to Richard in three or four years' time? The young king will inevitably lean towards his own family. Currently, Richard's arrested two of them, and the remainder are so terrified of him that they have either fled or taken sanctuary. They'll be looking for revenge in time.'

'Well, Richard could release Earl Rivers and the queen's son Grey and try to make peace with the Woodvilles now.'

'Buckingham wouldn't allow that and nor would Hastings and Stanley. The Woodvilles would demand a substantial share of power immediately and the only way that they could be satisfied is if other people had less.'

He groaned and put his head in his hands.

'On the one hand, Richard has the threat of the Woodvilles in the future but, on the other, he has the immediate problem that the council are not being particularly supportive. Maybe there is a way forward, Francis, but I can't see it and it would be useful to have a spy in Catesby. At least he could tell us what Hastings and his crew are thinking.'

★ ★ ★

Anne Neville listened intently to my analysis of the situation in London but made no comment. When I had finished, she continued to sit motionless in her tall carved chair. Presently she roused herself to look at me directly.

'Did my husband let it be known to anyone that he had sent you to me, Francis?'

'No, my lady. It was put about that I would be serving on Commissions of Peace in East Yorkshire, Northamptonshire and…'

'Excellent. Now tell me, did my husband remember to request the council to grant him an extension of the protectorship from four to thirteen years?'

He had and that was why I was with Anne Neville now. Richard had sent me to discuss the matter with Lord Stanley. Predictably, he heard me out in silence, the deep grooves between his eyes growing deeper.

'But why does Gloucester want such an extension, Francis?' he asked. 'I'll grant you that our young prince is a trifle young to become king at sixteen or seventeen, but why should he wait until he's twenty-five?'

'In thirteen years' time, the Woodvilles would be a spent force and there will be no revenge taken against Gloucester or Buckingham. Also, in fairness, the extension of the protectorship gives the young prince a chance to gain more experience. He'll be mature by the time he comes to the throne.'

'Assuming he does actually come to the throne! Francis, let me talk to Hastings. I'll revert to you.'

Surprisingly, Hastings' response was quick. I doubt whether he even bothered to think about it. He and the other lords in council were the devoted servants of the late King Edward. His heir had a legal right to inherit the throne. He, Lord Hastings, would have failed his late friend and master if the boy did not take up his crown when he was entitled to do so. With regard to the position of the Duke of Gloucester and Buckingham at that time, Lord Hastings regretted the situation but their role would come to an end then.

'That ungrateful old fool!' hissed Anne Neville. 'The extension of the protectorate would have made my husband safe.'

Her hand shook with fury for a moment until she composed herself.

'What message would you have me take back to Richard, my lady?' I asked a moment later.

Her fingers softly drummed the armrest of her chair and her blue eyes focused on the wall above my head; she ignored me completely as she marshalled her thoughts. I waited patiently until she was ready.

'There are three messages, Francis. The first one is the longest. Tell my husband that with the failure of the council to grant him an extension of the protectorate he has no choice but to pursue a path which he and I have already discussed. He should begin to make preparations immediately.'

'The second, my lady?'

'I will arrive to assist him early in June.'

'And the third?'

Her pale blue eyes shone with amusement.

'Tell him to make you chief butler.'

I must have looked puzzled. Anne Neville sat upright, smiling slightly at some secret joke before turning back to me.

'I understand that one of your ancestors was Chief Butler of Normandy.'

I had forgotten telling Richard the story that Henry Lovell had narrated.

'And, under the circumstances, it seems particularly appropriate that you become the Chief Butler of England. Now Francis, you'll have time to see your wife quickly before you return to London. Tell her that she's always in my thoughts.'

★ ★ ★

I waited with Ratcliffe outside the council chamber at Crosby Place; it was where Richard had based us while we were in London[20]. It appeared that the Duke of Buckingham was with Gloucester, and it was well known that when the two of them were together there could be no interruptions.

Ratcliffe brought me up to date on the situation in London. On the face of it, everything was proceeding normally. Merchants were going about their business, and the government was running smoothly. All the great offices of state – the justices, the heads of the Exchequers, the offices of Chancery and the Privy Seal – were functioning as before.

'The coronation committee under the new chancellor, Bishop Russell, seems busy too,' Ratcliffe continued. 'It's getting a bit awkward though since most of the next king's relatives are either fled, under arrest or still in sanctuary.'

'Is the situation with Hastings any better?'

There were raised voices now in the council chamber, although the words were indistinct. We looked at each other awkwardly.

'If anything it's getting worse. Catesby reports that Hastings, Stanley, Bishop Morton and the rest of them feel totally excluded from power now. They are demanding that Richard gets rid of Buckingham. But I suspect support for them is gradually beginning to erode. Did you know that Lord Howard has left Hastings and has joined Richard's party now?'

'Because he believes that Hastings is wrong not to extend the period of the protectorship?'

Ratcliffe chuckled.

'Catesby would have liked to hear you say that! No of course not, Francis. Lord Howard has ambitions to become the Duke of Norfolk; he has a claim that the late King Edward rather neatly blocked. Howard's price for his support of Gloucester is simple. He becomes Duke of Norfolk and his eldest son will be the Earl of Surrey.'

The council door was flung open and Buckingham emerged, snapping his fingers for his attendants. He nodded to me and, by the keen expression in his swarthy features, I guessed that he had a question for me. But then his eyes flicked to Ratcliffe and, changing his mind, he moved away.

Ratcliffe gestured to the council chamber.

'I imagine that Richard will want to see you first.'

CHAPTER 14

Ever since he had arrived in London, Richard had been in black. The natural assumption of any onlooker was that he wore the dark shade to mourn his brother, Edward. In reality it was part of Ratcliffe's strategy; he had argued that not only did the colour give its wearer a natural gravitas and air of authority, but its sombreness, when contrasted to the brightness of the clothes worn by many of the nobility, emphasised Richard's serious nature.

Catesby, whose tunics according to Ratcliffe were growing increasingly brighter, had naturally criticised the idea, but as I approached Richard I thought how well the colour suited him. His features were composed and he appeared calm, but I noticed that he played with the jewelled rings on his hands incessantly.

'Your message, Francis?' his voice was flat.

I reported the first two messages. He looked stern as he heard them, but then he glanced at me quickly.

'There was nothing else?'

'She said that you are to make me chief butler.'

A thin smile crossed his pale face. He was relaxed now and gestured to a large crossbow that lay on the table next to him. With curiosity, I moved over to examine it and then gave a gasp of surprise for, save its cord, the crossbow was made entirely of metal.

'It's the future,' Richard quietly advised me.

'Where did you get it? I'm not too sure about it being the weapon of the future though; it seems a bit heavy.'

'It was a present from Lord Howard. So I am to make you chief butler, Francis. Do you know what a chief butler's role is? He, among other things, has to provide service to the king at his coronation or at his coronation banquet.'

I thoroughly dislike ceremonial duties.

'I'm not really sure that I would be the best person for the job.'

'I am. Not many families can claim to have been chief butler in two different countries.'

I cursed my long-dead Norman ancestor and my own folly in mentioning the matter. Probably Richard thought that he was doing me a favour.

'So I am to be chief butler at Prince Edward's coronation?'

'Well, not exactly.'

His fingers stole back to his jewelled rings. He looked at me in silence. I looked back at him in bewilderment and then my heart sank as I finally understood.

★ ★ ★

He had the grace to hear me. In the spirit of friendship and loyalty, I had to tell him the fears that I harboured. He listened carefully as I put it to him that he was neither the lawful heir to the throne nor was he up to the task of being king. There are many times that I have to think before I speak but this was not one of them. I spoke simply and from the heart in order to persuade Richard not to do what he intended to do. He was calm, so calm indeed that by the time I finished speaking I was beginning to doubt my own argument. After I had stuttered out the last of my words, he invited me to be seated and systematically set out to refute the points I had made.

'Let me speak of the protectorate. Would you not agree that it was necessary for me to become protector in order to prevent the Woodvilles from taking over the government of England?'

'Yes I do.'

'And would you not agree that by becoming protector, civil war has been averted between Hastings' party and the Woodvilles?'

'Yes, that's true.'

'Then can you explain to me how I am to protect myself and my allies, Buckingham and Northumberland, from the vengeance of the Woodvilles in a few years' time?'

'No I can't.'

'I believe there are two possible methods. The first is practical but totally dishonourable. To save myself I could make an immediate alliance with the Woodvilles. They would probably agree to it but would want a substantial share of power immediately. This could only be achieved by taking such power from my own supporters; I would probably have to sacrifice the lives of men such as Buckingham to appease the Woodvilles. Surely you agree that to abandon men who have assisted me in order to save myself would be totally dishonourable?'

'Yes I do.'

'And even if I pursued this route, there would be no guarantee that in a few years' time the young king and his Woodville family might not seek to take belated revenge on me. Then the only other way I can look to safeguard myself and my allies is to extend the length of the protectorate, but the council has refused this. Seemingly they have little or no concern for my fate. Despite everything I have done to preserve order and uphold the rule of law, they are content to throw me to the wolves. Perhaps I am mistaken. Do you view the council's action – or lack of action – in a different light?'

'No yours is the only possible conclusion.'

'Have you considered another point which Buckingham has raised with me? In all the divisions that would arise in England in three or four years, when I step down as protector is it not possible that the Lancastrian claimant to the throne of England might take advantage of the chaos to make a bid for England's crown? Do you wish to plunge England back into the wars between Henry Tudor's Lancastrians and the divided House of York?'

'Of course not!'

'Nor am I alone in my belief that only through me becoming

king could all these dangers be avoided. The lords would support me. Buckingham would keep Wales safe, Northumberland could be relied upon in the North and Lord Howard could hold East Anglia. Of course, the northern lords would rejoice to have one of their own on England's throne and, in turn, I could help the North far more if I was king. Do you disagree with any of this?'

'No, except I mistrust Buckingham.'

'You'll find that you're wrong there, Francis,' he said with a smile. 'He was wholly supportive of my wife's idea when I went through it with him. His view was that I was merely doing my duty and had only the best interests of England at heart. He said that his role must be to ensure that I became king in order that I may fulfil my destiny.'

'Richard, can you not see that you're being used? Even if you feel it is your duty to be king, it will be too much for you.'

'But I will have helpers and advisors!' he protested quickly. 'I'll have honest men like you to tell me when I go wrong, faithful friends who will curb my faults. As well as my wife, I'll surround myself with straight-talking councillors. But Francis, I will not let your ill-founded concerns come between me and my duty!'

We stared at each other for a moment silently, then Richard smiled thinly again.

'You said that I was not the lawful heir to the throne, didn't you?'

'I did; you're not.'

'Tell me, Francis, was my brother Edward the lawful heir to the throne? Was he the eldest son of King Henry V or was he, in fact, the man who overthrew the Lancastrian King Henry VI and set himself up to rule in his place?'

'You know that he overthrew King Henry. But you know that he did so because the only way that the wars between the Houses of York and Lancaster would cease was if a strong man took over. He succeeded and your brother brought peace and stability to England.'

'So my brother was not the lawful heir to the throne?'

'No, but I suppose Edward felt it to be his duty to become king.'

'As it is mine!'

Richard was on his feet now and striding about.

'Francis, if my brother's son were to become king, there'll be civil war. England faces a disaster. This is no time to quibble on legalities – we need peace not war.'

He paced up and down quickly.

'Tell me, Francis; who is best equipped to take charge of the realm? There are but two candidates.'

He stopped and put his right hand out.

'The first is a mature man with an heir. He's a proven soldier, leader and administrator.'

He put out his left hand.

'The other is a twelve-year-old boy.'

He was right, but I hesitated. What he was doing was wrong.

'Do you imagine that my brother would wish to see all his achievements degenerate into the anarchy of civil war?' Richard demanded. 'Point to the candidate you think best able to preserve my brother's good works?'

I thought hard.

'Will you not help me to fulfil my destiny?' Richard asked sadly a moment later. 'The task that I face would frighten any man, let alone one as ill-equipped as me. You know that I have a no more faithful friend than you and that I need your help not just now, but at all times.

'Please, Francis.'

Whether Richard's proposed action was lawful, I did not know, but what I was certain of was that it was best for England. Besides, I was Richard's friend and he needed my help.

★ ★ ★

'The problem is, of course, that even if you and I agreed that Richard needs to be king for the good of the nation, it is going to be virtually impossible to persuade anyone else,' said Ratcliffe. 'King Edward was well loved, particularly here in London, and everyone would have expected his son to inherit the throne.'

I looked round the gloomy chamber in Crosby Place. The early June sunlight should have brightened it, but instead all it did was cast shadows.

'We could just have told everyone the truth,' I suggested.

'No one would have believed us. As soon as word got out that Richard was planning to become king, everyone would have said that he was exaggerating the situation to suit his own purposes. The Woodvilles are hated, Francis, but – as his father's son – the young prince is popular.'

'But Richard said that the nobles would support him?'

'Some would have – Northumberland, Buckingham and Norfolk, for example. He can probably rely on his brother-in-law, the Duke of Suffolk, but many of the others will stay neutral. Others, Stanley and Hastings included, would oppose him. No, to make Richard's ascent to the throne credible we need a convincing story as to why the young prince should not rule – a story that everyone will believe.'

He got up and paced round the room impatiently.

'How do you think Catesby is getting on with that damned cleric? Do you think the pair of them can come up with something convincing?'

'Possibly.'

We relaxed into companionable silence. It was curious how quickly Catesby had risen in Ratcliffe's service, I reflected. Mind you he had proved valuable in passing on information. Come to think of it, he was also harming Lords Hastings and Stanley by totally misleading them as to Richard of Gloucester's true intentions. But then it was not only his role as a spy which made Catesby so useful. It was his level of intelligence, which, Ratcliffe admitted sourly, easily exceeded his own and his sense of humour did tend to enliven weighty discussions.

I smiled as I recalled the occasion when Ratcliffe and I had discreetly advised him as to the reasons why the throne should pass to Gloucester rather than his nephew, the young Prince Edward. Catesby had listened to us with a face totally devoid of emotion and had pursed his lips.

'In acknowledging the undoubted truth of all that you have just told me, Sir Richard, there is perhaps only one tiny observation I can make,' he said primly.

'What's that?' snapped Ratcliffe.

'It would naturally be necessary to think of a more – shall we say – convincing reason for our high-flying duke to be elevated still further,' Catesby explained. 'While undoubtedly his motives and those of all who serve him would be applauded by the very angels themselves, mere mortals might perhaps struggle to comprehend them.'

'They would?'

'Certainly, my lord. And in their natural stupidity and brute stubbornness, it is conceivable that men might believe that he was taking the crown to serve his own purposes.'

'I agree with you.' Ratcliffe sounded grim. 'I worked it out a few hours after I was sounded out.'

'It took you so long, Sir Richard? Surely not?'

Catesby's amazement was plain to see, but then he smiled knowingly.

'Ah, but I see it now. You are exaggerating the time it took you, in order to make the rest of us feel less stupid.'

Timidly, he plucked at my sleeve.

'Is not Master Ratcliffe good to us, my lord?'

I bit my lip, but made no reply, so Catesby turned back to Ratcliffe.

'Will you not favour us by narrating the feasible fable which indubitably you will have fabricated by now, Sir Richard? The story of why Gloucester should become king.'

Ratcliffe scowled and rubbed his hands together angrily.

'Come, come, Sir Richard,' Catesby pleaded. 'There is no need to be shy.'

He glanced at me, his green eyes glinting with excitement.

'This will be a tale of the highest creative order, my lord.'

'It will?'

'Of course, my lord! It is widely known that our clever Sir Richard has a unique talent for conceiving complete untruths and conveying them so clearly and concisely that they come across with compelling conviction. A simple task such as this will have been meat and drink to…'

Ratcliffe slammed his hand on the table.

'You think of something!' he snarled. 'I haven't been able to.'

Catesby's green eyes twinkled with amusement.

'As you command, Sir Richard.'

★ ★ ★

But despite the seeming difficulty of the task, it was only the next day that Catesby sent word that he might have a solution. A time was agreed and he re-entered the chamber – a vision in white and blue – an excited smile lighting up his chubby features.

He explained that he had reflected on the matter and had instantly discovered one obvious problem. However credible the story, no one would possibly believe any tale put out by Richard of Gloucester or anyone close to him. Any such story would be perceived as an invention to allow Gloucester to secure the throne for his own selfish ends.

'Then we'll just tell the real reason why Richard of Gloucester should be king.'

'Such decisiveness, my lord,' beamed Catesby. 'But while I totally deplore the cynicism of this modern age, I regret that to the sceptical listener the truth might well be considered not wholly credible.'

'So what do we do?' demanded Ratcliffe in frustration.

Catesby regarded him with mock surprise.

'I fear you are teasing me, my dear Sir Richard. Surely, to a man of your intelligence, the answer is simple. Why a child could guess at it.'

A dangerous pause followed; with a bright laugh Catesby hurried on.

'The correct course of action would be to find a natural figure of authority – a man who believed that he had been cruelly used by the late King Edward and would be prepared to narrate a convincing story as to why his sons should not be able to inherit the throne.'

'You know of someone?'

'Certainly, my lord. There are any number of worthy men who would be prepared to fulfil such a patriotic duty. But the one I would favour would be Robert Stillington.'

'Who's he?'

'The Bishop of Bath and Wells, my lord, and a former chancellor of the late King Edward.'

'And he was ill-treated by the late king?'

'Shamefully so, my lord. It would appear that the unfairness of his treatment still rankles deeply with him. He was dismissed as chancellor for financial ineptitude. How ludicrous a decision when it is well known that our saintly bishop is so highly skilled in financial affairs that he has amassed a vast personal fortune.'

'Scandalous treatment!' agreed Ratcliffe with a twinkle in his eye. 'But was there not some story of him being an ally of Edward's brother Clarence at the time when Clarence was plotting against his brother and talking wildly against him?'

'His role was ill-defined and doubtless exaggerated, yet incredibly it brought him still further punishment. He was even accused of breaking his oath of allegiance to King Edward.' Catesby shook his head sadly. 'As if the poor man hadn't suffered enough and then, of course, he had his poor children to care for.'

'His children!'

A worried look came over Catesby's face.

'Both the Pope and the king had already reproved him about his six or seven illegitimate children, my lord. It would cause our celibate cleric considerable distress were you to allude to the matter.'

'Six or seven!'

'I think I have that right,' Catesby said anxiously. 'Let me see now, there's Juliana, John…'

'All right, all right. Are there any other negative points about Stillington?'

'Well apparently he studied law, like Catesby here,' Ratcliffe snorted. 'But maybe he can help us.'

'Do you want me to go and talk to him?' Catesby, seemingly unruffled, enquired politely. 'He lives in the Parish of St Clements.'

'What's the price for our dubious bishop?' Ratcliffe asked.

'For himself, I imagine a chance to obtain a position in government but I believe that he may well ask for something for his… um… nephew.'

'His nephew?'

'I understand our hard-done-to bishop learned the phrase while he was suffering during his visit to the Vatican, my lord. Apparently it is widely used there. Be that as it may, I do know that our family-minded bishop is particularly keen to advance John Nesfeld, his nephew.'

I hesitated. Stillingon hardly sounded the most appealing of men, but neither Ratcliffe nor I had an alternative so I gestured for Catesby to leave.

★ ★ ★

Catesby's scarlet satin robe introduced a welcome splash of colour to the gloomy chamber where Ratcliffe and I waited.

'So what did Stillington say?' Ratcliffe demanded. 'How did he react?'

Without being invited, Catesby seated himself and reached for the wine.

'Very well, I believe, Richard.' He turned to me. 'Would you like to hear what he said, Francis?'

We both stared at the chubby Catesby who gazed back at us with an expression of complete innocence. The challenge, though unspoken, was obvious. Catesby regarded himself as our equal now. Out of sheer habit, Ratcliffe and I glanced at each other. Catesby's lips twitched when he saw the conspiratorial look but he maintained his silence. We needed him and he knew it.

'Go on,' I told him. 'What did you and Stillington come up with?'

★ ★ ★

'Sweet Christ!' exclaimed Anne Neville. 'With all the resources that the Duke of Gloucester has placed at your disposal, all you can come up with is this unconvincing nonsense. The ravings of a madman, Master Ratcliffe, would be more plausible than your tale.'

'How so?' her husband asked. 'The way it was explained to me by Francis seems reasonably convincing.'

'I find that incredible!' Anne Neville interjected icily.

'It seems that I may take the throne because the two sons of King Edward are bastards. Why are they bastards? Because prior to marrying Elizabeth Woodville, my brother Edward undertook a plight-trothing ceremony[21] with one Lady Eleanor Butler. Now Lady Eleanor was still alive at the time of Edward's wedding, so it follows that Edward's marriage was illegal.'

'Bishop Stillington is prepared to swear that he officiated at the plight-trothing ceremony,' Ratcliffe added hurriedly.

Anne Neville's sharp intake of breath was clearly audible.

'And where is the elusive Lady Eleanor now?'

'She died about fifteen years ago, my lady.'

'How convenient! But doubtless there were children to console the king for his loss?'

'There were none, my lady.'

Anne Neville regarded Ratcliffe coolly.

'My brother-in-law was not generally renowned for being an advocate of purely platonic love, so permit me to say that I find the lack of issue both surprising and highly convenient. But tell me, Sir Richard, a ceremony involving the king would need to be witnessed, would it not?'

'Well Bishop Stillington officiated…'

'Who else was present, you idiot?'

'Well, we could pay a few people to swear they were there.'

Richard, Ratcliffe and I sat silently as Anne Neville digested this.

'Hitherto I have frequently wondered which of your blunders was the greatest, but now I know for certain! What you and Lovell are proposing is nothing short of total insanity.'

'It can't be disproved!'

In his anger, Ratcliffe forgot to use Lady Anne's title.

'Disproved! You're expecting people to believe that a dubiously witnessed, secretive commitment to marriage that happened twenty years ago and has never been mentioned before will be sufficient grounds to bar the sons of King Edward from the throne?' Anne Neville's voice was shrill with incredulity now. 'Do you honestly believe that all men are at your level of stupidity?'

A phrase used by Catesby sprung to mind.

'But King Edward's marriage to Elizabeth Woodville was bigamous, my lady. Therefore their children must be bastards.'

'If the plight-trothing actually took place, then you are correct about the marriage.'

'Thank you, my lady.'

Reassured, I smiled at Ratcliffe.

'But it doesn't follow that the children are bastards. After all, what was to stop King Edward and Elizabeth Woodville marrying again immediately after Lady Eleanor died? That would have made the, as yet unborn princes, legitimate.'

'But you still can't disprove this story about the princes' bastardry,' Richard turned to his wife.

'Of course I can, my lord!' Anne snapped. 'Not only can I, but so too can Lord Hastings. If there had been this ridiculous plight-trothing ceremony, do you not think that Edward's best friend and fellow lecher would have known about it? Think about it, my lord. If Hastings knew that Queen Elizabeth's children were bastards, he would have used that information against the Woodvilles when they were striving against each other after the death of King Edward.'

Anne Neville paused for a moment.

'That said, we can deal with Hastings.'

'But how do you know the tale to be false?' her husband persisted.

Anne shook her head irritably.

'Eleanor Butler was my mother's niece. When my father, the Earl of Warwick, rose in rightful rebellion against King Edward in 1469, he was rebelling against the king and the Woodvilles, whom he loathed.

'Do you not think that if he had known that King Edward's marriage was unlawful, he would not have used the information at that time?'

Ratcliffe glanced at her in desperation.

'Is it possible that your father was too chivalrous to do so, my lady?' he asked hopefully. 'I have heard much of his natural courtesy and sensitivity…'

'He was in rebellion at the time!' Anne Neville replied crushingly. 'Sweet Christ, he went on to kill two of the Woodvilles.'

She glared at Ratcliffe.

'Cannot you understand, you imbecile, that the simple reason my father failed to use what would have been a devastating piece of information is that it never happened.'

'But not everyone has your insight!' her husband objected. 'And it is possible that Eleanor Butler forgot to mention the matter to her uncle…'

'Forgot!' Anne Neville whirled round to face Richard. 'Are you seriously suggesting, my lord, that even if the apparently empty-headed Lady Eleanor had not mentioned the matter, other members of her family would not have seen fit to draw the issue to my father's attention?'

Richard made no reply so I tried to rescue him.

'My lord made an excellent point when he observed that not everyone would have your depth of knowledge on the matter.'

'Go on, Francis.'

Anne Neville's tone was slightly less frosty now.

'And it is unfortunate that, apparently, King Edward instructed Bishop Stillington not to discuss the subject during his lifetime.'

'Convenient, I would have said.'

'But the fact is he's a bishop.'

'A man of God,' Ratcliffe eagerly broke in.

'And has been for some time.'

'A truly holy man,' Ratcliffe added quickly.

'But the point is that he's prepared to swear that the story is true. Now I accept that the tale is a little weak at times, but given that it is the end result that matters and not the means which we use...'

A sudden smile from Anne Neville interrupted my narrative, so I paused for a moment.

'Go on, Francis, you're beginning to make sense,' she encouraged me.

I drew a deep breath.

'Well, under the circumstances, is it possible that you are being a little over-critical, my lady?'

The three of us looked at her apprehensively as she absorbed the criticism, but a moment later she smiled and raised her hands.

'That was bravely said, Francis, and I agree with you, but if we are to push on with this ridiculous tale of yours we must hurry.'

'Why is that?' Richard asked.

'Because, in the circumstances, my lord, I would imagine that Bishop Stillington's recollections will probably need to be referred to the ecclesiastical courts before your own claim to the throne can be entertained – and that is an issue best avoided. Also, of course,

Clarence's son probably has a better claim to the throne and we don't want people dwelling on that now, do we?'

Anne Neville turned briskly to Ratcliffe and me.

'We'll keep your plan but we need to think of other convincing reasons why the sons of King Edward cannot rule. In fact, the more reasons we have the better. Now, Sir Richard, spare no one's feelings and slander whomever you need to, regardless of rank, family or reputation. Better still, get the rainbow-coloured Catesby working on it while you step up your rumour-mongering to denigrate the Woodvilles still further. Is that clear? Good.'

She turned to her husband.

'Now my lord, there are other matters which require your instant attention. Might I suggest some appropriate stratagems?'

Once more, it seemed appropriate to withdraw.

★ ★ ★

With Anne Neville's arrival in London, Ratcliffe's campaign intensified. Rumours abounded about the evil-doings of the Woodvilles. It was already common knowledge by now that the queen and her family had attempted to seize the government of England. As a result, they now skulked guiltily in sanctuary. Until now though, no one had known that they had looted the treasury after King Edward's death. Nor was it fully appreciated how many of the late king's mistakes were caused by the folly of the Woodvilles and how, indeed, his brother Clarence's death could be wholly attributed to their vindictiveness. Yet still they had their supporters. Stillington's nephew was given the task of ensuring that they could neither escape from sanctuary nor be rescued. Within days, John Nesfeld had Westminster sanctuary blockaded by land and river.

With the Woodvilles effectively neutralised, Catesby was given the task of attempting to win over both Hastings and Lord Stanley to the idea that Richard should be king in place of his brother's eldest son. But even he had no success, neither Stanley nor Hastings would support Richard.

'I believe that they would oppose our peaceful Duke of Gloucester with their lives if need be,' an indignant Catesby told me. 'Of course they could probably muster 10,000 men if they had to. But is it not incredible that, given the danger facing England at this moment, they could both be so selfish?'

He wrung his hands in frustration.

'I used to view my Lord Hastings as an honourable man who served his master and his country. But now, Francis, I see the truth – clearly he is a self-seeking man, concerned only with holding onto power, caring nothing for anyone except himself. Why, there is talk that he will even ally with the Woodvilles!'

He chewed his lip in worry.

'I know my Lord Hastings; even now he'll be plotting against Gloucester and looking to strike against him. Tell him to have a care, my lord.'

I reported his concern to Richard and his wife. Richard was clearly disappointed, but Anne Neville merely shrugged.

'Then we have no need to dissemble further,' she remarked briskly.

'Why is that?' Richard asked.

'Currently the Woodvilles are weakened, my lord,' Anne Neville observed quietly. 'But it would be best to finish them off as a threat once and for all. Send Ratcliffe to the North; he should dispatch Earl Rivers and the queen's younger son, Thomas Grey. Let him also speak privately with Northumberland so that he can bring his troops south to overawe the Londoners. Now, Francis.'

'My lady?'

'To date all attempts to persuade Elizabeth Woodville to release King Edward's second son from sanctuary have been unsuccessful. It would appear that our flamboyant Duke of Buckingham is less persuasive than he imagines. Yet, for as long as that child remains outside our protection, he may serve as a figurehead for those who oppose my husband as England's rightful sovereign. Go and see Thomas Bourchier.'

'The Archbishop of Canterbury?'

'Of course, Francis. He should see Elizabeth Woodville without delay. Tell him to make the following points. Firstly, the boy is required for his brother's coronation. Secondly, King Edward's son is a child; he should not be in sanctuary since, being young, he cannot have committed a crime. As such, he can be forcibly removed from sanctuary without an offence being committed and undoubtedly he will be. Finally, tell Bourchier to offer his personal guarantees for the boy's safety.'

'Yes, my lady.'

'Thank you, Francis. Now with the Woodvilles finished and both young princes held safely, it will be time to deal with the final threat of Lord Hastings and his allies. It is essential that they are dealt with before they incite trouble and civil war. Indeed, as my Uncle Montague was known frequently to observe, it is far better for one man to suffer than many. So we'll strike at Hastings first, before he can land his own blow.'

★ ★ ★

I was not with the Earl of Surrey[22] when, in friendly fashion, he called at the house of Lord Hastings that Friday to suggest that they walked to the council meeting together. But when Surrey entered the small room in the White Tower, where I was waiting with my men-at-arms, one look at his face told me that he had been successful.

'Hastings didn't suspect a thing,' he chuckled softly. 'It was probably unnecessary to ensure that he actually came today...'

'Well, he has no reason to be suspicious,' I pointed out. 'The council is only continuing the routine business they began yesterday, and Gloucester's manner has given nothing away.'

'I suppose so.' Surrey began to arm himself. 'So what's the plan?'

232

'Gloucester's men will summon us. You make sure that Lord Stanley is secured. Pilkington here will get Bishop Morton and I'll make sure of Hastings.'

We relapsed into nervous silence, but, a short while later, I heard footsteps and glanced at Surrey.

'Ready?'

As quietly as it is possible in half armour, we followed Richard's man along the corridor. About twenty paces from the open door, I gestured to our men to wait. Carefully I listened until I heard Richard's ringing accusation that Hastings was a traitor.

I gestured to Surrey and we rushed into the room. I snatched a blurred glimpse of a group of elderly men, some seated in frozen immobility, others rising to protest at our intrusion. Frantically, I searched out Hastings, who was to be found seated next to Stanley. There was frantic confusion as scrolls were thrown about and chairs overturned. Shouts of fear and cries of surprise filled the room, but we grabbed Hastings and bustled him from the room.

A short while later, the men-at-arms brought out a white-faced Bishop Morton and a bleeding Lord Stanley. I signalled for the guards to seal off the council, as a stern-faced Richard glanced at my captive.

'Tower Green!' he snapped. 'Confine the other two.'

A short while later, Catesby and I stood on the lush grass overlooking the Tower of London, while at our feet Hasting's decapitated body twitched spasmodically.

'Such a speedy solution to our problem,' Catesby observed coolly.

Clearly the sudden demise of his former master had caused him little concern.

'But how do we explain Hastings' death to the Londoners?' I asked him with concern. 'He was popular among them.'

'Fear not, Francis!' Catesby's heavily padded shoulders shook with merriment. 'He was plotting with the Woodvilles, of course. I've already drafted out a story for the herald to tell the people.

Why it's so convincing you would have thought it one of Ratcliffe's fables! And my Lords of Gloucester and Buckingham will give suitable reassurances to the leading citizens that Hastings was planning to overthrow the government.' His green eyes glittered feverishly as he looked at me. 'There's nothing to stop us now, is there? Both the Woodvilles and Hastings are destroyed.'

I stirred uneasily. He was correct, of course; Richard could take the throne now and save England from descending into anarchy. Something didn't feel quite right though. Surely Catesby should show some remorse for the death of his former master?

Almost unbidden, an extremely nasty thought came to me; was it possible that Catesby had engineered the death of Lord Hastings to advance himself in the new regime? Certainly, by detecting Hasting's plot Catesby had made Richard's future more secure, but he had also done himself a lot of good in doing so. Come to think about it, how real had Hastings' plot actually been? I thought back. Hastings had told Catesby that he would not support Richard, but then not supporting was not exactly the same as threatening to oppose him by force. Then again, we only had Catesby's own report on the vehemence of Lord Hastings' refusal to back Gloucester. No one else had actually overheard or witnessed it. But then none of us knew Hastings as Catesby did.

On the other hand, I was hardly in a position to prove that Hastings had not been plotting. Indeed, his unswerving support for King Edward's son, combined with a desire to remain in power, made it entirely logical that he would have rebelled. If you took that point of view, then not only was Catesby's story entirely consistent, but he had done Richard a considerable service in identifying Hastings' plot so early. In all probability Catesby had been embarrassed by the scheming of his former master, I decided, and doubtless he sought to conceal his grief at his death by feigning indifference. He needed my help not my suspicion.

'It is just possible that some of Lord Hastings' former supporters might wish to take revenge on you,' I said awkwardly. 'It would be best for you to acquire some protection.'

Catesby nodded sadly.

'It pains me that men might wish to do me harm for merely doing my duty. But I too am a realist, my lord.'

He gave a piercing whistle and two men stepped out of the shadows of the walls of the Tower. The older was short and white-haired but broad. The metal bands on his arms glittered as he hefted his double-handed axe.

'Here is Bracher, and this is his son, also called William,' Catesby explained proudly. 'It's really very surprising that even with a squint he's so quick in combat. The scar on his mouth is amusing too, isn't it? It makes him appear as if he's always smiling.'

The two Brachers scowled at me malevolently.

Catesby smirked as he saw my look of revulsion.

'Every cat should have his own dogs,' he whispered as he tapped the spotted cat badge, which he always wore on his tunic. 'I do hope that you like mine.'

★ ★ ★

'Filthy wine this!' Broughton observed. 'But I'll try some more.'

I grinned at him. I hadn't realised how much I had missed him. Indeed, come to think of it, I hadn't seen him since before the Berwick campaign. I pushed the wine flagon in his direction as he gazed round the tavern in disgust.

'It's not much better in London,' I told him.

Northumberland's army was camped outside the walls, and entry to the city was forbidden to the soldiers.

'So what happened after Hastings' death?' he asked.

Broughton was totally trustworthy so I told him everything. He listened carefully and then groomed his wild beard with his finger.

'So Richard of Gloucester becomes king because his nephews are bastards. But, on top of that, Dr Shaa and Friar Penketh are saying that his brother, King Edward, was illegitimate as his mother had an affair with an English archer.'

'You haven't been listening, Thomas! They didn't say that; Buckingham primed the other preachers to say that.'

'The others!'

'Mm... I'm not sure that they didn't put in the bit about the Woodvilles using witchcraft to ensnare Edward into marriage too. Anyway, the Duke of Buckingham addressed the lords and gentry at the Guildhall and told them how far the country had deteriorated under King Edward and, with the threat of civil war, they should accept Richard as king.'

'Were they enthusiastic?' he wanted to know.

'Not particularly,' I replied truthfully, 'but they saw the sense of it.'

Then I remembered something else.

'Even Lord Stanley has accepted the situation; he's carrying the Lord High Constable's mace at the coronation procession.'

I smiled at Broughton across the table. To be truthful, it was a relief to have Richard's coronation organised, and to be able to look forward to an era of peace and tranquillity for England.

'It's all settled now, Thomas.'

But Broughton frowned at me.

'Maybe you're right, Francis, but I'm not so sure. I can understand why Richard needs to be king, but I rather wonder if everyone else will.'

I put his statements down to the wine.

'If the aim is correct, Thomas, do the methods really matter?'

Thomas put his mug down with exaggerated care and looked at me owlishly.

'Francis, it might be the best thing for England if Richard of Gloucester takes the throne, but it doesn't seem right.'

'Why not?'

'Kings inherit the throne from their fathers; that's the way of things and always will be. But this business of tales of bastardy and witchcraft doesn't seem natural. It just seems...'

He tugged at his straggly beard in frustration as he sought out the right word. At last, he lowered his hand and looked me straight in the eyes.

'It's like theft, Francis; it looks like Richard is stealing his nephew's throne.'

CHAPTER 15

Oddly enough, Broughton's comment seemed to sum up the mood of the whole of London at that time. Despite the glittering splendour of Richard's coronation, there was a curious air of sombreness in the city.

'You're starting at shadows!' Ratcliffe snorted angrily when I raised the matter. 'There's nothing to fear. People need time to accept the change, that's all.'

He must have seen my dubious expression.

'Listen, Francis, people are bound to be a bit bewildered. They were used to King Edward and his ways – it's only natural considering he ruled for twenty years or so. But, within a mere three months after his death, his wife's family have been disgraced and his children declared bastards. It's hardly surprising that men feel slightly disorientated. Give it a few months and everyone will accept the change.'

'You sound pretty certain.'

'Of course I am. In six months' time, no one will remember any king other than Richard.'

'The people seem resentful.'

'Sweet Christ, Francis! What does it matter if the people are a little unhappy? We're the ones with the power. We can count on all the major lords to support Richard – Buckingham, Norfolk, Suffolk, Northumberland. Of course Stanley's backing Richard now, as is everyone in the North.'

'Mm… I suppose you're right.'

'Of course I am. Now look on the positive side; Anne Neville has an ingenious idea of taking the king out of London and showing the new monarch to his people. The way I've planned it for her is that the royal progress will be so magnificent that folk will speak of it for years to come. Of course, in the early stages Anne Neville will remain here so as not to take any of the focus away from Richard, but she'll join him at Warwick and then they'll journey triumphantly up to York together.'

The vision of Richard and Anne's magnificent tour cheered him immensely, as he leapt to his feet and grinned at me.

'We're in the ascendancy now, Francis! Put away your fears of sulky southerners and imaginary enemies, and start enjoying the fruits of victory.'

★ ★ ★

I was temporarily reassured, but this feeling was put to an end when I found myself alone with Catesby. I remember seeking him out in the castle at Windsor just before we left to commence the royal progress.

He listened attentively to my proposed plan for Richard's personal security on the progress and made a couple of useful suggestions, since he was familiar with the country in the West of England and I was not. I thanked him for he was clearly extremely busy. The large number of scrolls on the table of his chamber indicated as much. But, to my surprise, as I rose to leave him he asked me to remain.

'I understand that Master Ratcliffe believes it unnecessary to watch the situation in the South while we accompany the king on his royal progress,' he said softly.

'Correct.'

He pursed his lips.

'A mistake, I would have said, Francis. The Woodvilles still have some support, as do the young princes. It would be prudent to take precautions.'

I thanked God for his loyalty and his foresight.

'I agree with you.'

We spoke of arrangements which would be required to monitor events while we were away. A great deal of work was required and I wondered in exhaustion whether we would not be better off abandoning the royal progress altogether. But Catesby was quick to point out that this would be construed by all as a sign of weakness.

'I suppose you're right,' I told him.

'But, even if I wasn't, the tour should still proceed.'

Catesby's eyes glittered excitedly and I sensed that his mood was changing. Clearly, the serious work had been dealt with, and now he was ready to play.

'After all, we must naturally consider Master Ratcliffe's feelings. Richard Ratcliffe is not only a friend and colleague, but, like all of us, he is one of God's children.'

He shook his head solemnly.

'How cruel it would be for poor Ratcliffe to return to his Heavenly Father prematurely! Believe me, Francis, the cancellation of the royal tour would be a death blow to the man.'

'It would? I accept he's put a fair amount into it.'

'It's his masterpiece!' exclaimed Catesby. 'Hitherto I had no inkling that behind those homely features and the humble trappings of a dear friend and colleague lay the mind of a genius.'

Catesby looked at me mistily.

'Believe me, Francis, the plan that he has created is of such scope and magnitude that it is almost of a divine nature.'

'You believe Ratcliffe to be divine?'

'Well I'm not suggesting that the infant Ratcliffe was actually born in a stable.' Catesby chuckled cheerfully. 'Although I grant you that, judging by the odour that clings so resolutely to his person, it is not wholly inconceivable that he spent many of his formative years in one. But, my lord, believe me when I say that it is hardly credible to think that a child born of human parents could have created such a plan.'

I thought for a moment. Presumably Ratcliffe was making the

royal tour as magnificent as he possibly could in order to advance himself still further. Certainly his strategy was sound provided the tour was successful. On the other hand, by so clearly identifying himself as its creator, he would receive the blame were something to go wrong.

I glanced at Catesby, who was now smirking at some secret joke.

'I hope you haven't encouraged Ratcliffe to make the tour too complicated,' I said suspiciously.

'Me?' Catesby was a picture of wide-eyed innocence. 'But why on earth would I wish to do anything to harm my good friend, the talented Master Ratcliffe?'

I must have looked dubious for he assumed a hurt expression. 'It really is too bad of you to think like this, Francis.' He pouted. 'Instead of contemplating such evil thoughts, you should be attending to the arrangements of how we will proceed to the first major point of the tour, Oxford University.'

★ ★ ★

I shifted uncomfortably on my seat, earning yet another disapproving glance from the rotund Bishop Dudley, who had been placed next to King Richard. Presumably Ratcliffe had put him there so that he could amplify the points made, but by this time I suspected that even Richard's interest in the proceedings had lessened.

I looked round the great hall of Magdalen College where, after three hours, the first of Ratcliffe's Great Debates was approaching the halfway stage. The young Oxford scholars were quietly awed by the presence of the king and his nobles, but I sensed that they were only pretending to pay heed to the sonorous tones of their Professor of Sacred Theology as he argued pedantically with his famous opponent, the eminently learned, albeit sharply spoken, Master William Grocin.

Thoroughly bored by now, I glanced up. The small windows

high up on the walls made the hall dark and oppressive. The high ceiling should have helped cool the room, but instead it seemed that the natural warmth of the summer, combined with the sheer numbers present, had turned the place into a furnace.

I looked at the wine and water which had been put on a small table next to Richard enviously, and licked my dry lips. Beside me, Lord Stanley stirred restlessly on our hard wooden bench.

'Tell me, Francis,' he murmured, 'have you any idea of what is to happen after this somewhat exhaustive examination of the various elements of moral philosophy?'

'Ratcliffe's second Great Debate.' I swallowed uneasily. 'Apparently it's even longer.'

'The thought of which almost makes me wish that I was back at Berwick,' he said wearily. 'Why does Master Ratcliffe insist on debates of such length?'

'Catesby told him that the longer the debate, the more scholarship you exhibit. So Ratcliffe was most insistent with the university about it; he even threatened to divert the royal tour to Cambridge.'

'Well, I suppose he'll succeed in his wish to make these debates unforgettable,' Lord Stanley observed dryly.

I was relieved when, finally, a hoarse Master Grocin stepped back from the podium. Both speakers bowed stiffly to the king and then to the chancellor of the university, Lionel Woodville.

Eagerly I made my way out to join the others in the warm sunshine. Beside us the river looked both cool and inviting, and it occurred to me that Minster Lovell must only be a few miles upstream. Nervously, I ran though the arrangements for Richard's reception there. Admittedly he was only going to be in my house for a day or so but, with Nan in the North, I was wholly reliant on the steward, Tawboys.

'Lord Stanley seems popular, doesn't he?' Broughton's cheerful tones broke into my thoughts.

He pointed to where a small crowd of scholars were clustered round my neighbour in the hall. Even as I watched, I saw Catesby approach him grinning; he was introducing yet another group of young people to Lord Stanley. That was kind of Catesby; the young scholars would never have dared approach him by themselves.

'I wonder why they all want to meet him.' Broughton muttered.

'I expect they want to ask him about his famous bears.'

'He keeps bears?' Broughton was amazed.

'Quite a collection apparently. He brought one up to Berwick while we were there to amuse his men. Big thing it was too; it needed four keepers.'

The sudden appearance of the tall chancellor of the university caused the young scholars to break off their questioning of Lord Stanley. Reluctantly, Broughton and I followed them back towards the hall.

Broughton pointed at the chancellor.

'I understand that his divinity lecture concludes the proceedings here?'

'I imagine that he'll say a few words of farewell to conclude the visit, but that will come after the divinity lecture. Ratcliffe felt it was essential that the visit concluded well, so he was adamant that the chancellor himself should speak so that this stage of the tour would conclude with appropriate gravitas.'

Broughton glanced at Lionel Woodville's retiring figure.

'I hope someone's told him which subjects he should avoid?'

'They have.'

Ratcliffe had been concerned that Lionel Woodville would use the opportunity of a public speech to play the martyr. After all, his brother, Earl Rivers, and his nephew had both been recently executed at the king's command. Currently, two of his other nephews – the sons of King Edward – were incarcerated in the Tower, while his sister and his nieces were in sanctuary. Conscious of this and the fact that there might be an element of personal animosity – since Ratcliffe himself had overseen the execution of Earl Rivers – Ratcliffe sought to obviate danger. And he had been wholly successful. It was true that the university chancellor was not pleased to hear talk of violent reprisals against the surviving members of his family, if anything untoward was said, but he was a man of sense. After due reflection, he promised not to instigate anything that could be construed as being derogatory to the king or, indeed, detrimental to the career of Sir Richard Ratcliffe.

'Nothing can go wrong,' I told Broughton as we re-entered the hall.

★ ★ ★

'It could have been worse.'

I tried to reassure Ratcliffe as we rode together towards Woodstock a day or so later.

He jerked his head round to look at me incredulously.

'How?' he bellowed. 'Just tell me how it could have been worse?'

'It's just an expression.'

Ratcliffe waved away my consolation and swung round to spit in the direction of the city of Oxford.

'It was a disaster and you know it. I bring the king to Oxford to establish him as an example of learning and scholarship. I go out of my way to present him as a paragon of generosity...'

'But Catesby's idea was brilliant! It was clever of him to suggest that you make the offer to Magdalen College on behalf of the king.'

'Of course it was a good idea!' Ratcliffe exploded. 'It was a perfect way to present Richard as a patron of scholarship. Sweet Jesus, with the king's gift those fools could have had anything they wanted – lands or money or endowments even.'

'Don't torture yourself.'

'And what do those idiots do? Anyone else would have just taken the money but not our university men. Oh no, what they want is to humiliate the king and make me look ridiculous.' Ratcliffe thumped the pommel on his saddle furiously. 'I can't bring myself to think about it.'

I shared his pain, as I cast my mind back to the college hall crowded with fellows and scholars who had gathered together to hear their chancellor's valedictory address to their king and his party. The speech had been both formal and brief and, much to the relief of our group, nothing was said which could be considered even slightly contentious. Indeed, as the speech progressed Ratcliffe had become more relaxed. But his ease was premature.

The king's offer to the college of any gift they desired had been relayed to Magdalen College and the fellows and scholars had debated among themselves as to what form the present should take. Having decided on a suitable gift, they had requested for the chancellor to convey their response to the king, which, the chancellor announced, he was pleased to do so now.

'I must admit to be surprised at their choice of gift,' Lionel Woodville continued candidly. 'But since Your Grace had made the offer to the college directly, it would have been inconceivable to have sought to influence their thinking and so regretfully I was powerless to intervene.'

'As regards the college's choice of gift, Your Grace, it would appear that my Lord Stanley's celebrated collection of bears has been the main subject of conversation in the college ever since your royal party arrived at the university.'

A tolerant smile lit up his austere features as he leant forward to address the king.

'By all accounts, Your Grace, since you have arrived at the college, all the fellows and scholars have talked about is these great beasts and, accordingly, Magdalen College humbly requests Your Grace to ask Lord Stanley to send some of his bears, together with their keepers, of course, to Oxford for a visit.'

A roar of spontaneous applause greeted the chancellor's request, which swelled as Lord Stanley rose with a smile to his feet. He raised a hand and the clamour ceased in expectation.

'I shall be pleased to arrange such a visit,' he announced.

Lionel Woodville allowed the rowdy cheering to continue for a couple of minutes before signalling for silence. He glanced at the stony-faced king.

'I would like to apologise for the seemingly frivolous nature of the college's choice of gift and provide a possible explanation for the choice,' he begged.

Taking an abrupt nod as a sign of permission, Lionel Woodville adopted a reflective stance.

'I have noted with pleasure that a number of visits have been made to the university of late, and I am extremely gratified, as such visits by distinguished personages have added further lustre to this great seat of learning.' A puzzled look came across his face. 'But while I assumed that mine was a viewpoint widely shared, I was distraught to discover that there is indeed a school of thought that runs contrary to my own.'

Lionel Woodville leant forward confidentially.

'It appears, Your Grace, that, if the rumours are true, such visits afford little satisfaction to Oxford. There have been complaints about the tedium of the proceedings of a recent visit.

'Indeed, unkind and malicious persons have been heard to remark that such visits were self-indulgent. Upon enquiring after the reason for these absurd statements, I was amazed to discover that this view originates from the erroneous belief that the only purpose of such visits is to attempt to promote the visitors as men of wisdom and patrons of scholarship.'

He gave a dry chuckle to demonstrate his contempt at such stupidity.

'Now clearly, Your Grace, these views are held by only a minority in the university, and you may be confident that the propagators of such evil gossip will be severely punished.' Lionel Woodville spread his arms apologetically, 'But it is just possible that this wrongheaded thinking has instigated a request for a visit by creatures, who naturally have no pretension to scholarship.'

Lionel Woodville bowed graciously to the thin-lipped king.

'I must, as chancellor, apologise for any offence that my words may have caused, but, painful though it is for me, my position demands that I give an account of the thinking behind the unusual nature of the choice of gift.' [23]

★ ★ ★

I turned to Ratcliffe who was still hunched in a state of misery.

'It will blow over,' I said to try to reassure him.

He looked at me dully.

'The whole visit was planned so that the university could be impressed by the king. Can you honestly say that they were?'

'It was certainly unforgettable.'

'For all the wrong reasons!' howled Ratcliffe. 'I tell you, Francis, I'm finished. They told him that they would rather have a visit from a load of bears than the king.'

We rode on unhappily for a while. After a while, he tugged savagely at his reins, and I moved over to hear his bitter words.

'I wouldn't have minded quite so much if I had been brought down by a rival,' he moaned, 'even if it had been that fat fool Catesby. But to have everyone laughing at me because my career has been ended by a bunch of bloody bears – it's just too much!'

I chose not to reply; I suddenly recalled the uncharacteristic pains Catesby took in troubling himself to introduce the shy scholars to Lord Stanley. I remembered that it had been Catesby who had suggested the idea of the king's gift to Ratcliffe. I tightened my hands on the reins. With Ratcliffe disgraced, Catesby would undoubtedly turn his attentions to trying to unseat me. Side by side, we grimly rode on through Woodstock.

CHAPTER 16

Ratcliffe's problems assumed less importance when we reached Woodstock later that day when Catesby, along with a messenger from London, found us. At the time the message seemed of little importance, but how could we have known that it was destined to bring about a catastrophic series of events.

On the face of it, the matter was simple. There had been a failed attempt to rescue the two sons of the late King Edward from the Tower of London. Despite creating fires in parts of London to serve as a diversion, the rescuers had failed completely – four of them had been caught. It appeared some of them were former servants of the late king.

'Initially, I viewed the report as inconsequential,' Catesby advised us. 'Indeed, it barely seemed worth bothering about. However, His Grace the King views the matter differently. He would appreciate it, Francis, if I could join him and you at Minster Lovell?'

'Naturally, you're both welcome,' I told him politely.

'Thank you. Now the king has commanded Ratcliffe to proceed to the town of Gloucester, so regrettably he cannot join us.'

Catesby smiled apologetically at Ratcliffe.

'Believe me when I say that I did all that I could to persuade His Grace that there was little chance of another repeat of Oxford, but His Grace insisted it would be best if you were personally to check, in detail, all the arrangements which you have made.'

★ ★ ★

It should have been a happy time at Minster Lovell even without Nan but, while Tawboys had done his work well, there was no assuaging Richard's worry. The humiliation at Oxford and the news from London was affecting him badly. I grew concerned as for the first time I realised how exposed and possibly vulnerable he was without the guiding hand of Anne Neville. She would have been able to get him to see both matters in perspective but without her Richard's anxiety was feeding on itself.

I tried to ease his worry; Catesby had more information about the plotters, and I was able to point out that a groom, a pardoner and two other low fellows hardly constituted major danger. All Richard had to do was write to the council in London and Bishop Russell could deal with them.

Still he was unsatisfied and anxious, so I suggested strengthening the cordon round Elizabeth Woodville and her daughters in sanctuary. After all, if an attempt had been made to rescue the young princes, another one could easily be made to rescue the young princesses.

I had not appreciated the scale of Richard's anxiety though. Hitherto he had sought to appear interested in Minster Lovell and had demanded that I show him the site of the half-built tower by the river. From there I had taken him to the hall to show him my most prized possessions, the pair of tapestries with their silver and gold threads depicting the first King Richard and his crusaders. But if I thought the chivalry of 'The Siege of Acre' might have pleased him, I was mistaken. Immediately after I had spoken about the princesses, he tightened his lips and abandoned his inspection of the elaborate salt cellar shaped in the form of a castle. In silence, Catesby and I followed him into the adjacent solar. His agitation was by now quite marked, so I waved away the servants.

'You've both failed me completely!' he snapped. 'I left Westminster reassured that an adequate surveillance system had been set in place to monitor possible trouble while I was away from the South. Yet, despite the costs it incurred, your allegedly efficient system failed to detect this insurrection.'

'But you don't know it was an insurrection!' I protested.

'Of course it was, Francis.'

Richard's face was very pale now against his black tunic.

'If it had been a revolt there are signs we would have noticed,' I told him. 'There would have been reports of armed men gathering, of supplies being arranged. We would have heard tales of dissatisfied nobles.'

'Yet His Grace might well be correct,' Catesby silkily interposed. 'After all, someone must have supplied money and weapons to those four traitors. There must have been people waiting to receive the two princes if the plotters had succeeded.'

I glanced at him in surprise. Until this moment I knew Catesby had viewed the attempted rescue of the princes as an ill-conceived venture by a few of the late king's former servants. Why was he suddenly trying to inflame Richard's worry?

'Of course, there was to be a revolt!' stormed Richard. 'Catesby's point is valid. It's only because you failed to detect any of the signs of rebellion, Lovell, that you are sticking obstinately to the view that it does not exist.'

'Of course I do! You're mistaking shadows for substance. Militarily it would be impossible to mount a rebellion without us knowing about it.'

Richard leapt to his feet. The ring which he had been rolling against his palm fell to the floor. I picked it up and handed it to him. He grabbed it away from my hand and glared at me.

'You would accuse me of seeing shadows? At least I have the nose to smell danger.'

'There isn't any!'

'Sweet Christ, Francis, why are you so stupid? Let me reiterate; four men could not suddenly have decided to try and rescue those two royal bastards. There must have been a larger plan. Catesby, you're supposed to be intelligent, do you not agree?'

'Absolutely, Your Grace,' Catesby replied smoothly. 'But while you and Lovell were discussing the matter, I did have a thought as to why the revolt…'

'There isn't a revolt!'

'Silence, Lovell! At least one of you is making some sense. Continue, Catesby!'

'The rebellion went undetected because it was planned in France or Burgundy. Regrettably, I have no agents in either of those two countries, but it is obvious that either of those states would wish to have the sons of King Edward to use against England. Indeed, Your Grace, the more I think of it, the more certain I become that, had the rescue succeeded, those young boys would have been across the Channel in a few days.'

A thoughtful silence greeted his explanation. It was so plausible that I found myself nodding slowly, but then I pulled myself together sharply. Surely Catesby could not be correct? Earlier on he had been inclined to be dismissive of the rescue attempt, but now he seemed to be blowing it out of all proportion.

'I don't agree with...'

'Be silent, Francis!' Richard shouted. 'You're only looking to hide your failure by displaying total ignorance. Now, be quiet you two while I think for a moment.'

I scowled at Catesby as Richard paced anxiously up and down, because I thought I could see his plan. He was using this situation to promote himself at my expense. With Ratcliffe and now me out of favour, he would rise to become Richard's closest councillor. Richard quickly came to his own conclusion.

'It fits!' he snapped at Catesby. 'Brittany has Henry Tudor, so obviously France would wish to have Edward's bastard sons as their own candidates for England's throne. You're right, Catesby; the French would have got the boys overseas and then mounted an invasion.'

'Possibly to link up with the supporters of the late king in the South of England,' Catesby interjected deferentially.

'Of course!' Richard suddenly paused. 'They would have come when we were farthest away from London.'

'At York, Your Grace!' Catesby was horrified. 'But we'll be there in a month. We must plan countermeasures immediately.'

'Body of Christ, of course we must!'

'There's another problem,' Catesby added hurriedly. 'Clearly the French have planned this very cleverly. But only one group of the men that they've hired to rescue the sons of King Edward has been caught.'

'You mean they will have employed more agents to rescue the boys?'

'It would have been prudent, Your Grace. They're probably already in London.'

Richard swung round hurriedly.

'You're right, we must move quickly. I'll write to Russell immediately, but...'

I stepped forward. Richard's fatal impulsiveness had seized hold of him now and he had to be stopped.

'This is lunacy! We have no proof of any of this. We've seen no evidence of a conspiracy; all we have is supposition.'

'What's this total lack of vision, Lovell? You seem totally incapable of grasping the scale of the crises.'

'Because it doesn't exist!' I shouted angrily.

Dear God, I had never seen Richard in such a state before. He was seething with anger, but at the same time his worry was visibly evident. He was pacing round the room and gnawing at his fingernails now.

'Look, let me go investigate. I know what to look for; if I'm wrong, I'll admit it, but then we can at least plan appropriate measures.'

'That's an excellent suggestion!'

Surprisingly Catesby agreed with me, but then a worried look came to his face.

'The trouble is, Francis, that I'm not sure how much time we have. The French plan is probably quite advanced by now and this is the best time to mount a campaign.'

'You're allegations about the French are fabrications and you know it.'

'Silence!'

Richard glared at me.

'How can you not see that the attempt to seize the two royal bastards is an obvious prelude to civil war? Jesus, even Ratcliffe would be able to see that!'

I heard him out and then stepped forward to try and calm him; his face was now white with strain, but Catesby was faster than me.

'Your Grace is shrewd to observe the dangers of a three-sided civil war,' he observed admiringly. 'While naturally the Lords of Buckingham, Northumberland and Norfolk would support you against the two royal bastards, their Woodville family and the French, Brittany would inevitably back Henry Tudor. Why, with three different parties involved, the war could go on for years.'

'You're talking nonsense again!' I snapped.

Catesby turned to Richard with concern in his voice.

'Your Grace, we must move quickly, I beg you. We're wasting time trying to explain the danger to Francis. I beseech you to ignore him in this matter. He's loyal and devoted to you, I know, but time runs against us and, with poor Ratcliffe not here to help explain matters to Francis, we're wasting time.'

It was the mention of my friend's name that made my anger suddenly explode. Ignoring Richard, I took a step forward and swung hard. There was an immensely satisfying moment as my fist made contact with Catesby's face. The next thing I recall, the solar was full of the king's bodyguard and I was hauled away past a prone Catesby.

★ ★ ★

It was not until the next day that Richard summoned me to the Great Hall of Minster Lovell. I went slightly shamefaced, but in the certainty that I had been right to prevent Catesby inflaming Richard's fantasies. As I crossed the courtyard, I wondered whether he would be less worried today. I doubted it, but I was proved wrong. There was colour in his cheeks and he was seated. When he spoke, his voice was calm.

For the sake of our friendship, he was prepared to overlook my violent attack on Catesby. Indeed, such was Catesby's nobility of character that he himself had pleaded that I should receive no punishment. He had argued well, pointing out that it was not my fault that I had been unable to grasp the gravity of the situation or the threat to the whole of England and its beloved monarch. Nor indeed did he resent the blow; it was merely a gesture of frustration from one who strove earnestly to keep up with slightly more advanced intellects.

I groaned.

'Richard, he's using you.'

He gave me a kindly look.

'You're wrong, Francis, but no matter.'

He got up and strolled to the window.

'We'll resume the exploration of Minster Lovell now, Francis.'

'Have you got time?' I asked bitterly. 'What about the rebellion? Or has Catesby suppressed that for you already?'

He showed no annoyance at my sarcasm, but began to walk towards the door. As he reached it, he turned and beckoned me to accompany him. Together we strolled out.

'The threat of rebellion was very real, Francis, believe me, but it's dealt with now. We have no need to fear civil war.'

It seemed best to humour him.

'Indeed? Well, that's good news.'

'It was Catesby who enabled me to come up with the solution last night. It's a clever plan.'

I was not in the mood to discuss Catesby's clever plans.

'Well, I'm glad it's all ended satisfactorily. Where's Catesby now?'

Richard glanced at me.

'He's gone to London. There is a need for a certain amount of discretion in my plan and Catesby thought it best if he attended to it personally.'

He nodded happily, all trace of worry gone.

'He's a clever fellow Catesby and a loyal man too.'

'He's using you to advance himself.'

Richard paused outside the door of the church.

'He warned me that you would say that, but Francis, you have no need to be jealous. You'll lose nothing by his rise in my service; I'll confirm your appointment as chamberlain and chief butler and you'll not lack for rewards.'

'I'm not looking for rewards. I'm just trying to help you as a friend.'

'Then act like one! Catesby's good and I need clever people around me. I want you and Ratcliffe to work alongside him.'

I wanted nothing less and imagined that Ratcliffe would feel the same, but I had committed myself to Richard at Berwick and was therefore bound to serve him as he saw fit.

'If you insist,' I said slowly. 'We'll try to work with Catesby for your sake.'

He was pleased to have got his own way.

'Excellent, Francis!' He smiled. 'And when we reach York you may leave me so you can spend some time with your wife.'

It would be good to see Nan again, but I hesitated.

'You will not require me at York?'

His smile was both open and honest.

'I'm not saying that I won't need you, Francis, but with the revolt averted I can spare you for a while.'

This was not, however, to prove the case. I had only been with Nan for a few days when the summons arrived.

★ ★ ★

It was a grim-faced Ratcliffe who greeted me at Pontefract Castle. His manner was usually brusque, but today he was curt in the extreme. His own instructions, he advised me crisply, were simple. The moment I arrived I was to be brought straight to Anne Neville.

There was no time to refresh myself or to change my clothing. She required me at once.

'Is it rebellion or invasion?'

'Worse!' he grunted, as we clattered up the stairs.

I stopped in amazement.

'What is it then?'

'She'll tell you herself. Come along.'

At the top of the stairs, he indicated the chamber.

'In there,' he said sternly.

Ratcliffe drew his sword.

'This will be one conversation that no one else will overhear.' He jerked his head towards the door. 'Go on in, Francis.'

Mystified, I tapped softly on the chamber door.

★ ★ ★

Anne Neville sat motionless in one of her typically tall-carved chairs. She made no greeting as I bowed but gestured for me to be seated on the wooden seat opposite her. Her pale blue eyes rested only fleetingly on me; I guessed that her thoughts were elsewhere. Judging by the absence of attendants or any other people, I suspected that she had probably been brooding for no small amount of time.

'I require a full account of my husband's visit to Minster Lovell.'

Her words, when they came, were clipped and precise.

'From when we arrived, my lady?'

'Of course,' she said testily.

I told her everything I could remember about our stay. When I had finished, she sighed deeply.

'But you were certain there was no rebellion?'

'I was.'

'And you said that the next day my husband was much calmer?'

'Certainly. He told me that due to his planning, the rebellion would not happen and forgave me for hitting Catesby.'

'You should have killed Catesby!' she hissed.

I was shocked.

'My lady?'

'You should have killed him! You should have torn out that poisonous tongue of his and ripped out whatever manhood that effeminate fat fool possesses!'

'But why?'

'Why?' Her voice was incredulous. 'I'll tell you why. That mincing self-server sought to use my husband to advance himself and the gullible idiot believed him.'

'So there was no rebellion?'

I probably sounded slightly smug by now.

'Of course there wasn't and stop grinning like that! How anyone can smile after the damage that Catesby has caused us is totally beyond me.'

She relapsed into brooding silence, but presently another thought must have struck her as she raised her head and demanded to know why I had not bothered to ask the king what his plan had been.

'His plan?'

Her palm smacked the arm of her chair.

'To end this and all future rebellions, you idiot! How many plans do you think he had?'

'Your husband was not himself that night. He was worked up and wouldn't listen to reason, although I tried to counsel him. I think I was also angry that he had been so easily duped by Catesby and furious that he locked me up in my own home. So, the next day, since he seemed calmer, the last thing I wanted to do was to rekindle his anger.'

Anne Neville compressed her lips.

'Would to God that I had been at Minster Lovell!'

Her finger pointed at me.

'You're a coward, Lovell! If you'd been a proper man you would have braved my husband's anger and prevented this folly.'

'Prevented what folly?'

She ignored me.

'You could have ridden after Catesby and stopped him.'

'Stopped him from doing what?' I cried in exasperation.

Anne Neville eyed me incredulously.

'You mean even now, you haven't guessed what the plan was?'

Abruptly she gestured to a table where a pitcher of water stood. I filled a glass and handed it to her. For a few moments, she nursed the glass in silence. Then her mouth tightened.

'You failed him and you know it!'

'How can I have failed him when I had no knowledge of what the king was planning to do? Richard would not listen to me; he was determined to be guided by Catesby. I thought that they were both wrong.'

'You failed completely!' Anne Neville snapped. 'God knows all men fail ultimately, but you managed to bungle it at the very first opportunity. You knew that my husband requires firm guidance and you neglected to provide it.'

'You're being totally unreasonable!' I burst out. 'All right, Richard has presumably made a mistake. Maybe eventually you'll actually tell me what he's done, but don't start blaming everyone else!'

'Oh why are men such fools?' she burst out in sudden fury. 'God, why do you fashion men in your own image yet deny them even the smallest fraction of your all-knowing intelligence? And tell me, sweet Lord, why you provide them with pride instead of brains, so that in their vanity they are incapable of listening to those who are better assisted to guide them?'

She rose from her chair and gestured at me with her glass.

'You're no better than he is!' she said furiously. 'You sit there so proud and uncaring. Doubtless you believe that we should fall on our knees daily to give thanks for our husbands, don't you? Well, you try giving thanks for a husband when all the time you're wondering why God has saddled you with an idiot! And you try to express gratitude for a man whose impulsiveness is such that it causes him to rush into a course of action without even thinking of the consequences.'

'My lady, this is hardly fair or appropriate.'

'Of course it is, you fool! It's time you heard the one question that all married women ask God at some stage – what sin have I committed to deserve such an idiot for a husband?'

There was sudden crash as her wine glass smashed against the wall behind me, and then the only sound was a violent sobbing as Anne Neville fell to the ground. I moved towards her and lifted her up. For a moment she struggled, then went limp as I carried her back to the chair. I fetched her more water and then moved to the window to allow her to compose herself. Gradually her crying subsided and she regarded me sullenly with reddened eyes as I sat down again.

'You've no idea what's happened, have you?'

Her voice was cracked.

'Perhaps if you could just tell me.'

Her hands fluttered wildly.

'But your loyalty to Richard? Will it, that is, will you?'

I cut her off.

'I gave my loyalty to your husband at Berwick, my lady. To my mind loyalty, once given, can never be retracted. Whatever Richard has done, I will always serve him. So, come now, tell me what has happened?'

Anne Neville dabbed her tears and took a deep breath.

'In order to prevent what he wrongly believed to be a major revolt and stop future attempts to support the sons of King Edward, he had the two boys killed.'

My heart went out to the two young boys. What a terrible way for the young innocents to perish! What needless cruelty and waste!

'Don't waste your tears on them! News of their deaths is already circulating. The reaction of people is so great that there will be a huge rebellion against us and we will all be swept away.'

She wrung her hands in frustration.

'Now do you see where my husband's foolishness and impetuosity has landed us?'

I said nothing. I felt slightly sick.

'But with your skill you can defeat the rebels,' she continued quickly. 'Ratcliffe already has information to assist you to help you plan your campaign and we can easily muster support.'

She looked at me anxiously.

'You will serve Richard, won't you, Francis? You'll stay faithful to him, despite what's happened.'

Loyalty is a heavy cross, but it has to be born.

'I will, my lady; in spite of what has happened, I believe that the reasons to place your husband on the throne are as valid now as they were previously. Additionally, as I have said, I will always be loyal to Richard. But there is one aspect of your speech that has distressed me, my lady.'

She frowned momentarily but then, smiling wanly, she spread her hands.

'It is possible that I was a trifle distraught, dear Francis. Perhaps I made some unfortunate remark that caused you pain? It was certainly not my intention to do so.'

'No, it wasn't that.'

Anne Neville regarded me blankly.

'Conceivably, I spoke too harshly of my husband. Now naturally he was foolish, but that is not to say…'

Dear God; was there not an ounce of humanity left in the women or had her lust for power destroyed it completely?

'It wasn't that either,' I said wearily. 'What upset me was that the only reason you regret the deaths of the princes is because of the threat that their murder poses to you and your husband.'

She looked at me enquiringly.

'Well, what else is there? Naturally any death, even that of Woodville blood, is to be regretted; but…'

'But their murders were not just any death! These were children, my lady, small defenceless children sleeping peaceably until they woke with a start at the sound of strange footsteps climbing the stairs towards them. Young boys, my lady, who would have clung terrified to one another in the gloom of the night, as slowly the door creaked open…'

She waved her hand feebly, but I continued.

'They would have been petrified as their killers came out of the darkness into their room. They would have cried out in terror as they saw the pitiless looks on the faces of the two Brachers. But the children's pleas for mercy would have gone unheeded, wouldn't they, my lady? And their feeble attempts at resistance would have been to no avail. Two small lads would not have stood a chance against two grown men determined to earn their blood money.'

I looked down at her contemptuously and she lowered her eyes.

'I don't suppose the two young princes were much older than your own son, my lady. Try to think of them when you next see him.'

She made no response as I turned to leave. I quietly cursed her, Richard and Catesby. Above all, though, I cursed the bind of my own loyalty.

CHAPTER 17

Ratcliffe, it appeared, had known about the princes for three weeks. Having heard the rumours that had been circulating in York about the deaths of the boys, he had requested Richard to allow them to be paraded through London to suppress such malicious gossip.

'But then she sent for me, told me what had happened and asked me how best we could deal with it.'

'What did you recommend?'

'Nothing. If it had been one boy, we could have blamed it on a fever – but two and at the same time? No, the best thing was to say nothing and let people believe that they had been secretly moved out of London.'

'But if there are rumours of their deaths, it doesn't sound as if it worked.'

'Agreed, but it was worth a try. Anyway she then told me to write to Catesby in London. She said that you would want as much information as possible to plan your campaign.' Ratcliffe smiled grimly. 'Her language in relation to our dearly beloved colleague is quite colourful, isn't it? But she did point out that the only way he could hope to regain favour was if he helped to prevent the rebellion that he'd indirectly created. I've got his reports here; they arrived yesterday.'

'All right, I'll read them tonight and we'll talk tomorrow.'

★ ★ ★

It was several hours later that I pushed back the chair and stretched. Realising I was incredibly hungry, I called for food. As I waited for its arrival, I reflected on what I had read.

I was impressed by the efficiency of the documents I had studied and was certain that the content was correct. Indeed, it was hard to find fault in any aspect of Catesby's objective reporting. He was clearly brave too; a lesser man might simply have relayed the information that he had received from his agents and simply sent it without trying to reconcile conflicting stories or venturing an opinion himself – but not Catesby. In his desire to try to rehabilitate himself, he had used his considerable intellect to build up a highly detailed picture of the curious combination of Yorkists, Woodvilles and Lancastrians who were ranged against us.

The major opposition, Catesby began, was from the followers of the late King Edward in southern England. Many of these were important men who had been trustingly left in their positions, as sheriffs and crown officials at the time of Richard's accession. Most of these men had been hostile to the new king taking the throne and might have been planning to try and replace him with the late king's eldest son. However, whether they were or were not, the current rumours of the murders of the princes had turned them solidly against the king.

With the two royal bastards believed dead, these potential rebels lacked a leader. Diligent research had, to Catesby's surprise, revealed that the former supporters of King Edward had no wish to replace King Richard with either of his two nephews – the young Earl of Warwick or John of Lincoln. Instead, they planned to transfer their allegiance to the last Lancastrian claimant to the throne, Henry Tudor, and wished him to marry King Edward's eldest daughter, Elizabeth. Catesby added that, despite the absence of any royal blood in Henry Tudor, he believed this to be a clever ploy since it would put an end to the wars between the Houses of York and Lancaster.[24] He understood that the Woodvilles supported this particularly as, by themselves, they were incapable of overthrowing King Richard.

On the subject of the Woodvilles, Catesby noted, he suspected the active involvement of Elizabeth Woodville's eldest son, Dorset, and her brother Lionel Woodville, together with their adherents, in the plot. At this stage, Catesby felt unable to give precise estimates of rebel numbers but judged that they would be substantial. Preliminary information indicated three or possibly four major mustering points; he hoped to be able to provide the specific locations within a few days. With regard to Henry Tudor, information was less detailed. There had been no reports of large numbers of ships being provisioned in Brittany; hence he judged it unlikely that Tudor would seek to land backed by a sizeable Breton contingent. Likewise, he regretted not having precise data but he thought it likely that Tudor would seek to land in the West Country, which was still the most pro-Lancastrian part of England. In conclusion, Catesby promised to provide further information as it became available and humbly begged that if I or Sir Richard Ratcliffe had any specific questions we should send him a message immediately.

The arrival of a page with bread and goats cheese momentarily caused me to break away from my thoughts, but with his departure I returned to Catesby's analysis of the rebellion, and the more I thought about it, the more concerned I became. So I re-read Catesby's reports for a second time since it was possible that the feeble light from the flickering candles could have caused me to miss something. But when eventually I finished, I was still confused. While the reports were detailed and probably accurate, they failed to address the obvious question – how on earth could the rebels hope to win?

★ ★ ★

'But why do you say that?' Richard asked me.

I gave him a surprised look. At least conversation flowed more easily between us now. Initially both of us had been guarded, possibly even nervous of the other. After a while we found ourselves being frank and honest with each other; since that which had happened could not be undone, both of us wished to move away from it.

'Their tactics are wrong. Let's assume Catesby's latest information is correct. We know that the rebels are planning for simultaneous uprisings – in Exeter, Salisbury, Newbury and Kent, and we know the timing too – St Luke's Day.'

'It's going to be hard to deal with four outbreaks.'

I shook my head impatiently.

'No it's not. Firstly, remember that the South of England has few major lords with armed followers, so while I agree that these rebels are men of local importance, they haven't got the resources that we have. Secondly, they are too spread out.'

'But they would look to join together when Henry Tudor lands?'

'That would take considerable co-ordination and we're not going to just wait for them. Don't forget they have no overall general either and, most important of all, they are not being supported by a substantial number of Breton soldiers.'

Richard looked puzzled.

'I suppose you're right, but if Catesby is correct, the men leading this rebellion are sheriffs, JPs and landowners. Men such as these are not stupid. They must know that all our own loyal lords can deal with them easily. Why, Norfolk can move his men out of East Anglia and crush the Kentish rebels. Buckingham's troops can deal with the ones in Exeter.'

'And I'll move down to Oxford and raise men to deal with the rest. But it's too easy, isn't it? We're missing something.' I paused for a moment. 'Write to Norfolk, Richard, and tell him to be prepared to defend London and to take all the necessary measures to prevent the rebels from crossing the Thames. Then give orders to increase the number of men guarding Elizabeth Woodville and her daughters in sanctuary.'

'Wouldn't it just be easier to drag them out of sanctuary?' he asked irritably. 'Then they could be safely hidden away.'

There was a loud tap at the door.

'Particularly the older one whom Tudor's supporters want him to marry; then no one would try to rescue them.'

The knocking on the door became more persistent.

Richard wheeled round in fury. At that moment the door was flung open and Catesby rushed in. He was filthy and looked exhausted.

'Your Grace. The Duke of Buckingham has risen in revolt! He's raised 3,000 men and plans to join the southern rebels!'

★ ★ ★

Catesby panted while he gave us his news. He admitted to mistrusting the Duke of Buckingham, since he had always feared his ambitions. Accordingly, directly after the royal tour had commenced, he had instructed his agents to watch the duke's behaviour closely.

Initially, he feared that he might have misjudged matters, as nothing untoward had occurred, but as he investigated the southern rebellion more closely, one item in particular caught his attention. It was a report of a meeting at Thornbury between Lionel Woodville, who he knew to be involved in the revolt, and the Duke of Buckingham.

His suspicions aroused by now, he checked his agents' most recent reports regarding Buckingham and it appeared to him that there was evidence of military supplies being gathered. He could find no trace of men being summoned, but doubtless that was proceeding. Not trusting anyone else with the message, he had ridden to tell the king personally.

Richard was incredulous.

'Are you insane? On the evidence of one meeting between Buckingham and Lionel Woodville – who happens to be his brother-in-law – you're seriously suggesting that the man who did most to put me on the throne has become a traitor?'

Catesby's hands shook nervously.

'I could get more evidence if I had more time, Your Grace, but I fear that the duke is already summoning his men.'

'Bah! There you go again trying to rush me into something foolhardy.'

Behind him, the chamber door swung open and the guards ushered in Anne Neville. Seeing Catesby, she curled her lips contemptuously and dismissed her two attendant ladies.

'And what is that doing here?' she demanded witheringly.

Richard gestured to Catesby.

'Tell the queen your ridiculous story!' he commanded.

At the second time of telling, Catesby's tale sounded even less credible. Anne Neville was clearly unimpressed.

'So, once again, you seek to poison the king's mind in order to further your own ambitions. Yet again, you invent plots and traitors to build yourself up.'

'But, my lady, it's the truth!'

She ignored his protest.

'I had been led to believe that you are clever,' she remarked scornfully. 'Doubtless such praise was awarded to you by your fellow men, since they naturally view anything that is not mediocre as exceptional. But, be that as it may, what truly amazes me is that you have the arrogance to assume that anyone else could possibly believe you.

'Tell me, you fat fool, before the guards drag you away, why should the Duke of Buckingham risk all his titles, lands and honours that the king has given him to back a nobody like Henry Tudor?'

Catesby's hands flapped wildly.

'I cannot understand his reasoning, my lady. The only possible reason there could be is that he has noted the hostility that some men showed when your husband seized... um... that is, inherited the throne. Then when the news of the princes was sounded out abroad, he worried that, in placing King Richard on the throne, he had made a mistake and backed the wrong man. Possibly he feared that men would associate him too closely with the king and the death of the princes.'

'Call them the royal bastards, you idiot!'

'Quite so, my lady, but maybe he thought as a result – were the rebels to be victorious – he would lose his lands. Conceivably, he may have feared for his very life.'

'You have no idea, do you?'

Anne Neville's acid tones cut through Catesby's frightened babble.

'For all your fine words, there are too many "ifs" and "buts". Now I recall that in the past you expressed the belief that Buckingham seeks to wear my husband's crown. So tell me, you ridiculous apology for a man, why would he back Henry Tudor to become king? Why would he support a man, who has a lesser claim than his own?'

I stepped forward.

'There is one major point…'

'Sweet Christ, Lovell, will you not interrupt! Had you spoken out half as much at Minster Lovell, we would not be in this situation.' She turned to her husband. 'My lord, if you listen to this fat slug's advice and march against Buckingham, all you will achieve is to turn your most loyal supporter into an enemy.'

Richard nodded.

'I'll tell Buckingham to move against the rebels in Exeter and Salisbury. Francis, you'll gather men here and then move south to reinforce him.'

'No.'

For a moment there was a stunned silence as Richard and his wife stared at me in total disbelief. Even the white-faced Catesby shot me an amazed look. I pointed at him.

'He's right, Your Grace.'

I ignored the storm that swept over me and blotted out the furious voices of the king and queen. I had little love for Catesby; once, possibly twice now, he had fooled people with his tales of imaginary plots and, had it not been for one thing, I would have readily accepted that this was a third attempt to do just the same thing. I waited patiently, reflecting how unfortunate it was that true loyalty can often involve opposing those whom you serve when you believe them to be wrong, but such is the way of things. Despite the vitriolic words and furious glances flung at me, I knew it was the best way to help Richard. Eventually something like calm settled in the chamber, so I asked if I could depart as there was much to be done and not much time left.

'And what, pray, are you intending to do?'

If anything Anne Neville's tone was more scathing than earlier.

'I'm going to stop Buckingham and his men from crossing the Severn to get into England,' I said grimly. 'I've no idea why Buckingham has joined the revolt, but now the rebel tactics make sense.'

'How?'

'Before you arrived, my lady, the king and I were discussing the rebellion. To our minds, a series of localised outbreaks could have been fairly easily suppressed and, as such, the rebel strategy made no sense. But now, with a large force to serve as the nucleus of an army, their strategy is obvious. Buckingham will advance into England and move eastwards across southern England. He'll get reinforcements from the rebel mustering points and move towards London. By the time we have assembled our own men, he might have outnumbered us.'

'But if you're wrong, you will have turned an ally into an enemy!' objected Richard. 'You'll have stopped him coming to our aid.'

'I'm not wrong!' I told him. 'In fact, I know I'm right. Now if you want to suppress this revolt, the only way to do it is to stop Buckingham's force from linking up with the southern rebels. That means holding him with inferior numbers until we can bring our major force against him. We need to drive a wedge between him and the other rebels and that means stopping him at the Severn River. I'll do that while you bring the rest of the troops south. If we can stop Buckingham, the rest of the revolt will fizzle out.'

There was a silence while husband and wife looked at each other uncertainly.

'We could travel down to Lincoln as planned,' I suggested, 'but what we could do is to gather our own men as we go. I'll leave you there and raise my own troops. I'll collect more troops in Banbury. I strongly recommend that you ask for the Great Seal and declare the Duke of Buckingham a traitor.'

★ ★ ★

But this was to prove one campaign that I did not need to fight to help Richard. As I moved towards Gloucester, it became apparent that not only were the rains in the South-West of England excessively severe, but also they had caused substantial flooding in the region. With all the bridges across the Severn already having been destroyed, the Duke of Buckingham's army was unable to enter England. Reports began to come in from our forward scouts. They spoke of plunging morale among Buckingham's men as the combination of driving rain and floods took their toll on his army. Communications later confirmed this. Additionally it appeared that it was impossible to bring supplies to his force.

I smiled grimly when I heard the news. By now Buckingham's own spies would have reported the news of our own advance. If morale was already low in Buckingham's force, it would sink like a stone when his men realised that they would soon be fighting the whole royal army themselves. I slowed the pace of our advance and waited for the inevitable.

Two days later I heard the news that I expected. There had been wholesale desertions. Buckingham's army had imploded and was no longer an effective fighting unit.

Satisfied I turned my attention to dealing with the English rebels.

★ ★ ★

In truth, there was not much to finish. Devoid of Buckingham's army, the southern revolts fizzled out. Buckingham himself was betrayed by one of his own retainers and was executed. Henry Tudor, arriving late, sailed disconsolately back to Brittany. Richard was triumphant.

Working in comparative harmony, Catesby, Ratcliffe and I established a strategy to build on our king's success. Loyal supporters were rewarded with crown posts, as now there were more than sufficient to satisfy those who had proven loyal. Others received lands, since naturally all of Buckingham's estates fell to the king. Predictably, the king's most powerful supporters, Northumberland and Stanley, received the lion's share but Richard's followers had no cause to complain of their spoils.

With all opposition swept aside, the parliament that formed to justify Richard's title as king in the following January was merely a formality and, with his title fully authorised, Richard was wholly on the ascendant. Certainly the Woodvilles believed so; in March of that year Elizabeth led her daughters out of sanctuary and bowed to the inevitable.

Whether King Edward's widow simply despaired of Henry Tudor ever replacing Richard as king or she had just suffered sufficiently in her cramped and uncomfortable quarters in sanctuary will never be known. For whatever reason though, she reached an agreement with the king and, in return for a pension and promises of suitable marriages for her daughters, she surrendered to Richard. With that, all opposition against him ended.

Gradually, we strengthened our grip on England. The South of the country was an obvious weak area for us. Almost half the sheriffs and many of those holding crown posts had been involved in Buckingham's revolt. Consequently, they needed to be replaced; as such faithful men from the North were sent to fill those positions of authority.

How successful this proved was hard to say. Our men were not readily accepted by the local landowners. They were not from the area and did not know it as the locals did. There were no ties of friendship to integrate them into these communities. Richard had called on me to establish myself in a similar way as he wanted me to build up a power base in the Thames Valley. But I had no desire to settle there; my home was in the North and I imagined others who had come south felt the same.

But still we tried to build support for the king. The London merchants were courted – they did not love Richard as they loved King Edward, but they were to prove a useful source of revenue. Richard's own family members were used to trying to build up territorial influence. His bastard daughter's husband, Huntington, was given lands in Wales. In an effort to reduce the influence of the loyal, albeit over-powerful, Earl of Northumberland, Richard's nephew, John of Lincoln, was dispatched to head up the Council of the North, which was finally established in July.

With opposition at home crushed and Henry Tudor an impotent imposter languishing in Brittany, victory was ours.

★ ★ ★

Soon though, dark clouds gathered to cover the brilliant sun. In April, Richard's young son died unexpectedly. His death drove both parents into paroxysms of grief, exacerbated by the fact that he was an only child. There were unkind people who whispered that the boy's death was simply the vengeance of the Lord. The tragedy seemed to mark a turning point in our fortunes as, unless Anne Neville could produce another heir, Richard's dynasty was doomed.

Across the Channel too, Henry Tudor was slowly beginning to develop as a potential alternative. Further to the failure of the Buckingham revolt, a number of influential southern rebels had joined him. It had been to this crowd of supporters that Henry Tudor had promised that when he became King of England he would marry Elizabeth, the eldest daughter of the late King Edward.

Of course, we made every effort to force Brittany to surrender Henry Tudor, but neither diplomacy nor bribery worked and somehow word of our best plan leaked out and Tudor fled to France.

★ ★ ★

'It's all turning out very badly,' I told Nan on one of my hurried visits. 'Pressure is mounting on us as Tudor builds up quite a credible court in exile. Meanwhile, if you believe the gossip, rather a lot of people are beginning to favour the union between Tudor and King Edward's daughter.'

'I suppose they believe that it would unite the Houses of York and Lancaster forever,' she mused aloud. 'Then again, the murder of the poor princes has rekindled the love that people had for King Edward. All his former supporters would be keen to have his daughter as their queen, even if it meant accepting Henry Tudor as their king.'

I nodded gloomily; I was beginning to believe that many people in the South detested our regime so much that they would back anyone to force Richard from the throne. Nan saw my expression and gently stroked my hand.

'Is my cousin Anne any better?' she asked gently. 'I fear for her because she has not responded to either of my letters.'

'Her illness has been troubling her…'

'What form does it take?' Nan demanded.

'It's reported to be wasting sickness. She tires easily; she is short of breath and has lost a great deal of weight.'

It was an understatement, but I did not want to upset Nan. The truth was that the immensely vibrant Anne Neville was slowing down. All her strength and vitality were being used to fight her illness.

'Dr Hobbys and the other physicians swear that in time she will recover,' I added reassuringly.

We needed her well again, I thought despairingly. It was not simply that Richard needed her guidance, but for peace and security the country needed an heir to the throne. For as Ratcliffe had pointed out grimly, given the choice between Henry Tudor and a young Yorkist wife, and King Richard without an heir, most men would opt for Tudor.

'I'm sure Anne will recover soon,' I said confidently.

★ ★ ★

But I was wrong. Gradually that indomitable will that had built Richard up in the North began to fail and the fiery spirit that had secured the crown for him started to burn less brightly.

She was rarely seen these days and devoid of her advice Richard was at a loss until, seemingly effortlessly, Ratcliffe moved in to fill the power vacuum that Anne Neville's illness had created.

For my part, I was indifferent to Ratcliffe's rise to power. Certainly he was as ambitious as ever, but what mattered at this critical time was that we all supported Richard in his hour of need. Catesby publicly concurred with this viewpoint. However, such was his own ambition that he secretly resented his rival's rise to the top and continually sought to find a way to oust him.

That Christmas in 1484 he almost succeeded. He went privately to the king and proposed a course of action which, I believe, might have found favour with Richard. I can recall Ratcliffe's anger as he explained it to me. The plan was a simple one.

Despite the carefully managed public appearances of Anne, it was becoming apparent to everyone that she was extremely ill. Indeed, such was her condition that Richard had been urged by the doctors to shun his wife's bed. Under the circumstances, Anne Neville was clearly not going to produce an heir. Equally there was the strong possibility that Henry Tudor would invade next year and, due to his promise to marry King Edward's daughter Elizabeth, he would gain support from many former Yorkists. Catesby's solution was to deny Tudor this support and, instead transfer it to the king. On the death of Anne, Richard – not Henry Tudor – would marry Elizabeth, his brother's eldest daughter. The more Catesby worked on his plan, the more attractive it seemed to him. With Elizabeth married to Richard, not only would Henry Tudor lose the Yorkist support that the marriage would have brought him but Richard gained it. The South of England would be satisfied now that King Edward's daughter was on the throne. It would also stop the harmful rumours about the fate of the young princes, King Edward's sons. After all, while people might assume Richard had killed them, the marriage would make them reconsider their views. Surely no female would willingly marry the murderer of her two brothers!

Ratcliffe was uncertain as to how Catesby had managed to persuade King Edward's widow, Elizabeth Woodville, to agree to the scheme, but he was shrewd enough to make an accurate guess.

'She would see it as a way to rebuild her own family's power base,' he observed. 'It would not only give her the prestige and influence she's always sought but, of course, it would enable her eldest son, Dorset, to return to England.'

'And with her eldest daughter as queen, Elizabeth Woodville makes her family into a force again.'

'Which is exactly what that scheming bitch wants!' Ratcliffe said bitterly. 'In such a scenario, the king gets an immensely popular – not to mention fertile – young wife and Henry Tudor is denied all the support such a marriage would have brought him. Furthermore, Elizabeth Woodville dances on the grave of Anne Neville and returns to power. Her daughter, of course, gets the crown she craves and Catesby will have negotiated his own position in this arrangement.'

His face fell.

'And will, of course, ensure that I am excluded.'

I ignored his selfishness.

'But are you really sure that the daughter is as keen as her mother on the marriage?' I asked incredulously.

'Haven't you seen how much yarrow she's carrying!' Ratcliffe snorted, 'She's practically wreathed in dried flowers these days[25]. Don't be fooled by those simple fresh-faced looks, Francis. She's as cunning as the fox in the Aesop's Fables she's always reading. She has every intention of becoming queen, and why should she wait for Henry Tudor? He might not invade or he might invade and be beaten.'

I leapt to my feet.

'I'll go and see Richard immediately. He must be made to see that he is being manipulated and what he is contemplating is completely wrong.'

Ratcliffe raised a hand to stop me.

'Just wait a moment, Francis, before you rush off. We face powerful adversaries all with vested interests in this proposed marriage. Let us plan our strategy to prevent it carefully.'

For a fleeting moment I thought of leaving; I would return to Nan and the clean air of the North. I would go away from this sordid court full of sin and greed. Let Richard fend for himself.

Ratcliffe watched me closely.

'You won't help him if you don't oppose this marriage, Francis. If you are loyal to him, you'll help me stop it.'

I wanted to go, but he was right.

★ ★ ★

It was a vicious power struggle that was fought out between Catesby and Ratcliffe in the opening part of 1485. It was a war without weapons fought in the battlefield of a palace against a backdrop of a dying queen and a faltering king.

Initially the tactics used by both sides were predictable. Both parties attempted to justify their positions on the proposed marriage through judicious use of the scriptures. But that proved inconclusive, with both parties claiming victory over the appropriate section of Leviticus.[26]

After this stalemate, Catesby moved onto the offensive. The benefits of the marriage for Richard and the country were carefully dissembled. Ratcliffe counterattacked by using my influence in the North and, on my return, I was pleased to tell him that not only was there a total repugnance to the idea, but men objected very strongly to anyone taking the place of Anne Neville, daughter of their beloved Earl of Warwick, in Richard's affections.

But all these arguments caused rifts among Richard's followers at the very time when we needed to be unified to face the threat from Henry Tudor. The Woodvilles must have recognised this too, as they proposed a meeting to resolve our differences.

Two days later Ratcliffe and I met with Catesby.

★ ★ ★

To Catesby, Henry Tudor posed a very real threat, but only, he emphasised, if Tudor could count on the support that would come to him from those disaffected Yorkists who wanted him to marry King Edward's daughter.

'Sheer common sense tells us that if she marries her uncle, King Richard, Henry Tudor cannot invade,' Catesby concluded. 'So may I ask why you two oppose the marriage?'

'It's a sin,' Ratcliffe said simply.

Catesby raised his eyebrows.

'That is a very definitive answer, isn't it? Even when our clerics and divines debated the matter they could not agree with one another. All right, suppose for a moment that I agree with you. I can still show you how the wrongdoing might be mitigated by the good it produces.'

'Go on,' said Ratcliffe dubiously.

'Well, if Richard does not marry his niece, we all agree that Tudor will invade, don't we?' Catesby continued. 'So there will be war.'

We nodded, and satisfied, Catesby leant back and placed his fingertips together.

'But then suppose Richard does marry his niece? There will, of course, then be no invasion by Tudor and consequently no battles, no killings, nor any widows and orphans.'

It was not an argument I had heard before and, for a few tempting seconds, I almost accepted it, but then I shook my head. Catesby looked amazed.

'But why do you still object, Francis?'

'Because you are causing Richard to sin!'

'The political realities of the situation make that inevitable,' Catesby retorted. 'Through this marriage, which, I repeat, though sinful brings good along with it, Richard retains his throne.'

'But it's wrong.'

'Oh stop being so hypocritical, Francis!'

I blinked in bewilderment.

'What do you mean by that?'

'Well you accuse me of leading Richard into sin, but if I am, then I am only following your example!' Catesby snapped. 'After all, just think back to your time in the North and tell me what you did to help Richard every time he and Anne Neville were threatened politically.'

'I tried to protect them!'

'Very commendable,' purred Catesby, 'but the trouble, of course, was that your notion of protecting Richard always seemed to involve the slaughter of large numbers of people. Indeed, it might be said that you proved incapable of helping Richard and Anne without killing people on a wholesale basis.'

I sat stunned.

'And you were pretty indiscriminate about the deaths,' Catesby continued inexorably. 'It didn't matter to you how many Scots and French were murdered provided Richard benefitted politically, did it?'

He paused and looked down at the table.

'And there were the English too, weren't there, Francis?'

'What English?' I asked shakily.

'Your own troops who died in battle,' Catesby said gently. 'You were responsible for their deaths in the same way that you were for those of your enemies.'

His green eyes met mine.

'It does not seem to have occurred to you that every death that you caused directly or indirectly was a sin which at Judgement Day will be laid not just at your door but also at Richard's.'

He turned to face Ratcliffe.

'Richard knew about the lies and calumnies you spread on his behalf and the men whose reputations you so maliciously slandered, so he is guilty of those too.'

Catesby had us spellbound by now and he knew it, so we sat silently while he continued.

'Both of you have already carried out more hellish deeds on Richard's behalf than I intend to, so how on earth can you two hypocrites object to the marriage on moral grounds? You might agree, of course, that all of your actions were designed to help and protect Richard. You could say that you were merely fulfilling your roles to the best of your abilities, and if, at times, you committed sins and caused Richard to err, it was regrettable, but still a political necessity.'

He drew a deep breath.

'If you argue that way, it would be complete double standards to reject my marriage plan for Richard and his niece. What is the difference between what I am doing for Richard now and what you two sanctimonious bastards have already done for him?'

The vehemence of Catesby's attack had shaken me badly. Hurtful though it was, I could not fault his logic.

'Could we move away from the moral side of the marriage?' Ratcliffe said meekly. 'It is possible that you have a point, but there is the political aspect that needs to be considered.'

Sensing a pragmatic ally, Catesby gestured expansively.

'By all means, Sir Richard, I would welcome your views.'

I listened distractedly as Ratcliffe spoke of the danger from the North, as I sensed that there was something wrong in Catesby's argument. The trouble was that I could not identify it.

'How many people live in the North?' Ratcliffe interrupted my thoughts.

'Only about one in five, I think.'

Catesby chuckled delightedly.

'So you see, my dear Ratcliffe, that even if all the people in the North oppose the marriage, they will be powerless against the rest of England. Furthermore, as you so shrewdly pointed out, they have no leader.'

The discussion between Ratcliffe and Catesby drifted onto the Papal approval which would be required for the marriage of two people so closely connected. I returned to Catesby's words; I was convinced that there was a flaw in his argument, but I could not make out what it was.

'When the Woodvilles return to power after the marriage they will seek revenge on Francis and me,' I overheard Ratcliffe say.

Catesby's genial laugh filled the little room.

'So that's what has been really worrying you, Ratcliffe! Have no fear on that score. Agree to the marriage and there will be no reprisals against either of you.'

'And my lands?' Ratcliffe demanded.

'You'll keep them all,' Catesby reassured him.

'And my position in government?'

Catesby shrugged regretfully.

'The Woodvilles will want their own people in power.'

He turned to me.

'So do you accept the marriage too, Lovell?'

'No.'

Catesby's eyes narrowed.

'Why not?'

'Because your argument is flawed. You said that because Ratcliffe and I caused Richard to sin for political purposes, it is entirely logical that you should be able to do the same.'

'Surely you don't deny the fairness of that?'

'Yes, I do, actually. There is one very major difference between what we did for Richard and what you are planning to do.'

'And what is that?'

'All our actions, whether right and wrong, were designed to help

Richard. In this instance, your marriage plans for him are to benefit yourself. You and the Woodvilles want to control and manipulate the king which, without Anne Neville, Ratcliffe and myself in the way, you would be able to do.'

I glanced down at Catesby.

'So, for that reason, not only will I not agree to the wedding, I will do everything I can to prevent it.'

He did not respond. I decided I needed to provoke him further.

'A lot has been said about the sinful nature of the proposed marriage of Richard to his niece,' I told Ratcliffe. 'In reality, I'm not so sure that the actual union would have been so terrible. After all, as Catesby pointed out, a greater good would have arisen as a result of it, so perhaps God might have overlooked it. But, do you know, I rather think that all this talk of it being sinful has obscured the far greater sin.'

'Which is what?' Ratcliffe asked curiously.

I pointed at Catesby.

'His motivation in proposing the marriage.'

Catesby rose with surprising speed and strode furiously towards the door. When he reached it, he turned to glare at me.

'It will be impossible for you to stop the marriage!' he hissed. 'We will not let you influence the king or prevent that which is planned.'

He smiled maliciously.

'There is one further point of which you are unaware – the king himself believes the marriage should proceed.'

With that parting shot, he was gone, followed a moment later by Ratcliffe.

I sat down wearily. Plainly it was my duty to protect Richard from what would be on all counts a wrongful marriage, but how?

I mulled over various alternatives but rejected them one after the other. At last I was left with only one.

The more I thought about it the more I hated it, but I had no choice.

I got up abruptly; I could not be a coward when Richard needed me.

CHAPTER 18

As chamberlain, theoretically at any rate, I controlled access to the king. In practice, Richard saw whom he wanted, when he wanted. But for all that, it was a simple enough matter to arrange for his private chambers to be closed off and suitable guards posted to discourage visitors. I arranged matters carefully before I saw him. I wrote the letters myself, trusting no one else with their content.

★ ★ ★

It was late when I entered Richard's chamber. At the sight of me, he jumped up anxiously from his chair by the fire and demanded to know what was amiss.

'Nothing! I merely wished to talk to you.'

'I can think of more suitable times.'

I ignored him and returned to the door. I closed it firmly and slid the bolt across.

'Now we won't be disturbed,' I told him. 'Not that there is much chance of that; I've put my own men off guard duty tonight.'

He eyed me coldly.

'Leave me, Francis!'

'I want to talk to you about this proposed marriage. You've been ignoring me because you don't want to hear my view. Unfortunately for you, I'll not be silenced because I believe that, as a friend and servant of yours for many years, what I have to say is important.'

He resumed his seat and shrugged.

'I take it you object to the proposed marriage?'

'Of course I do!'

'I did too,' he volunteered surprisingly. 'Like you, I viewed the matter as unnatural. But then it was put to me that my own views were unimportant since, where duty is concerned, how can a king's own thoughts matter? The marriage of Edward's daughter denies Tudor the support that she would have given him. If he cannot gain her support, he cannot invade. If he cannot invade, England has peace and security.'

He rose and stood in front of the fire.

'Given that it's the duty of the king to provide his country with peace and stability, what do my own feelings matter? The king is always to be the servant of his country. Hence for the sake of my country, I must marry my brother's daughter.'

'You could always marry her off to a third person. That way *neither* Tudor *nor* you get to wed her.'

'And their child? Their brat would always be a threat to my heir.'

He pulled off his topaz ring and began to slowly roll it between thumb and forefinger.

'No, Francis. As it has been explained to me, it is essential that I have an heir or else England slides into anarchy and, for reasons that are obvious, my brother's daughter is the best person to provide such an heir.'

He eyed me earnestly.

'Given that you have never known me to shrink away from duty, surely you must recognise that my forthcoming marriage is the correct course of action?'

I felt great sadness as he advanced the corrupt arguments of others.

'The only thing I recognise, Richard, is incest.'

His mouth tightened.

'If your king is prepared to make such a sacrifice for his people, who are you to disagree?'

Dear God, how malleable he was without Anne Neville!

'Listen, you fool, it's not just going to be me who objects; it's going to be everyone. Who's going to support a king who marries his niece? Who's going to acknowledge his son who is also his great nephew? Can't you see for a moment that that which you're planning – or, to be precise, what is being planned for you – is morally wrong by any standard and loathsome to all your countrymen?'

He moved towards the door in anger, but I hauled him back to face me. He struggled furiously in my grip, but for all his strength he lacked both my size and weight. I pushed him firmly back into his seat and stood over him.

He made to rise, so I bent over and pushed his shoulders back; our faces were very close now.

'Marry the girl and how many of your subjects will follow you?'

He squirmed in my grasp.

'The people of the North…'

'They will follow me!'

He ceased struggling and looked up quickly.

'What do you mean?'

I let go of him and gazed down at the man whom I had promised myself that I would always serve.

'I'm leaving you, Richard.'

'You're leaving me?'

'To join Henry Tudor.'

'You traitorous bastard!'

'And when the invasion comes, Tudor can head south to join his supporters there. I'll go to the north country. When I get there, I'll tell men how you planned to marry your own niece, while your wife – the daughter of their great Earl of Warwick – lay dying close by.' I gazed down at him. 'Believe me, Richard, men will come flocking to my standard.'

He leapt up reaching quickly for his knife.

'You, of all people – a traitor!'

I slapped him as hard as I could across the face; he staggered, dropping his knife as he did so.

'Then ask yourself why. Have the courage to look at yourself and see what you've become.'

Apart from a vivid mark on one cheek, his face was very pale and his mouth worked furiously.

'I'll have you hunted down and destroyed!'

'That wouldn't change a thing! I've already arranged to have letters sent to friends in the North telling them exactly what you've been planning and how you've treated their own Anne Neville. Once they know that you've had me killed for speaking the truth, I imagine that they'll raise the North against you.'

Richard glared at me.

'You wouldn't dare to do all these things!'

I bent down and picked up his dagger; his eyes widened for a moment in fear.

'I'm not going to kill you,' I reassured him, 'although it would probably make life a lot easier for Henry Tudor. But believe me, Richard, I'm completely serious in all that I've said. Unless you swear, here and now, to give up this obscene plan to marry your niece, I'm leaving you. What's more, I'll use whatever skills I have to defeat you.'

His mouth tightened as we stared at each other; then slowly he moved to his seat by the fire and sat down. Watching his narrowed eyes and slow hand movements as he rotated his ring, it was obvious that he had not considered the possibility that I would desert him and was hastily calculating the threat that such a departure posed.

I guessed his immediate reaction would be to judge that I was bluffing. I was faithful Francis, after all, and had served him loyally all these years – surely I wouldn't really contemplate leaving? But then to his knowledge I had always completed everything I had set out to achieve.

He had to consider how my defection would cause men to question their current loyalties to him. Possibly he thought he could accommodate my loss to him as a soldier as he thought there would be other men to take my place. But were they up to my standard?

Also the king had to consider the threat from the North. Catesby might have assured Richard that everyone in that part of the country would ultimately accept the marriage to his niece for the sake of peace and stability, but the king knew that I knew the fighting men there better than Catesby. Equally, if it came to a test of honesty, Richard would believe me rather than his other advisors.

'So what happened to your famous loyalty?' Richard mocked me bitterly. 'Faithful Francis, the king's own dogge!'

'You should be grateful that I showed you enough loyalty to come here tonight. At least I proved sufficiently faithful to come and tell you that what you're planning is wrong.'

'You came here to threaten and blackmail me!'

I was beginning to grow angry.

'Only because I'm not prepared to just sit by while you let yourself be manipulated and used for the benefit of others!'

'I'm not being used!'

I bent down and hauled him to his feet.

'Come on, Richard; all your life you've been used by others – sometimes it even suited you! It benefited both King Edward and yourself that you made a success of the North; then it suited both you and Anne Neville to marry. Although I grant you that her manipulation of you in the North was for your own benefit as well as her own.'

He struggled furiously in my grip, but I ignored him.

'But what happened after the North, Richard? Whose idea was it for you to become king? Your wife's, I believe. Now why should that be?'

Furiously he tried to move his arms, so I tightened my grip.

'It was to prevent civil war!' He gasped.

I bent my face to him.

'Are you sure?' I asked cynically. 'Yes, I agree that is what we all believed at the time, but do you know I have recently come to wonder if that was truly the case.'

I glanced down sadly at his white face.

'You see, with the benefit of hindsight, I have started to think that perhaps you becoming king owed far more to Anne Neville's ambition than the true needs of England at the time. Possibly, just possibly, she saw the opportunity when King Edward died and used you, along with the rest of us, to take advantage of the situation.'

He opened his mouth to speak, but I was determined to make him see sense.

'Then think of all the others who have used you. Buckingham, Northumberland and Norfolk all supported you to become king because they all stood to gain personally, not because they believed in you. They used you as Catesby has.'

'The princes were killed to prevent civil war.'

'And more recently the Woodvilles have done the same.'

'The proposed marriage will make the country secure!' he protested.

I pushed him back into his chair in disgust.

'You're just repeating what you've been told!' I said contemptuously. 'Try thinking for yourself for a change! Doesn't common sense tell you that civil wars are avoided and peace and tranquillity gained through good leadership, not infanticide and incest? Can't you see how the Woodvilles are using Catesby, who's misleading you for his own advantage?'

He sat in silence studying the flickering fire. He made no movement, nor for once did he play with his rings. He simply sat and gazed into the flames. In the half light, he looked a solitary figure and, for all his jewels and rich apparel, a strangely vulnerable one. For a moment, I thought to cushion the harshness of my words with a comforting phrase; in my frankness, I must have hurt him. But then I hardened my heart as matters were too far advanced now. Either Richard faced up to the truth or I could no longer serve him.

★ ★ ★

'I believe that the king has privately decided against marrying his niece,' a smiling Ratcliffe advised me a few days later. 'Poor Catesby is quite chastened, it would appear!'

He glanced at me inquisitively.

'His decision appears to have coincided with your discussion with him?'

'He had already made up his mind. He simply told me that there would be no marriage.'

He looked at me with disbelief but wisely kept silent. The Woodvilles weren't able to hold their tongues though. Informed of the king's decision and devoid of Catesby's support, they petitioned a number of nobles to intercede on behalf of the Princess Elizabeth but to no avail. Eventually, to suppress the whole business, at my suggestion, the king publicly denied that he had ever intended to marry his niece.

★ ★ ★

On my advice, Richard made Ratcliffe his chief advisor with a subdued Catesby supporting him and myself watching the both of them. Despite my dislike of Catesby's conspicuous lack of morality, he had been cut down to size and had unparalleled intellect. Equally Ratcliffe's undoubted skills in propaganda should not be wasted.

I tried to be with Richard as often as I could; while neither of us ever talked of that fateful night, I knew that what I had said had shocked him and, in a curious way, I felt both guilty and responsible for him. Moreover, the death of Anne Neville left him morbidly dejected. I believe he saw his own mortality in hers and increasingly turned to God for consolation. I think it helped him to have someone to listen to him as he talked of his faith and I heard him out as he spoke of his plan to come to grace.

As far as I could see, his confession was total. He made no attempt to conceal anything; he even blamed himself for his brother Clarence's death.

'But you can't be responsible for that!' I protested. 'It had nothing to do with you.'

'The sins of omission are as great as those we commit,' he

corrected me gently. 'I could have saved him from being killed; Edward would have listened to me.'

'You're being too hard on yourself.'

He smiled at me with childlike innocence.

'Perhaps, but at least I can make restitution to his son. I've decided that Clarence's boy, the young Earl of Warwick, should be my heir.'

I thought for a moment; Clarence had married the older daughter of my first master, the Earl of Warwick, while Richard had married the younger. This made Clarence's son the grandson of the old Earl of Warwick. The thought pleased me and I smiled. Richard noticed it and shrugged.

'To be honest, the boy has a better right to the crown than I do,' he said awkwardly, 'so it seems only fair that he should at least reign after me.'

He glanced at me.

'Will you do something for me, Francis?'

'Of course.'

'Swear that you will make sure that Clarence's son reigns after me in case... well, that is...'

His morbidity had to be discouraged.

'You'll rule for a long time yet, Richard. But if it makes you feel better, of course I'll swear to it.'

He smiled at me shyly and tugged at his England ring, which he had worn since his coronation. A moment later he passed it to me and I looked in awe at the lions engraved upon it. I made to pass it back, but he shook his head.

'Keep it to remind you of your promise.' He looked at my hands. 'You'll probably need to wear it on a chain.'

He laughed.

I grinned at him and we relapsed into companionable silence with the troubles of the past behind us. We were not to feel secure in the present though; all the while rumours of Henry Tudor's invasion were growing, and I had no doubt that soon we would be at war, a war that would decide for once and for all whether Richard had a right to the throne. I tightened my mouth as I looked at the small figure beside me. One way or another, I vowed I would protect him by defeating Tudor.

CHAPTER 19

'If you expect me to defend Southampton against Henry Tudor, I'll need more cannon.' The broad northern tones of John Hoton cut through my thoughts. 'There's not enough time to patch up the land walls or to make repairs to the castle, but give me more cannon and I can hold Tudor at bay.'

I smiled at the enthusiasm of the newly appointed Constable of Southampton Castle but made no reply. Below us the babble and bustle on Westgate Quay evidenced the growing prosperity of the port, but neither the sounds nor the sights on the dockside afforded me pleasure. It was at the horizon that I gazed; for the fifth day running there was no sight of a fleet.

Where in hell's name was Tudor? It was already approaching mid-August, so he was long overdue. Catesby's spies had been specific. They knew Tudor's numbers, the likely date of landing and even the location near Southampton. According to them, Tudor should have been here by now.

There was no danger that he could have come ashore secretly, I reassured myself. We had paid agents a fortune to watch all the hidden bays and concealed coves along this part of the coast. Even if our agents had played us false, there would have been others to tell us of the landing of Tudor's French troops and the 500 renegade English serving under him. Dear God, for a bounty the size we were offering, a man would have betrayed his own father. But if Tudor was not here, where was he?

The empty horizon was mocking me, so I indicated that we should return to the castle. Followed by our escort, John Hoton and I descended from our position by the customs house and started to walk back up English Street. I ignored the sullen faces and hostile stares of the townsfolk as our escort elbowed them from our path. I was used to their enmity by now – too many of them had sympathised with the traitor Buckingham and, given the opportunity, would back Tudor now. Well, they were not going to get the chance.

As we passed the Church of Holy Rood, I wondered whether Catesby's forecast of Tudor's landing place was correct. Ratcliffe had doubted it. He had pointed out that Tudor would be more likely to land in Wales where, despite his long absence, his Welsh blood would attract support. Personally I doubted this, but conceded the possibility.

So we had taken precautions in Wales, but it was in the South of England, where support for Richard was weakest, that we had put in the greatest effort. I had created three military zones: John, Lord Scrope my neighbour and fellow soldier from Yorkshire held the South-West region; another Yorkshire man, Brackenbury, together with the loyal Duke of Norfolk held London and the South-East; while I took personal charge of the central zone. Ahead of us, the imposing castle gatehouse loomed and our escort fell back to guard the rear as Hoton and I entered. We halted in the courtyard and he glanced at me.

'Do you want to continue your inspection of the castle?' he asked.

I shook my head.

'I've come to the conclusion that, in Tudor's place, I would not bother trying to capture Southampton. It would slow him down and he needs to press on inland and muster his supporters in England.'

'So how will you stop him?' Hoton wanted to know.

I explained the strategy that I had designed for all three military zones.

'Firstly, we work on the assumption that Tudor's fleet is not intercepted and destroyed by our own ships, which have been patrolling the Channel since April, and that his army manages to land unopposed. So, as soon as we hear of a landing, we use the fast courier system to notify the king in Nottingham. He will immediately muster the main army.'

There was the sound of a disturbance from the gatehouse, but I paid it no heed. The guards there could deal with the mutinous townsfolk.

'Now while the main army is concentrating in the centre of England, we slow Tudor down in the South. We attack their foraging parties and prevent sympathisers from joining them. Then we deny Tudor food and shelter.'

'How?'

'All livestock in their path are slaughtered; all habitations are torched. The enemy will find dead sheep polluting rivers and streams.'

I broke off as a mud-splattered rider forced his way through the fracas at the gatehouse and spurred his horse towards us. Even as he slid off his sweating horse, the messenger's hand was inside his tunic.

'From Master Catesby, my lord,' he panted.

I seized the scroll and reeled in shock. How in hell's name could it have happened?

'Get your men ready!' I ordered Hoton. 'Tudor's in Wales and is approaching Shrewsbury.'

He looked at me, mouth agape.

'But how? You said that all precautions had been…'

There was no time for this. I tossed a coin to the messenger.

'Refresh yourself quickly and return to Master Catesby. Tell him I need to know the numbers and composition of Tudor's army. I also want his estimate as to their direction and state of morale. Now repeat what I have said.'

He did so immediately and I was impressed by his efficiency. Clearly Catesby had used one of his best people.

The messenger eyed me shrewdly.

'You'll be moving north, my lord. Where should Master Catesby send this information?'

I thought briefly. The recipient would have to be a man that I trusted completely at a point between here and Nottingham.

'Tell him to send it to the Abbot of Our Lady in Abingdon,' I told him. 'His abbey is near Oxford.'

★ ★ ★

Despite the need for haste, our march to Nottingham was no mad scramble; to have hurried too much would have exhausted the men and lamed the horses. I needed time to think too. I let John Hoton dictate the pace of our ride north and, as I knew him to be prudent, unquestioningly obeyed his measured orders to ride, walk or rest the horses. I spent the time pondering what lay ahead. The hardest part was that, until I received Catesby's second message, I had no hard facts. All I knew was that Tudor had inexplicably breached our defences in Wales. What would he do when he got to Shrewsbury?

He had two choices. Assuming he had attracted considerable support in Wales, he could head straight down Watling Street towards London. I chewed my lip nervously. Richard's army would not be fully mustered, but he would be unable to ignore the threat to his capital. In this scenario, we would be forced to fight against a rebel army whose numbers would undoubtedly exceed our own. But Tudor had another choice, which would favour us. If he had not got the support he needed by the time he reached Shrewsbury, he would not dare to try for London. He would probably head to the North-West and try to enlist the support of his stepfather, Lord Stanley. But he would get an unpleasant surprise because…

'Halt!'

Hoton's sharp command caused me to jerk hard at my reins and, looking up, I followed the direction of his pointed finger. Ahead of us in the distance, a large party of horsemen were heading north.

He wheeled round.

'I can't make out their banners, my lord. Can you?'

'No.'

He narrowed his eyes.

'We'll treat them as hostile then and, since they easily outnumber us, we'll try to avoid them.' He raised his voice. 'Dismount and rest!'

It would delay us, but it was the safest choice. I slid off my horse wearily. All over England, I reflected, men would be stirring and moving purposefully towards the centre of England, but to fight for whom? I recalled a discussion I had had with Broughton uneasily.

★ ★ ★

'You mean everyone would have still supported Gloucester if he had been content to remain as protector?' he clarified.

'Yes.'

'Course they would,' he slurred. 'No one would have backed Tudor. That's why he never dared to invade until Richard became king.'

I trusted Broughton as I trusted no other man, but I found it hard to believe that men could think in this way.

'Are you sure?'

He looked at me sadly, pitying my ignorance.

'Come down from the lofty heights of the court, Francis, and see facts the way ordinary men see them. Richard of Gloucester split the supporters of the House of York when he became king. He may not have found the promotion from protector to king difficult, but it was hard for a number of other people.'

I made no response, and he traced two circles in the spilled wine thoughtfully.

'Then again,' he murmured, 'two young princes might have been little problems for Gloucester, but they became large ones for many of his subjects.'

'But would you risk your life and your lands fighting for an unknown Welshman? Henry Tudor has no right to the throne.'

Broughton shrugged.

'How much of a right does Gloucester have?' he asked quietly. 'Francis, I don't know who will fight for Tudor, but then I can't say who will fight for Richard either.'

★ ★ ★

'Abingdon, my lord!' Hoton pointed ahead.

I grunted in acknowledgement.

'Do you reckon that Master Catesby's messenger will have arrived there yet?' he asked conversationally.

I shrugged. I was in no mood to talk. Ever since I had thought back to what Broughton had said, I had recalled a number of other conversations and incidents and none of them had cheered me. For a start, Broughton's assessment had been devastatingly accurate. In taking the crown, Richard had divided the followers of the House of York; support for him was ebbing away as the malicious rumours against him multiplied and spread. I suspected that by now our regime was a minority one, and one which was growing progressively weaker. For all that, Richard's own position was tenable provided the great nobles backed him. The problem was that too much power was concentrated in the hands of but three of them, so it would be the troops of the Duke of Norfolk, the Earl of Northumberland and Lord Stanley who would comprise the majority of our army. Catesby doubted the loyalty of Lord Stanley though, arguing that he would be unnatural to fight against his stepson, Tudor. Ratcliffe and I disagreed. We argued that Lord Stanley had proved loyal to Richard since his coronation; he had made no attempt to support his stepson at the time of Buckingham's revolt and, we pointed out, there was no evidence to suggest that he was going to do so now. While Catesby had agreed grudgingly, we were all privately suspicious of Lord Stanley's intentions, which was why, when matters came to a head, neither Ratcliffe nor I had known what to do.

★ ★ ★

'So what do we do?' asked Ratcliffe frantically. 'Stanley's asked permission to leave court and administer his estates.'

'The timing is curious. At court we can keep an eye on him, but let him go and he may join Tudor if he chooses.'

'I know that!' howled Ratcliffe. 'So what do you suggest, Francis?'

I was saved the necessity of answering as at that moment Catesby sauntered into the council chamber. He had clearly overheard us, as an amused smile lit up his features.

'If you forbid Lord Stanley to return to his estates, it is, of course, just possible that the perceptive peer might conceive the idea that you don't entirely trust him,' he began in his normal teasing voice.

Ratcliffe snorted impatiently.

'Anyone could work that out!' he snapped. 'But let him go and he could lead 6,000 men to back Henry Tudor when he invades.'

Ratcliffe glared at his rival.

'What's your suggestion then?'

Catesby waved his hand airily.

'Let Stanley go,' he said cheerfully. 'Show him you trust him.'

Ratcliffe snorted.

'Even from you that's foolish in the extreme.'

'Foolish?' Catesby regarded him with an amused smile. 'Yes, I suppose you would see it that way. But then, of course, we all have our limitations.'

I interposed myself between the two of them.

'Tell us your whole plan.'

Catesby grinned malevolently.

'We'll release Lord Stanley, Francis. We'll let him return to his estates, but on one condition.'

'Which is?'

'His son, Lord Strange, comes to court in his place before Tudor's invasion.' He smirked. 'We'll call him a guest, of course, but others may see him as a hostage.'

Catesby shrugged fair-mindedly.

'Naturally men will always disagree on terminology, but we'll all agree on one thing.'

'What's that?'

He clicked his fingers delightedly.

297

'Is it not obvious? Why, at the precise time that Lord Stanley declares for Henry Tudor, his son will be dispatched to the divine realm.' His eyes twinkled as he beamed at us. 'How likely is it that Lord Stanley will join Henry Tudor now?'

'Knowing that if he does so he'll be causing his own son to be executed?' Ratcliffe said slowly.

'Executed!' Catesby's voice was shrill with surprise, and he gave Ratcliffe an amazed look. But then he raised his hands in apology.

'My dear Ratcliffe, you must forgive me, but I do not know how it is that, even after working alongside you for two long years, your lack of vision still has the capacity to astonish me.'

'What are you proposing?' I asked horrified.

Catesby gave me a friendly pat on the shoulder.

'Something more likely to catch the imagination, wouldn't you say? After all, Lord Stanley might see his son's martyrdom as an acceptable price for securing the throne for his stepson, Henry Tudor.'

'I would very much doubt it.'

'But why take chances, Francis?' Catesby's genial chuckle filled the chamber. 'Now, put yourself in the place of Lord Stanley and tell me are you going to rebel against the king when you knew that such an act would cause your son to be blinded?'

I winced.

'Then castrated.'

Ratcliffe shut his eyes.

'Before being put on the rack to be finished off!' Catesby's glittering glance swept over us. 'Now surely you will agree that such a threat with its lengthy – or should I say lengthening – conclusion will prove a sufficient deterrent.'

★ ★ ★

'There's a message for you, Francis.' John Sante, the elderly Abbot of Our Lady rummaged through an untidy mass of scrolls on the table next to him.

I waited in a fever of anxiety, but eventually the short-sighted Abbot recognised the royal seal and passed the parchment over.

I skimmed through it quickly. Predictably Catesby's information was detailed. Tudor had already entered England at Shrewsbury and was moving slowly in an easterly direction. So, Tudor lacked the numbers to march on London. That was excellent news. I read on, cheered. Despite reports of Tudor's army numbering more than 10,000, Catesby's own assessment put the rebel numbers at around 5,000. Reports from deserters, he added, indicated that the majority of these were French and Scottish troops. So Tudor had not added significantly to the numbers he had landed with. This was far better than I had hoped for. I glanced through the rest of the report in delight, but there was nothing of substance.

'I am commanded to join the king and his army at Leicester!' I told John Sante.

He eyed me gravely.

'I trust that everything is satisfactory?' he enquired.

'Of course.'

He made no response, but his courteous silence pricked my conscience. John Sante had known my family a long time and, having worked with him on a couple of occasions, I knew him to be both intelligent and discreet.

I handed him the scroll. He studied it myopically and at length returned it to me.

'It would appear to be a straightforward matter,' he said quietly. 'Surely 5,000 rebels cannot prevail against the might of England. Nevertheless, I shall pray for you, Francis.'

I thanked him and knelt for his blessing. When I rose, he smiled at me and pointed to Catesby's scroll.

'There is one phrase in Master Catesby's report that puzzled me,' he began.

I handed him the scroll and he pulled it close to his eyes. Satisfied that he had selected the right sentence, he pointed at it. I read it carefully for, in my haste, I had overlooked it and now it made my blood ran cold.

'I trust that our northern contingent will join us soon…'

Alone in my guest chamber, I read and re-read the line that the short-sighted Abbot had spotted. On the surface, it was a mere factual statement that our men in the North had not joined the main army yet, and this was what I had told John Sante. But Catesby was never superficial – the key sentence was a coded warning. Catesby did not believe that Northumberland and his men were coming to join Richard's army. I cast my mind back wearily to the time when Catesby had first shared his misgivings with me.

★ ★ ★

'I hear that Northumberland is unhappy,' Catesby simpered.

'Dear God, why's that? He's already benefited far more than anyone else through Richard being king.'

'The ingratitude of our loyal lord beggars belief,' agreed Catesby indignantly. 'But it could, of course, be connected to the fact that he has not retained responsibility for all three marches in the North.'

'He's not competent enough.'

Catesby narrowed his eyes.

'I could not agree with you more. But naturally, as a lawyer, I feel obliged to point out – with the utmost reluctance you understand – that in every dispute there are always two viewpoints.'

He gave me a sideways glance.

'You've heard, of course, that the Council of the North is another problem for Northumberland?'

'I hadn't.'

'I'm surprised. Well, apparently there's a rumour that the Earl believes that its sheer existence impinges on his authority.'

'He's a member of it!'

'Do you know, Francis, I'd have to say that it's not precisely the same as heading the Council of the North.'

'Well no, John of Lincoln – the king's nephew – leads the council. Now I admit that he has limitations, and people don't like working with him.'

'Oh, but I have complete confidence in our understanding Earl of Northumberland's ability to tolerate the inexperienced Earl of Lincoln,' Catesby hurriedly assured me.

'You do?'

'Certainly!' Catesby gestured expansively. 'His tolerance is renowned throughout the land. He'll put up with the king's nephew as enthusiastically as he welcomes his monarch's visits to the North. I am reliably assured that at the end of each visit our hospitable earl implores his beloved monarch to extend his stay.'

I realised that he was mocking me now. Northumberland had hoped to have the North to himself when Richard became king and hated his presence there.

'By the way, Francis, there is one matter you could clarify for me,' Catesby continued merrily. 'With your knowledge of the North, I mean.'

'I'll try.'

'Excellent!' he beamed. He took my arm and we moved forward slowly. 'You'll forgive me from mentioning it, but I was reflecting just now what an excellent impression you would make in a court of law. You seem so honest.'

I waved away the compliment.

'What's the question?'

'Am I right in thinking that our noble king is from the Neville family and that Northumberland's family are the Percies?'

'You are.'

'So succinctly put!' Catesby cried delightedly. 'Juries would love you, Francis! No "ifs" and "buts", just the plain truth every time.' He chuckled delightedly and I laughed too at the ridiculousness of the suggestion that I could charm juries.

'And just how well do the Percies and Nevilles get on?' Catesby asked pleasantly.

My smile faded abruptly. The Nevilles and the Percies had always been bitter rivals and loathed each other, but I was growing tired of his insinuations and allegations.

'You're absurd!' I snapped. 'Northumberland worked with Richard when they were in the North together. Why, he helped him become king.'

301

'So did Buckingham! Francis, can't you see that we must take nothing for granted. Not everyone has your honest stupidity and plodding loyalty. Recognise that Northumberland might possibly be regretting giving his support to our naive king.'

His green eyes flashed angrily.

'God knows, I've told him about this enough times, but he just maintains that Northumberland is completely trustworthy. Will you tell him as much? It might eventually get through to him.'

'I'm not sure I believe you either!' I told him flatly.

Catesby stamped his foot in frustration.

'All right, don't believe me, but consider two points. Firstly, where is the king's primary source of support?'

'The North.'

'And who is entrusted with bringing all that support to our expectant monarch?'

'Northumberland.'

We parted on bad terms. Later that day, I pondered on his words and reported his fears to Richard, but he waved my words away – he had faith in Northumberland. I returned to Southampton unhappily.

★ ★ ★

I turned in my bed restlessly and tried to tell myself that I was making myself afraid of shadows rather than anything of substance. Catesby was jumping to conclusions. He would not have known that the distances in the North are so great that it takes longer to gather men together. Consequently, Northumberland's muster would have been far more protracted than, say, Norfolk's.

Then again, once Northumberland had actually raised his men, it would take him a considerable time to march south to Nottingham. Being no solder and being unfamiliar with the North of England, Catesby would not have known these things. His worries had to be groundless, surely?

'I trust our northern contingent will join us soon…'

But what would happen if Northumberland's mustering took too long and he failed to arrive before the battle? Devoid of the support of the men from the North, we would be in considerable trouble. Then again, what if Catesby's insinuations were correct? Suppose Northumberland joined Tudor? Angrily I tossed and turned. All this could have been avoided if Richard had listened to me and mustered his army before Tudor's invasion, but he would not because he was overconfident. This was not caused by an overly optimistic assessment of our military situation that I could have corrected for him, rather his confidence stemmed from a much deeper belief that I could not get him to abandon. It was Ratcliffe who illuminated me when I came to Nottingham to report on the southern defences.

★ ★ ★

'You'll find that not a great deal has been done,' he snorted angrily after I had enquired how the preparations for the army were proceeding.

'Dear God, why not?'

Ratcliffe's shoulders sagged.

'The king believes that he's protected by God now,' he said wearily, 'so now he's content to let matters take their natural course.'

He looked at me hopefully.

'Maybe you'll be able to talk some sense into him?'

I tried, but I failed. I argued that we should muster our troops earlier. It was already mid-July and the campaigning season would not continue much after September. If we concentrated our forces before Tudor landed, we would be in a position to fall on him before he could attract too much support. It could be expensive to summon men prematurely and doubtless they would resent it, but it would deter men from joining Tudor. But Richard was reluctant to take men from the harvests; nor would he issue personal summons to the northern lords. True, some were already with him, but many were not.

'Northumberland will bring our northerners,' Richard assured me. 'With him, Norfolk and Stanley, I have more than enough men.'

'But…'

'In any event, Francis, either you'll halt Tudor in the South or he'll be destroyed by our followers in Wales.'

'Look, Richard, I accept that, in theory anyway, we should be able to halt Tudor on the coast or in Wales, but I can't guarantee it. Surely the obvious thing is to start planning for a scenario where Tudor penetrates our outer defences and starts to move inland. We need to arrange this now as it takes time to organise. Bring up the serpentines and other cannon from the Tower and the castles near here immediately rather than waiting to hear that Tudor has landed. Start assembling your followers now. The earlier you start the greater number of men you'll gather.'

'There is no need,' he announced calmly.

'How can you be so certain?' I demanded furiously.

He disregarded my anger and showed no offence at my tone. Instead, he rose from his elaborately carved chair and moved slowly towards me.

'You still have your ring?' he asked.

I touched the chain around my neck.

'And you will still keep your promise?'

'To put the Earl of Warwick on the throne if you die before you can ensure his succession? You know I will.'

He smiled and for a moment his pale face lit up with happiness.

'Faithful Francis.' But then he turned and moved to the window. 'Yet for all that, I am certain that you will not be the one to ensure that Clarence's son rules after me.'

I sat silently, not understanding. He turned and saw my enquiring look.

'God will allow me personally to attend my nephew's succession,' he explained.

This was beyond my comprehension.

'How do you know?'

I think my question interested him for he resumed his seat and placed his fingertips together.

'Tell me, Francis, what do you recall of the process whereby we may hope to earn remission from our sins?'

I was growing tired of this.

'Nothing.'

'You are still to come to grace,' Richard chided me gently. 'But first we bring to mind all our sins, admitting all and concealing nothing. Then we confess them daily in a manner which is both humble and penitent, and we beg for forgiveness. Indeed, it is as our very tears wash away our evil-doings that we seek to make restitution and hope to earn Our Lord's favour by doing good works.'

He touched the cross he wore lovingly, its jewels burning fiercely against the sombre hue of his tunic.

'There are some who argue that restitution is unnecessary and faith alone can bring us to salvation, but they are wrong to think like that, I am certain.'

This was not the Richard I knew.

'Why is that?'

He smiled at my seeming interest.

'God rejoices in our desire to make restitution,' he explained. 'And, indeed, He helps us to do so. He is truly content that I seek to make amends to my brothers by placing Clarence's son on the throne to rule after me.'

'Well, He won't be very pleased if, due to your inactivity, Henry Tudor gets to the throne first.'

My bitter remark was probably both sacrilegious and treasonable, but I was past caring. Somehow Richard had to be dragged back to reality, but he just shook his head sadly.

'You still fail to understand don't you? Listen, Francis, the Almighty knows that I wish to make recompense to my brothers, and He is both fair and generous. How can you believe that He will deny me this chance to do so by allowing a usurper to steal the throne, which will rightfully belong to my nephew Warwick when I am dead?'

He began to pace up and down in his frustration at my inability to understand. Suddenly he stopped and whirled round to face me.

'Francis, can you not see how God is already helping me? By allowing Henry Tudor to invade he is ensuring my nephew Warwick's inheritance.'

This was ridiculous.

'Well I've heard that He moves in mysterious ways, but really.'

'Just think, Francis!' he howled and sprung towards me to seize my arm. I winced for, despite his lack of stature, he was strong. 'While Tudor was in

305

France he was safe. I could never have persuaded the French to have handed him over, but now God has delivered him into my hands in England.'

He released his grip and beamed up at me.

'Surely, Francis, by doing so the Almighty, in his loving goodness, will ensure that I will now defeat Tudor, and with him dead there is no one to prevent Warwick from succeeding me.'

He nodded happily and watched my expression.

'Surely you see it all now, Francis, as indeed it was revealed to me. By killing Tudor, I begin to earn absolution for my sins.'

I made a final effort to make him see sense.

'But that's even more reason for organising everything properly now? Summon your troops immediately.'

'And have their families starve in the winter because I denied them the chance to tend their fields and harvest their crops?' Richard rebuked me. 'Surely that would be a poor way for me to earn my own salvation?'

I sighed in sheer frustration; Richard had retreated into a world where I could never reach him.

'Trust me, Francis, when I say that God is already helping me to make amends, I speak nothing but the truth. Our victory is certain and, since this is the case, let all other matters take their natural course.'

There was no way to argue with him.

'When do you intend to proclaim Warwick as your heir?' I asked curiously.

'When Tudor has been killed, of course. I would not have it said that I was forced to name my heir because I feared I would be defeated,' he answered swiftly. 'Such talk would offend the Almighty.'

★ ★ ★

I turned in my bed. Richard might have been confident, but others were not. And then Catesby's words cropped up in my thoughts again. It had been one of our last meetings together and he had been as efficient as ever. The business was swiftly concluded and I recalled him leaning back in his seat as he dismissed the clerks.

'Have you thought of transferring part of your estates to your wife?' he asked casually.

'Why?'

He sniffed.

'It seems to be quite the fashion at court these days.'

He saw my bemused expression and condescended to explain.

'It's a precaution in case Henry Tudor wins. Obviously, a man like you would lose all his lands, but your wife can legally retain those lands that she holds in her name.'

'It would look disloyal to Richard.'

He raised a cynical eyebrow.

'Naturally it would, but your wife or widow would need somewhere to live.'

He had a point, so I agreed unenthusiastically.[27] Catesby made a note of the manors that I suggested and nodded briskly.

'I'll have the papers drawn up for you,' he said as we rose. 'It won't take long; I've become quite an expert at it by now.'

I thanked him, but curiously he made no sarcastic comment. Instead his gaze was unfocused as he stood completely still. Presently he shook his head, as if to clear his thoughts, and gave me an embarrassed glance.

'There's no need for thanks, Francis.'

It was so uncharacteristic a remark that I was curious.

'You seemed so distracted just now?'

He gave a light laugh.

'I was merely thinking of these land transfers and reflecting how prone men are to look to their own affairs at times like these.'

It seemed a commonplace observation, so I turned to go. But, as I reached the door, he spoke softly again.

'But then, I suppose, a truly wise man would provide as much insurance for himself as he possibly could.'

At the time I assumed he was still referring to the land transfers so I walked on.

★ ★ ★

I rose at the first hint of dawn, hoping that light and movement would sweep away the dark fantasies of the night. It was, I thought in impatience, time to end speculation on men's motives and possible actions, and to confront the reality. Above all it was time to face Tudor in battle. I strode out purposefully to rouse Hoton and his men.

CHAPTER 20

Catesby sniffed ostentatiously.

'You could have the decency to have cleaned yourself up, Francis, before rushing in here.'

I ignored his fastidiousness.

'I see that Northumberland's troops have arrived; so what's the overall situation?'

Catesby's eyes narrowed as he carefully selected a scroll from a number that lay on the table in his tent. Even on campaign, he seemed to delight in surrounding himself with paperwork. His green eyes flickered down the scroll.

'We'll start with Tudor,' he began. 'The latest estimates put their force at about 6,000 men under the generalship of the Earl of Oxford.'

'Only 6,000?' I gasped.

'Apparently so. Now Tudor is currently camped a few miles west of here.'

'But in your first message you said that Tudor was approaching Shrewsbury and a week or so later he's only got as far as here. What has he been doing?'

Catesby grinned.

'I imagine that the pace of his advance slowed somewhat as he realised the paucity of his numbers. Doubtless he spent the time looking for allies.'

I smiled back at him.

'Well he does not seem to have had much success, does he?'

Catesby regarded me thoughtfully.

'I would urge against over-optimism, my lord. I am not wholly convinced that our own situation is perfect. Morale is not high and there have been desertions.'

I shrugged. On the eve of battle that was unsurprising.

'And while the Earl of Northumberland has arrived,' Catesby went on, 'the number of men with him is somewhat low.'

'How low?'

'4,000.'

'Is that all?' I asked aghast.

Catesby eyed me neutrally.

'Naturally, it would be wholly inappropriate for me to venture an opinion, but I hear that the Earl of Northumberland is claiming,' and Catesby lingered on the word, 'that there was inadequate time to muster all the men of the North. Accordingly, most of the men who accompanied him here are his own personal followers.'

I ignored Catesby's insinuation. He knew nothing of the North and still less about the problems of mustering men quickly. Still, Northumberland and his men were here, as was Richard's most loyal magnate, the Duke of Norfolk and the men from London under Brackenbury. We probably vastly outnumbered Tudor.

'On the face of it, Lord Stanley appears loyal to the king,' Catesby advised. 'Initially he declined the royal summons claiming that he had fallen victim to the sweating sickness, but since then he has raised his men and placed them in front of the advancing Tudor army falling back slowly towards us.'

Lord Stanley could have been acting as a screen for Richard's army or, alternatively, he could have been doing the same for Tudor so that he could receive fresh recruits without reinforcements.

'What about his brother, Sir William?'

'Already declared a traitor. We know that he has been in contact with Tudor, but he has not joined him. At present, the forces of both brothers are camped to the south of us.'

This was a conundrum. If Sir William was a traitor and Lord Stanley supposedly loyal, why were their two forces allied together?

'But even without the Stanleys we must easily outnumber Tudor's force?'

Catesby pursed his lips.

'By about two to one, Francis.' He smiled without humour. 'But were Lord Stanley and his brother to fight for Tudor, both armies' numbers would be broadly even.'

'Do you think they will?'

Catesby rose and began to saunter about.

'While we were at Nottingham, Lord Stanley's son tried to escape. We recaptured him and, under interrogation, Lord Strange confirmed that his uncle, Sir William, was a traitor, but swore that his father was loyal.'

Catesby stopped and grinned at me.

'Did I believe him? No, of course not, but I knew what to do. So I put Lord Strange in the hands of my two dogs.'

'Why?'

Catesby looked amazed.

'Do you seriously imagine that I would entrust such a key hostage to the incompetent royal guards again? Had Lord Strange escaped, his stepfather would have immediately declared for Tudor. Now, safely chained night and day to my man, Bracher, there is no chance of that happening.'

That was true and, undoubtedly, with Lord Strange in our possession, Lord Stanley would not dare join Tudor.

'Make sure you keep him safe!' I said. 'Now I will go and inspect the likely battleground before we all meet in the king's tent.'

★ ★ ★

As I walked down the grassy slope towards the great marsh, I tried to put myself in Tudor's mind. He had advanced to a position less than half a day's march west of us. He would be upon us tomorrow. But how could he hope to win? His own spies would have told him our own numbers, and he would know by now that we held Lord Strange hostage. Surely Henry Tudor was not expecting his stepfather Lord Stanley to sacrifice his eldest son? Against odds of two to one, assuming that both Lord Stanley and his brother remained neutral, why was Tudor advancing? I pondered this as I stood for a while by the side of the great marsh; then it suddenly struck me – this was Tudor's final throw of the dice. He had tried once before and failed. If he ran away now, no one would support him a third time. Well, clearly he had courage, but it would be to no avail tomorrow. I carefully started to construct my battle plan to defeat Tudor's general, the Earl of Oxford.

★ ★ ★

It was crowded in Richard's tent and I had to raise my voice to make myself heard above the babble.

'Tudor will be upon us tomorrow,' I began.

'We should advance on him now.'

For an old man, the Duke of Norfolk had a surprisingly strong voice. Next to him his son, the Earl of Surrey, nodded belligerently.

'My men are exhausted,' Northumberland said sulkily. 'We should remain here and let Tudor come to us.'

'What do you think Tudor's tactics will be, Francis?' Ratcliffe tactfully intervened.

'Assuming we remain here, Tudor will attack either our left or right flanks.'

'He'd come straight at our centre!' bellowed Norfolk. 'I dare say you do things differently in Scotland, Lovell, but...'

'He can't cross that marsh!' I snapped irritably. 'Have you inspected it? A man could cross if he was careful, but for an advancing army it's a natural obstacle. Horses and men-at-arms would be fatally slowed, while we showered them with arrows.'

'But there's an old road which runs through the marsh!' someone objected.

'You could cross there if you were marching in column,' I responded, 'but not if your army was extended in full battle array.

Tudor will either head north or south when he comes to the marsh and work his way round it to fall on us.'

'If he takes the southern route then Lord Stanley will deal with him,' Richard observed.

'Assuming he's loyal!' Norfolk boomed. 'He might just join forces with him.'

The noise inside the tent intensified as speculation regarding Lord Stanley's true intentions was hotly debated. I turned to Richard, who stood beside me with a look of anger on my face.

'Enough!' he snapped and the noise was instantly subdued. 'It is time to end this issue once and for all. Send a messenger to Lord Stanley and tell him that we require his oath of loyalty or his son will perish!'

There was a thoughtful pause. Clearly such a message as this would need to be carried by someone of authority. Equally, in view of the content, the risk to the bearer was considerable; he himself might be held as a hostage or suffer a worse fate.

Ratcliffe stepped forward tentatively.

'I'll go,' he said gruffly to conceal his nervousness.

The king quickly nodded, but, before he could speak, William Catesby stood up and turned to Ratcliffe. There was no trace of scorn or mockery as he faced his rival.

'Your courage has never been in doubt, Richard,' he remarked quietly. 'Indeed, I have long admired it, but might I suggest that I take the message? You have many strengths, but it is possible that my own – which lie more in the field of diplomacy than martial abilities – might be more suitable on this occasion?'

Catesby had few friends, but his bravery and praise of his rival drew approving glances from those in the tent. Undoubtedly, his mental ability and persuasive tongue made him the most suitable person to act as messenger.

'Leave immediately!' the king commanded. 'Now Francis, how do you see the battle tomorrow?'

'If Catesby succeeds in his mission, Your Grace, I would suggest that Lord Stanley remains in his present position and acts as our left wing. You, my Lord of Norfolk, will take the right wing.'

'And my men?' Northumberland broke in.

'The centre, my Lord. Now, I suggest that we maintain the high ground tonight, but in the morning move all our troops down to the plain – except for the king's own men, who we'll use as a reserve.'

Richard frowned.

'But why will we not take advantage of our defensive position here? All the cannon are in place and Tudor would be forced to fight uphill.'

'Because we have superior numbers, Your Grace. The space here is too confined for us to deploy our greater numbers to the best advantage. On the plain, we can spread our men to surround Tudor whether he attacks from the north or the south.'

All men know themselves to be great generals, so it was not unexpected that the debate on the next day's tactics went on for a considerable time. In the end, though, I had my way.

★ ★ ★

Richard gestured for me to remain behind when the others departed. Devoid of men, I noticed how opulent his tent was with its tapestries, carved stools and golden cups set on a large table.

'I want you to stand beside me tomorrow, Francis,' he said quietly. 'Norfolk, Northumberland and Stanley will only take orders from me, but I would welcome your advice.'

'Of course, Richard.'

He smiled gratefully, but, before he could speak further, the tent's flaps were flung open and Catesby stepped in. One look at his smiling face was sufficient to tell us that he had been successful.

'Lord Stanley's sworn his loyalty!' he announced happily. 'He'll fight for his king tomorrow.'

'Was it difficult?' I asked.

Catesby's green eyes gleamed and he bore himself proudly; he knew that he had accomplished something that must have taxed even his own considerable abilities.

He grinned at me.

'Let's just say, Francis, that after some time the loyal Lord Stanley was made to see where his best interests lay.'

I smiled back. With Stanley on our side, we outnumbered Tudor by almost three to one.

★ ★ ★

Dawn's glimmer was only just visible as I raged through the camp, ignoring the chaotic scenes that surrounded me. Dear God, our sentries must have been drunk or asleep to have allowed Tudor to get this close.

I pushed my way through the crowd in front of the royal tent, shouldering aside clerics, servants and sentries indiscriminately and burst into Richard's quarters.

'Tudor's caught us by surprise!' I shouted as I waved his priest away impatiently.

'I have not yet taken communion!' he protested in shock.

'There's no time for that now!' I told him as I chivvied the priest toward the tent's flaps. 'We need to move quickly. We must get Norfolk's men down the hillside. You must send word to Northumberland to advance his men.'

'The men will not have eaten.'

'They can eat later!' I told him desperately. 'The important thing is to advance our troops.'

Ratcliffe hurried in.

'Tudor's turning back. He's now heading to the northern end of the marsh.'

A feint by Tudor – pretend to advance on Stanley's troops and then turn north instead. Clever, but wholly unnecessary, for we had not even got our troops down to the plain, let alone arrayed them to face south. Tudor would have done better to have come straight at us. I turned to Richard frantically.

'Give the orders now while I make sure that your household knights get their retinues ready.'

'I'll help, Francis,' said Ratcliffe. 'We can use Harrington and Marmaduke Constable to assist us.'

'Right.' I glanced at Richard. 'I'll send your squires and clerks to you now. You can dictate your orders while you get armed.'

★ ★ ★

I ignored the loud bangs of the serpentines; they were proving useless, I reflected. Despite the best efforts of the Flemish gunners, Oxford's force was too far away for their guns to have any effect, nor was there time to move them down the hill. Still, at least Norfolk had got his men onto the plain and I could see them deploying in long lines about half a mile below us. Brackenbury's troops followed him.

'Why did you insist that Brackenbury's men fought in the rear rows?' Richard asked me.

'Lack of morale,' I told him in resignation. 'They are mostly Londoners and, given a choice, probably would not be here at all. I've put horsemen behind them to stop them running away. But it doesn't matter because, as soon as Northumberland's men move up, we'll put them behind Norfolk.'

'But we have men here. Why not use them to reinforce Norfolk and Brackenbury?'

'Because as soon as Northumberland is in position, we'll take our men from here and move north-west. Then we'll attack Oxford's left flank in a hooking movement. Oxford will be hit from the front and from the side. Outnumbered two to one, he'll be quickly defeated.'

I turned to an attendant squire.

'His Grace requests my Lord of Northumberland to quicken his advance and take up station in support of the Duke of Norfolk.'

I beckoned to another.

'Ride to Lord Stanley and request him to move his force to the north-west of his current position. He should be ready to cut off Oxford's retreat.'

I watched carefully as Norfolk and Oxford inched towards each other. As far as I could see, Tudor had concentrated all his force in one compact division that was advancing on a narrow front. Our scouts advised that there were a small body of horsemen behind the marsh who presumably were either a flank or rear guard, but numbering less than 100, their effectiveness would be debatable.

I turned back to the main battle anxiously. Norfolk had sacrificed depth of line for length, doubtless trying to intimidate Oxford. This was a mistake since many of his men would not actually be facing an enemy when battle was joined.

'Norfolk puffs himself up like a bullfrog,' I told Richard. 'But once Northumberland gets in behind him, we'll have the victory.'

★ ★ ★

Dear God, why was Northumberland so slow in his advance? Already Norfolk and Oxford's lines had crashed together after a volley of arrows had been fired by both sides. Though the din of battle was plainly audible, in that mass of men it was impossible to make out what was happening. Fortunately, Norfolk had enough experience to send back messengers. The first had advised that their initial assault had pushed Oxford back. The second, a short while later, reported stubborn resistance and requested reinforcements.

Richard looked at me but I shook my head. We would need all our troops for the devastating right-hook assault.

I turned to the messenger in his white lion tunic.

'His Grace requests that my Lord of Norfolk contains Oxford while we prepare to take the enemy in the flank.'

I chewed my lip nervously. The squire who had been sent to Lord Stanley had not reported back yet, but by now his force would be preparing to advance to the North-West. As soon as

Northumberland got into position behind Norfolk, it would be time to spring the trap shut. Richard gestured to our immediate left.

'Northumberland has halted to reform his men into assault formation.'

The right-hook manoeuvre could begin very soon now. I willed Northumberland to hurry.

★ ★ ★

'The duke is dead!' Norfolk's messenger panted out. 'The Earl of Surrey commands the van now.'

What in hell's name was Northumberland doing? No one could take so long to perform such a simple manoeuvre.

'He fears that his flanks are being turned.'

Northumberland was not manoeuvring at all. He had simply halted his men.

'And he begs for reinforcements.'

I swung round to Richard.

'Command Northumberland to continue his advance and fall in behind the Earl of Surrey's men!' I thundered.

I turned back to face the messenger.

'There will be no reinforcements. Tell Surrey to hold his position until we can attack Oxford's flank.'

★ ★ ★

'My Lord of Northumberland believes that His Grace's interests are best served if he maintains his current position,' the squire informed us.

I glanced at the static body of men to our left. They were at least a quarter of a mile from where we needed them. I stared at him.

'But why?'

The squire squirmed.

'He gave no reason, my lord.'

'Possibly he fears that were he to leave his current location it would expose Surrey's flank to a possible attack by the Stanleys,' Ratcliffe hazarded.

I rounded on him.

'That's nonsense! The Stanleys and their division have left their position and should be heading north-west to cut off…'

'Can you see them?' he interrupted.

From our vantage point on the hill in excellent light, it would be impossible to miss 6,000 men marching up past the marsh. But where were they?

'Try looking south.'

These words came from Harrington, who had arrived with Ratcliffe. We all peered to the south. Sure enough, about two miles south, beyond Northumberland's troops on the sloping terrain, a large number of men were in static formation – Stanley's men.

'So Stanley's finally shown his true colours!' I burst out angrily and wheeled to face Catesby. 'I thought you said he was loyal.'

'He still might be,' Harrington, observed nervously.

But Catesby looked at us in despair. All traces of the clever lawyer had disappeared and he gesticulated wildly.

'He swore his loyalty to his king,' he babbled. 'He's…'

'A traitor!' Richard snapped.

Catesby looked shamefaced.

'Would you like me to try to persuade him again?'

Dear God, Catesby was brave; Lord Stanley would slaughter him.

'No,' said Richard, 'he's shown himself to be disloyal, and your life is too valuable to me.'

He glanced at Ratcliffe, who nodded slightly.

'Kill Lord Strange!' Richard commanded Catesby.

'Are you certain, Your Grace?' Harrington interrupted. 'Surely, after the battle…'

'After the battle?' I echoed incredulously. 'Richard, we are losing. Northumberland is not obeying orders and Stanley could attack Surrey presently.'

'But he won't while Northumberland is blocking his path. So what's your strategy?'

My mind raced furiously, trying to ignore the hubbub around me. If Northumberland was loyal to Richard, we could probably still manage the decisive right hook, which would bring victory. After all, provided that Surrey could hang on, the sheer unexpectedness of a flank attack, even by a few fresh troops, would be enough to shatter Oxford's men. It would be a massive risk though. Such reinforcements as we had also protected the rear of Surrey's division. The moment we moved to mount the hooking manoeuvre we were exposing Surrey's troops. If Northumberland was not loyal, he could take advantage of our absence to tear into the back of Surrey's men. Caught between Oxford at the front and Northumberland at the rear, Surrey's force would be slaughtered before we were ready to mount our attack on Oxford's flank.

I explained this to Richard.

'I cannot recommend a strategy until I know which side Northumberland is on,' I concluded.

Richard had already removed his gauntlets and was tugging at his rings. Watching his strained expression and tightly pressed lips, I had an inkling of the mental agony he was going through. He had always trusted Northumberland and, until a moment ago, all that trust seemed fully justified. The next decisive move in the battle depended on one key question: was Richard correct in his assessment of Northumberland's loyalty?

To my mind, Northumberland's lack of urgency in his advance and his refusal to obey orders indicated that Richard was incorrect, so I tried to help him.

'You will be exposing Surrey's rear if you move our men from here.'

'But if we don't make the attack on Oxford, we cannot defeat Tudor!' he protested angrily. 'Northumberland is loyal, I am certain.'

'As was Buckingham!'

Our angry glances locked. I charged my gaze with every ounce of willpower I could muster. He had to understand that the risk of mounting a flank attack on Oxford was simply too great in the current chaotic circumstances. Richard's mouth worked furiously for a moment and then he was still.

'Our troops will remain in their present position,' he said bitterly.

I heaved a sigh of relief, but then frowned. We had to do something to assist Surrey who was clearly under considerable pressure. Surely we could release a few men from here to assist him. With their aid, he might still be able to batter his way through Oxford. I put this to Richard hesitantly.

★ ★ ★

'Stanley's manoeuvring!'

A white-faced Catesby pointed to the south. I tore my gaze away from the main battle reluctantly. Oxford's line was beginning to bow under the weight of the extra troops, which we had flung against him, and I was beginning to dream of victory. But sure enough there was movement in the south.

'Northumberland's turning to face him.'

Richard pointed excitedly at the troops to our left and turned to me.

'Francis, advance the rest of the reserves. We'll sweep Oxford away while Northumberland holds off Stanley.'

I glanced at Northumberland's men.

'No.'

'No?' His bewilderment was yet to turn to anger and for a moment I felt desperately sorry for him. I gestured at Northumberland's soldiers.

'They are forming a column, Richard, not a line. They are getting out of Stanley's way.'

In shocked silence we watched Northumberland's troops abandon their king and march away from the battlefield.

★ ★ ★

'Look!' I think it was Pilkington who spotted the little cavalcade slowly advancing across the marsh. 'Look at those standards; it must be Tudor himself!'

'Can't be more than sixty men with him.'

'I thought he was with Oxford.'

'Never mind that! He must be heading to join Stanley.'

'We can reach him first. Bring up the horses!'

'All knights forward!' Richard shouted. 'Ratcliffe, get Harrington, Percy, Ashton and Grey. Hurry, man, hurry!' He was beside himself with excitement now. He grabbed my arm. 'I told you that Tudor would be delivered into my hands, didn't I?'

He broke off to shout orders to his household knights, but I hesitated. Something seemed wrong. Why was Tudor so exposed and with such a small escort? And why was he moving so slowly?

'We can reach Tudor long before the Stanleys do!' bellowed an exultant Ratcliffe. 'Oxford's too far away from him to help either.'

'My lord!' A frightened messenger tugged at my arm. 'The enemy has reinforced his line. My Lord of Surrey begs for more men.'

Richard laughed when he heard this.

'Take all the men, Francis, and lead them yourself. Once Oxford's men hear that Tudor's dead, they'll flee, but just secure the northern flank until that happens.'

He turned to his squires and prepared to mount. Still I hesitated; something was very wrong, but I did not know what it was. Impulsively, I snatched his horse's reins from his groom.

'Let me lead the charge, Richard. You stay here.'

He laughed savagely.

'No, Francis – God has chosen me for this task.'

He gestured imperiously; reluctantly I passed the reins to him. At that moment, the trumpets blew.

Despite my fears, I could not but admire the magnificence of that charge. Sunlight glinted on silver armour and the colourful banners billowed out as the pace of the horsemen quickened. There was no line or order to the knights, but all bore themselves proudly as, with lances outstretched, the king's elite thundered towards the enemy.

Tudor's escort belatedly seemed to realise the danger and increased their pace towards the advancing Stanleys, but the distance was too great and, realising this, Tudor's men turned to face the charging knights. Prudently, they too began to urge their horses forward, as to receive a charge while stationary is to court disaster. Even at this distance I could still distinctly hear the drumming of hooves as their powerful horses swept Richard's knights towards their prey, but then that sound was lost as with a series of crashes the two sides collided.

The impact of the charge drove Tudor's men back towards the marsh and a number of his men were toppled from their mounts. I saw one of Tudor's standards start to sway and then it fell completely as the charge disintegrated into a swirling melee. Our knights discarded their shattered lances and hacked at the enemy with their swords.

Through the dust cloud, I could see a number of riderless horses aimlessly galloping hither and thither, but my gaze focused on the scene at the side of the marsh where men clashed furiously together and sought to find the weak parts in their enemy's armour. At this distance, it was impossible to discern who was friend or foe.

★ ★ ★

I made a final circuit to ensure that no men remained behind when I joined Surrey but there seemed to be no one apart from four figures on horseback.

I moved towards them to order them into battle.

'Keep away, Lovell!' Catesby's voice was shrill.

I stared at him in bewilderment; then I saw the two Brachers on either side of the fourth man whose hands were tied.

'I thought you were ordered to execute him!' I said, pointing at Lord Strange.

Catesby tittered.

'My dear Lovell, why on earth should I wish to do such a thing?' he asked.

So Catesby had decided to disobey orders to ingratiate himself with Lord Stanley. I reached for my sword. Seeing this, the two Brachers slowly dismounted.

'Lord Stanley won't save you because you spared his son,' I said.

'But he already has!' Catesby laughed. 'Ever since I took Lord Strange into my safekeeping, he's been totally secure and, due to my messages, Lord Stanley was well aware of this. Naturally, he has been obliged to act with circumspection so as not to throw suspicion onto me, which would have endangered his son, but he has been careful and presently his son will be safely returned to him.'

'And your price, Judas?'

Catesby's lip curled contemptuously.

'How old-fashioned you are, Lovell! But, since you enquire, Lord Stanley was good enough to confirm yesterday that the new government would require men of ability such as myself, and they would welcome a wise head like mine.'

A surge of anger swept through me.

'God help you then if Richard kills Tudor down by the marsh.'

For a moment, Catesby's face assumed a puzzled look, and then, incredibly, he broke into a delighted roar of laughter. He was still chuckling a moment later when he glanced down at me.

'You seriously believed that it was Henry Tudor himself who was down by the marsh, didn't you, Francis?'

I gaped at him.

'Who is it then?'

'A few of them are personal attendants of Henry Tudor, of course. The remainder of them are French mercenaries – small in numbers naturally, but sufficiently tough and experienced to keep fighting until Lord Stanley's troops can rescue them. The real Henry Tudor is in a safe place.'

He smiled complacently.

'Of course, as I pointed out to Lord Stanley yesterday, an impersonator in full armour is hard to detect.'[28]

I moved forward very slowly my hand inching towards my sword.

'Of course, Gloucester was impetuous at the best of times,' Catesby continued, 'but, given such a tempting target, I knew that he would go for it and, with Richard dead, my new master's throne is much more secure.'

I was almost within striking distance of Catesby, but still the Brachers were positioned on either side of him.

'What about Northumberland?' I asked Catesby to distract him.

His lip curled.

'He believes that a Percy should rule the North and his heart was not for Richard. Now whether it will be for my new master King Henry remains to be seen. You see…'

I sprang at him, but the younger Bracher was quicker and blocked my way. I swung at him and felt a jolt, but my blade rebounded off his breastplate. He straightened himself and raised his axe in both hands – but I struck first. I caught him at the join between neck and shoulder and he started to sway. I pushed past him as his knees buckled.

There was a sudden movement to my left but then my head seemed to explode and I knew no more.

★ ★ ★

When I came to, Catesby was standing over me. As my vision cleared, I saw his familiar sneer.

'You really had no idea, did you, Francis? You're just like the rest of those boneheaded idiots. None of you could see that Richard of Gloucester was finished even before the battle began.'

'You traitorous bastard!' I croaked.

'How unfair you are, Francis,' he gently chided me. 'After all, I cautioned you about Lord Stanley and warned you about Northumberland.'

He spread his hands.

'Under the circumstances, it seemed to me prudent to make my own arrangements and look to serve a different master in the future.'

Just as he had with his last master, Lord Hastings, I thought miserably.

Catesby glanced down at me.

'Your problem, Francis – well, one of them anyway – was that you were always so wrapped up in your dog-like concept of loyalty that you were totally incapable of realising the true nature of the men around you.'

He broke off as the elder Bracher interrupted him by pointing down towards the marsh. Catesby narrowed his eyes.

'It would appear that Lord Stanley's troops are almost up to what remains of the decoy and Gloucester's knights,' he observed. 'So, if you will excuse me, dear Francis, I believe that I will now withdraw, since I am reliably informed that in the first flush of victory, soldiers can be somewhat indiscriminate in their slaughter.'

The two Brachers hefted their axes and moved towards me. I made no move to rise. After what I had heard, I would welcome death. Catesby's piercing whistle halted them abruptly.

'Guard Lord Strange at all times!' he commanded them, and they turned away from me reluctantly.

Catesby sauntered over.

'I'll leave you for Tudor, Francis. Of course, you'll be executed, but you can take comfort from one thing.'

'What's that?'

His face lit up happily.

'When it comes to the moment of your beheading, you will see a dear friend close at hand. After all, with my high position in the new regime, I am certain to be given one of the best seats for the occasion.'

And then he was gone.

★ ★ ★

I rose unsteadily and looked down towards the marsh. Red-coated billmen were among the knights now, their sharp weapons cruelly raking the horses' flanks and pulling their riders down. I glimpsed a few of the knights turn and flee, but knew instinctively that Richard would not be among them.

Hot tears welled uncontrollably as I watched the remaining household knights fight on defiantly in small groups. As more and more of Stanley's troops poured into the battle, so the paragons of Richard's army scorned them and fought on bravely, but the odds against them were lengthening. Not only did Stanley's troops vastly outnumber the handful of surviving knights, but their longer weapons easily outranged their shorter swords. Realising their advantage, the billmen redoubled their efforts and attacked the tiring knights from all sides, battering at them savagely until one by one their opponents slowly dropped. I forced myself to watch the slaughter knowing that their deaths and that of Richard were my fault.

I cursed myself. I had scented danger all right, but being unable to recognise the nature of the threat, I had done nothing to avert it. I had kept silent when I should have shouted out. Through my hesitancy and cowardice, I had failed Richard and his knights, and I was just as responsible for their deaths as Stanley's soldiers.

It took a painfully long time, but the numbers of knights dwindled until there were no more and the red-coated infantry swarmed over their bodies to pillage them. I made the sign of the cross, confident that such loyalty to Richard would earn them a place with him in the hereafter, and turned my attention to the plain. Already Lord Stanley's main force was up to the place that Northumberland had so recently vacated and was moving steadily forward to mount a flank attack on Surrey's unsuspecting division. I groaned quietly as I knew what must follow. In a moment, Surrey's men would spot them and alert their comrades with panic-stricken cries. Terror would spread quickly, and Surrey's force would degenerate into a mob of desperate men fleeing in all directions. And so it would be, as they were at their most vulnerable, that the true butchery would begin.

I looked away in total disbelief. Within the space of only a few hours, the army that Richard had entrusted me with had been annihilated and not by the enemy but through treachery. And it was by a traitor's plan, and through my own negligence, that the man whom I served was dead. Tears welled in my eyes as I grieved him. Even as I mourned, I had a moment of inspiration. Richard had been killed, but did I not carry part of him with me? I pressed hard against the armour on my chest and sighed with relief as the ring that he had given me dug into my skin. I smiled as I visualised its crown and lions insignia – it was clearly the token of a king. It had been too small for my finger, so I wore it on a chain to remind me of my promise.

I traced a circle on that part of the armour under which the ring lay and considered the course of action that I was indebted to pursue. To make Richard's heir, the Earl of Warwick, king, it would be necessary first to unseat Henry Tudor.

I grimly surveyed the battlefield for a final time; I was not going to be able to salvage much from the wreckage of our army. Our defeat had been total, and the House of York was in complete disarray. But, I assured myself, it had not been annihilated.

I moved towards the horses. Today was our nadir, but it was not the end. Our cause could be rebuilt, and, in time, I could rally enough people behind it to make it strong enough to defeat Tudor.

It would not be an easy task, though; I brooded on the difficulties that lay ahead. Then, in self-reproach, I dismissed my concerns as irrelevancies. A promise is a promise, after all.

POSTSCRIPT

What happened to the key protagonists?

Ratcliffe: Richard Ratcliffe was killed at the Battle of Bosworth. Due to his close association with Richard III, it is probable that he joined the king in his final charge and perished with him.

Catesby: Contrary to his expectations, Catesby was not given a position in the new regime. Instead, he was captured and executed in Leicester a couple of days or so after the Battle of Bosworth. Catesby was given sufficient time to write his will in which he bitterly acknowledged, that the trust that he had placed in Lord Stanley was ill-founded.

Lovell: Francis Lovell's story continues in Volume II, *The Last Rebel*.

NOTES

1 The Battle of Towton resulted in a decisive victory for the Yorkists.

2 Richard Ratcliffe was knighted after the Battle of Tewksbury, 1471.

3 At that time both the English and the Scots divided their border regions into three administrative and defensive regions called Marches. Broadly speaking, the West March covered modern Cumbria, formerly called Cumberland and Westmorland.

4 Curiously enough, Richard's words were truly prophetic. The following year an English army sailed to France to wage war there. There were no battles, since Louis XI elected to buy off the invading English rather than fight them. As such, there were no casualties. There was, however, one fatality; Henry Holland, Duke of Exeter, disappeared mysteriously overboard on the return journey from France. It was never established whether he had fallen into the Channel or been pushed into it.

5 Whereas there were supposed to be procedures on both sides of the borders to settle disputes, these appear to have been totally ignored by Richard of Gloucester and Lovell. There appear few, if any, records of meetings between representatives of the English and Scottish West March officials at this time.

6 Dumfries was the capital of the Scottish West March.

7 The lack of evidence that the Woodvilles worked directly against Richard, Duke of Gloucester and Anne Neville could possibly be explained by the subtlety and cunning of their plotting. So skilful were the Woodvilles that none of their attempts to destabilise Richard and Anne and encroach into the North have ever been proven. Although many historians freely concede that the Woodvilles were extremely ambitious elsewhere.

8   Whereas the conventional war hammer of the period was a short weapon comprising a hammer and two spikes, Lovell's own war hammer was different. From his description it appears to have been a longer, two-handed bludgeoning weapon.

9   Lovell's half armour probably comprised full armour for his upper body, with thick padded material to protect his upper legs.

10 Broadly positioned where Belgium and a part of Holland is today, medieval Burgundy was a large and prosperous independent duchy.

11 The wool and cloth trade in 15th century England employed a vast number of people. It was the country's largest export by far. A considerable number of different tradespeople were involved in the production, transport and treating of both wool and cloth.

12 Now called Boulogne.

13 At this time (early 1482) Berwick was in Scottish possession.

14 The harvest in the preceding year had been particularly bad in England and the winter of 1481-2 was extremely severe.

15 The Battle of Grandson (1476) resulted in a heavy defeat for Duke Charles.

16 Lovell's account of the defeat of the Scots is interesting insofar as it was previously believed that the Scots only made one attempt to relieve Berwick and break the siege. This attempt resulted in the Battle of Hutton Field. While the details of Hutton Field are sparse, it was certainly not the action narrated here by Lovell.

17 At that time the Order of the Garter was awarded for the highest chivalric achievement. It must be assumed that Lovell's admission to the Order was a reward for services over his military career, rather than solely for his efforts at Berwick. It might have been difficult to reconcile the concept of chivalry with the more ruthless tactics he employed at the Battle of Berwick.

18 For political reasons, the Scottish Army declined to fight the invading English Army. The English under Richard, Duke of Gloucester entered Edinburgh unopposed and a peace treaty was arranged. The invasion gained none of its original objectives – the only prize being Berwick itself.

¹⁹ In this Richard and his wife appear to have been remarkably successful. By a grant of parliament of 18 February 1483, Richard, Duke of Gloucester was awarded a number of crown posts and lands in the West March. Additionally, he was granted the hereditary wardenship of the West March. He was also granted whatever lands he could conquer in Scotland and the right to naturalise any Scots whom he subdued. This enormous bestowal of power and territory is sometimes referred to as Richard of Gloucester's Palatinate and it gave him more influence in the North of England than any man before or since. Despite not beating the Scots in battle, Richard of Gloucester emerged from the campaign with an enhanced military reputation and the titles and control of territory that Anne Neville sought for him.

²⁰ Presumably so they were easily accessible. Lovell had his own property, a manor in Ivy Lane, whilst Ratcliffe lodged in Stepney.

²¹ A firm commitment to marry rendering a further marriage bigamous, unless both parties agree to break off the plight-trothing first.

²² Lovell makes a mistake with the title here. Lord Howard was not made Duke of Norfolk until June 28. His eldest son was made Earl of Surrey the same day. Lovell predates Surrey's earldom by two or three weeks.

²³ The eagerly awaited visit of Lord Stanley's bears apparently took place in the Michaelmas term of 1483. Their keepers are reported to have dined with the Fellows.

²⁴ Technically it was not quite right to say Henry Tudor had no royal blood. While he had none from his paternal grandfather (Owen Tudor), who married the widow of Henry V, his mother (Margaret Beaufort, Lady Stanley) was descended from John of Gaunt, son of King Edward III. What little royal blood Henry Tudor did have came from the maternal side, but there were other people who had a better claim through birth to becoming King of England.

²⁵ Yarrow was regarded as a particularly lucky plant and as such was sported by young girls hoping for a husband. It would have been more conventional to have discreetly worn only a single sprig of yarrow.

²⁶ Leviticus (Chapter 18) expressly prohibits the marriage of a man to his aunt, but it does not specifically forbid the marriage of a man to his

niece, despite detailing a fairly comprehensive list of family members who one should not marry. It is likely that Catesby would have claimed that the lack of this particular prohibition was sufficient grounds for the marriage to be legal, while Ratcliffe and Lovell's clerics would have argued that if it was wrong for a man to marry his aunt, it must, logically, be wrong for an uncle to marry his niece.

27 The meeting, as described by Lovell, must have occurred prior to 10 June 1485 since it was on that date that he conveyed his manors of Halse and Brackly to Nan. The transfer of only such a small part of his vast landownings can only be construed as a gesture of loyalty to Richard III.

28 Curiously enough, it was the largely pro-Tudor historian, William Shakespeare, who was the first to refer to the impersonation of Henry Tudor (or the Earl of Richmond as he was named until he became king). Shakespeare gives King Richard the lines: 'I think there must be six Richmonds in the field/Five have I slain today instead of him.' (Richard III, Act V, Scene iv.)